DARKHEARTS

Praise for *Darkhearts*

'Laugh-out-loud and tearful at the same time, Sutter's *Darkhearts* combines real characters, smart prose, and an emotional journey into one fantastically relatable read'
Charlie N. Holmberg

'A messy, joyful story about what happens when rockstars meet reality, and about finding the part of yourself that makes you whole. These boys and their love story filled up my heart – I couldn't stop reading, and I didn't want to'
Amie Kaufman

'*Darkhearts* is a delightful, boy-centric YA that doesn't shy away from Romance with a capital R. Chance is a soulful, ethereal mystery to the reader, and David a down-to-earth, weighty mystery to himself, but wherever your tastes lie, you'll find it in *Darkhearts*. Sutter has created a world that will feel starkly familiar to teens, layered with exploration and an unflinchingly real glimpse into the sometimes elusive world of the teen boy. Top everything off with an insta-fave quirky best friend, and a setting steeped with musicians' culture – Sutter is an author to watch'
Aprilynne Pike

DARKHEARTS

JAMES L. SUTTER

ANDERSEN PRESS

First published in 2023 by
Andersen Press Limited
20 Vauxhall Bridge Road, London SW1V 2SA, UK
Vijverlaan 48, 3062 HL Rotterdam, Nederland
www.andersenpress.co.uk

2 4 6 8 10 9 7 5 3 1

British Library Cataloguing in Publication Data available.

ISBN 978 1 83913 337 4

Printed and bound in Great Britain by Clays Ltd, Elcograf S.p.A.

For my mother, Mary Lafond.

Thirty-nine years, and I still constantly find new reasons to admire you.

1

It's hard to know what to say at a friend's funeral. It's even harder to know what to say at an enemy's.

So what do you say when it's both?

I chose the coward's way out and said nothing. When the rabbi finished his eulogy and called for stories from the mourners, I stayed silent. Honestly, it would probably have been the right choice even if I hadn't been chicken. Save for a few texts, I hadn't spoken with Elijah in over two years. Who was I to him, anymore?

It wasn't like there was a dearth of speakers. There were plenty of people who wanted to talk – family, friends, even a couple other celebrities. They said the sorts of things you always say when a kid dies: he was so bright, so talented, so full of potential. Except in Eli's case it was actually true. He wasn't just poised to do great things – he'd done them, and had the Grammys to prove it.

Chance waited until last, of course. Always the showman, never wanting to risk being upstaged, even at his best friend's funeral. He told a story about Eli getting so distracted writing a new song that he accidentally locked himself out of his hotel room in just his underwear. Security caught him trying to climb up to his own balcony, thinking he was some sort of crazed stalker. Everyone laughed through their tears, big sobbing gasps of relief.

It was the perfect ending note. But of course it was – everything about Chance Kain was perfect, from the slim black

1

suit to the asymmetrical flop of his straight black hair. It was what made him America's favorite asshole.

The rest of the service was a blur. I kept my distance from most of it, not wanting to intrude. At the cemetery, I joined the other mourners in forming a ring around the family, trying to shield them from the paparazzi waiting like vultures, giant camera lenses balanced on headstones.

Then it was back to Eli's parents' house for the shiva visit, taking off my shoes and rinsing my hands with the pitcher of water outside the door. If the temple had been awkward, the house itself was stifling. Eli's parents and sister shook my hand, but their eyes were far away. All the mirrors were covered with black cloth, which I knew was another Jewish tradition but just reminded me of the whole Darkhearts vampire shtick. Nobody really spoke, other than brief murmurs of sympathy and muffled tears.

When standing around in their living room got too uncomfortable, I found myself drifting away without really intending to. Nobody noticed as I wandered past the bathroom and down the stairs, retracing the route that had once been second nature.

The furniture in the rec room was right where it had always been, minus only the black bulk of the PA speakers on their spindly stick-stands. The lights were off, and the afternoon sun coming through the big picture window was so achingly familiar that it stabbed straight through me, pinning me to the bottom of the stairs.

"Weird, huh?"

I turned to find Chance tucked into the corner of the old couch, sprawled with his tailored jacket unbuttoned and legs outstretched. Even with eyes red from crying, he looked like a cologne ad. Whereas I looked like exactly what I was: a seventeen-year-old acned ogre wearing his dad's suit.

At some point in the last two years, Chance had gotten a tattoo – a tiny silhouette of a crow in flight, just below and outside his right eye. Because of course he had. He was holding a vape pen, but the lack of candyfloss stink said he knew better than to use it in here. He waved it vaguely at the room.

"It's all the same." He looked up at the ceiling, where the footsteps of mourners clumped and dragged. "Up there, outside, everything's different. But in here, it's like we're still fourteen."

I didn't want to have this conversation. Didn't want to have *any* conversation with him. But my mouth had other ideas.

"Almost," I said.

He raised a professionally groomed eyebrow.

I pointed past him. "They fixed the drywall."

"Oh shit! You're right." He laughed, leaning forward and staring at the spot where the hole had been. "I'd forgotten about that. You jumped off the coffee table and put your guitar's headstock straight through the wall."

"Only because Eli ran into me." I smiled in spite of myself. "We tried to cover it with that poster from the Vera Project."

"Yeah, because that wasn't suspicious at *all* – just one little poster on a giant blank wall." He pulled a knee up to his chest, revealing a flash of purple dress sock with tiny black skulls. "I was sure his mom would kill us for that one. Or remember when we got all those people to come film the video, and someone backed up the toilet?"

I nodded. "The Poonami."

3

"There was like an inch of water soaking the carpet. My parents would have had me in boarding school like *that*." He snapped his fingers. "But Eli – " His voice cracked, and he fell silent. There were no tears, but I could see a muscle working in his jaw.

"Yeah." Eli had been able to talk his parents into anything. I sat down on the other arm of the couch, not looking at him, the old perch still so natural.

"Hey, remember Mrs. Miller?" He pointed at the neighboring house across the tiny backyard, his tone artificially light. "Always banging on the door and yelling at us to turn down. Remember what she always used to say?"

"'My father played with Louie Armstrong! If he didn't need to be this loud, neither do you!'" It had been a running joke between the three of us. Whenever someone flubbed a note or was too loud in the mix, we'd throw something at them – a guitar pick, a couch cushion – and yell *Louie Armstrong!* Eventually it had become an all-purpose battle cry. Our own private yeet.

We both fell silent, staring out the window.

When he spoke again, his voice was tight. "We had some good times here, huh?"

"Yeah," I repeated.

Another long silence.

Suddenly Chance kicked the coffee table, heel slamming into the wooden corner and spinning it halfway around. "God *damn* it, Eli!" He covered his face with his hands.

I still had no idea what to say.

"I just wish he'd *talked* to me." The words were muffled, reverb-y. He pulled his hands away, blinking rapidly. "I knew

4

he was drinking too much, that he was tired of touring, but *everyone* gets tired of touring. I didn't know . . ."

He took a shuddering breath, then stood. He pulled the table back into place, then pocketed his vape and walked to the stairs. At the bottom, he turned to take a last look around the room, searching it for an answer.

"Dammit, Eli," he said again, softer. "How could you just leave us?"

Then he was up the stairs and gone.

I let out a breath. My hands unclenched, and I was suddenly flooded with gratitude that Chance had left when he did. I knew he was hurting, and as much as he pissed me off, I didn't want to make it worse. But if he'd stayed another minute, I might not have been able to keep holding my tongue.

Because I knew the answer to his rhetorical question.

How could Eli leave him behind?

The same way you both left me.

2

All right, let's rip the Band-Aid off:

My name is David Holcomb, and I was almost famous.

When I was thirteen, I started a band with my two best friends. Chance sang, I played guitar, and Elijah programmed everything else on his MacBook. Eli loved big, fake eighties drum sounds, and Chance loved vampires, and between the two we ended up at a sort of poppy goth-rock. We called ourselves Darkhearts, and titled our self-recorded demo *Sad Shit You Can Dance To*.

We got good quick, and for a while it was all I wanted to do. We played every all-ages club in the greater Seattle area, my dad dutifully hauling us and our gear around in his construction van. It was fun to rock out, and there's definitely something to be said for hitting puberty while playing guitar in your middle school's only band. When we won the eighth-grade talent show, you'd have thought we were BTS the way kids screamed. And when we played the Fremont Abbey, Maddy Everhardt threw *actual panties* onto the stage. So yeah, that part was good.

But the thing nobody tells you about being an underage band is that you hit the ceiling pretty quick. It's a ton of work just to play the same handful of all-ages venues over and over. You can't tour, because even if you could convince your parents to take time off work and drive you, who's gonna come see you? Your friends can't drive, either. And to be honest, after the initial novelty of seeing someone they know onstage, most of them

6

don't actually want to see you play the same songs again and again. Sure, there's always YouTube or TikTok, but do you know how many teen bands there are online? The answer is *all of them.*

Add in Eli growing steadily more tyrannical about the songwriting, plus Chance embracing every annoying lead-singer cliché ... well, you get the picture. So when freshman year arrived, with all the new pressures of high school, I proposed taking a break.

Words were exchanged. Birds were flipped. When I walked out of the practice space, nobody followed.

Two months later, a rep for Interscope saw the new two-piece version of Darkhearts at a Neumos early show and signed them on the spot.

Six months after that, they were the hottest new band in North America. *Rolling Stone* described them as "if Chris Cornell returned from the dead to front the Cure." Chance leaned into his vampire act, changing his last name to "Kain" – a biblical reference I found deeply ironic, given how we'd ended things. *Entertainment Weekly* called him "the next David Bowie," while *Pitchfork* compared his glam-rock sex appeal to St. Vincent and Prince. Billie Eilish took them along on her stadium tour.

Meanwhile, I was trying not to fail social studies.

Fortunately, becoming pop stars meant the two of them dropped out of school almost immediately. Between that and the fact that we'd barely hung out since the night I left, I could almost pretend they didn't exist. Sure, it was hard to hear girls talking about how Chance Kain was the best thing to happen to eyeliner, or to hear a car drive past blasting "Midnight's Children." But it wasn't like I'd spent every moment of the last two years jealously stewing about how my life should have been different.

That *certainly* wasn't what I was doing two days after Eli's funeral, lying on my bed recovering from a long day of stacking lumber. Junior year had ended weeks ago, and I'd consented to spending the summer working for my dad's contracting business – a fate which, if not actually *worse* than death, occasionally bore a striking resemblance to Dante's vision of Hell.

My phone chimed from where I'd dropped it on the floor. I stretched out an aching arm and flipped it over, revealing a new text.

> I'm bored. Wanna get dinner?

The number wasn't in my contacts, but it seemed like a weird sort of spam, unless the robocall bots were getting lonely. On the *exceptionally* small chance that a cute girl had somehow gotten ahold of my number without my knowledge, I texted back.

> That depends. Who's this?

The reply was immediate.

> Chance. Had to change my number.

Chance? I let my body go limp again. On the big list of people I didn't want to grab dinner with, Chance was at the top, tied with my mom and Mr. Ullis, the skeezy gym teacher.

The dude had driven me out of my own band with his prima donna bullshit – constantly upstaging me at shows, vetoing my ideas, making unilateral decisions for the whole group – then gotten famous and never looked back. This was literally the first time he'd texted me since the breakup. And now he was hitting me up like nothing even happened?

I was about to text back and tell him exactly what he could eat when an image of a disappointed Eli flashed through my mind.

It shouldn't have mattered. Eli hadn't invited me back aboard the Darkhearts fame train, either. But at least he'd kept in touch a little. And while Eli might screw you over, you at least knew he'd have the grace to feel bad about it. Eli felt bad about *everything*.

More importantly, he'd always been the peacemaker in the band. I knew he'd want me to play nice.

If he were still alive, I might have told *him* to get bent as well. But that's the thing about dead people: it's hard to argue with them.

My fingers seemed to move of their own accord.

When?

The phone chirped.

Now. Pick me up?

The message came with an attached Google Maps link.

The presumption of it set my teeth on edge. He assumed I'd drop everything *and* pick him up? But I shot back a thumbs-up emoji and hoisted myself out of bed. *This is for you, Eli.*

My room was technically the house's attic, which had pluses and minuses. On the one hand, it was big, running the length of our little house. On the other, the slope of the roof to either side meant there was only a six-foot-wide corridor in which I could stand without hitting my head. I grabbed a hoodie from the not-so-dirty pile and hauled open the Floor Door, the trapdoor my dad and I had installed when I was twelve. Except for the angle, it looked exactly like an ordinary door, complete with doorknob.

Downstairs, Dad was splayed out shirtless on the couch, rewatching *Stranger Things.* He saw me come down the stairs and paused the show. "Where are *you* headed so late? I thought you'd be dead after unloading that trailer."

"Gonna go grab pizza."

"Oh yeah?" He sat up. "Want company? I could even put on a shirt."

"I'm actually meeting somebody."

"Oh *reaaaally.*" He grinned and waggled his eyebrows. "Anybody I know?"

I briefly considered lying, but decided it wasn't worth it. "Chance Ng." I wasn't about to use his stupid stage name around Dad.

"*Chance?*" Dad scowled like he'd bitten into something rotten. "What does *he* want?"

"Dad, come on." I hated this topic. "His best friend just died of alcohol poisoning. He probably just wants to talk to somebody who knew Eli as well as he did." As I said it, it suddenly seemed obvious.

"Shit. Right. Sorry." His frown evaporated, replaced by guilt. "Eli's poor parents . . . Well, that's good of you to talk to him." He gave me a sympathetic look. "How are *you* doing with all that?"

I shrugged. "Fine? I dunno. I hadn't seen him in two years."

"I know, I just . . . If you ever want to talk about it . . . I'm here, okay?"

"Yeah."

The ticking of the wall clock filled in as Dad searched for something else to say. Finally he gave up, shaking his head. "You're a good kid, David."

"I know." I opened the door, saving us both from further conversation.

Outside, the night was crisp, despite the fact that the Fourth of July had already come and gone. A streetlight shone down on my truck where it sat at the curb.

"My truck" – two of the most beautiful words in the English language. It wasn't a particularly *nice* truck – was, in fact, the same beat-up F-150 I'd been riding in since I was born, its red paint scratched all to hell by two decades of construction sites. I wasn't even a Truck Guy, one of those faux cowboys trying to stand out from the sea of Priuses and Camrys in the Franklin High School parking lot. But the day Dad handed over the keys for my exclusive use, everything changed. It was no longer *the* truck, it was *my* truck. And that, as Robert Frost wrote, made all the difference. It rumbled awake like a sleeping dragon as I turned the key.

Instead of his old house, Chance had sent me an address up near the Arboretum, where half the driveways had gates and hedges to hide from the prying eyes of normal people. Chance was leaning against one such gate, face illuminated by his phone as he scrolled, the rest of him a slim shadow in a black denim jacket. Making doing nothing look cool was one of his primary talents.

I pulled over and rolled down the passenger window. "Hey."

"Hey." Chance pocketed his phone and peeled himself off the wrought iron. He opened the door and swung up into the cab, taking it in with an appraising eye. "Nice truck."

He probably had a Porsche parked behind that hedge, if not a Lambo. I bit back a retort and pulled away from the curb. "Where we going?"

"Orbital?"

"Sure." I tapped my phone and threw on some music.

"Hey! Bleachers!" Chance let his arm hang out the window, slapping the side of the truck to the beat. "You know we actually recorded with him?"

"Oh yeah?" I kept my tone light, but my dentist would have had some choice comments about the way I was grinding my teeth.

"Yeah, his real name's Jack Antonoff. The label brought him in for a single we did, for that movie with Saoirse Ronan. Dude's a wizard."

"Cool." I cranked the volume, making it impossible to talk.

Orbital Pizza was down in Georgetown, an old industrial district still only halfway gentrified, and thus a maze of warehouses and factories turned into art spaces. Orbital fit the dive flavor to a T, with a crust-punk clientele and active train tracks running through its parking lot. We went inside and slid into a booth across from a kids' airplane ride that had been broken since I was young enough to ride it.

A heavily tattooed waitress with green hair slid us some menus. "You need drinks?"

I ordered a ginger ale, while Chance just got water.

"Will this be separate or together?" she asked.

"Separate," I said, at the same moment Chance said, "Together."

He smiled at me and held up a credit card. "This one's on me."

Irritation flared. "No thanks." I turned back to the waitress and said, "Separate checks, please."

"Sure, hon." She looked vaguely amused, then squinted at Chance. "Aren't you ...?"

He gave her a thousand-watt grin. "Yup."

She studied him a moment longer, one hand on her hip, then shrugged. "Cool." She turned and sauntered back to the bar.

I felt a brief flush of validation at seeing him so thoroughly dismissed, but Chance turned the same grin on me.

"Thank god for punk waitresses." He flipped up one of the menus. "I could be George Clooney and she still wouldn't give a shit."

"You *like* that?" I couldn't quite keep the surprise out of my voice.

"It's refreshing." He didn't look up from the menu. "You want garlic bread? I want garlic bread."

The idea that he could be so famous that *not* being fangirled over was a luxury did nothing to soothe my raw ego. Fortunately, the waitress returned with our drinks, forcing us to stop and order – a meaty pizza-beast called the Brooklyner that had always been our go-to. When she was gone, Chance sprawled out across his side of the booth and put his feet up, dress shoes shiny black against the red vinyl.

Sitting sideways like that perfectly displayed the little crow tattoo, swooping along the edge of one knife-sharp cheekbone like some sort of corvid prison tat. I wondered if he arranged the flop of his bangs specifically to point toward it. Anyone who gets a face tattoo is desperate to be asked about it.

I resolved to die before mentioning it.

Chance looked me over, taking in my brown Carhartts and blue plaid button-down. "You've changed up your style."

"Yeah. Guess I outgrew the eyeliner goth phase." In fact, I'd dumped it the moment Darkhearts got signed – the painted nails, the black clothes, the dye and wax to transform my wavy brown mop. The last thing I wanted was to see Chance and Eli every time I looked in the mirror.

"Ouch." Chance grinned and splayed a black-nailed hand against his chest, acknowledging the hit. "Well, at least you've still got the ghoul-pale thing going."

"True." That part of the Hot Topic look had come naturally.

"It works for you. Farmer Holcomb. Very rugged." He looked up at the old show posters on the walls, the cow skulls and retro beer ads. "Man, I miss this place. Remember when your dad used to bring us here after gigs?"

Of course I remembered. It had only been two years. "You don't come here on your own?"

He shrugged. "I'm always on the road. And whenever I'm not, Mom's so starved for family time that she wants us to either cook together or go off on vacation somewhere."

"She doesn't travel with you?"

"And leave her job? Nah. Dad comes on tour – I guess technically I'm homeschooled now. But Mom stays here with Olivia. She says at least one of us kids should have a normal life."

"I don't know what's so great about a normal life," I muttered.

"You'd be surprised." He stretched languorously, folding his hands behind his head. "I know it sounds cool, but most of touring is just travel. Getting up at four in the morning to fly somewhere, or trying to sleep on a bus while you haul ten hours through the middle of nowhere. You don't realize how much of the country is corn until you've driven from Denver to Omaha. Ninety percent of this job is sitting around waiting for bathroom breaks."

"Yeah, and the other ten percent is playing stadiums and going on talk shows." I rubbed my fingers together. "Lemme bust out my tiny violin."

To my surprise, he laughed. "Fair enough." He swung his legs around under the table and sat up, leaning forward. "Enough about me. How's life? What's been going on?"

I squirmed beneath the force of his gaze. That was the thing about Chance: when he turned the spotlight on you, you felt the heat. It was part of what made him a great frontman.

"Nothing much," I said. "Working for my dad this summer, doing construction. Other than that, just, you know, school."

"Yeah? What's that like?"

"Seriously?"

"Seriously what?"

"You really want to hear about high school?"

"Dude, I was at Franklin less than nine months – my knowledge of high school comes primarily from teen movies. And I'm pretty sure nobody's getting laid as much as those suggest." He shot me a calculatedly devilish look. "Or *are* they? You ever ask Maddy Everhardt out?"

I flinched. "What?"

"Dude, she threw her panties at you."

"She threw them at *us*. And that was just a joke."

"Yeah, it's always a joke till it's not. And now two of us are gone. You've had two years of wide-open runway."

I barely kept my mouth closed. That bald statement – the way he so casually mentioned their abandonment of me, the not-so-subtle implication that I only had a chance with Maddy because he'd left the picture – froze over any part of me that had started to thaw under his attention. And never mind that he'd flirted shamelessly with Maddy when he'd known I liked her – the way he flirted with *all* the girls at our shows, making sure none ever had time for the rest of us, because who could compete with that dazzling smile? It had been one of the last straws that drove me out of the band.

As it turned out, I *had* dated Maddy. For three months, sophomore year. She'd been my first real kiss, and more.

And then she'd ditched me without a backward glance, like everyone eventually did. All because of – who else? – Chance Kain.

But I wasn't about to tell Chance any of that. I sat back and crossed my arms. "Yeah, well, it's not quite that easy."

He nodded sympathetically. "I feel you, bruh."

I snorted. "Sure you do."

"What? You don't believe me?"

I raised an eyebrow.

He held his hands up in surrender. "Dude, okay, yes – I meet a lot of girls. But you know what the gossip sites *don't* show? My dad and my manager chilling in the corner, waiting for me to get back on the tour bus. I'm in a different city every night. How am I supposed to date anybody?"

I hadn't really considered that angle. He ran a hand through his hair, somehow managing to mess it up while still looking like he'd just walked off a movie set.

"Trust me, man: there's freedom in staying in one place.

Your friends are always nearby. I've got a lot of numbers and mutuals, and get to hang out with a lot of cool people, but at the end of the day, it's just me and Eli." He grimaced. "Or at least it was."

"Shit."

Silence descended over the table. I folded my straw wrapper into an accordion while Chance toyed with his silverware.

"He hated the parties," Chance said at last. "I'd always try to get him to come. 'Come make friends,' I'd say, and he'd be like, 'Why would I want more friends?'"

I fought back a smile. That did sound like Eli.

"I'll never understand that," Chance continued. "Like, shy I get. If you're scared of talking to new people – okay, fine. But Eli wasn't shy. I mean, remember the Penis Game?"

The Penis Game, which had been all the rage in fifth grade, had been simple: seeing who was willing to yell "penis" loudest in a public area. "He always won."

"Every. Time. It didn't matter if you were on the bus or in a store or *what*. He's the reason people *stopped* playing." Chance shook his head. "He didn't care what anybody thought. I wish I had that kind of confidence."

I rolled my eyes. "Says Chance Kain."

"Man, I care what *everybody* thinks. All frontmen do. It's why we're out in front."

The sudden honesty caught me off guard. "Huh."

He pointed a fork at me. "You've got it too, you know. That confidence."

I scoffed. "Yeah, right."

"No, seriously." He looked me in the eye, and it was like getting blasted by Cyclops from the X-Men. "You've had it since the day we met. You were ten years old and ready to kick my ass over Magic: The Gathering."

I grinned in spite of myself. "You traded Eli two Pitchburn Devils for a Kalonian Hydra. Someone had to teach you a lesson."

Chance grinned back. "It's not my fault he didn't look up the price guides! But you set up that whole sting operation to get them back. You were fearless."

Eli had wanted to drop the issue, but I wouldn't let him. Chance wasn't in our class, so I'd made Eli take me to the park where they hung out.

"And then you sucker-punched me," Chance said, with satisfaction.

"I did *not*! I gave you a choice! It's not a sucker punch if I tell you I'm gonna do it."

"Yeah, but I didn't think you *would*. And then I hit you with my card binder, and Eli faked that asthma attack and made us carry him all the way home."

I chuckled. Eli had gone as rigid as a wooden plank, in a preteen guess at what an asthma attack might look like. By the time the two of us managed to carry him the three blocks to his house, Chance had agreed to give Eli's cards back, and we'd all gone to eat Otter Pops and play Xbox.

"What a legend," Chance said. Then, quieter, "I still can't believe he's gone."

In that moment, the boy across the table didn't look like Chance Kain, International Sensation. He looked like a slightly larger version of Chance Ng, the boy who'd stopped in the middle of a fight to help one enemy carry another. Looking at him now, I felt the same thing I'd felt that day: that maybe there was more to this kid than just the grinning huckster. I wanted to reach out and put a hand on his shoulder.

A plate of garlic bread slid between us, breaking the moment.

"Oh, *hells* yes!" Chance grabbed a slice, bobbling it between fingers. "Hot! Hot!" He flashed his magazine smile, sliding back into character. "Hey, did you know that when you do anything in Hollywood, they're required by union rules to have a massive catering spread? We shot this video last year, and they had like ten thousand dollars of just *snacks*. The girl in the video with us – Clara Shadid, you probably saw her in the new Bond movie – anyway, she'd been flirting with me the whole shoot, right? So she takes this whole chocolate-dipped banana, and I swear to god—"

I sighed and psychically willed the pizza to cook faster. It was going to be a long dinner.

3

"You had dinner with Chance Kain?!" Ridley crouched in the tiny garden of her parents' house and pointed a gloved finger at me accusingly. "And you waited until *now* to mention it?"

I lounged in an ancient lawn chair, the vinyl strips pressing zebra lines into my arms and legs. "It's not a big deal."

"Um, *yeah*, it is." Ridley tossed another weed on the pile. It was hot today, and sweat glistened along the dark skin of her arms, staining the armpits of her sleeveless shirt. My own untoasted Wonder Bread complexion was already noticeably pinker than it had been this morning. "He's in the top ten hottest guys in America. I mean, objectively – that's not me, that's *Teen Vogue*. They're basically a peer-reviewed journal of celebrity hotness. I knew you used to play together, but that was knowing, like, *intellectually*. This is different." She wiped her forehead, smearing dirt across the pink scarf restraining her cloud of kinky black hair. "So spill some tea. What's he like?"

Ridley McNeill had moved down to South Seattle sophomore year, and was thus one of the few people in our grade who hadn't had at least a passing acquaintance with Chance and Eli. If I was being honest, it was probably one of the things that drew me to her initially – the chance to be around someone who didn't automatically associate me with them.

"He's kind of a dick." Though even as I said it, I had to admit it wasn't entirely fair. There had been moments last night when it had almost been like the old Chance, from back when we'd spend all summer playing video games and swimming in the lake. But it was easier to go with the preloaded answer.

"But a *hot* dick, right?"

"Do you even listen to the words you say?"

"Whatever." She threw an uprooted dandelion at me. "It's just such a waste. Chance Kain spending the evening with the one person on the planet who doesn't want to jump his bones, while I'm stuck here pulling weeds."

"There are like ten weeds. We'd already be gone if you worked a little faster."

"You could help, you know."

"Sorry, I'm otherwise occupied. Isn't that right, Artoo?" I addressed the question to the McNeills' basset hound – full name Artoo Dogtoo Leeloo Dallas Multipass McNeill. He was puddled next to the lawn chair, accepting my scritches like the flatulent emperor he was. "Besides, they're your chores. I'm just moral support."

"Then support. Keep me entertained while I'm in Yard Jail." She dug another weed out of her mother's strawberries, making a face at the tiny slug clinging to it. "Hit me with the hot goss. Is he dating anybody?"

"What? I don't know."

"You didn't even *ask*? You have no sense for the sensational. What does he go for? Is he actually bi, or is it just a stage thing?"

"Dude, I wasn't building him a dating profile."

"It's just that his public image makes it this big mystery. Is he straight? Is he queer? What's his deal?"

I thought back to years of sleepovers, telling secrets in the dark. "I'm pretty sure he likes girls. Or at least he did. I dunno if that's expanded. Like I said, I didn't ask." The idea of hearing Chance talk about his sex life was intensely uncomfortable.

Ridley shook her head. "You're killing me, Smalls."

"Smalls?" Ridley's primary goal in life was to become a professional film critic, which meant she was constantly quoting things nobody else had seen. She even had her own blog-slash-newsletter, *Modern Lens*, where she wrote about old movies and how they did or didn't hold up in the modern era. (*Fight Club*, for instance, remained a nihilistic masterpiece despite its contributions to toxic masculinity, while *Ace Ventura* was transphobic garbage.) Her most popular posts actually rewrote key scenes to bring them up to date, and she was starting to think about doing creative writing in college as well as film studies.

"You haven't seen *The Sandlot*?!" She gave me an incredulous look, then waved it away. "That's basically child abuse. But never mind – we'll deal with your tragic upbringing another time. The point is, I need *details*. Some grade-A Chance Kain specifics. They really help set the scene when I'm rubbing one out."

"Dude!"

"Okay, okay – cool your tool. I'll keep my private time private." She tossed a slug-eaten strawberry to Artoo. "So if you weren't getting me juicy celebrity-hookup gossip, what *did* you guys talk about?"

I frowned. "Mostly Eli."

"Oh." Ridley sat back onto her butt, barely missing a ceramic lawn gnome. She looked embarrassed. "Shit, I'm sorry. Here I am, thinking with my lady boner, and you were just at a funeral. How're you doing?"

"Okay? I guess?" You'd think I'd have had a better answer,

given how often people kept asking. I picked up the dandelion she'd tossed and twirled it in my fingers, watching its cottony ball spin. "I mean, I didn't really know him anymore. But it's still weird, you know? He's the only kid I've known who's died. And like, he was always kinda melancholy, but he didn't even drink when I knew him. It's strange to think that someone I have all these memories about is gone. It both changes things and doesn't. I dunno." I rubbed my eyebrow. "Can we talk about something else?"

"Sure." She nodded sympathetically, then grinned. "Hey! Here's something fun: I haven't told you yet, but my family's going to visit my grandparents in Yakima next month."

"Lucky you ...?"

"No, you don't get it: *My family* is going to Yak-in-the-Crack. *I'm* staying here, because we've got the SAT that Saturday." She gave a magician's flourish. "Which means that Saturday *night*, we'll have the house all to ourselves."

"Oh yeah?" I sat up straighter.

As sexual tension went, Ridley and I were about as low as possible for two theoretically compatible, sexually frustrated teenagers. Which was honestly a little weird, as she was objectively cute – prodigiously curvy (what she called "Rubenesque"), with skin like a mahogany stain on red cedar and a constant mischievous smile. Yet for reasons I couldn't entirely explain, ever since her first whispered joke during precalc, we'd fallen immediately into an easy, sibling-style friendship. A "mixed-gender bromance," as she termed it.

But platonic or not, when a girl says you should come over because her parents aren't home, it suggests certain possibilities.

Before I could dig into that statement, two red dots appeared on the grass beside me. Giggles rang out from above as they tracked over onto Ridley.

I made a big show of noticing them, then leaped out of my chair, covering Ridley's body with my own. "Madam President! Get down!"

A barrage of Nerf darts rained down, rubber suckers thwapping against my back. I dragged the lawn chair over us, using it as a shield.

Ridley wriggled out from under me, laughing. "Get off me, you knob-goblin!"

Artoo shambled over, unable to resist the call of the laser, and began licking my face like he was trying to find the center of the Tootsie Pop. I tried unsuccessfully to hold him at bay, craning my head to avoid the slobber. "Good god, Artoo! Your breath!"

"Well, for the last half hour, he's been eating his own butthole, so." Ridley slapped dirt off her own posterior and glared up at the second-story window, where two giggling gremlins peered down, laser pointers taped to Nerf guns. "Does Mom know you're opening windows?"

"No," Kaylee yelled back.

"That was rhetorical, dingus."

"You swore!" Malcolm accused gleefully. "I'm telling!"

"'Dingus' isn't a swear, you quisling."

"Quick," I said, gathering darts off the lawn. "What bad guys are we? Orcs?"

"Right, because the hobbits *totally* had automatic weapons. Plus the whole orc thing is racist."

"Fine." I stood up from behind my lawn chair barricade and began whipping darts up at the window. "For the Fire Nation!"

Most of the darts bounced off the house, but one sailed

satisfyingly through the window, clipping Malcolm on the ear. The kids yelled with delight and disappeared, cranking the window shut behind themselves.

Ridley put her hands on her hips. "They only do this with you, you know."

"I know." I righted the lawn chair.

"You're like five times nicer to them than they deserve."

"Maybe." Personally, I thought her siblings were pretty cool, as first and second graders went. But that was probably my only-child status talking. I was sure the constant running and screaming would get old if I were trapped in the same house with them every day. "Anyway. You were saying they're gonna be gone?"

"Yup." Her canary-eating smile returned. "And I'm going to throw the biggest, most clichéd party you've ever been to. Everything Hollywood shows teenagers doing that never actually happens? We're doing it."

I paused in collecting the last few darts. "Wait, really?"

"Hundred percent. We'll make it movie-themed, naturally – come dressed as your favorite film character. We're gonna get wasted and play strip Twister and make questionable romantic decisions and it'll be *epic*."

That *did* sound pretty epic. But I frowned. "Where are *you* gonna get alcohol?"

"Jackson's on it."

"You're inviting your brother?"

"No!" She chewed her lip. "Though, actually, now that you say it, having some college guys here might be cool. But no, his roommate has a fake ID. He promised to get us a bunch of White Claw and shit."

"Damn, nice. What'd you promise him?"

"Nothing." Smugness radiated off her like a space heater. "He still owes me for smoothing over the Great Valentine's Day Debacle."

I raised an eyebrow. "You've been holding that over him all this time?"

"Are you kidding? After all the work I put into Operation Not-a-Scumbag? Dude was never gonna save that on his own."

She had a point. "I guess the bit with the baby rabbit rental *was* pretty impressive."

"Damn straight. Honeys love bunnies. And by my calculations, him still having a girlfriend is worth *at least* one illicit beer run."

I shook my head admiringly. "You're always keeping score, aren't you?"

"It's why I'm the boss, baby. Like the Godfather but sexy. Don Corleone in capris." She pointed her trowel at me. "Which reminds me: *you* still owe me for letting you use my research on Ms. Schiffrin's take-home final."

I sighed and got to my feet. "Fine. Which ones are weeds?"

"Okay, one, you're a little late to that party, and two, do you really think *weeding* is an equivalent favor? I'll let you off easy, but not *that* easy." She paused for effect. "I want you to invite Chance to my party."

"What? No!" I glared. "Did you not hear anything I just said?"

"I heard you say he's a jerk. That may be so. He's *also* the most exciting thing to happen around here all year, and I want a piece of it. Think how much cooler our party will be with some star power! Who's gonna skip that one?"

"No. No way."

"Come *on*, Davey! Don't let your beef get in the way of epic party times."

Was there any part of my life that was safe from Darkhearts bullshit? "He's probably not even going to be here in a month. He's always either out on tour or down in L.A."

"Hmm." She crossed her arms, thinking. "Okay, new plan: set up a chance for us to hang out, just the three of us."

I rubbed my eyes. "You're really not going to stop with this, are you?"

She frowned. "Look, I get it: you hate that Chance got famous and you're stuck bumming around here with the queen of the nerds. I know you don't like talking about Darkhearts, so I never ask about it. And I won't after this, I promise. Just bring him by my work or something so I've got bragging rights. I can feel fancy, and afterward all my co-workers can wonder what other tantalizing mysteries lie inside the girl scrubbing congealed grease out of the griddle tray." She opened her eyes super wide and clasped her hands together. "*Please?*"

There was no fighting it. "Ugh, fine. Just stop giving me anime eyes."

"*Yusss!*" She gave a Napoleon Dynamite fist pump.

"Now can you please finish your prison sentence so we can go swimming already? Gabe and Angela are probably already out on the boat."

"You got it." She bent over and began ripping up weeds and weed-like greenery with hitherto unseen gusto. She looked back slyly over her shoulder at me. "You know, this really *would* go faster if you helped."

I picked up another dandelion and blew on its puff, showering her in a thousand floating seeds.

"Oh you *dong-weasel*," she said good-naturedly. "If any of these sprout next year, I'm busing over and leaving them in your bed."

"Sticking with the *Godfather* theme, I see."

"Don Corleone, baby. Don. Corleone."

4

It killed me to ask Chance for anything, but a favor was a favor, especially where Ridley was concerned. So the next afternoon, I walked the few blocks from my house to Bamf Burger.

Unlike Ridley, who lived down near the strip of restaurants and shops along Rainier, I lived in a mostly residential neighborhood, with one tiny pocket of commerce. There was a bookstore, a pet-supply place, a hair salon – and Bamf Burger.

A car with an illuminated Lyft sign idled by the curb out front. As I crossed the street, the door opened and Chance unfurled out of the back seat.

He looked like he'd stepped out of a music video. The clothes were admittedly understated for him – a charcoal dress shirt with a skinny black tie and skinnier black jeans. On anybody else, they might have said "coming straight from church," and maybe he even had, given that it was Sunday. Yet there was something about the *way* he wore them that made all the difference: shirt straining against broad shoulders, tie loose and top few buttons undone, sleeves rolled up across wiry forearms. It was the sort of artfully disheveled look you saw all the time in ads, but that just looked sloppy when *you* tried it. Unless you were Chance Kain.

He pulled dark aviators halfway down and grinned wolfishly. "Figured I'd wait out here for you, so we can make our grand entrance." He tapped the side of the car, which pulled away.

"Thanks?" I hauled open the restaurant door.

Inside, the air hung thick with sour grease and onion. Pages from old comic books papered every wall of the cramped dining area, and a TV off to one side played a fight scene from a Marvel movie.

"Christ, I've missed this place, too." Chance clapped me on the shoulder. "I'm gonna get fat hanging out with you, Holcomb."

We made our way to the counter, where a pimply dude with a name tag reading JEFFREY was working the register. I ordered a Colossus Burger with yam fries and a Coke. Jeffrey looked past me to Chance, his eyes widening in recognition.

Chance had learned his lesson, and stood a few feet back, waiting for me to pay before stepping up to make his own order. I turned away to find a table, but not before I saw him tuck a twenty into the tip jar.

Asshole, I thought, and immediately felt ridiculous. While I might not enjoy him flaunting his wealth, I had to admit that tipping well did not, traditionally, make one an asshole.

"You came!" Ridley launched herself out of the kitchen, still wearing her apron. Her usual majestic mane was locked up in a protective bun. She tackled me in a hug redolent of fry oil, knocking me halfway into a booth. Then she turned, suddenly shy, and gave Chance a little wave. "Hi. I'm Ridley."

"Hey Ridley. I'm Chance." He nodded to the booth. "Want to join us?"

Despite the fact that they both knew the entire *point* of this was so they could meet each other, Ridley beamed like Prince Charming had just invited her to the ball. She slid in beside me.

Chance leaned back against the window and put one leg up,

resting his arm on it like he was posing for a photo shoot. He was still wearing the aviators. I didn't know if that was part of the whole Darkhearts vampire gimmick, or just the standard "celebrity incognito" look, but it annoyed me either way. The fact that they looked great on him only made it worse.

"Ridley," he said smoothly. "That's a cool name."

Ridley rolled her eyes. "I guess. My parents are big nerds. They love Star Wars, so if I'd been a boy, they would have named me Fisher, after Carrie Fisher. But I was a girl, so they named me Ridley after Ridley Scott, the guy who directed *Alien*."

"Wicked." He flashed her a smile. "So which is better, Alien or Star Wars?"

"Oooh! Um …" Ridley tapped her lips, enjoying the challenge. "If we're talking the whole franchises, they've both got some genius and some garbage. But I think Star Wars. It's certainly less transgressive – *A New Hope* is literally just Campbell's hero's journey. But it's obviously had a greater impact on society as a whole, and the twists in *Empire* pretty much set the standard for every trilogy that came after. Plus there's just more to the universe, and more characters that stick with people. Leia, Han, Lando, Yoda. Alien's pretty much just got Ripley and the xenomorph."

Chance nodded, but like he was considering rather than agreeing. "Interesting."

Ridley's eyebrows rose in challenge. "You disagree?"

A kinder person would have warned him that he'd just challenged a black belt to a bar fight, but I wasn't feeling particularly generous.

Chance shrugged artfully. "You're not wrong. Star Wars is a modern pantheon – the iconic villain, the badass princess, the

31

scoundrel, the farm boy destined for greatness. Plus there's Muppets. It's Henson's Law: CGI will always show its age, but puppets are forever."

"*Right?!*" Ridley smiled. "Salacious Crumb for the win."

"*But.*" Chance raised a finger pedantically. "I'd argue that Alien's the better art. Giger's creature design is so alien because elements are so disturbingly *familiar.* Like all of Giger's work, it plays on the inherent connection between darkness and sexuality."

Now it was my turn to roll my eyes, but Ridley's face lit up like a jack-o'-lantern.

"Yes!" She leaned forward. "I've got this theory that regardless of how you dress it up, all horror comes down to the same fundamental human fears. Like, the alien's entire life cycle is a direct metaphor for fears of rape, infestation, and pregnancy."

"Exactly." Chance sketched a curve in the air. "Just look at the creature's head. It's basically a giant penis."

"And now we're talking about dicks in public. Lovely." I looked around to see who was watching, which was pretty much all of the occupied tables.

Chance pulled his foot down off the seat and removed his sunglasses, giving Ridley a contrite look. "Sorry. I hope I'm not getting you in trouble."

"No, it's cool, I'm on break." Ridley leaned out of the booth and yelled "*I'm on break!*" at nobody in particular. She turned back, and her eyes widened. "Hey – you got a tattoo!" Then she slapped a hand over her mouth. "Oh my god! Does it make me a total stalker that I know it's new?"

Yes, I thought, but Chance just smiled graciously. "If I didn't want people to notice, I wouldn't have put it on my face. I got it when I turned eighteen a few weeks ago."

Ridley dropped her hand, looking relieved. "Can I ask what it means?"

Chance flashed a smile, mystery and sass in equal parts. "It's my psychopomp. He shows me where to go."

"Your spirit guide?" Ridley leaned forward eagerly.

"Like Virgil in Dante's *Inferno*," I said, just to establish that I, too, had taken AP English, and was thus also Very Smart.

"Exactly." Chance gave no hint of embarrassment. "A reminder that we're all wandering in a dark wood, looking for someone to help us on our way." He pointed to the tattoo, as if we weren't already talking about it. "That's why I got it beside my right eye – because we read left to right. So when I look in the mirror, he reminds me to look to the future, not the past."

Gag me, I thought, but Ridley was enraptured.

"Wow," she said, then looked suddenly sympathetic. "I'm sorry about Elijah, by the way. I should have said that sooner."

"Thank you." Chance bobbed his head solemnly. "So, Ridley . . . Holc here tells me you go to Franklin?"

"Yeah, I switched schools two years ago." She shot me a confused look. "But hold up – 'Holc'?"

I grimaced. "Some people used to call me that." Most people, actually. I'd made a point of dropping it at the same time I'd stopped wearing all black.

"They don't anymore?" Chance looked surprised. "But it's so perfect!" He reached out and grabbed my bicep. "Look at these guns. Holc smash!"

I shrugged him off, blushing and annoyed. There was a time

when the fact that I was taller and heavier than Chance and Eli had been something we could all joke about. Now, coming from this designer-clad, Hollywood-polished version, it felt suspiciously like a fat joke.

Fortunately, Jeffrey approached with a tray before I had a chance to brood properly. He set the food down, then stayed standing there, staring. "You're Chance Kain."

"And you're Jeffrey." Chance shot him a wink and finger-gun, then leaned close and tapped the guy's name tag with a stage whisper. "*I cheated.*"

"Wow." Jeffrey gaped. "I mean ... wow. You probably know all the hot famous chicks, huh?"

"I don't know about 'all' ..." Chance demurred.

"Do you know Taylor Swift?"

"We've met."

"What about Carmen Elizalde?"

Chance winked. "A gentleman never tells."

"Thank you, Jeffrey," Ridley said pointedly.

"Wow." Jeffrey finally moved, but only to dig out his phone. "Do you think ...?"

"Of course." Chance leaned in and bared flawless teeth as Jeffrey mugged for the selfie.

"*Thank you, Jeffrey.*" Ridley's foot pressed firmly down on Jeffrey's.

At last the boy took the hint. With a final "Wow," he returned to the counter.

"Sorry about that," Ridley said.

"Don't be," Chance said. "It happens."

"I can't believe he threw up a west-side sign in that picture," I said. "We're not even *on* the west side."

Ridley ignored me. "So what do you do when you're not touring?"

Chance had ordered fries and a milkshake, and he popped the lid in order to dunk one. "Oh, y'know. Interviews, acting, work on new music. Read poetry."

"Poetry?" Ridley looked intrigued. "Like what?"

"All sorts of things. I love Billy Collins's *Art of Drowning*. Or Stephen Crane. Do you know Crane?"

Ridley shook her head. Chance leaned forward, staring deeply into her eyes, and said:

> *"In the desert*
> *I saw a creature, naked, bestial,*
> *Who, squatting upon the ground,*
> *Held his heart in his hands,*
> *And ate of it.*
> *I said, 'Is it good, friend?'*
> *'It is bitter – bitter,' he answered;*
>
> *'But I like it*
> *'Because it is bitter,*
> *'And because it is my heart.'"*

He finished and leaned back.

"Whoa," Ridley breathed.

"Can you believe he wrote that in 1895?" Chance spread his arms out across the top of the booth, still holding the milkshake. "It's so dark, so raw. Timeless in its melancholy. It really speaks to me."

The drama of this pronouncement was spoiled somewhat

as he tried to take a sip of milkshake, only for the straw to collapse. After a second of fruitless sucking, he gave up. "I'd forgotten you can't drink these with a straw."

"Yeah, sorry," Ridley said. "We make 'em thick."

"That's okay." He gave her a suggestive smile. "I *like* 'em thick."

Ridley actually *giggled*, and any remaining positive feelings I might have been harboring toward Chance since our pizza night evaporated. I tore into my burger.

The rest of lunch continued in that vein, with Chance giving dramatically intellectual or enigmatic answers to every question. With Jeffrey having broken the seal, three other restaurant patrons came over, two for selfies and one with a napkin that Chance dutifully signed, flirting easily and shamelessly with all of them.

At last the food was gone, and Ridley looked up regretfully at the clock. "My break's over."

"Well, it's been lovely to meet you, Ridley." Chance slipped his sunglasses back on. "I'm glad David introduced us. I'll definitely check out your newsletter."

"Me too." Ridley still had a stupid grin on her face. "I mean, I'm glad he introduced us, not that I'll check out my newsletter. I already check it out regularly." She laughed awkwardly. "Hopefully he'll bring you around again."

I bristled internally – our deal was for *once* – but Chance said, "I'd like that."

We got up and left, Chance giving a little wave to all the eyes following us.

Outside, I said, "Well, catch ya later," and turned to walk home.

A touch on my arm stopped me. "Hey. Want to go for a walk?"

I must have shown my shock, because Chance quickly removed his hand, turning it into a vague gesture down the hill. "I mean, I already Ubered all the way here. Come on, let's go to the park." He smiled encouragingly.

The last thing I wanted was to spend the rest of my Sunday with Chance, but something – maybe basic politeness, maybe the surprise, maybe the fact that even *I* was flattered by Chance Kain wanting to hang out – made it hard to say no. I shoved my hands in my pockets. "Yeah, sure."

We began walking down the hill toward Lake Washington. Chance's head swiveled constantly as he drank in the rows of picturesque craftsman houses, the smell of trees and gardens.

"Man. I love summer here. Everywhere else, people hear 'Seattle' and go" – his voice went high and whiny – "'Eww, doesn't it rain all the time?'" He shook his head. "They have no idea. I mean, look at that shit." He jerked his chin toward a madrona leaning out over the sidewalk, its papery red bark curling up in long strips, framed by the blazing blue sky.

"I guess," I grumbled.

He looked over at me. "What's up?"

"*Dude.*" The word was out before I knew it, dripping venom. I pointed back up the hill toward the restaurant. "Why'd you have to be all fake?"

He looked startled. "What?"

I put a dramatic hand on my chest. "*This poetry . . . so deep, so timeless in its sadness . . .*" I dropped it. "Since when do you read poetry?"

He shoved his hands in his pockets. "I read some."

"Fine, but it's not *you*. That whole time – flirting with everybody, acting all mysterious and intellectual. You weren't even *talking* like you. You weren't like that the other night."

"That was different."

"How?"

Chance leaned back against someone's fence and took his sunglasses off. Without them, he looked suddenly tired.

"Look, dude. Hanging out with you is one thing. You already know me. But other people don't want me. They want Chance Kain."

"Bullshit."

"Oh really?" Chance sneered. "You got a lot of experience being Chance Kain?" I flushed with anger and embarrassment, but he didn't wait. "Trust me on this. This is just how it is. People don't want to meet celebrities – they want to meet the *image*. You think Johnny Depp is really Captain Jack Sparrow all the time? That Chris Evans is really Captain America?" He shook his head. "Go on any 'Who's met a celebrity?' thread on Reddit. It's all people mad that some famous person wasn't who they thought they were. You've gotta show them what they want to see. Dudes like Jeffrey want to think I'm wrecking hotel rooms and banging every hot chick in Hollywood. Girls like Ridley want to think I'm brooding and thoughtful. So yeah, it's poetry or whatever. You think they want to hear about me playing *Animal Crossing* and doing homework for my dad?"

I crossed my arms, unconvinced. "Whatever. Just don't do it to Ridley, okay? She's cool."

He sighed and pushed off the fence. "Fine. Just for you. But don't blame me when she's disappointed."

We started walking again. He hung his sunglasses off his

half-buttoned shirt. "So. Are you and her ...?" He let the suggestion hang in the air.

"What? No! She's just a friend."

"You sure?"

"Positive." I looked over at him. "Why? Are you actually interested?"

He shrugged. "Just curious. I hadn't heard from you in a while."

My hackles rose. "Heard from *me*? You didn't exactly reach out."

He gave me a cool stare. "Yeah, well, given how you left things, it seemed like maybe you didn't want me to." Then he looked away. "Anyway. I'm glad we're hanging out now. It's good to see you again."

The sincerity in his voice caught me off guard. It was so easy to be mad at him when he was doing his rock star bullshit, but as soon as he wasn't, it felt petty and small. I was starting to get emotional whiplash.

"Speaking of which," he said, "there's a memorial concert for Eli on Saturday night. You should come. I'll put you on the guest list."

The look on my face must have said everything, because he rolled his eyes. "Oh, come on. It's not just me – it'll be a bunch of other artists doing tributes. I'm barely even in it."

As fun activities went, watching Chance prance around being adored was somewhere below "wisdom teeth removal" and "getting my junk caught in a zipper." But if it was for Eli ...

"I might be busy," I said.

"Sure, whatever. Just text me if you want in."

We reached the bottom of the hill, where Seward Park

jutted out into Lake Washington, a walking path circling the base of its thickly forested hill. I started toward the path, but Chance stopped me once again with a touch on the elbow.

"Uh, could we do the woods instead?" He nodded up at the hill, then shot a look at the crowded path. "There's just a lot of people here . . ."

I started to mock him, then remembered the fans in the restaurant. "Okay." We crossed the parking lot and headed up onto the trails.

Within moments, the sounds of the city cut off, swallowed by giant trees and thick beds of fern. Narrow trails split off in every direction, and we followed one at random, switchbacking upward. Every so often we'd catch glimpses of the lake, with its distant bridges and flotilla of boats.

"Man," Chance said, "remember when we played laser tag out here?"

"Yeah." For my twelfth birthday, my dad had rented the equipment, and we'd brought it down to the park, hunting our friends through these woods.

"You, me, and Eli – we were unstoppable. Your dad had to split us up so the other kids would have a fighting chance."

I smiled at the memory. "Yeah. We were pretty good."

But Chance's own smile was small and tight, his eyes turned toward the underbrush. As if he might still find us hiding there.

We came across a huge tree that had fallen, smashing a little clearing out of the dense brush. Its surface was a solid bed of moss, and Chance flopped down on it, lying with arms outstretched like Christ on the cross. "I miss being outside."

"You don't go outside?" I plucked a fern, stripping the tiny brown spore dots from beneath its leaves with my thumbnail.

"Tour, man. Wake up, work out, school with my dad, get to the venue, do press, meet and greet, play the show, then do it all over again the next day."

"You don't get days off?"

"I mean, sometimes. We fly home whenever we can. But Benjamin – that's my manager – he says teen acts have a shelf life. If we want a chance at still doing this when we're twenty-five, we need to tour as hard as we can now to build up the fan base." He frowned. "Or at least, that was the plan."

I didn't want to ask, but couldn't help myself. "So what happens now? Without Eli."

"Who the hell knows? Everybody's still trying to figure it out." He picked up a pine cone and threw it sidearm into the bushes. "So you're working for your dad this summer?"

"Yeah."

"You like it?"

"It's okay."

"What all do you do?"

"Whatever needs doing."

He sat up, laughing incredulously. "Jesus, Holcomb. Work with me here."

A flash of anger. "Sorry I'm not as interesting as your celebrity friends."

"Dude, what did I just tell you?" He gave me a hard look. "Celebrities aren't actually interesting. We're all just faking it, everyone doing the same job and pretending to have a good time. But yeah, I've got a lot of rock stars in my phone. If I wanted to talk to them, I could." He pulled up a clump of moss and chucked it at me. "Instead, I'm out here talking to *your* truculent ass. So what does that say about you?"

In spite of myself, I felt my anger melting away, replaced by a hot flush of pride. "Truculent, huh?"

"You're not the only one studying for the SAT."

I chucked the moss back. "I'm a gofer."

"Excuse me?"

"What I do at work – that's what it's called, a gofer. I go get stuff for them. Lunch, supplies, whatever. Plus cleaning and carrying. On good days, I get to learn actual carpentry."

"Gofer, huh? Now I'm imagining you building stuff in a Chuck E. Cheese costume."

"Don't give my dad any ideas."

Chance smiled. "Remember that time we were like ten, and he was still remodeling your house, and he paid us for each dropped nail we picked up?"

"And we realized we could just take them from the nail bucket and sell them back to him."

"I bought so much candy I threw up." Chance lay back down on the log, hands behind his head.

The log was plenty long enough, so this time I did the same, lying with my heels almost touching his. The moss was surprisingly soft, and the sun filtering down through the leaves and needles high above gave a pleasant sense of vertigo as the trees swayed. They reminded me of a phenomenon I'd read about called crown shyness – the way some trees deliberately keep a gap between themselves and the trees around them, so they don't injure each other during storms. Stopping their own growth rather than allowing their branches to touch.

From the other end of the log, Chance asked, "You ever think about coprolites?"

"What's a coprolite?"

"Fossilized shit. Dinosaur poop."

I gave a startled laugh. "Uh . . . no? Do you?"

"I am right now."

"Clearly. Why?"

"I was just thinking . . . so it's literal shit, right? But give it enough time, eventually it becomes this thing people will pay thousands of dollars for, especially if whatever made it isn't around anymore." He waved a hand toward the sky. "I think maybe life is like that."

"Life is shit?"

He snorted. "I mean, yeah, sometimes. But that's not what I meant. I just mean that you have all these moments that don't really seem important. It's just one after another, so you take them for granted. But then enough time goes by, and they go from being stuff that happened to being *memories*. And you look back, and suddenly they seem valuable."

I considered. "I can see that."

There was a quiet moment, and then he said, "I think people are like that, too. You discount the ones that are always around, but the ones from your past seem more important."

I took that in, turning it over in my mind. Then I sat up. "Did you just call me a piece of shit?"

He grinned up from the log. "There we go. There's the Holc I remember."

I had no choice but to smile back.

5

The next day was Monday, which meant Dad banging on my door at 8:30 A.M.

"Up and at 'em, boyo. Time for church."

St. Walpurga's Catholic Church perched atop Beacon Hill, tucked away in one of the residential sections. To me, as someone who hadn't spent much time in churches, it looked like a stock photo, an emoji come to life – sloped roof, stained glass, and a tall bell tower coming out the top.

At the moment, it also had a chain-link fence wrapped around the property. I prepared to hop out and unlock the gate, but it was already open, with Denny's van and Jesús's pickup parked in the lot.

Inside, the church was a mess. Pews had been shifted around to make room for sawhorses and scaffolding, and the walls and ceilings had been opened up in several places, the toasted gold of unstained lumber a sharp contrast to the coffee brown of the original wood.

A wiry woman with a rockabilly haircut and paint-spattered coveralls sat cross-legged in one of the church's side rooms, running blue tape along the edge of a window. "Heya, boss."

"Hey, Denny," Dad called back.

Jesús was over by the altar, walking beneath his namesake with an armful of lumber. Mexican pop blared from Bluetooth speakers.

My heart lifted. As a general contractor, Dad worked with a

lot of different folks, but days with Denny and Jesús were the best.

As I deposited Dad's tool bags on the bench, Denny popped her head out of the conference room. "Hey, check it out – I finally looked up the name of this place last night." She raised her voice. "Yo, Savior! Cut the yodeling – I'm about to educate you all!"

Jesús – a short guy old enough to be my grandfather but with biceps like cantaloupes – smirked but paused his phone.

"So get this: apparently Saint Walpurga was a virgin who – wait for it –" Denny held up her hands. "– *exuded oil.* That's it. That's the miracle." She grinned hugely. "I mean, shit – by that definition, I was a saint all through high school. Where's my church, huh?"

Jesús shook his head, but he grinned as well. "So blasphemous."

"Psht. Says the owner of 'Jesus Is a Carpenter, LLC.'"

"Hey, that's just good marketing." Jesús spread his arms wide. "Everyone knows you can trust in Jesús."

Jesús never got tired of the joke, and honestly, neither did I. He turned to me. "You working with me today, pard?"

I looked to Dad, hopeful.

He nodded. "Sure, at least for a bit. I need to take some measurements."

"Thanks, Dad." I was already moving.

We'd been on the church remodel long enough that Jesús had brought out a decent assortment of tools. There was a table saw, and a miter, and the stained plastic buckets full of drills and nail guns. Still, I knew that his workshop contained rarer beasts – jointers and lathes and alien machines I was desperate to see in action. All of it smelled of sawdust and machine oil, like Jesús himself.

"What's today?" I asked.

He motioned over at the eastern wall, which was currently impersonating an old-school platformer game with its maze of scaffolding and temporary supports. We'd spent part of last week tearing out lath and plaster to reveal the studs, a filthy job that was also deeply satisfying, in a postapocalyptic sort of way. How many people get to attack a church with a crowbar?

"Now that we've cribbed the roof so it won't come down on us, we can start replacing studs, or sistering up those that can stay." He squatted, drawing me down beside him. "See here?" He pointed to the base of the wall, where the old wooden boards were cracked and discolored. "That's dry rot. These old buildings, nothing's treated. You get moisture in here, it's game over. The whole sill plate needs to go, and probably most of these studs. You see how they just go straight into the sill here, no bottom plate?"

I nodded along. I loved the way he used jargon around me. It felt like being part of a secret society. Wood wizards.

"This whole place is old-school stick frame, nothing standardized, so we're gonna have to cut each board to fit." He gestured to a stack of two-by-fours. "I'll yell out measurements, you figure out the most efficient cuts and make 'em. Once you're done, we'll start tearing out and replacing. Okay?"

"Sure." As far as actual carpentry went, it was pretty mind-numbing, but lumber wasn't cheap, and I appreciated Jesús's faith in me.

"More interesting stuff soon, I promise." He pointed to the rippled ribbon of wood where the intact walls met the slant of the roof. "See that crown molding?"

"Yeah?"

"That's custom work, and old – you can't just buy it from

Home Despot." *Home Despot* was another of his standard jokes. "We're gonna need to match it once the wall's complete." He gave me his appraising-sensei look. "So how would you do it?"

"On a router table," I said quickly.

"Sure – if you've got the perfect bit. But let's say you don't. Look at all those different ridges. And that angle – how the whole thing curves to fill the gap. How you gonna do that?"

I thought it over. An ordinary router couldn't give you a big negative-space curve like that, and even if it could, it'd be a sin to carve out a whole block of good wood just to get that little curved edge. Which meant—

"Multiple pieces. We do each shape on the edge of its own board, staggered so they fit together to make the curve, then glue them."

Jesús nodded. "And the bits? What kinds do you need?"

I peered up at the decorative ridges and scallops. "Cove, round-over, and . . ." I racked my brain for the correct term. "Beading?"

Jesús's eyes crinkled with satisfaction, and he raised his voice. "Your boy's a genius, Derek!"

"Yeah, yeah," said my dad. "Just don't let him know, or he'll end up as cocky as the rest of you." But he sounded proud.

"By the time you're my actual apprentice, I'm not even gonna need to tell you what to do. I'll just sit in my truck and eat Takis."

My chest inflated, but I just smiled and shrugged. "Works for me."

"Let's get to it, then." He handed me some safety glasses. "Eyes on."

Most people don't think of woodworking as musical, yet

that was the best way I had to describe how it felt. The high-pitched scream of the miter saw felt the same as turning on a guitar amp and hitting a chord – not in the notes, but in the *power*, the way the sound hit you in every cell of your body. But it was even more than that. It was about creation, and precision, and fitting things together just right.

In the years since Darkhearts, I'd barely touched my guitar. There was just too much wrapped up in it. But in carpentry, I'd stumbled upon that same rush – this time in something that was mine alone. I couldn't wait to be done with high school and working for Jesús full-time.

With all the pieces cut, he and I set to work pulling rusty nails and ripping out dry-rotted timber.

"I saw in the paper about your friend," he said.

"What?" It took me a second. "Oh, Eli?"

"The benefit concert." He pried loose a spacer and tossed it onto the pile, shaking his head. "Such a shame."

"Yeah." I still hadn't decided if I wanted to go to the show or not. Every time I came close, I thought about how it would feel to be standing in that crowd, looking up at Chance. To have *him* looking down on *me*, literally.

Yet at the same time, a part of me knew I was being ridiculous. This wasn't about Chance, it was about paying respects to *Eli*. And whether or not I saw the show wasn't going to change anything. Either way, Chance Kain would still be famous, and I'd still be me. At what point did refusing to acknowledge that fact become cowardice? A little kid covering his eyes to make the monster go away.

"You talk to him?" Jesús asked. "Before, I mean. Or the other one?"

From across the room, Dad grumbled, "More than they deserve."

"Derek." Jesús's thick eyebrows drew together.

Dad held up his hands. "Not speaking ill of the dead. What happened with Elijah was a tragedy. Just saying David's been more supportive than I would be, if they'd stolen my songs."

My stomach curdled. "They weren't my songs, Dad."

"Bull*shit* they weren't. You *founded* that band."

I sighed. It didn't matter how many times I tried to explain that Eli had written most of the songs, and that they hadn't used any of mine on the album. Dad wasn't interested in understanding.

"*I* wanted to take them to court," Dad said, rolling into his usual rant. "Get our cut of the royalties. David convinced me not to."

"Dad ..." I really didn't want to do this in front of Denny and Jesús.

"If they and their families had any shred of honor, they'd have cut you in. And like I said – Elijah, that's water under the bridge. But the other one, Chance – I drove his punk ass to gig after gig, and he hasn't even shown his face around you in two years. He took your band without so much as a thank-you. As far as I'm concerned, he's a thief."

"Dad!" I caught the sharpness in my tone and immediately reined it back. "He's not that bad."

What was I doing? Why was I defending *Chance*? Half the things Dad was saying were things I'd said myself. All I knew was that I wanted this conversation over as quickly as possible.

Dad finally seemed to catch on to my discomfort, checking himself with an effort. "Yeah, well, like I said, you're a more generous man than I." He gestured at the church around us. "Maybe they should call this place St. David's."

I busied myself prying another nail.

"Well." Dad hid his own embarrassment by clapping dust off his hands, then pulled the tape measure off his belt. "Hey, Denny! Wanna gimme a hand over here?"

She poked her head out of the other room. "What's up?"

He pointed to a horizontal support beam running across the open nave of the church, a dozen feet above the floor. "I need somebody to get up there and hold a tape on the corner of that window."

"Ooh – sorry, boss." Denny attempted to look contrite. "No heights for me today. I'm blazed as hell."

Dad's jaw dropped. "You're *high*? It's ten in the morning!"

"What's your point?" She held up a roll of blue tape. "Today's a masking day, and masking is boring. Weed makes it better."

Dad shook his head. "I will never understand how you're as good as you are." He tucked his thumbs into his tool belt. "And why are you masking already? We haven't even closed up the walls out here."

"Because you're done in *here*. And because I wanted to get baked, which means it's a masking day. Any more questions?"

Dad waved dismissively and turned to me. "All right, then. You're up, kiddo."

Jesús looked to the floor beneath the beam, where we'd shoved all the pews. "We're gonna need to move those to get a ladder up."

"Nah, it's fine." Dad tapped the ladder leaning against the wall next to him, across the room from his target. "He can go across the beam."

Jesús frowned. "You sure?"

"What are you, OSHA? That beam's ten inches wide. He wouldn't fall off if it was on the floor." He made a hurry-up motion at me. "Let's go."

"It's cool." I set my crowbar down and made my way over to the ladder. "I don't mind heights."

In fact, it was the opposite. As I climbed the ladder and stepped off onto the beam, I felt a familiar sense of pride. I'd never gotten into rock climbing, and I wasn't an adrenaline junkie. I didn't fantasize about skydiving or bungee jumping. Heights just didn't affect me the way they did most people.

And like Dad said, the beam was plenty wide. If you could walk a straight line on the ground, you could walk it in the air.

I took the end of the tape measure and walked it across.

"Look at that," Jesús said approvingly. "Cool as a cat."

I held the tape in place while Dad moved his end around, noting measurements, then let go and walked back across.

As I came down the ladder, Dad gripped my shoulder.

"See?" he announced, squeezing my shoulder and displaying me to the others like a trophy. "That's what I'm talking about! It's all about confidence. With enough confidence, you can go anywhere."

And as the warmth of their praise seeped in, I made a decision.

Dad was right: confidence *was* everything. I liked having the guts to go where other people couldn't.

It was time to apply that to other parts of my life.

6

"This is *literally* the coolest thing that has ever happened to us," Ridley announced.

Seattle is a city of neighborhoods, and there isn't really a reason to go downtown unless you're a tourist or work for one of the megacorp overlords. Seeing shows was my primary exception to this rule, and thus I'd come to associate the hot-bleach-and-diapers smell of the light rail with excitement.

Next to me, Ridley practically vibrated in her plastic seat. She'd set her hair free in a dense black halo and wore a tight T-shirt with a chopped-out neckline, its blue a perfect match for her eye shadow. She grabbed my arm and shook me with her.

"I can't believe you're getting us backstage!"

Technically, *Chance* was getting us backstage. While it had galled me to accept, I told myself this was a special case – and also that Ridley would totally lose her shit. The latter had certainly proven true, and the way she kept treating me like I'd pulled off some impossible coup was rapidly softening my default resentment – something she no doubt knew, master manipulator that she was. But sometimes it's nice to be manipulated.

The light rail pulled into Westlake Station, and we joined the crush of Saturday night revelers storming the escalators. Panhandlers drumming on buckets perforated the salty waterfront air as we walked the four blocks to our destination.

The Moore was the oldest theater in Seattle, a big squared-off brick of a building with an attached hotel. Plastic letters on the light-up marquee proudly proclaimed SONGS FOR ELIJAH BENEFIT CONCERT: SOLD OUT. Doors were still more than an hour away, but the line of people waiting already stretched down the block and around the corner.

Ridley ran up to the will call booth, towing me behind her like a balloon. "We're on the guest list!"

The bored guy inside checked our IDs, then pointed. "Go around to the alley. Wait by the fire door."

Ridley marched us past the line of ordinary ticket holders with enough pomp for several European monarchs, the effect only slightly spoiled as we turned into the alley and its steaming stench of summer dumpsters.

We found the fire door, a blank gray rectangle with no external handle. After a few minutes, it opened, revealing a redhead a few years older than us wearing all black and a headset.

"IDs."

We handed them over a second time, and she checked them against a list on an iPad. "All right, come in." She held the door open and tapped her earpiece. "I've got two VIPs off the Dark-hearts list at the north door."

Inside, it looked less like a theater than a loading dock, with concrete floors and a ceiling of metal struts. A forklift sat parked against one wall.

A handsome man in his thirties with curly brown hair and a sleek plaid sport coat strode briskly toward us, dress shoes echoing in the cavernous space. The blue LED of an earpiece flashed.

"You must be David and Ridley." He gave a smile so warm it was unsettling, looking each of us straight in the eye as he shook our hands. "It is *so* good to meet you. I'm Benjamin,

Darkhearts' manager. I'll take you back." He turned and began walking, without waiting to see if we'd follow. I got the impression he did that a lot.

Ridley grabbed my arm once more. "We're *VIPs*!" she hissed happily.

"I know." I carefully peeled her fingers out of my bicep.

Benjamin led us down a hallway that felt a little less industrial, with normal-height ceilings. We emerged into a big room with carpeted floors and a long snack table in the middle. Maybe twenty people stood around talking or lounged on ancient leather couches.

"Oh. My. *God.*" Ridley stared at a middle-aged white guy in a flannel shirt. "Do you know who that *is?*"

But my eyes had already found Chance. He leaned against a wall, chatting up a gorgeous Black girl in a tube top and glasses. He was dressed in tight black everything, all the way to the black eyeliner trailing artfully down like tears. The only splotch of color was a pink anatomical heart across his chest, ringed by an asymmetrical spiderweb of leather straps and buckles. He looked like a god, perfect and poised.

He spotted us as we came in and broke away with a smile, sauntering over to us. "Welcome to the circus. You guys get in all right?"

"Definitely!" Ridley chirped. "Thanks for inviting us!"

"My pleasure," Chance said, but he was looking at me. I tried to give him an everything's-cool smile.

Ridley stepped in closer to Chance, looking around a little wild-eyed. "Is everyone here famous?"

He grinned conspiratorially. "Mostly. The label put it together fast, but they were able to get a bunch of folks in on it – all people who knew Eli. Billie's here, of course, and Finneas. Sub-Radio was already coming through on tour, and Janelle flew in from Sweden or somewhere. But we've got local folks, too – all different styles. UMI, Macklemore, Jay Park . . ." His smile faltered. "It's a benefit show fighting teen substance abuse. Who doesn't want in on that?"

Ridley nodded sympathetically. "That's really nice."

Benjamin clapped his hands. "Two minutes, everybody!" Then he strode quickly out of the room.

I snagged a personal-size bag of chips from the snack table. "What's in two minutes?"

A guy I didn't recognize with full-sleeve tats reached past me to grab a wrap. "The meet-and-freak," he said, and turned back to a couch.

Chance nodded. "You two got here just in time."

"Meet-and-freak?" Ridley raised an eyebrow.

"The meet-and-greet. It's some press, plus superfans who pay a ton to come backstage and meet some of the performers. It's a good way to raise extra money."

I crunched a handful of barbecue chips. "So why 'freak'?"

Chance winked. "Watch."

A door opened, and two big guys wearing hazard-yellow security shirts stepped inside.

"Here it comes," Tat Guy muttered.

"Time to earn my keep." Chance slapped my shoulder and moved away. "Have fun!"

A mob of people surged through the door.

And the screaming began.

To be fair, it wasn't a *lot* of screaming. But in an enclosed room, any amount of squealing is plenty. The most enthusiastic freak-outs came from a knot of teenagers who immediately surrounded Chance, several of them wearing Darkhearts shirts or tear-streak makeup to match his. Chance, for his part, perched majestically on the back of a couch, smiling enigmatically down at them as he used a Sharpie to sign whatever they handed him.

Other fans – of which many were surprisingly ordinary-looking adults – clustered around the room's other celebrities. Ridley immediately tugged me toward the guy she'd noticed earlier. "Come on! Let's meet some stars!"

"You go," I said. The whole thing made me uncomfortable, and I couldn't tell whether I was excited or embarrassed to be there. To join the mob getting autographs felt like admitting defeat – putting myself forever on the "fanboy" side of an invisible line, while Chance stood shining and untouchable on the other. I grabbed a sparkling lemonade from the snack table. "I'll catch up."

Ridley hesitated, clearly debating dragging me along, then shrugged and joined the fray. I retreated to a couch away from the scrum.

Tat Guy was still sitting there eating. He gave me a nod. "You a friend of Chance's?"

A question that seemed to be getting more complicated every day. But I nodded.

"He's a good kid." He took a long slug from a can of beer. "Fucking shame about Elijah. That kid had more talent at seventeen than I'll have at seventy."

"Yeah." He wasn't wrong. Elijah had always been the genius in the group.

"You performing tonight?"

The fist in my guts twisted. "No. You?"

"Yeah, we're covering 'Photo Burn.' I'm the guitarist for Godhead Immolator."

"Oh, cool." I bobbed my head as if I'd heard of them.

He smirked. "Don't worry, nobody else has heard of us, either." He gestured to the crowd that was ignoring us. "We're thrash-pop, nowhere on the level of these folks. But Elijah was a fan. He brought us out to open for a couple of gigs on their last tour, and Chance remembered." He finished his beer and belched loudly. "So how do you know them?"

"I used to play guitar for Darkhearts."

"No shit?" The man peered out from behind his curtain of greasy blond hair with renewed interest. "This must be extra messed up for you, huh?"

"You have no idea."

A college-age kid in a tattered Spiritbox shirt approached nervously. "Jason Elkis?"

The guy next to me straightened. "Yeah?"

"I'm from the University of Washington *Daily*. I was hoping I could interview you?"

"Well ho-lee shit!" The man grinned, and I stood, ceding my couch spot to the kid.

I rejoined Ridley as she made the circuit, letting her drag me into selfies with various celebrities, but my attention kept creeping back to Chance, holding court with his entourage.

He looked so comfortable. It was hard to imagine introverted Eli doing this every day. But I guessed that was why you had frontmen: to stand in front. For the first time, I wondered if Chance's aggressive spotlight-hogging might have been as much about protecting Eli as stealing all the glory for himself.

Or, as the meme says: Why not both?

At last the lights flashed and the security guys moved in, ushering the fans back out into the theater. Ridley and I followed, but hands on our shoulders stopped us.

"Not you two." Chance pulled us back out of the pack. "I've got something special for you."

He waved, and the redhead from the back door appeared. "Emma, right? Benjamin said you could hook my friends here up with some of the *special* seats." He gave her a dramatic cartoon wink.

The girl glowed, and to my surprise winked back. "Absolutely." She beckoned for us to follow her.

For the second time, Chance held me back.

"Hey," he said quietly, in a voice that was no longer Chance Kain, Showman. "Thanks for being here, dude. I think it would have meant a lot to Eli."

"Of course." I tried to look as if it had never been in question. The sudden brunt of his earnestness was disconcerting, and I didn't know quite what to do with my hands.

He smiled and let me go.

Emma led us out into the theater proper, onto the steeply sloped floor that was rapidly filling with the general-admission crowd. I'd assumed we'd be headed up to one of the giant overhanging balconies, but as we approached the exits back out to the lobby, she turned and unlocked a door marked STAFF ONLY.

The crowd noise cut off as the thick door closed behind us. Inside was a narrow staircase, looking significantly rattier than the rest of the theater. We followed Emma's flashlight up it and down a sloping, unlit hallway, its walls missing chunks of plaster. At its end, the left wall suddenly opened up into a series of glassless, arched windows supported by pillars. Beyond, the whole theater spread out before us.

"Whoa." I leaned my head out.

"This is the old gallery," Emma said, pulling two folding chairs from a stack against the wall. "It hasn't been properly renovated, so nobody's allowed back here except staff."

"I see." I kicked lightly at the not-so-safety rail that only came up to my thighs.

Emma unfolded the chairs and set them in front of the view. "You're getting the secret seats all to yourselves tonight. Don't hang any limbs over the railing or my manager will have all our asses. Got it?" She waited sternly for our nods. "All right then. If you've gotta pee, I can take you out now, but once the show starts you're stuck here until I come get you – you can get out the door, but you won't be able to get back in. Either of you need the facilities?"

We shook our heads. Ridley said, "Thank you, Emma."

The girl flashed a grin. "No problem. Enjoy." Then she was gone.

The gallery had no lights of its own, leaving us half in shadow, lit only by the house lights outside. Across the theater, I could see a matching row of dark arches high up along the theater wall.

"This is *so rad*." Ridley leaned out to look, then quickly jerked back, taking one of the folding chairs. "Way cooler than front-row seats."

I had to admit she was right. It was like being Batman, watching over Gotham from a rooftop.

The house lights began to go down.

"Oh *shiiiiiiit*," Ridley squealed.

I ignored the chair Emma had left me and perched sidesaddle on the gallery's railing, my back against a pillar.

Somewhere up in the mess of rigging, a projector clicked on. The backdrop of the stage came to life with a three-story-tall picture of Eli with his skull-stickered laptop, one headphone pressed to his ear.

The audience cheered.

The show that followed was a tour de force, with guest after guest covering Darkhearts songs – sometimes faithfully, sometimes reinterpreting them in their own diverse styles. I made a point of hooting loudly when Godhead Immolator did their shredding, brutal take on the music, fronted by an incongruous pixie of a dude with cotton-candy hair and Christina Aguilera vocals.

Yet the star of the show was undeniably Chance. He emceed the whole thing, peppering the introduction of each act with funny anecdotes about Eli or somber reminders about the dangers of binge drinking and the importance of reaching out for help with addiction. He gave the spotlight operator a workout, stalking around like a panther. At one transition the lights went out and he appeared atop a speaker cabinet in a puff of purple smoke.

I couldn't take my eyes off him. He'd always been good at working the crowd – one of those singers who's always getting down in the audience's faces or pissing off the sound guy by swinging the mic around by its cable – but this was another level. He *owned* the stage. When he flashed that devilish smile, you felt like he was your best friend.

Except, of course, that he *had* been my best friend. I'd been a crucial part of his transformation into this ascended being.

Which raised the question: Was this what I might have become, had I stuck with the band? I'd never had Chance's natural showmanship, but even a pale reflection of godhood still made you immortal. Jealousy and pride warred inside me.

After the sixth or seventh such introduction, Ridley whispered, "When's he going to sing?"

I smirked. "Just wait."

I was right. After two hours of star-studded spectacle, the lights went out again. This time they stayed out, unaccompanied by any music over the massive speakers. The crowd's roar faded slowly to respectful silence, then to confused muttering as the darkness stretched on.

"Did the power go out?" Ridley asked.

"Shh."

At last, as the crowd's rumble built to a peak, a ring of crimson floor lights sprang up in the center of the stage.

Chance stood in the middle, like a demon in a summoning circle. In the shadows, he seemed taller, every line of his face drawn in ink as he slowly raised his head.

Bass thrummed through the theater, deep sub-rumbles that shook like the steps of an approaching kaiju. An airy choir of ambient guitars and synths joined it from above, weaving around and through each other in offset loops. I recognized the opening of "Asleep at the Altar," the final track off Darkhearts' first album.

Chance raised his mic and began to sing, low and slow. His voice was a subterranean river, dark and unhurried. He didn't dance now, didn't strut – just rode the rising swells of the bass, flirted with the fluttering electronic skitter of the music. *Eli's* music. The wall of sound lifted Chance up, presenting his voice to the audience like an offering. Eli's music was a ring, and Chance was the diamond in its center.

His voice built, rising in pitch, growing more powerful. You didn't even need the lyrics to know what it was about. You could hear it in Chance's voice – the grief, the universal *why?* that everyone asks at some point.

That question rose with the music, and the instruments drew back, letting it hang alone in the air. The theater held its breath.

Lights slammed on as the beat dropped, smashing into my chest. Onstage, Chance flared like a phoenix, clutching the mic with both hands as he howled out the chorus. The notes were a bandsaw, barbed and cutting, his body curling in on itself with the strain. In his voice was everyone who'd ever raged at a god who lets bad things happen, everyone who'd ever stood on a cliff and screamed themselves raw. It was a shivering, living thing that grabbed you by the spine even as Eli's beat forced your body to move.

And then it was over. Chance straightened, sweating, and brushed the hair from his eyes – perfect in his imperfection. He kissed three fingers and held them up in a *Hunger Games* salute.

"Thank you, Eli," he said.

And the lights went out for the last time.

The audience applauded. When the house lights rose, he was gone, the picture of Eli once more taking up the back wall. People began filing toward the exits.

Ridley turned to me.

"Well," she breathed. "*I'm* pregnant now, how 'bout you?"

7

Three days later, I texted Chance.

ME:

Hey. What are you doing right now?

His reply was immediate.

CHANCE:

Dinner with the fam. Why?

In my imagination, he sounded surprised. But to be fair, so was I. My thumb swiped arcane symbols across the virtual keyboard.

ME:

There's this thing I want to go
to called Death Putt. Like mini golf,
but punk rock. Totally underground.
It pops up in random warehouses,
then disappears before the city
can shut it down.

CHANCE:

Ooh! Intriguing!

I felt a swell of pride. It was nice to know normal people could still impress celebrities.

ME:

I got the address off Reddit.

Anyway, tonight's the last night
they're doing it. Wanna come?

CHANCE:

Hell yeah!

I was about to send him the address when my phone chimed
again.

CHANCE:

Think there'll be a lot of
people there?

ME:

Probably? The pictures make
it look like a big party.

I waited for the little ".." of him typing to resolve. It took a
surprisingly long time. At last he sent:

CHANCE:

Going out in public isn't
always great for me.

I rolled my eyes.

ME:

Dude. Google some photos.
They've got a hole that
SETS YOUR BALLS ON FIRE.

Besides, people recognized you
at the burger place. It was fine.

CHANCE:

I know, but in a restaurant
there's usually only a few
people. Crowds are different.

I gritted my teeth.

ME:

Man, get over yourself.
You're not THAT famous.

CHANCE:

I kinda am, though.
¯_(ツ)_/¯

The arrogance of this asshole. I wondered why I'd ever thought this was a good idea.

ME:

You know what? Forget it.

Good show the other night.
Thanks for getting us in.

I'll see ya around.

I was shoving my phone back into my pocket when it began dinging frantically.

CHANCE:

Wait!

Let's do it.

You're right, I'm sure it'll be fine.

I read the messages over. Was this victory? I wasn't sure.

ME:

Yeah?

CHANCE:

Yeah.

I mean, how can I say no to
having my balls set on fire?
🔥 🍆 🔥

I smirked.

ME:

Okay. I'm thinking we get there at 8,
right after it opens.

CHANCE:

Sounds good. Pick me up
again?

I still didn't understand why he was being such a scrub. Did he get off on making me chauffeur him around? But I figured I'd already pushed him far enough out of his comfort zone for one night.

ME:

Sure. Be there in half an hour.

Chance replied with a string of skulls, flames, and golf emojis.

I hit the road, and soon was once again pulling up at his curb. He slipped out through the motorized gate, its bars wheeling closed behind him, and I was surprised to see him wearing blue jeans and a roughed-up gray hoodie – incongruously boring going-out clothes for him, even before he got famous. Not that he'd ever needed fashion to stand out, but the drab outfit made his dark eyes and the sharp lines of his face a more approachable sort of handsome – homecoming king rather than fallen angel.

He hopped up into the cab, craning his neck to look into the tiny back seat. "Just us?"

"Ridley was gonna come, but her parents are making her babysit. And Gabe and Angela are down in Tahoe for a wakeboarding thing."

"Ah." He nodded. "Hence my sudden recruitment."

I shrugged.

"Well, it sounds great," he said. "Thanks for picking me up."

I pulled out into the street. "Yeah, what's the story with that?"

"With what?"

"Me picking you up. Afraid to park your Lambo in a bad neighborhood?"

He made a face. "I don't have a Lamborghini."

"Whatever. You must drive *something* nice."

He looked out the window and muttered something.

"What?"

"I said I don't drive." He shrank back in his seat. "I don't have my license."

"Wait, *what*?" I glanced over at him in shock. "You don't know how to drive?!"

He glared back. "I know *how*. I mean, mostly. I've got a learner's permit. I just don't have my license."

"How? *Why*?"

"There's just never a chance to practice on tour. When

you've already got a bus, it doesn't make sense to bring a car, and Dad isn't going to rent one just so I can practice for an hour in some city I don't know. So I just use Uber and shit."

"Wow."

"Look, it's not a big deal, all right?" The defensiveness in his tone said he absolutely knew how big a deal it was.

"Sure, yeah. Totally." I thought of how much time I spent cruising around in my truck, alone or with Ridley riding shotgun, roaming the back roads east of the city. Getting my license the day I turned sixteen had been the greatest sense of freedom I'd ever encountered. The idea of Chance being able to afford any car he wanted but unable to drive any of them was at once sad and bursting with juicy, delicious schadenfreude. I felt my shoulders relax and draped my elbow out the window to catch the summer breeze.

The address led us down to Georgetown again, a bizarre section where streets cut across each other at all angles and factories stood side by side with ordinary houses. I tried to keep one eye on my phone as it talked me through the mess of divided streets.

"It's supposed to be in a decommissioned post office or something," I said. "Some arts collective took it over."

After several tense minutes of circling, Chance pointed. "Think that's it?"

Down one of the alleys, half illuminated by a tall streetlamp, a big dude with a shaved head guarded the door of a squat building with boarded-up windows. A knot of people stood nearby, smoking.

"Only one way to find out." I parked the truck and we walked over.

Now that we were out of the truck, I could hear the muffled pulse of bass from inside the building. The bouncer wore a Utilikilt and a glittery plastic tiara, which did surprisingly little to decrease the threat of his massive crossed arms.

"Is this Death Putt?" I asked.

"That depends," he said. "Are you eighteen?"

I froze, my heart sinking. Nothing on the website had said it was an eighteen-and-up thing. Why did everything cool hate minors?

Chance was smoother. He gave a high-octane grin and said, "Would we be here if we weren't? I *love* the tiara, by the way."

"Right." The man eyed us dubiously – and then his face went suddenly soft. "Hey, wait a second – are you Chance Kain?"

If Chance's smile had been gasoline before, it was rocket fuel now. He winked. "That's between you and us."

The man grinned back. "My husband and I danced to 'Till Death' at our wedding." He opened the door and stepped out of the way. "Enjoy."

Inside was a carnival on acid. The building was one giant open space, crammed full of people and bizarre structures. Laughter and sirens punctuated a background buzz of death metal. A middle-aged woman with a *Clockwork Orange* bowler hat and eye makeup sprawled on a couch just inside the door, guarding the swinging saloon doors leading into the rest of the chaos.

"Heya, droogs." She held out two clipboards. "Disclaimer time! No papers, no party."

We took the clipboards, Chance reading the opening aloud.

"'I hereby acknowledge that everything in Death Putt is profoundly unsafe, and that I'm a reckless dumbass just for being here.'" He grinned. "Awesome."

We both signed quickly and dropped some cash in the big box marked DONATIONS. The woman handed us two putters and a scorecard, then pointed. "First hole's over there, but go in any order you like. Don't be a dick, and don't hit anyone with your balls unless they're into it." She waved us through.

We passed through the doors, and I struggled to take in the barrage of flashing lights and noise. "Fucking A."

"I know, right?" Chance craned his neck, still grinning like an idiot. "I feel like the ball in a pinball machine."

"Totally." Grudging respect forced me to add, "Thanks for getting us in."

"Fame has its uses." He tapped me with his putter. "Come on, let's play!"

The first hole was just opening up, an older punk couple wandering off as we approached. While the turf was the same carpet of fake plasticky green you'd find at any mini-golf place, the hazards were decidedly different. For this one, someone had found two blow-up sex dolls – one male, one female – and posed them in compromising positions, with golf-ball-sized tunnels running between their various orifices. A sign next to the tee read HOLE 1: BALLS DEEP.

"Beautiful." Chance gave a chef's kiss, then took a ball from the basket hanging off the sign. He lined up his shot and yelled *"Fore-some!"*

The course only got crazier from there. One hole had an industrial shredder waiting to destroy your ball if you missed. One had a series of pneumatic hamster tubes that sucked up your ball and sent it hurtling to different points around the room. One let you shoot your ball out of an air-powered cannon, trying to get it into a toilet bowl, while another had enormous metal dragon puppets that allowed your opponents or anyone passing by to play Hungry Hungry Hippos with your ball. And of course, there was the hole where an attendant in a top hat and rabbit mask dunked your ball in something that burned blue as you putted it through little flaming geysers.

The crowd was all different ages – I saw a grandma go past in a leather jacket bedazzled with the words BLACK ROCK CITY – but most had the standard artsy underground look, with piercings and neon hair. There was plenty of cosplay, and half the attendees seemed content to just hang out, chatting at the apocalypse-themed bar or trying on communal costumes for a photo booth.

For the first few holes, everything was normal – or as normal as it can be when you're trying to hit a ball between whirring saw blades. But as we waited for the girls in front of us to finish their hole, one of them turned and noticed us.

"Oh my god!" she gushed. "It's Darkhearts!"

My stomach dropped at the half-truth of it. Did they maybe remember us from back in the day, when I could claim that title? Or did they just assume I was Eli? Before I could figure out how to respond, Chance stepped in, graciously posing for their selfies.

"Do you want to join us?" the taller of the girls asked.

There wasn't really a polite way to refuse, given that unless we went out of order we were going to be standing behind them the whole way through. Chance looked to me, and I shrugged.

The girls – Yumi and Claire – turned out to be a couple of years older than us, roommates at UW who'd decided to stay in town over the summer. They were both undeniably cute, and I was surprised to find they talked to me almost as much as to Chance.

What they were *not* was discreet. By the time we'd made it to the seventh hole – MR. T FRIED MY BALLS, where crackling Tesla coils shocked special foil-coated balls – we'd begun to gather a crowd. Chance had to tear himself away from admirers each time it was his turn to putt, and it was slowing us down considerably. Not that anyone seemed to be complaining.

A slender, good-looking millennial in a purple suit with the shirt unbuttoned to the navel sidled up beside us. "Hey, Chance. Buy you a drink?"

A shadow passed across Chance's face, and I realized he must be thinking of Eli – of all the drinks that had carried him away in the bleak anonymity of a hotel room. But it was only a flicker. By the time he turned to the man, his camera-ready smile was back in place. "Amaretto sour, if they've got it."

"Sure thing."

One hole later, the man was back – and not with one drink, but two. He handed the second one to me and touched the small of my back. "You boys have fun tonight." Then he slipped off into the crowd.

I stared at the drink, then at Chance. "Whaaaaaat the eff?"

He smiled and clinked my glass. "Cheers."

I'd never even heard of amaretto, but the drink was shockingly good – simultaneously tart and syrup-sweet. "Wow."

"Right?" Chance raised his glass. "It's like a lime Otter Pop."

"It's like the Earl of Lemongrab just came in my mouth."

Chance barked a surprised laugh, as did several of our entourage. I felt a buzzing glow that might have been the alcohol.

As the evening went on, though, the attention started to get old. Everybody wanted to talk to Chance, and while some of them followed Yumi and Claire's lead and talked to me as well, most were focused on soaking up every iota of Chance's attention. Even weirder were the people who didn't say anything, just stood there recording us with their phones.

By the time we reached the final hole, where a water jet cutter sliced our balls in half, I could see that entertaining the whole crowd was wearing Chance out. The way he had to constantly laugh and smile at each new person reminded me of my cousin's wedding in California, the way my aunt had insisted on introducing me to an endless stream of people I'd never met before and would never meet again. It raised a strangely protective instinct in me, and I did my best to block the more aggressive fans as we returned our putters and made our goodbyes, politely turning down offers of after-parties (though I *did* let Claire give me her number). Chance shot me a grateful look as we made our way to the door.

My head was still spinning a little from the drink, and the shock of fresh air after the packed club was ambrosia. The doorman waved good night.

"That was *incredible*," I declared. "Even better than—"

The world erupted in light.

I blinked and saw two people – a Black man with a giant camera, and a white woman with a smaller camera and a cell phone.

The camera flashed again, shutter chattering like a machine gun.

"Shit." Chance held his hands up, one blocking his face, the other blocking mine. "Paparazzi. Professionals."

"Seriously?" It didn't seem like a big deal – plenty of folks inside had taken pictures – but Chance was grimacing like he'd just stepped in dog poop. "Okay, no problem. We'll just go to the truck and leave."

"No!" He pulled me back out of the streetlight, trying to keep our backs to the paparazzi as they circled for a better angle. "Don't let them see your truck. They'll run the plates, find out everything about you, and we'll never get to hang out normally again. They're the friggin' FBI of gossip."

I still didn't exactly see the problem. So what if some tabloid had pictures of me? But I hadn't seen Chance this agitated since Eli's funeral. "Okay, so what do we do?"

He glanced back over his shoulder, then gave me a sudden, savage smile. He grabbed my wrist and yanked me into motion. "Run!"

I stumbled, and then we were sprinting down the alley, away from where we'd parked. I looked back and saw the two photographers start running as well, cameras clutched to chests. "They're chasing us!"

"That's what they do!"

We sped up, dodging dumpsters and gross puddles. Ahead, the alley opened up onto an empty street.

"Which way?" Chance asked.

Right led back toward the lights of the main commercial strip, left deeper into the industrial wasteland. I chose at random. "Left!"

He didn't hesitate, just turned and kept going.

And suddenly it didn't matter why we were running. It was enough just to be young, and fast, and moving as a pack. Chance whooped as we leaped up onto the concrete ramp of a loading dock, shoes scraping against pavement, then soared off the other side.

Behind us, the paparazzi were still following, but they weren't teenagers. Our lead grew as we hauled ass across a playfield.

We rounded a corner, passed a dairy plant, then quickly juked around another corner and down a sidewalk lined with a tall green hedge. I didn't do a lot of running, and the exhilaration was starting to give way to a burning in my lungs. "Where are we going?"

"Good point." Chance stopped, glanced around, then yanked me sideways through an arbor.

"What—?"

He put a finger to his lips.

Inside the hedge stood a weird, tile-roofed stone house that looked like something out of ancient Rome, surrounded by elaborate landscaping and a statue of a mermaid. Engraved over the door were the words THE CORMAN BUILDING. Light shone faintly from the windows, joining with streetlights peeping through the hedge to cast shadows across the yard.

Chance pulled me down into the darkness behind a large bush, out of sight of the entrance.

We squatted in silence, thighs and arms sardined together in the shadow of the shrub. I could feel the warmth radiating off him through his hoodie, the silent heave of his ribs as we caught our breath.

Soon enough we heard running footsteps approaching. They paused just on the other side of the hedge.

"Shit." The woman's voice. "Whaddaya think?"

"Maybe that way?"

The feet ran on, receding into the distance.

After several more minutes, Chance finally stood. But instead of going for the entrance, he moved deeper into the garden. I lurched to catch up, my eyes on the building's old-timey windows.

"What're you doing?" I hissed. "What if someone's in there?"

"Then we tell them the truth." Chance leaned close enough that I could feel the breath of his whisper. "That we were running from some creepy adults who were stalking us."

I had to admit, it was a pretty good excuse. And between Chance's fame and my pasty, corn-fed complexion, maybe the cops would even give us a warning before shooting us.

The hedge completely enclosed the property, making a little triangle of privacy. In back, a pergola draped with vines and the hanging stars of festival lights stretched out over a stone patio and two long wooden tables. I shrank back from the light, but Chance crept right up to the building's glass doors and peered inside.

"It's cool," he said softly. "It's some sort of event space. There's nobody there, just a night-light."

My shoulders unclenched. I let my breath out in a whoosh and sank down onto one of the tables' benches. Chance came and sat beside me on the tabletop, his feet on the bench.

"Okay," I said when my blood finally stopped pounding. "I'm willing to concede that maybe you *are* that famous."

He laughed. "Thanks, man." He waved a hand. "For all of this. After the last few days, I needed some fun."

"What happened the last few days?"

He frowned. "Just business stuff. I don't really want to talk about it."

"Okay."

He leaned back on his elbows and stared up at the string lights twinkling down between leaves. "They look like fireflies. Have you ever seen real fireflies?"

I shook my head.

"They have them in Nanjing. I got to see them once, when we visited Nai-Nai – my dad's mom. We went to this park where they fly all around the temples." He sighed. "I wish we had them out here. There's something so poetic about them, you know?"

I let my head loll back dramatically. "Not poetry again."

He shoved my shoulder. "Oh shut up. You telling me the metaphor doesn't resonate with you? Searching through darkness, shining your light so briefly, hoping someone sees you before you die?"

"More like flashing your ass trying to get laid." But he was right – there was something about his image that struck a chord.

He laughed. "Is that how you do it?"

"Do what?"

"Get laid." He looked over at me and smirked. "You must have hooked up with *somebody* in the last two years."

I blushed, hoping the dim light hid my color change. "Maybe."

"Yeah?" He sat up, leaning forward eagerly. "How far are we talking here? Did you *hook up* hook up?"

My face was a furnace. "We fooled around."

"Nice, dude." He leaned back on his hands. "So who was it?"

I still had zero interest in telling him about Maddy, and being put on the spot made me suddenly angry. "Why do *you* care? You could have banged either of those college girls tonight. Or both at once."

He rolled his eyes. "Don't go projecting your fantasies onto me. You sound like that burger guy."

"You telling me you haven't?" It suddenly seemed very important that he admit it. "I saw those groupies flocking around you at the meet-and-greet. You expect me to believe you never get any backstage action?"

"Can't," he said. "It breaks the rules."

"*What* rules?"

"My manager's. Benjamin's Rules of Stardom." He raised a finger. "Rule One: No sex with fans." A second finger. "Rule Two: If breaking Rule One, always take the condom with you when you leave."

"Ew, what? Why?"

"So they can't use it to get pregnant after the fact." He said it so matter-of-factly. "You think you're protected, and then after you leave …" He made a graphic gesture. "The fan decides getting pregnant is a way to make you marry them, or pay child support, or just blackmail you."

"Jesus. That's sick."

"Yeah. So. No hooking up with fans."

"Damn." I considered that for a moment. "So you really never do *anything* with them?"

Now he looked uncomfortable.

"Aha! So you *have* done it."

He nodded slowly. "Once."

The grim way he said it drained any remaining anger. "Yeah?"

"Yeah." He went back to staring up at the lights, skin dappled with their glow. "There was this one … Emerson. They worked at the venue. We'd had to get there early for some preshow thing that got canceled, so there was nothing to do but sit around the green room. They were assigned to be my handler – get me water, take me where I needed to be, whatever – but mostly we just talked. And they were cool, you know? I felt like we connected." The regret in his voice was a physical weight.

"But?"

He shrugged helplessly. "But they were a fan. They thought they knew me, and they didn't. They knew *Chance Kain* from a hundred interviews, but they didn't know *me*. I was a fantasy. And when we hooked up, I could feel it. Their disappointment." He shook his head. "They say never meet your heroes, right? Well, *definitely* don't put your tongue in their mouths."

"Ouch."

"Yeah." He forcibly lightened his tone. "But hey, nobody knowing my sexuality is part of my brand now. Everyone loves a mystery." He spread his hands. "Can't date a mystery, though, so . . ."

"Damn," I said again. Then: "It's like cars."

His breath exploded out of him. "*What?*"

I waved vaguely. "You could buy any car you want, but you can't drive any of them. Same thing."

"*Wow.*" He stared, head bobbing slightly as he studied me. "Really trying to make me feel better, huh?"

"Guess you'll just have to wipe your tears with hundred-dollar bills." But I smiled as I said it.

He laughed. "Asshole."

"Somebody's gotta be. Everyone back there thought you were Jesus in skinny jeans."

"You saying I'm not?" He put a hand on his chest. "You wound me, Holc."

He moved the hand to my shoulder and pushed himself to his feet.

"Come on, let's sneak back to your truck. Jesus needs a ride."

8

After our adventure running from the paparazzi, I didn't see Chance again for the rest of the week. Which wouldn't have been remarkable except for the fact that, somehow, incredibly . . . I kind of *wanted* to?

It wasn't just that we'd had fun at Death Putt. That didn't mean anything – I could have been hanging out with one of the blow-up dolls from the first hole and that place would still have been awesome. But there'd been something about running and hiding together – working as a team – that felt different. For those few minutes, it had been almost like the last two years hadn't happened. He hadn't been Chance Kain, but just Chance, the kid I used to play *Fortnite* and talk about girls with. The one who'd made starting a band seem like fun. The Chance who'd been one of my best friends.

It was an uncomfortable feeling. It was one thing to hate Chance. It was something else entirely to miss him.

I managed to repress the urge to contact him for a while, spending my days working at the church and my nights building my own projects down in the basement, or watching Netflix with Dad. But by Saturday morning, with Ridley scheduled to work all weekend and my next-best friends Gabe and Angela still on vacation, it was starting to seem a little ridiculous.

What exactly was I afraid of? I wasn't some fan clamoring for his attention – if anything, it was the opposite. After all, *he'd* texted *me* first. With his (perhaps justified) fear of going out in public, it seemed like he was bored in Seattle. I'd be doing him a *favor*.

So I gave in and texted him.

ME:

Hey, you wanna hang out tonight?

To which he replied:

CHANCE:

Can't. Busy all weekend.
Music stuff.

It was almost a relief, the way the resentment flooded back in.

Of course Chance didn't want to hang out. He was too busy being famous and important. What had I been thinking? The dude hadn't texted me once in the *two years* since I left the band, and now we hung out a few times and suddenly I was wistful for the good old days? It was pathetic.

My phone chimed again.

CHANCE:

Actually, want to come work
out with me? Right now?

I hesitated. Working out wasn't something I really did. Between manual labor for my dad, PE at school, and walking up Seattle's hills, exercise was something that happened *to* me rather than something I sought out.

But what the hell else did I have going on?

Sure, I sent back.

*

I parked on the street outside Chance's house and pressed the button on the gate's speaker box.

"Hello?" Chance's mom's voice.

"Uh, hi. It's David Holcomb."

"David! Come in!"

The box beeped, and the gate rolled open with a squeak.

To call the house a mansion would be overkill. While it was easily twice the size of the one my dad and I lived in, I'd been to houses just as big in my own neighborhood. South Seattle was a rapidly gentrifying mishmash, with modern Lego-brick Yuppie Cubes squatting Borg-like next to sagging shacks with bars on the windows. So the Ngs' new house wasn't unusually huge.

What it was was *nice*. The whole thing was made of red brick, with peaked roofs that gave it the air of a Victorian manor. It rose up from between landscaped terraces on the side of the steeply sloping hill, giving every window on the east side a full view of Lake Washington. The cobblestone driveway slanted down to a roundabout with an elevated stone vase like some sort of *Mario Kart* trophy. As if anyone walking in needed a reminder that winners lived here.

The front door opened. "David!"

Mrs. Ng looked exactly the same as the last time I'd seen her: an aggressively fit Korean-American woman in her midforties, with a round face and long black hair pulled back in a ponytail. Since it was Saturday, she'd traded her usual business wear for some REI hiking thing that looked like cargo pants had decided to make a dress, and it fit her better than I was entirely comfortable with.

Yet all of that was secondary to her smile. Mrs. Ng had the

most vibrant expressions of anyone I'd ever met, and her smile was on full blast as I hustled down the driveway.

"Look at you! You're huge!" She had to reach up to grab my shoulder. Her grin didn't waver, but her eyes sharpened meaningfully as she said, "We haven't seen you in a while."

As mild as it was, the rebuke stung. There had been a time when Mrs. Ng was the closest thing to a mom in my life – if not actually mine, then one I could stand near for a bit, letting her mothering reflect off Chance and onto me. When I'd walked away from the band, I'd walked away from her, too. It had seemed like the only option, but it had still hurt.

"Yeah, long time, huh? Crazy." I rubbed uncomfortably at the back of my neck.

She took pity on me, drawing me inside. "Come in, come in!"

Somehow the view from inside was even better than the view outside. I gaped at the way the open floor plan ended in a wall of solid glass.

"Not too shabby, huh?" Mrs. Ng's accent was pure NYC – blunt and fearless, with a casual intensity that was simultaneously thrilling and terrifying.

"It's amazing."

"We moved out of the old place last year. Though honestly, with Chance and Lawrence gone all the time, it's probably more than we need. But right now, it's perfect." She opened the gleaming steel fridge. "You want a La Croix or something? We've got leftover lasagna. Or pot stickers?"

"Thanks, but I probably shouldn't. Chance wants to work out."

"Right, of course. God forbid he be allowed to *relax* on a weekend." She turned and leaned back against the stone countertop, crossing her arms. "So. David. Catch me up. Still at Franklin?"

"Yeah."

"Applying for college?"

"I'm actually gonna do an apprenticeship instead. Carpentry."

Thin eyebrows rose with curiosity. "Really?"

"Yeah, with one of my dad's contractors." I rushed to justify, getting in all my arguments before she could pass judgment. "I've been learning from him for about a year, and I'm working for them all summer. I'm getting pretty good at it."

She considered this, then nodded once, decisively.

"Good for you. I always say more kids should get into the trades. The world has enough unemployed lit majors." She gestured at the opulence surrounding us. "Not that I should talk smack about the arts. I'm twenty years into public-policy jobs and living in a house my teenage son bought me." She cocked her head. "You playing any music?"

I struggled to keep my shoulders from hunching. "Not really."

She saw it and switched subjects, only to pin me like a butterfly with fresh scrutiny. "Girlfriend?"

I laughed uncomfortably. "No."

Mom Gaze intensified. "Boyfriend?"

"What? No." I blushed.

She grinned mercilessly. "Tinder hookups?"

"Mom! Christ. Cut him some slack."

Chance came down the stairs. He was wearing ordinary track pants and a white Sub-Radio T-shirt with the sleeves cut off, yet somehow managed to make the outfit look a hundred times more stylish than my basketball shorts and Seahawks jersey.

I turned toward him in relief. "Hey, dude."

"Hey."

"Holc!"

I turned just as four feet of kinetic energy in a pony-print package slammed into me, wrapping her arms around my waist.

"Hey, Olivia!" Suddenly I knew how Mrs. Ng must feel looking at me. Chance's little sister had grown six inches since the last time I'd seen her. God, was she in kindergarten already?

She immediately let go and lifted her arms. "Crowd-surf me!"

"Olivia, come on." Chance frowned, embarrassed. "Leave him alone."

The look of perfect confidence she shot him was a startlingly miniature version of their mother's. "Holc doesn't mind."

Mrs. Ng smirked. "Do I want to know . . . ?"

I looked helplessly to Chance.

With a sigh, he came over and grabbed the girl beneath her armpits. "Ready?"

"Ready!" she yelled.

I grabbed her feet. With a heave, we lifted her straight-armed above our heads. With Chance in the lead, we ran into the living room yelling "*CROWDSUUUUUUUUURF!*" Olivia howled with laughter.

After several laps of the posh living room and a dining table made from a medieval church door, we finally dropped her dramatically – but carefully – onto the couch.

"Oof," I said. "You're heavier than last time!"

Chance's grin faltered, and suddenly I knew exactly what he

was thinking: that the last time we'd done this, there'd been three of us to carry her.

Olivia was mercifully oblivious. She bounced up off the leather cushions. "Again!"

"Enough, Livi." Mrs. Ng was smiling. "I'm sure the boys want to go do their *actual* workout." She looked to Chance. "Unless Peter's got you doing sister-lifts? She makes a pretty good kettlebell."

"Seriously." Chance waved to me. "Come on, we'll work out in the basement."

He led me down a flight of stairs, into a tile-floored room that could only be called a basement in the sort of house with statues in the yard. The view was as expansive as in the living room upstairs, with the jagged line of the Cascades looming purple beyond the lake.

Workout equipment packed the space. A rowing machine, a weight bench, a giant metal rack, a long line of dumbbells – it looked like somebody had walked into a gym and asked for one of everything.

"Jeez," I breathed.

"I know." Chance looked embarrassed again. "But it's better than going to a public gym every day."

After the response at Death Putt – let alone the photographers – I could see how that would be a problem.

He moved over to the bench. "This is actually perfect. Peter's got me on a seven-day rotation, and today's upper body. You can spot me."

"Who's Peter?"

"Personal trainer."

"Of course." He said it so casually. Who didn't have their own personal trainer?

"Here, I'll go first." He slid a steel weight plate off a rack and slipped it onto the end of the bar. "Grab a forty-five for the other side, will you?"

I did. The plate was surprisingly heavy.

"Do you bench?" he asked.

"Not really." I'd only lifted a couple of times. "The school gym is all machines."

He pointed to the head of the bench. "Just stand there and try not to fart. If it looks like I'm about to die, grab the bar."

"Okay."

I moved into position, and he lay down on the bench. I took a half step back so I wouldn't be teabagging him, but all his attention was on the bar, jaw clenched and laser-focused. With a lurch, he shoved it up off the rack, held it for a second, then lowered it to his chest.

"One!" I felt the percussion of his breath, mint-tinged, as he pistoned the bar back up. He did eight reps, grunting with each push, then settled it back into its cradle with a clang.

"All right!" He swung to his feet and stepped to the side, hands going to the weight plate. "Your turn. What do you want?"

"I'll do this."

He cocked his head. "You sure? Free weights are a lot different than machines. You gotta engage all the little stabilizer muscles."

I outweighed Chance by probably thirty pounds. I'd spent all summer stacking and hauling. Defiance rose up inside me, snarling. "I've got it."

"Okay." He lifted his hand off the plate in surrender and moved behind the bench. "Ready when you are."

I lay down on the bench and gripped the bar, still seething at his intimation that I couldn't do it.

The bar came up out of its cradle easily enough. With a surge of vindication, I brought it down. The steel hit my sternum with a thud.

And stayed there.

"Come on!" Chance encouraged. "Push!"

It was like there was a car on my chest. The bar pressed down, threatening to cut me slowly in half, like a cheese slicer.

"You got this!" Chance insisted.

My arms shook, but it was like those dreams where your limbs don't work. The finger of God stabbed down on my rib cage.

Chance's hands snaked beneath the bar to either side of me. "Breathe out as you push. On three. One . . . two . . ."

I shoved with all my might. With Chance's help, the bar rose, wobbling. It slammed back into the cradle.

"Nice!" Chance said.

My face burned with more than just exertion. Chance saw it.

"Look, man, you're big, but bench is hyperspecific. Nobody uses their pecs this way unless they're actively targeting them. It doesn't mean anything."

The only thing worse than being shown up by Chance was being patronized. I gritted my teeth and let him swap the plates for some half their size.

After several sets on bench, we moved on to the big black rack thing.

"Pull-ups!" Chance announced. "Wide-grip, to focus on

lats." He hopped up and grabbed a bar that curved like the handlebars of a giant tricycle, swinging back and forth as he walked his hands out to the ends. He hung there with his feet a foot off the floor, body forming a perfect Y, then took a deep breath and hauled himself up, arms and shoulders bending into a W. Then he did it again.

"Just do . . . as many as . . . you can," he grunted.

The muscles of his arms and shoulders corded and bunched, the sleeveless shirt displaying them to great effect. Without any fat to hide them, every fiber stood out stark and defined, like line art in a comic book.

He did maybe ten reps, then dropped back to the floor, breathing heavily.

"Wide-grip *sucks*," he panted. "It took me a while to even do one. You can skip it if you want."

There was no way this was going to go well, and we both knew it. Yet I couldn't just give him that win without trying. I jumped up and grabbed the bar, managing to swing out until I was holding the handles the way he had.

I didn't normally worry much about my weight. While I was bigger than average, and had some extra padding, I didn't get bullied for it, most of the time. If you were picking teams in PE, I'd probably be somewhere in the middle of your list. But hanging from Chance's pull-up bar, I felt every extra pound sucking me downward toward the Earth's core.

I set my jaw and pulled, but I might as well have been trying to cast a spell. *Wingardium leviosa*. My shoulders refused to budge.

Yet they weren't the only thing being stubborn. I continued to hang there, straining for all I was worth.

And then Chance was hugging my legs.

"Dude, what—?"

"Pull!" Chance commanded.

I obeyed. And mercifully, I rose. With Chance helping to lift my lower body, suddenly my chin was over the bar.

"Again!" Chance commanded.

We did two more like that before Chance let go and stepped back. I dropped heavily to the floor.

"Good!" Chance gave me a thumbs-up.

My face burned so hot, I probably looked like the Kool-Aid Man. This had been a bad idea. "Maybe I should go."

Chance looked wounded. "Dude, I told you – nobody's good at wide-grip to start. Peter had to lift my legs like that for like six months."

I wished Chance would stop being so damn encouraging. Mockery would be easier than pity.

"Look, I promise you'll like this next one." He turned and grabbed a pair of dumbbells off their rack. He held them out to the side, arms bent ninety degrees, the weights even with his head and making his biceps pop obscenely. "Military press." He lifted them up over his head until his arms were completely straight, then lowered them again. He did a set of ten, grimacing, then handed me the weights. "Now you."

I was prepared for another round of embarrassment, but this one *was* easier. I did several reps, the motion smooth and solid.

Chance grinned. "See? I told you."

Suspicion loomed. "What weight would you normally do this with?"

"This one." He saw my skepticism and raised his hands. "I'm not screwing with you! I knew this would be easy for you – you've got huge shoulders. I bet you can max more than me without even practicing."

"Huh." My anger sputtered and stalled.

"Here." Chance pulled me over to a mirror on one of the walls. "Watch yourself to make sure you keep good form."

I put the weights up. Chance stepped behind me, fingers touching my triceps as lightly as moths. "I'll spot you. Just go until you burn out."

I lifted. To my surprise, the mirror actually made me look pretty great – with the weights in my hands, you could see the lines of my own muscles moving, better than I ever looked flexing in the bathroom after a shower. Chance stood just behind me, watching over my shoulder with a smile that sent a wave of pride washing through me. As the reps mounted and my arms began to shake, the pressure of his hands strengthened, keeping me from wavering.

When I felt on the absolute edge of collapse, I let the weights fall forward, lowering them to the ground with a grunt.

Chance stepped back and grinned. "Damn, dude, you're a beast!"

"Yeah?" I couldn't stop myself from smiling.

"Totally. You're built for this." He pressed his forearm against mine, inviting me to compare. "I spend most of my time just trying to stay lean without looking like a scarecrow, but you could go full swole if you tried."

People had remarked on my frame before – Dad's contractors asking why I didn't play football, relatives noting how big I'd gotten – but it was different hearing it from Chance. Muscles in my neck relaxed. "Thanks."

We moved on to other lifts, Chance naming and explaining

each in turn. Upright rows, dumbbell flies, overhead triceps extensions. I was pleased to discover that I wasn't as pathetic as I'd feared. Chance might look like a movie star while he lifted – sweat slicking his black hair down across his forehead, arms bulging like tennis balls in a tube sock – but at least I could hold my own. Sometimes, anyway. Moreover, now that I wasn't embarrassing myself with every exercise, it felt good to be here with him. Exciting, even. I'd long hated the idea of Chance Kain, Celebrity. But if I was his equal – if he wanted me here with him – then what did that say about me? It was flattering.

He frowned as I did a hammer curl. "You're swinging your arms."

"Am not." I did another rep.

"You totally are." He put one hand on my bicep, in the crook of my elbow, and the other on the back of my arm. His hands were fever-hot. "*Now* do it."

My arm tried to move forward, pushing against him, but he held me firmly in place. It felt weirdly nice.

He grinned. "Harder this way, huh?"

"Okay, yeah."

He held me for a few more reps, then let go and stepped back. Air rushed in to fill the shadow his fingers left behind, like the afterimage from a flash.

"All right," he said. "I'm worked. Now we finish by doing crunches till we want to throw up."

"I thought this was upper-body day."

"*Every* day is ab day." He patted the flat drum of his stomach. "Muscles are nice, but all photogs care about is shredded abs."

I frowned. "I've never even seen my abs."

He shrugged. "Eh, abs are overrated. They're basically just a giant sign that says 'I don't get to eat carbs.' *Your* muscles actually *do* stuff." He pointed to a mat on the floor. "Here, you go first."

I flopped gratefully down onto the mat, sweat trickling down to sting my eyes. "You seriously work out like this every day?"

"Every day." He gave a rueful smile. "Can't afford to get fat with the whole world watching."

"Right." Given our relative body shapes, the way he said "fat" stung.

It must have shown in my face, because he followed quickly with "Not that there's anything wrong with that! It's just the job, you know?"

"Yeah, I get it." In truth, I couldn't help but respect. I worked hard for my dad, but while there was occasionally heavy lifting, a lot of construction was fetching things or standing around holding a chalk line. And at least I got weekends. It had never occurred to me how much work Chance must put into maintaining heartthrob status.

"Seriously," he said. "It's dumb. People imagine celebrity as all champagne and groupies, but it's more like chicken breast and cardio."

I lay down in sit-up position, then twitched in surprise as Chance knelt on my feet, leaning forward and folding his arms over my knees.

"So you don't flop around," he explained, and slapped my thigh. "Get to it!"

I began crunching.

He slumped down, resting his chin on his forearms. "Honestly, man, nice work. You're good at this."

As much as his encouragement puffed me up, the contrarian in me still said, "Not as good as you."

"Dude, weren't you listening? I do this *every day*. This is your first time, and you're crushing it." His smile was exhausted, a little strained, and all the handsomer for it. "So give yourself some credit, okay?"

A rush of warmth. "Okay."

And something in the back of my brain said:

You could kiss him right now.

I froze, my back sticky against the mat.

Chance sat up, concerned. "What's wrong?"

"Nothing." I quickly started doing crunches again, closing my eyes so he wouldn't see anything in them.

Where the hell had that come from? I didn't even *like* dudes. And even if I did, I wouldn't like *Chance*. Not like that.

It was obviously just a random thought. Like when you're looking down over the edge of a tall building and feel the urge to throw yourself off. The call of the void – that's what the French call it. Everybody gets that. It doesn't mean you actually want to jump. It's just an acknowledgment that you *could*.

This was clearly like that. At the top of each crunch, my face was a few inches from Chance's. So yes, technically, I *could* lean forward and kiss him. It was a physical possibility. That's all.

Like jumping off a building.

"You okay, dude?"

"Yeah," I grunted. "Just … harder than I thought …"

"Good." He grinned again. "The more you hate something, the better it is for you."

And just like that

    everything

        shifted.

You ever do those optical illusions online? The kind that

don't look like anything until you focus on the dot in the middle, and then the whole image seems to start moving, or colors swap, or what looked like one image is revealed to be another?

This was that. In one firework flare of insight, I understood exactly why that thought had popped into my brain:

I'd thought about kissing Chance Ng because *I wanted to kiss Chance Ng.*

It was absurd. I'd only ever liked girls. I had crushes on girls. I watched porn *of girls.* Sure, I could recognize Chance's attractiveness – the action-hero line of his jaw, the dark and piercing eyes, the way his hair was always perfectly imperfect – but it was in the same way you admired a painting.

Which wasn't even getting into the fact that I'd spent the last two years hating him. We'd only just started talking again. I hadn't even seen him since we were fifteen. None of it made any sense.

And at the same time, it made terrifyingly *perfect* sense. Didn't it sometimes feel like I was the only person in the world who *didn't* want to kiss Chance Kain? He was hot. He was rich. He was talented.

He was currently pressing his entire body against my legs.

My feet were literally wedged under his ass, separated from his junk by about two molecules of polyester. I was suddenly terrifyingly aware of my toes.

In the Tetris game of my brain, the last piece fell into place, blinking out an entire row.

This whole time we'd been working out, I'd thought it was jealousy that made me notice every muscle in Chance's arms.

But jealousy doesn't give you a boner.

"I, uh . . . I think I'm good." I scrambled out from under his grip as casually as I could.

"Okay." Chance gave me a curious look, then lay back on the mat with his knees up. "Hold my legs?"

The thought of sitting on his feet that way – of my crotch pressed up against his ankles – sent blood to more than just my cheeks. I shoved my hands into my shorts pockets, playing defense. "Oh! Um, actually, I—"

Footsteps down the stairs. *Oh thank god.*

"Chance?" Mr. Ng leaned into the room, eyes widening as he saw me. "Oh! Hello, David. Good to see you again." He turned his attention to Chance, who sat up on the mat. "Chance, you'd better clean up. Benjamin will be here in half an hour for your Skype meeting." He looked back at me. "Sorry to run you off, David. Chance has a packed schedule this weekend."

"It's cool," I said. In fact, it was more than cool. Suddenly there was nothing I wanted more than a little distance between me and Chance.

Chance looked to me. "Good workout, man. Let's do it again when I'm not so busy, yeah?" Was it just me, or did his smile look hopeful?

"Yeah. Sure. Absolutely." I turned and fled for the stairs.

Mr. Ng patted me awkwardly on the shoulder as I passed. "Don't be a stranger!"

"I won't, sir."

But even as I let myself out the front door, I knew it was a lie. I *was* a stranger.

Maybe even to myself.

9

"Conundrum. Noun."

"Something you can't figure out."

Ridley made a keep-going gesture.

"Umm ..." I closed my eyes. "A confusing problem or question."

"Good." Ridley tossed the flash card onto the pile on the floor.

It was Sunday evening, that melancholic hour when the weekend isn't over but you can see the end coming. Sunlight shot through the blinds at an angle, stacking gold bars across the wall.

We were lounging on opposite ends of Ridley's bed. In a house full of chaos and geekery – commissioned art of RPG characters, Game of Thrones Lego sets, a Death Star waffle maker – she'd rebelled by having the sort of pristine room you only saw in hotels and hospitals. Bed made, clothes on hangers, a white wooden desk with laptop cord coiled and all the pens lined up. The only evidence of her parents' nerddom was a geometric mural of the Lonely Mountain from *The Hobbit*, which her parents had painted before she was born. I was glad she'd left it – the clean angles and blazing sunset made the room feel like an escape. It was matched on the opposite wall by printed-out photos of people jowling – Ridley's trademark practice of leaving your lips loose and shaking your head from side to side while taking a picture, creating bizarre faces. There were pictures of her jowling at the beach, jowling at school, the whole family jowling at Disney World. It was a weird thing, but it was hers.

Ridley picked up another card. "Façade. Noun."

"An illusion. A false appearance."

"Correct." She tossed the stack down in front of me and flopped over onto the bed. "Okay, now do me."

"You gotta work on your pickup lines."

"Says you."

I sighed and collected the cards. "Aren't we done yet?"

"We're done when the stack is done."

I leaned back against the wall. "This is so pointless. You already got the highest score of anyone we know, and I don't need to take them at all."

"Yeah, but I want a *better* score. And you do too need to take them."

Technically, she was right. While the SATs didn't matter for my apprenticeship, Dad had made me promise to take them anyway, just in case. That way if I decided I didn't like carpentry, I could always go back and get a degree. It seemed like a fine enough trade – the future I wanted, in exchange for one Saturday of testing.

Except that Ridley wasn't about to let me get away without studying.

"Okay, fine." She grabbed a stuffed dolphin and bounced it off the ceiling. "So you worked out with Chance yesterday. Dish. Is he really as ripped as his pictures, or is it all Photoshop?"

I remembered his shoulders as he did pull-ups, each individual muscle standing out in stark relief. "It's real."

"*Ungh.*" She clutched the dolphin against her groin. "My

ovaries can't take it. A golden ticket to the Chance Kain Gun Show, and it's wasted on an unappreciative audience."

If only. Life would have been so much simpler if that were true. After returning home, I'd spent the whole afternoon hiding in my room, trying to figure out what it all meant. Porn sites confirmed that I definitely wasn't attracted to random naked dudes. So why did thinking about Chance's hands on my arms keep sending sparks through me?

But I couldn't say any of that. Instead, I tossed a pillow at her and said, "Stop molesting Flipper."

"Whatever, he likes it. Dolphins are perverts. Did you know they wrap eels around their junk to masturbate? And they have prehensile dongs." She made a squiggling motion with one hand.

"God! Why do you know this?"

"Why do you *not* know this? I thought boys were obsessed with their dicks. Did you know echidna penises have four heads? Which is extra weird because the females only have two vaginas. I guess God loves echidna threesomes?"

By now I was blushing furiously, which was of course what she wanted. I managed to keep my cool enough to say, "Really going for uniqueness on those essay questions, huh?"

She grinned and rolled over to face me, chin pillowed on the dolphin. "All right, so, tell me more about Chance's mansion. I want details."

"It's not a mansion."

"You said there was a statue. Was there a statue?"

I frowned.

"See? Mansion."

"Look, I don't want to talk about Chance, okay?" It came out angrier than I intended. I didn't want to even *think* about Chance, and the fact that I couldn't seem to stop was driving me nuts.

Ridley's smile soured. "Okay, jeez. Don't get your manties in a twist." She nodded to the stack of vocab words.

I drew one. "Despondent. Adjective."

"You since you got here."

"Very funny."

She sat up. "Seriously, Davey, what's eating you? If it's Chance, okay, I get it – you're still pissed about Darkhearts. But if you hate the guy so much, why do you keep hanging out with him?"

It was a good question, and one I would have desperately loved an answer to. But I knew Ridley well enough to know that if I gave her even a crumb of the truth, she'd ferret out the whole story, and then I'd never hear the end of it. Not that she'd make fun of me – exactly the opposite. Her enthusiasm would be a million times worse. She'd go into Plotting Mode and micromanage every detail. The last thing I needed was her planning my and Chance's fantasy wedding.

"It's not that," I said.

"Then what?"

I waved the flash cards at the workbooks and laptops. "I'm just sick of studying. It's stupid."

"*You're* stupid. By which I mean you're smart, which is why it would be stupid not to study." She frowned, suddenly all business. "Seriously, David. This is important. You only get one chance at this."

"You're taking them a second time."

"I mean *metaphorically*. Going to college – or not – is one of the biggest decisions of your life." She tilted her head. "You *sure* you don't want to at least apply to UW with me? See what happens?" She waved expansively. "We could get an apartment together. I'll bring home theater girls for you, and you can find me all the cute woodworking boys from the art department, and we'll have big bohemian salons like it's Paris in the 1700s. We'll both get jobs at the same quirky coffee shop, and you can build furniture for them, and I'll host monthly movie nights . . ." She trailed off, lost in her own story.

That's how it was with Ridley. Life was a film, and we were all her actors. Normally I didn't mind – her flair for the dramatic made everyday events feel a little more epic – but this particular argument was old and tired. I kept my face perfectly flat, staring at her until her eyes refocused and she returned to Earth.

She held up her hands in defeat. "No shade, I know." She sighed. "I just want you to be happy."

"I *will* be happy, Rid. I *like* woodworking. I'm good with my hands."

"That's what *she* said." She gave an impish smile. "And I wouldn't mind working *Chance Kain's* wood."

"Dude! What did we just agree?"

"Oh come *on*! *Valar Morghu-lust* – all girls must thirst. The boy is a total smokeshow. It was one thing when you hated him, but now that you two are cool, it's game on. I need you to help me plan how to make him fall in love with me." She rolled over and held the dolphin above her, staring into its plastic eyes. "Maybe we could all drive out to the mountains, and you could pretend your truck broke down, and Chance and I could offer to watch it while you walk back to the nearest gas station. We'll do it at night, somewhere high elevation, and it'll get cold enough that the two of us will have to huddle together for warmth . . ."

"You're being ridiculous," I snapped.

"Of *course* I'm being ridiculous." She glared at me upside down. "Dude. I know I don't *actually* have a chance with Chance. But you miss all the shots you don't take, right? So let me dream a little." Her look turned penetrating. "Unless you know something I don't . . . ? Is there a reason I shouldn't chase him?"

Yes. Except that wasn't really true. Whatever I might be feeling – and that was still an open question – it was clearly one-sided. Chance and I had been *lifting*, not flirting. Activities didn't get any bro-ier than that. The dude just wanted a friend, and I wasn't about to make things any more awkward than they already were.

Which meant there was no reason to shit on Ridley's parade. None I was willing to admit to, anyway.

"No," I grumbled.

"All right then. Scheming hats on." She bit her lip. "Maybe the three of us could go out on his yacht—"

"He doesn't have a yacht."

"Are you sure?"

I was not.

"So we'll go out on his yacht, and I'll pretend to drown, so he has to dive in and save me and give me mouth-to-mouth. And then I'll be like, 'How can I ever repay you?' and he'll be like, 'It's nothing,' and I'll be like, 'No, I insist, let me take you out to—'"

My phone chimed. I checked the text.

CHANCE:

Can you hang out right now?

102

Ridley noticed my surprise. Her mouth opened in shock. "Wait – is that *him*?"

I nodded.

"*Ohmygod!*" She flailed her hands and feet in the air like a dying bug, then rolled up onto her knees. "What does he want?"

I told her.

Both hands flew up to cover her mouth. "This is some *The Secret* shit! Active manifestation! I put my desires out into the universe, and the universe is providing!" She grabbed my shoulders. "Ask if I can come too!"

"Dude."

"*Please!* I'll owe you a favor."

From Ridley, that was the biggest bargaining chip there was. I sighed and texted back.

ME:

I'm hanging out with Ridley. Can she come?

His reply was immediate.

CHANCE:

Just you. Come pick me up?

"What'd he say?" Ridley demanded.

I was trying to figure out how to respond when my phone chimed again. I looked down to find just one word. The last word I ever expected to see from Chance Kain.

CHANCE:

Please?

10

Ridley was disappointed, but adamant that I should go anyway. "The king of goth-pop needs you."

"He needs a ride somewhere," I grumbled.

"That's what Lyft's for, dorkus." She gathered up my study materials and shoved them into my hands. "He clearly needs *you.*"

When I pulled up outside Chance's house, he was waiting by the gate again, wearing a tightly tailored maroon dress shirt with military-style epaulets and black slashes across the chest. His hair was perfectly arranged, and he looked like he'd just stepped off either a talk show or a spaceship. Either seemed possible.

He ran over and got in. "Hey."

"Hey." I pressed in the clutch. "So where we going?"

"Anywhere." He leaned his head against the window. "Just drive."

I didn't appreciate the whole chauffeur routine, but something was clearly wrong, so I let it slide. I shifted into first and started rolling.

We were already pointed north, so I went with it. Before long we were winding through the leafy tunnel of the Arboretum. Just beyond it, the road split, offering an on-ramp for the freeway. On impulse, I took it, letting the truck yowl pleasantly as I slammed through its gears and shot us out onto the bridge.

At a mile and a half, the 520 Bridge was the longest floating bridge in the world. The low sun behind us caught every tiny wave as we sailed across Lake Washington. To the south, the mountain was out, looming over us like the opening credits of a movie.

Chance still hadn't said anything. I could practically hear his teeth grinding as he stared out the window.

I pulled my phone out of my pocket and synched it to the stereo. I thought for a moment, debating which album to put on, then settled on the obvious choice.

Guitar feedback faded in, the soft slap of brushes, and then the thick acoustic groove of the Cure's "Out of this World" filled the truck. I rolled my window down and hung my arm out, cranking the music to let it roll over the top of the wind noise, the gusts chuffing inside the cab like a caged animal. Air slapped rhythmically at my outstretched hand.

Chance didn't speak, didn't change expression, but from the corner of my eye I could see his head start to bob against the window, moving involuntarily to the beat. The sort of rocking people call "self-soothing" in autistic kids, but which everyone has in them somewhere, if they'll just let it run.

Bloodflowers: the classic Cure album all three of us had agreed was perfect, start to finish. The album that made us want to start a band. Shuffling, morbid, smooth and languid in a way that hit harder and heavier than any metal. "Out of this World" wasn't my favorite song, but it wasn't up to me – if you were going to play more than one song off an album, you played the whole thing in order, as the artist intended. That had been Eli's rule.

I turned south down 405 as the song ended, through the

gleaming towers of Bellevue, then east again on I-90. Skyscrapers turned to suburbs, then to trees. The Cascades rose up huge and craggy, their tops crowned in gold, feet lost in shadow.

With each mile we put between us and the city, I could see Chance unclench, slowly reinflating. He rolled his window down and hung his hand out as well, turning it at angles to feel the pressure of our passage.

"Maybe Someday" came on as we wound up into the foothills proper, and he slapped the dashboard in time with the drum drop. "Fuck!" But he said it with relief. He slumped back against his seat and finally looked over, giving me a little half smile.

I nodded. I might not know the specifics, but I absolutely knew the feeling.

We chased the last rays of daylight up the mountains, gaining elevation at eighty miles an hour. We hit the crest of Snoqualmie Pass just as the album trailed off into a final squelch of screaming guitar. Chance let out a long breath.

"Man." He nodded to the abandoned chairlifts marching up the grassy slopes to our right. "Remember when your dad used to bring us snowboarding up here?"

I nodded.

"You guys still come up?"

"Some, yeah." Though in truth, we hadn't come up nearly as often since I'd split with Darkhearts. While I occasionally tagged along with the Martinez twins, Dad had never gotten beyond the zigzag falling-leaf method. He usually spent the day in the lodge cafeteria, reading books on his phone and eating ten-dollar crinkle fries – the only bad French fry shape. He never complained, but I still felt guilty. And anyway, it wasn't as fun to board alone.

"Those were good times," Chance said wistfully.

We drove on, my phone randomly kicking over to Boy Is Fiction's *Broadcasts in Colour*. The air went from crisp to cold as we coasted down the eastern side of the peaks. Instead of rolling up the windows, I turned on the heater.

As we passed through the momentary flash of a one-gas-station town, Chance asked, "So how far are we going?"

As if this were all my idea. I shrugged. "As far as it takes."

Chance grinned, his first real smile of the night. He studied the mostly empty highway, then pointed to the sign for an upcoming exit. "That one."

"What's there?"

"That's what we're gonna find out."

I exited. There was nothing at the end of the off-ramp, just a bare junction lined by trees. I took a turn at random, then another.

In moments we were out of sight of the highway, driving down a straight, two-lane road. There were no lights out here, not even the glow of distant farmhouses. Only empty fields and scrubby hills, revealed in filmstrip flicker by the narrow cone of our headlights, the edges of which suddenly seemed far too close.

The music stuttered and died. Chance leaned over to look at my phone. "No signal."

"Huh." The idea that you could just *drive* to someplace without cell service was something I theoretically knew, but had never personally encountered.

"Must be the mountains. We're in a valley or something."

We drove on in silence. After a minute, Chance said, "Man, there's really nobody out here, huh?"

"Guess not."

"It's like one of those roads from a horror movie. Like, where we break down, and the only house is full of murderous hillbillies."

The thought sent a chill through me, but I laughed. "Yeah, or some serial killer with a mask and a meat hook."

He laughed as well.

We kept driving. We still hadn't seen another car yet.

After a minute, he said, "You know what? I was wrong. This isn't mutant territory. It's totally the hitchhiker girl who doesn't say anything, and when we get back to town we find out she's been dead for twenty years."

"Or an alien abduction. This is prime crop circle territory."

"Hope you're ready to get probed."

We both snickered. But in the silence that followed, I heard him check the door locks.

We continued on in that vein, tossing suggestions back and forth, the unacknowledged fear crackling between us.

At last lights appeared in the distance, breaking the tension. I slowed as we approached.

Small spotlights along the rocky ground shone up at a wooden sign in the shape of Washington and the words STONE FOREST STATE PARK.

"We're here," Chance declared authoritatively.

"Guess we are." I nodded to a smaller sign with no-nonsense bold type. "Closed from dusk to dawn."

"Good thing someone forgot to lock up."

He was right – a few car lengths down the entrance road, the big metal swing-arm gate hung open. Chance looked at me expectantly.

I shifted back into gear and turned in.

The drive dead-ended in an empty, unlit parking lot. Headlights revealed nothing but a few picnic tables and interpretive signs. When I parked and killed the lights, darkness dropped over us like a weighted blanket.

We sat for a moment, letting our eyes adjust. Then Chance popped his door, and I followed. I took a step outside and stopped short.

Above us were more stars than I'd seen in my life. They stretched away in every direction, sky curving huge above the black waves of the surrounding hills.

"Holy shit." Chance craned his head back, spinning slowly. His voice was soft and reverent. "This is *insane.*"

They were bright enough to navigate by, and Chance walked over to the nearest picnic table. He lay down across the top, spread-eagled, and I perched on one of the attached benches, the rubberized metal diamonds digging into my palms.

"I wish I knew some constellations," Chance said.

I was taken aback. "You don't know *any?*"

"I mean, I know names, but I can never find them."

I pointed. "Well, that's the Big Dipper right there."

"Where?"

I pointed harder. "There."

"You said that already."

I leaned over until our heads were side by side, then pointed again. "That rectangle of four stars is the cup, and then those three are the tail."

"Oh shit! Okay, I see it."

I moved my finger. "And if you continue the line of those

front two stars – the edge of the cup – it points you toward the North Star. That's also the tail of the Little Dipper."

"Damn, dude. How'd you learn so much about stars?"

I thought of camping with Dad, that first summer after Mom left. I'd been supposed to spend part of the break with her. But of course she'd never showed.

"Just picked it up, I guess."

"Cool."

There was another long silence as we watched the sky. When I couldn't take it anymore, I asked, "What are we doing out here, Chance?"

He gestured. "Having an adventure. Looking at stars."

I resisted the urge to let my irritation show, but only barely. "You know what I mean."

He was quiet again. This time I waited him out.

Eventually he sighed. "The record company's pushing me to get back to work – a new tour, a new album, something."

"Jesus. Eli hasn't even been gone a month."

"I know. But everybody lost a shitload of money when we canceled the tour halfway. I don't have time to be sad, unless that sad's making them cash. I tried to explain that Eli was the songwriter – I've been in meetings all weekend – but they don't care. They wanna just buy songs for me. Hire producers. Benjamin says as long as I'm still the face of the band, most of the fans won't even notice."

My stomach clenched. I tried to tell myself the sudden rage was for Eli, for them treating him as disposable. But it was all too familiar. *The fans won't even notice.*

"But it's not just that." Chance waved angrily at the air. "I mean, maybe they're right. Maybe I can keep doing it alone. But what if I can't? What if Eli was the secret sauce, and everybody hates the new stuff? The tour, sure, maybe people will be fine with it. But if the next record tanks, the label will drop me, and Benjamin's always talking about how quickly audiences move on. I'll be a has-been at eighteen."

The casual way he said it – *a has-been at eighteen* – took that knot of anger in my guts and shredded it, parceling it out to every part of my body. My limbs buzzed.

"God," I said flatly. "How horrible."

Chance didn't even notice my tone, too wrapped up in his own drama. "I know, right? Everything we built, and it could all go *poof.*" He snapped his fingers. "Just like that. And then what?"

I knew what. I was living it.

Quietly, evenly, I said, "So this is your big crisis. That you might have to stop being a rock star."

Chance's head snapped around, meeting my gaze in the darkness. "That's not it! I've got people relying on me now. My whole team, Benjamin, the label. My parents might have to move!"

"It must be a lot of work, moving out of a mansion."

He jerked upright. "Why are you being such an asshole? I thought we were friends!"

"Are we, Chance? Are we *really*?" The worst part was, I had almost started to believe it myself. Started to act like maybe this time would be different. But Chance was still the same arrogant, self-centered prick he'd always been. The shame of it stung – fool me twice, shame on me, et cetera.

The words came vomiting up out of me, burning and bitter. "Because last I checked, we haven't been friends in years. You've been off touring the world, being Mr. Famous, while I've been stuck here watching it happen. Now you call me up, have me drop everything I'm doing to come listen to you cry about the idea that you *might* – *maybe* – have to be a *normal* person again. Well, guess what, Chance? You're right! Being normal *does* suck! But don't worry. We both know that as soon as you're done slumming it with me, reliving your middle-school highlights reel, you'll forget all about it and be right back hanging out on private jets with all the shiny fancy people. And I'll still be here." I shoved myself angrily off the bench. "So fuck that. And fuck you."

"Jesus, you really can't get over yourself, can you?" Chance shook his head, sliding down off the table. "After all the fun we've been having, everything I've done to try and rebuild bridges, you still can't go five minutes without being jealous. Some jab about my fame, some topic I can't talk about without you getting all sullen." He spread his arms wide. "When you look at me, do you even see me? Or do you just see a big mirror reflecting your own mistakes? Because I've been real with you." He smacked his chest. "*I'm* trying to be friends again. And all you do is blame me for your own choices."

"My *choices*? You left me behind!"

"You *quit* the *band*!" Chance's shout echoed off rocky slopes. "What was I supposed to do, chain you up in Eli's rec room? You wanted to stop, so you stopped! And it screwed me and Eli over pretty well, by the way – not that *you* cared. We had to scramble to figure out how to be a two-piece. But fine, *what*ever." He raised his hands in a theatrical shrug. "And you know what? You were happy enough with your choice until we got signed. It's only now, after he and I busted our asses doing the work, that you regret it." He snorted and shook his head in disgust. "You *do* realize we would have let you back in, right?"

I froze. "What?"

"We talked about it, me and Eli. Even after you stormed out and left us hanging. Even after we got the record deal. You were our *friend*, Holc." He huffed again. "If you'd asked, we would have taken you back."

The world went muffled and distant. My ears rang with a faint, high-pitched tone, like when you get hit with a flash-bang in a first-person shooter. I felt dizzy and grabbed the picnic table, just to have something to hold on to.

They would have let me back in.

"But you didn't ask." Chance stepped close. "You didn't want to do it anymore. And everything we built from there on out was me and Eli. So don't come around acting like we stole from you. *You* left *us.*"

He leaned in, head tilted, until our noses almost touched.

"If you have a problem with that, Holc – take it up with the mirror."

My arms shot out, shoving him backward. His eyes widened, and then his own palms hit me in the chest, knocking me away.

I lunged without thinking, tackling him and driving him back onto the table. He rolled with surprising strength, and my funny bone hit the edge of the bench, sending sparks shooting up my arm.

Nobody threw a punch. It wasn't that kind of fight – neither the posturing of a lunchroom showdown, nor the life-and-death struggle of a gang beating. This was something different: frustration made physical. We grabbed at each other, each unsure what we were trying to do, only knowing that it needed to happen. Fists balled up in each other's clothes as we strained to pin each other's flailing arms. Buttons from his shirt popped free beneath my fingers.

My knee clipped the side of the bench, and we went down in a tumble, slamming sideways onto the table's concrete pad. My elbow screamed as it took the hit a second time.

The shock of the impact knocked the fight out of us. We came apart as if by mutual agreement, rolling away onto our backs, breathing hard.

Above us, the stars wheeled their slow rotation.

I could have asked. Could have turned my whole life around with a phone call. Chance was right – it would have been so easy.

So why hadn't I?

From his patch of ground, Chance panted out, "Truce?"

I was glad it was too dark for him to see my guilty flush. "Truce."

"Christ." He groaned and sat up, brushing at his mangled dress shirt. "We haven't fought like that since fourth grade."

I half smiled, pushing myself up onto my bruised elbows and immediately regretting it. "Not since Eli and the Magic cards."

"Yeah." Chance gave a wheezing laugh.

And burst into tears.

11

I sat frozen, paralyzed with surprise. The silence of the night magnified Chance's gasps – big, ugly sobs that shook his silhouette. He hunched over, clutching his stomach.

After way too long, I ventured, "Chance?"

His voice was choked. "I killed him."

"What?" Nothing was making any sense tonight.

"I killed him!" He grabbed his knees, head hanging like he might throw up. "I killed Eli."

My brain was still numb from too many shocks, yet it didn't stop an icy dread from seeping in. I shoved myself up into a cautious squat, feeling the rocks and dirt embedding into my palms. "What are you talking about?"

"I knew he was depressed." Chance hiccupped, voice quavering. "Being away from home, away from his other friends – it was harder for him. He started drinking. Getting it from stagehands. I didn't tell anybody."

Relief flooded through me. "Chance, that's not—"

"I *knew*!" His snarl sent me toppling backward. "Eli *hated* touring. By halfway through the first tour, he was done. He just wanted to stay home and write music. But we were under so much pressure." He ground palms against his eyes. "He could have done it, too. Just gone home. Eli didn't give a shit about the money, or the label, or anything. He could have done whatever he wanted. But he didn't want to disappoint *me*." He looked up at the sky, starlight playing across the beautiful shipwreck of his grief. "I kept pushing him. Just a few more dates. Just a few more interviews. Gotta do that video. Might as well stay in L.A. – more convenient for everyone. It got to the point where he'd go straight back to his room and get hammered after every show. Just drinking till he passed out, alone in the dark. I told people he was working on new material." He hacked out a laugh, cold and angry. "I saw all the warning signs. And I covered them up. Because I was selfish."

He looked down at his hands, then up at me, his face naked and vulnerable. In a hoarse whisper that was the furthest thing from Chance Kain, Rock God, he said:

"I killed my best friend."

"Dude – " I reached out and touched his shoulder.

Chance lurched forward, collapsing into me. His body shook against mine, and my arms wrapped reflexively around him. He buried his face in my shoulder, hugging me tight as a fresh storm of sobs took him.

I was surprised to find that I was crying too – big, silent tears, leaking down my cheeks into Chance's hair. Maybe it was just the proximity of his grief, triggering my primate mirror neurons. Maybe it was the knowledge that he and Eli had never betrayed me after all. But suddenly the careful distance I'd built evaporated, and I had to face not the theory of Eli, but the reality. The shy, sweet boy who'd stayed up all night playing games with me. Who'd made me a custom ringtone for my thirteenth birthday. And who'd been so sad that feeling nothing had seemed better than feeling anything.

We sat that way for long minutes, me squatting awkwardly, Chance clinging to me like a drowning victim. I'd never hugged another boy before, and certainly not like this. I had no idea what to do with my hands, and after a while settled for patting ridiculously at his back, as if he were a dog.

"Dude," I said. "It's okay."

Chance just cried harder.

When the sobs finally gave way to long, shuddering breaths, I loosened my hold and drew back until I could see his face. "Hey. Chance. I need you to listen to me, all right? You didn't kill Eli. You know how I know?"

His eyes were dark pools, not quite daring to hope. I waited, making him say it.

He took a slow breath and asked, "How?"

I smiled. "Because you've *always* been obsessed with yourself, and it's never killed anyone before."

Chance gave a surprised laugh, thick with snot, and dropped his arms. "Jesus, dude."

"I'm serious." I squeezed his shoulder. "This isn't your fault. So you wanted to keep touring – so what? Like you said, Eli never had a problem doing his own thing. He could have walked away if part of him didn't want it, too."

He grimaced. "But he knew I—"

"You're proving my point, dude. Stop making this all about you. Could you have done more to help him? Sure. It sounds like everybody could have. But Eli was his own person. You wanna call me out for leaving the band? Tell me to take responsibility for my own choices? Fine." I pointed a finger at him. "But that means you gotta do the same for Eli. What happened is on him, not you. Okay?"

He stared, unblinking.

I shook him by the shoulder, not gently. "*Okay?*"

Breath rushed out of him. "Okay."

117

"Okay." I sat back onto the ground beside him, but kept my arm around his shoulders. He didn't pull away.

"Thanks, Holc." His arm went around my back, clasping my shoulder as well. He turned toward me. "You're a good guy."

The last of my resentment drained away. I might still be mad about the way things went down with Darkhearts. I probably always would be. But in that moment, I wasn't mad at Chance. Not anymore.

"You're a good guy, too."

Chance looked down at my shoulder, which was quickly turning cold as his tears evaporated. He wiped his wrist across his face. "I think I snotted on you."

"Now *that* you're responsible for."

He laughed, then held up his free arm. "Bro hug?"

We hugged, pounding on each other's backs with all the force of our previous fight. Chance's hair brushed against my ear. He smelled like sweat, and lavender laundry detergent, and the kind of neon deodorant with a name like Brutal Ice.

But as the thumping ended, he didn't pull away. Neither did I. We sat side by side yet twisted together. Beneath my hands, his back was solid and warm. His own arms were tight, pressing me close enough to feel each ragged breath he took.

I felt hollowed out. Exhausted. My limbs were as heavy as Chance's dumbbells from the previous morning, yet he didn't object as they pressed down across his shoulders, letting him take the weight. We leaned into each other.

And all of a sudden, I didn't want him to let go.

But soon enough his arms loosened. This time it was he who leaned back, just far enough to look at me. The wind off the foothills tousled his already disheveled hair. I could only see suggestions of his face – a cheek, the point of his chin – but they glowed in the starlight like the city at night: elegant, mysterious, and utterly familiar.

"Holc?" The word puffed against my lips, still warm from his mouth.

My breath faltered.

"Yeah?"

And then we were kissing.

I can't tell you who moved first. It seems important, doesn't it? Who kissed who. Who was brave enough to be first over the top of that trench. But maybe it's better this way. No points to be scored.

His lips were shockingly soft, and hesitant – barely more substantial than his breath. Yet as that first touch cascaded up my nerves and into my brain, it was like someone threw a switch on an electromagnet, smashing us together. My lower lip was between his, the faintest hint of his teeth behind them. My hand came up to cup his cheek, hot and smooth, then slid around to the back of his neck, venturing up through the brush-straight bristle at his nape and into the product-thickened mane above. Somehow, having my hand in that perfect hair was as exciting as the kiss itself.

After an infinity of back-and-forth – each of us receding as the other pursued, like waves on a beach – we finally broke apart. We stared across the sudden space between us.

"Holy shit," Chance breathed.

We cracked up, the excitement and relief and fear exploding out of us in manic laughter. Yet still he didn't let go of me.

When we'd stopped laughing, he looked up at me, face going serious. "So what does this mean?"

My armpits were cold with sweat. My insides tensed happily, like we were a roller coaster climbing toward the drop.

I answered honestly.

"I have no idea," I said.

And leaned back in.

12

My phone had a seizure as we hit the freeway, a dozen vibrating text dings and voicemail chirps all stacking atop each other as we reentered cell reception. I tugged it out of my pocket and thumbed quickly through, keeping one eye on the empty freeway.

With the exception of three from Ridley, all of the texts were from Dad, summed up conveniently by the last one:

DAD:

WHERE ARE YOU?!

"Oh *shit.*" I glanced at the clock on the stereo. 1:17 A.M.

"What's up?" Chance had his fingers in front of a vent, warming them in the engine's excess heat.

"I didn't check in with my dad."

"Oooh." Chance made a face. "Buuuuuustedddddd . . ."

I laughed. I knew I should feel guilt, or dread, but I just couldn't. Not right now.

I told him to make himself useful and see how long it would take us to get back. He tapped at his phone.

"Jesus – an hour and a half? It didn't feel that long getting out here."

I could probably cut that down by speeding, but not by much. I held my phone up to my mouth to be heard over the road noise and said, "Hey phone, text Dad."

When it beeped acknowledgment, I said, "Sorry for not texting. I'm okay. Headed home now – be there around three. Send text."

121

The phone read it back to me for confirmation, then sent it.

Chance watched from where he leaned against the passenger door. "So how much trouble are you in?"

"Unclear." I didn't have an official curfew, and Dad was normally pretty chill. But 3:00 A.M. was a bridge I'd never crossed before. "You?"

"Nah, it's fine. Since Dad and I are gone so often, whenever we're actually home, he and Mom disappear into their bedroom and lock the door as soon as Livi's bedtime hits. They'll never even notice I'm gone."

"Oh god." The image of Mr. and Mrs. Ng having sex was uncomfortable in a variety of ways, and even more so with Chance right beside me. He snickered.

My truck snarled up over the pass. My eyes felt dry and gritty, and my whole body hummed, as if from too much caffeine.

Chance and I didn't say much. Maybe neither of us wanted to break the spell. Yet every so often our eyes would meet, and we'd both start grinning uncontrollably.

I wanted to reach over and take his hand, but already the anxiety was creeping back in. If I tried – would he accept? In my exhausted haze, our kissing was starting to feel like a dream, the product of an overactive imagination. Everything about this night seemed to belong to the darkness, and now we were driving back out of it.

Only, he kept giving me that smile.

At last we pulled up in front of his house. He took off his seat belt, and we sat for a moment, staring at each other.

"So . . . uh . . ." I said.

He darted forward and kissed me, a quick peck on the lips. He recoiled, smirking.

"Bye, Holc."

Then the door was closing behind him.

I drove home, held awake only by endorphins and the desperate need to pee. I debated parking a block away, to avoid waking Dad if he was asleep, then decided that if he *had* gone to bed, the best thing would be for him to see my truck outside when he woke up.

The lights in the kitchen and living room were on as I parked, but that didn't *necessarily* mean anything. He could have left them on for me. I slunk to the house and slid my key stealthily into the dead bolt, then eased open the door.

A hot gust of cinnamon rolled over me, and I knew I was screwed.

Dad sat at our tiny kitchen table, the phone in his hands dusted white. More flour covered the kitchen counter, and the pans of cinnamon rolls in front of him joined cookies on the stove and a loaf of banana bread atop the microwave.

Shit shit *shit.*

"How's Chance?" he asked.

This was bad. Dad only baked when he was stressed. For him to make cinnamon rolls *and* banana bread . . . "Uh. He's fine."

"That's good." His voice was dangerously light. "Don't you want to know how I know you were with Chance? After all, you told me you were studying at Ridley's."

"Dad, I—"

"You said you thought you'd be home by nine. When you didn't show up, I figured, hey, whatever – maybe they're watching a movie or something. When it got to ten, I texted you. But I guess you were busy."

"Yeah, sorry—"

"So at *eleven*" – his voice rose easily over the top of mine – "when you still weren't responding, I had to contact Ridley. Except I don't have her number. I didn't even really remember her last name. So I had to go stalk your social media until I found her. When she didn't respond to my messages – because she was probably asleep, like *I* should have been – I had to stalk *her* profile until I found her parents. But of course they weren't checking Facebook messages, so I had to pay forty dollars – which is coming out of *your* paycheck – to find out their phone numbers through one of those online detective sites."

I felt myself shriveling, but said nothing. He'd clearly been rehearsing this speech, and wasn't about to be interrupted.

"So I called up some people I've never met, who probably have work in the morning, at *damn near midnight,* and finally got her mom to pick up on the third try. Fortunately, she was very understanding. She went and woke Ridley, which is how I learned you'd gone off with Chance Ng. I tried to call *his* parents, but of course their numbers have changed, and the creeper site couldn't find them." He scowled. "I guess when you're rich and famous, you pay someone to scrub that data. So I was just debating how long to wait before calling the police when you finally texted, letting me know you'd be home at *three in the goddamn morning."* His hand had made a fist around his phone, and he carefully unclenched and laid it down on the table. His face went sad. "What the *hell,* David? I've never gotten up in your shit about staying out late. All I ask is that you keep me informed. A little basic courtesy."

"I know," I said quickly. "And I'm sorry. I would have texted, but it was sort of an emergency, and then we lost cell reception."

"You lost reception?" Dad looked startled. "Where in the hell were you?"

"Um." Suddenly I saw our little adventure through his eyes. Guilt coiled inside me. "Near Ellensburg, I think?"

"*Ellensburg?!*" His eyes shot comically wide above his beard. "You drove *across the pass* and didn't think to tell me?"

"We didn't plan to!" I insisted. "It just sort of happened. Like I said, it was an emergency."

"What kind of emergency makes you drive *a hundred miles* each way?"

"It was Chance. He was having a hard time."

"Oh, of course." Dad crossed his arms, leaving flour-white fingerprints on his flannel shirt. "It's gotta be hard, being that rich. More money, more problems."

"Jesus, Dad. Not everything's about that." The unconscious echo of my own fight with Chance was disorienting. "Why can't you cut him some slack?"

"Cut him slack?! You told me yourself the kid was a pretentious dick – so much so that he drove you out of your own band. Then he gets rich off of your work, but you won't let me sue for your share. For two years you mope around, and then as soon as he shows up needing a friend, you go out of your way to support him." He leaned forward and gripped the table. "I just don't want to see him take advantage of you again."

My temper flared. "He's not taking advantage of me!"

Dad fixed me with a stare. "Are you sure?"

Was I sure? Everything had been such a whirlwind. Tonight had felt different, like everything had shifted. And something *had* changed. But what did it mean? Had I really been wrong to resent Chance all those years? Or was I just finally falling prey to the same desperate crush as all of Chance's fans?

I didn't think so. But honestly, I was so tired I could barely think. My brain felt twisted around like a Red Vine.

"I've gotta piss." I walked past the table toward the bathroom.

"Hey!" Dad shot up out of his chair. "I'm not done talking to you!"

"You'd rather I pissed on the floor?" I didn't look back, just reached for the bathroom doorknob.

"Goddammit, David!" Dad slapped the wall in frustration. "Fine! Go ahead – walk out! Just like your mother."

The words exploded into the room, blowing all the air out. My hand froze above the knob. I turned.

Dad stood stricken, as if I were the one who'd said the unforgivable. As I stared, his shock melted to shame. He reached up, fingers splaying across his beard and the bridge of his nose, as if to cage words that had already escaped. Flour turned his brown hair white and old.

An eternity passed. Finally, he spoke.

"Get cleaned up and go to bed," he said quietly. "You've got work in five hours."

I could only nod slowly, then turn and enter the bathroom. When I emerged, the lights were off, and his bedroom door was closed.

I climbed the stairs to my own room in the dark, anger and shame clinging like the smell of vanilla glaze, wondering how everything had gotten so complicated.

13

Dad took pity on me and stopped at Starbucks the next morning. I wasn't normally a big coffee drinker, but my eyes felt like wrinkled grapes, and at least the bitter burn kept them open.

Neither of us spoke much on the drive, last night's words still sloshing silently around the cab. After fifteen of the longest minutes ever, we pulled in next to Denny's van. Where Dad's was the plain white cargo van of contractors everywhere, hers was an airbrushed acid trip, complete with a cartoon of herself riding a dragon, using a long paint roller as a lance.

Denny was up a ladder when we got inside, but came sliding down in a rush as Dad began setting out the byproducts of the previous night's disaster.

"Oh snap! Is that banana bread?!"

"And cinnamon rolls." Dad cleared a section of the workbench. "Homemade."

"Dude. Derek. *Dude.*" She grabbed a slice of banana bread, pointing it at me. "Pay attention, Dave-o. This, right here, is why your dad is the best general in Seattle." She took a bite, and her eyes rolled back in her head. "Oh, holy *tits.*"

"Thank David," Dad said evenly.

Denny looked at me in surprise, cheeks bulging. "You made this?"

I shrank down between my shoulders. "Not exactly."

"Chow down, Denny," Dad said. "It's just us today, and I don't want to take any more home than I have to."

"No Jesús?" I tried to hide my disappointment.

"He's got another job he needed to work in." Dad didn't look at me. "You're helping Denny today."

"Okay." That was normally almost as good as helping Jesús, but there was something ominous about the way he said it.

"Toss me a scraper, Den."

Denny juggled baked goods long enough to oblige. Dad handed me the paint knife – a tool like a metal spatula with a broad, flat blade – as well as a respirator.

"Paint scraping. Outside. No ladders, just whatever you can reach. Start on the east wall, and clean up as you go."

"Oh dip! Thanks, boss." Denny smirked at me with friendly malice. "I don't know what you did, but I'm glad you did it. Hope you've got headphones."

"You remember how?" Dad asked.

"How could I forget?" I muttered.

"Lunch is at one." He turned back to the bench. "Get scraping."

I wanted to shoot back something cutting, but thought better of it. With a sigh, I grabbed my water bottle and headed outside.

Judging by the snippets of Dante's *Inferno* that I'd read for English class, I didn't think scraping paint was *technically* a circle of Hell, but I was pretty sure that was just an oversight. On its surface, scraping seems like no big deal – maybe even satisfying, in the way some kids like pouring Elmer's glue on their hands in elementary school, just to peel it off. But that doesn't take into account the circumstances. When you scrape paint, you don't get to just clear a patch. You have to scour everything that's going to be painted, searching out every little crack and bubble, scraping it so it can be sanded and primed. What's fun for five minutes becomes tolerable after twenty, and excruciating after a few hours.

I'd spent two very long days scraping walls for Dad at a bar in White Center last year, but this was even worse. Because the real killer on scraping was the cleanup. While Dad was pretty sure this paint wasn't full of toxic lead, the clients still wouldn't want a bunch of paint chips getting ground into the soil. Which meant you had to make sure you picked them all up.

Every.

Last.

Flake.

The monotony of the task gave me plenty of time to think – but honestly, I wasn't sure that was a good thing. Part of my brain was still riding high from the previous night's adventure, even as my exhausted body decomposed around it. Yet every hour that passed left me with more questions.

Why exactly was I lusting over Chance Ng, of all people? Why *now*, when I'd never had a hint of it in the years we'd hung out? I'd never expected to kiss a boy, so what did it mean that I had? And while I'd believed Chance when he'd said they would have let me back into Darkhearts, Dad might also be right, in that I was setting myself up for a fall. Because whatever had changed between us, Chance was still Chance, which meant any day now he'd be gone again. And I'd still be here, scraping paint and trying to figure out what it all meant.

I'd finished the east wall and was down on my knees picking chips out of the grass when Denny came out to check on me, a cinnamon roll in either hand.

"These things are the *shit*," she announced. She appraised

my wall with a critical eye. "Not bad. You might actually get through this today." She kicked at the long grass along the wall's foundation. "Should've laid down a tarp first, though. Makes cleanup a lot easier."

I stared up at her from the ground.

A tarp. How the hell had I overlooked that?

She laughed. "Don't worry, you're not the first." She sat on a nearby stack of lumber and held out a cinnamon roll. "Want one?"

For everything Dad's cinnamon rolls represented, there was no denying they were delicious. And I *definitely* wanted the break. I stripped off my gloves and sat down beside her.

"So." She handed me the bun. "What'd you do?"

I shrugged. "Stayed out too late. Didn't call."

She nodded agreeably. "Been there. You grounded?"

"Not yet."

"Lucky. Your dad's chiller than most."

"Yeah." But I couldn't explain the truth: that by invoking Mom, Dad had committed a sin every bit as bad as my own.

When I was seven, my mother announced she was done – done with her job, done with Dad, done with Seattle. She wasn't sure where she was going, just away. They gave me the choice: go with Mom, or stay with Dad.

I, in my infinite seven-year-old wisdom, chose Dad, on the theory that if I stayed, Mom would have to stay nearby to see me, and thus I'd get to keep both of them. In choosing Dad, I'd called her bluff.

And she'd called mine. In the decade since, I'd seen her exactly three times. She didn't even text unless I texted her first, and somewhere around age ten I'd quit bothering.

None of that was anything I could talk to Denny about. But as my mind started to turn back to the questions buzzing around it, I recognized an opportunity.

"Hey, Denny . . . Can I ask you a personal question?"

She leaned back, elbows propped on the stacks of two-by-fours. "Dave-o, for cinnamon rolls like these, I'll give you the nuclear launch codes."

I steeled myself, then said, "How did you know you were gay?"

She didn't seem surprised, just tongued a molar thoughtfully.

"Honestly? It was never really a question." She smirked. "I remember in first grade, trying to kiss Claudia Demopolis at the top of the slide at recess. She slid down right as I leaned in, and I somersaulted all the way after her. Had to get three stitches in my lip."

"Ah." Not helpful. "Interesting. Thanks."

"No problem." She lifted her roll for another bite. "So have you kissed him yet?"

"*What?!*" I bobbled my own roll, catching it an inch before it hit the dirt. Frosting squished between my fingers.

"Kid, I'm a butch working construction. I've had this conversation before." She took a bite, then shoved it into her cheek. "So this boy you're into. Have you made a move?"

"Maybe." My face burned. "Yes."

"Good for you. Did you like it?"

This was excruciating. Why exactly had I thought this conversation was a good idea? "Yeah . . . ?"

"There you go, then. That's all you need to know."

"But I've never liked guys before."

"So?" She turned to face me. "Take it from me, dude – don't

get wrapped up in the labels yet. Sexuality is ..." She looked around for a metaphor, then lifted what was left of her cinnamon roll. "Like this cinnamon roll. You see it, you think, 'Damn, that looks good,' so you eat it. If you like it, you do it again. Everything else – whether you're bi or pan or sapiosexual or whatever the hell – that's about labels, and politics, and creating shorthands for *other* people. That can be useful, and important for society, but you don't have to pick a flag right out the gate. Just let yourself like who you like." She took another bite. "This boy – is he out?"

"Not exactly." And then, because I had to tell *someone*, I blurted, "It's Chance Kain."

"No shit?" Denny's eyebrows rose appreciatively. "You don't start small, do ya, Dave-o? I bet half the guys in America would go gay for Chance Kain. Boy is *hot.*"

Sudden panic gripped me. "Please don't tell anyone."

She smiled. "Trust me, bud. The first rule of Queer Club is you don't out other people – and that goes double for you with Chance, all right? That shit can be hard enough without the whole world watching. You take your time, and let him take his."

I nodded. She clapped me on the shoulder again.

"You got any questions, you hit me up, okay?" She pulled out her phone and texted me her number. "And don't take any shit about it from anybody – straight *or* queer. Whether you go full-on boy crazy or never kiss another boy again, you're in the family now. Got it?"

Relief expanded in my chest. "Thanks, Denny."

"No problem." She sucked the last of the frosting off her fingers, then looked at them. "I probably should have washed my hands before this." She shrugged and stood. "Whatever. Enjoy your Easter Egg hunt, Dave-o."

Right. Paint.

With a sigh, I knelt back down beside the church and resumed my penance.

14

So are you grounded?

It was the question on everybody's mind. Ridley's text had already been waiting for me that morning, and in its excessive punctuation I could hear her maniacal delight, our summer having been remarkably low on gossip. Chance's more restrained text arrived while I was on my lunch break, back already aching from hunching over cleaning up paint.

My answer was the same for both of them:

ME:

I don't *think* so . . . ?

Chance responded immediately.

CHANCE:

So you're free to come out swimming
with me after work tonight. :)

The craziness of the previous night came pouring back, a giddy tsunami that swept away all other concerns. But I texted back only:

ME:

Probably not a good idea, if I want to *stay*
ungrounded.

Another ding.

Tomorrow, then?

We'll see, I typed. But I could already feel myself grinning.

Dad may not have officially grounded me, but it also wasn't like we'd had a conversation about it. Aside from him condemning me to Paint Purgatory, we'd barely spoken. Yet either way, I knew that going out that night would only dig me in deeper. And besides, I wasn't a *complete* asshole – he might have lost the fight by bringing up Mom, but I knew I'd been wrong to make him worry. So when we got home that night, sweaty and filthy, I let him have first shower. By the time he'd gotten out, I'd already made popcorn and queued up *Over the Garden Wall* on the TV.

I held up the bowl, looking as sheepish as possible. "Movie night?"

The corner of his mouth quirked up slightly. He knew a peace offering when he saw it. But he said only, "I'll order a pizza."

I made sure to turn my phone to silent, so no one could interrupt. By the fourth episode, we were both asleep on the couch.

The next morning, I was sore from sleeping half draped over the armrest, but the mood felt closer to normal. I spent the first part of the day being a model employee, trying to predict what Dad would need before he asked, so by the time lunch rolled around I figured my odds were as good as they were going to get.

"Hey, so," I said casually. "Would it be okay if I went out swimming with some friends after work tonight?" I added quickly, "I'll be home before dark! It's just so hot out today."

Just the act of asking was already a huge concession – I hadn't needed to ask permission to do stuff since I got my driver's license, and even before that, the issue had been more transportation than authorization. Dad was a loud proponent of treating children as autonomous individuals, and thus as long as I wasn't cutting class or getting arrested, my schedule was my business.

Yet all that seemed to be forgotten for the moment as he raised an eyebrow. "With who?"

I wasn't about to lie. "Chance."

He frowned.

"... and maybe Ridley, and some other people." Which wasn't technically a lie. On a hot day like today, there were bound to be other people at the beach. Maybe one of them would even be Ridley. Who could say?

He held the frown another moment, then sighed and shook his head. "Fine."

"Thanks, Dad!" I quickly began gathering up our trash from lunch, getting back to work before the conversation could go any further. As soon as I was safely out of sight, I whipped out my phone and texted Chance.

ME:

We're on.

It really *was* a perfect day for a swim. The air-conditioning in my truck had never worked, and by the time I pulled up at Chance's house, sweat had soaked through my shirt. I peeled away from the cracked vinyl seat back with a squelch.

This time there was no Chance waiting to leap desperately through the passenger door. As I walked toward the gate, I felt my armpits redoubling their output – and not just because of the heat. My heart was hammering.

Which was stupid. I'd been here before, just a few days ago. Yet somehow everything felt unfamiliar. When we were friends – or frenemies – I'd felt like I'd known what I was walking into. But now ... were things different? Did I *want* them to be different?

I pressed the call button.

"Hello?" Chance's voice.

"Hi, yeah, I've got a delivery here for one Chance Ng? The package says it's seventeen plus-size dildos, plus something called 'The Annihilator.' I'm gonna need a signature."

"Very funny. I'd tell you where to shove them, but I'm assuming they come with instructions."

The gate buzzed.

Chance met me at the door. He was wearing red-and-orange board shorts, sport sandals, and a black T-shirt with a logo of a burning van beneath the words TOMORROW WE DIE! I was suddenly very aware of my sweat-stained work shirt and too-large camo-patterned swim trunks – the only thing left with same-day shipping when it had finally gotten hot enough to swim. Apparently a lot of people were weirdos who bought their swimsuits in March.

"Ready to go?" Chance threw a towel over his shoulder and held a second out to me. "You need a towel?"

"Oh." In my rush to change and get into my truck as soon as I'd gotten home, I'd totally forgotten. "Yeah, actually. Thanks."

"No problem." He tossed it to me, then stepped out and closed the door.

"So where we going?" As soon as I said it, I realized our problem. In Seattle, people busted out the bikinis as soon as it hit sixty-five. On a truly hot day like today, the beaches would be packed. If Chance couldn't go to Death Putt without being mobbed, how could we go to a park? And why hadn't I thought about that at any point in the previous five hours?

Maybe because you were too busy trying to figure out how you felt about Chance in a swimsuit?

But Chance wasn't heading toward the front gate. Instead, he turned down the side of the house, through the edge of the landscaping. "This way."

Oh, of course. "You've got a pool?"

"Nope."

"Private beach?"

"No."

I thought of Ridley. ". . . Yacht?"

He threw back his head and laughed. "Jesus, Holc, you really don't do surprises, do you?"

Below their house, a path of paving stones zigzagged down the terraced slope, past young fruit trees and decorative shrubs. At the bottom stood another tall hedge and a shed the size of some apartments.

Behind the shed was a more normal wooden gate. We stepped through and found ourselves on a cement staircase, turned almost into a tunnel by another hedge and overhanging trees.

"Huh." I craned my neck as we descended, trying to peek through the hedges and neighboring fences. "Is this private?"

"Nope. Though the people here act like it. This area is full of these little secret easements – places where it's too steep for streets, so they just become staircases."

"Ah." There were some of those near my house as well, but they felt more open and public, always full of dog walkers or people running stairs.

At the bottom, the stairs intersected with a cul-de-sac. Chance walked toward what looked like a driveway, with a NO TRESPASSING sign nailed prominently to a tree above another sign warning about a neighborhood watch. Chance blew past both.

I followed a little more hesitantly. "Do you know these people?"

Chance shook his head. "Like I said, people *act* like they own it, but this is public right-of-way. I checked Google."

The road dead-ended in the lake, and sure enough, there was a sign saying PUBLIC ACCESS. Though what it accessed wasn't much: just a bench scrimshawed with graffiti and a thick thatch of bushes and lily pads, with the sparkle of the lake beyond.

"See?" Chance beamed. "Total privacy."

"And such a lovely view." I kicked at the bushes. "Did you bring a machete?"

"Oh, don't be a wuss." He dropped his towel, kicked off his shoes, and peeled off his shirt. The sight of his lats moving beneath his skin, the curved creases of his hips pointing down into his trunks like pistols waiting to be drawn, did something inside me. I turned away, pulling my own shirt off slowly to hide my blush.

To cover the awkwardness, I said, "At least the paparazzi won't think to look for you here. Everybody knows vampires hate water."

"That's actually only running water. Also, don't be a dick."

When I turned back, Chance was already moving between

the bushes, out into a narrow path through the lily pads. I followed, stepping down into the lake. The water closed cool and perfect over my feet.

Followed by six inches of muck as I sank into the bottom.

"Oh, *gross.*" I pulled my foot up with a squelch, feeling the slime between my toes. "It's like stepping in dog shit!"

"More like duck shit." Chance was fifteen feet out now, and still only up to his thighs. "Come on, Holcomb!"

"Great. Now I've got duck-herpes ..." I kept wading, silt blooming in a muddy cloud with each step.

Chance reached the edge of the lily pads and dove. His body glided effortlessly beneath the surface, half visible through the mirror-bright waves, before surfacing like a dolphin maybe forty feet farther out. He whipped his head, flipping hair back out of his eyes, and treaded water, arms moving in lazy arcs.

God, he was handsome. The squared-off line of his pecs, the chin like a goddamn Disney prince. How had I never recognized it before? I mean, I *had,* but not like this. Not in this compulsive, ball-clenchingly horny way. Or had part of me always known, and just buried it under jealousy and resentment? Even back when we were still in the band, how much of my irritation at Chance's preening had been a defense mechanism? An attempt to bury other feelings I was less prepared to deal with?

Weirder yet, had *he* felt the same way about *me*?

"Holc?"

I dove. It was nowhere near as graceful as Chance's, more of a glorified belly flop. I surfaced and thrashed my way out to his depth.

He grinned. "Pretty nice, huh?"

"Yeah." Looking back to the shoreline, I could see fancy

houses climbing the hill in a wall of green and glass. To the north, the bridge we'd driven over a few nights before was a buzzing line across the water, while farther out ski boats towed their namesakes in noisy circles. Yet right here, we were the only two people around.

"I'm really glad your dad didn't ground you," Chance offered.

"Me too." A strand of hair had slipped loose from his mafia slick-back and curved in a perfect arc down across one eye.

When I didn't say anything else, Chance flicked water at me. "Hey. What's bugging you?"

"Nothing."

"Liar."

I blushed, outraged and embarrassed to be so transparent.

He frowned. "Are you feeling weird about the other night?"

Yes. "No."

"Look, it's okay if—"

My mouth opened before I could stop it.

"Is this a date?"

As soon as the words left my lips, I wished I'd sucked in a lungful of water instead. Or maybe just sunk down into the mud and stayed there, like one of those hibernating frogs.

Chance's frown deepened. "Do you *want* it to be a date?"

"Do *you*?"

Chance gave an exasperated snort and shook his head. "You never make anything easy, do you?"

I stayed silent.

"Okay, fine – I'll go first. As usual." He sighed and locked eyes with me. "Yes, Holc, I would like this to be a date."

"Oh." Even though I'd known it was coming – *hoped* it was coming? – the answer hit like I'd stepped in front of the light rail.

I momentarily forgot to tread water, and got my original wish as a wave filled my nostrils. I flailed and coughed.

Chance's face flattened with disappointment. "Dammit, dude, you could have just said—"

"No!" I nearly swallowed more water in my effort to interrupt. "No, it's good! It's great!" Something inside me seemed to have been waiting to hear him say it, and now clicked into place. "I do, too. Want it, I mean. To be a date."

He searched my face. "Yeah?"

"Yeah."

He laughed with relief, tipping over backward into a spread-armed float. "Jesus, man. Way to leave me hanging."

I smiled. "Sorry. I'm not very good at this."

"Dating? Or swimming? Because they're both pretty obvious."

"Screw you."

"Come on, let's get back where you can touch bottom before you inhale a salmon."

Such was my relief at the sudden clarity – *I was on a date with Chance, and it felt good!* – that I didn't even argue, just followed him back in until I could float with my toes barely touching bottom, oscillating up and down with the wake of distant boats. Chance found a submerged rock to perch on, rising slightly out of the water, baring his collarbones.

"There," he said. "Now you won't drown every time I ask you a question."

"Ha ha."

His smile got a little lopsided. "So . . . I'm gonna go out on a limb and assume you've never kissed a dude before?"

"No." Insecurity shot through me. How was it possible to feel simultaneously weird about having kissed a boy and weird about *not* having kissed one? "Have you?"

"No." He said it so easily.

Another wave of relief, albeit completely unwarranted. "So you're saying I'm the hottest guy you've ever kissed."

"Technically." He grinned. "If you want to win by default."

I pumped my fist like Homer Simpson. "*De-fault! De-fault!*" I might be out of my depth with all this, but at least Chance was right there with me. "You've kissed girls, though. You went out with Jennifer Marse for like two months. And you kissed Grace Kim after that show at the Black Lodge."

"Yeah. And there was Emerson, that fan I told you about – they were nonbinary. But those were different."

I knew what he meant. Kissing Chance had been at once familiar and alien. The lines of his face were sharper, his skin rougher. He *smelled* different – a boy smell, all sporty and mentholated and . . . *warm*, somehow.

And yet his lips had been just as soft, his mouth just as gentle and insistent. The essence of it was the same. Like the old song said, maybe a kiss was just a kiss.

He tossed a strand of lakeweed at me. "Anyway, you never told me who *you* dated while I was gone."

I blushed, and his eyes widened.

"It's someone I know, isn't it?! Who?!"

I looked away and told the truth. "Maddy Everhardt."

"*I knew it!*" Chance swung his arm, slapping a wave of water across my face. "I *knew* she had a thing for you! How long did you guys date?!"

I swiped water from my eyes. "Three months. Sophomore year."

"Three months!" His brow furrowed. "Why'd you break up?"

"It, uh . . ." This was awkward. "It was over you, actually."

"What?" Chance looked puzzled.

I gritted my teeth at the memory. "When you came through on your first big tour, and played the Paramount. A bunch of our old crew went to see you."

"Yeah, I remember." Chance frowned. "Maddy was there."

"Yeah. She wanted to go."

"And you didn't."

"Yeah." It suddenly seemed petty, but everything had been so fresh at the time. So raw.

Maddy had seen that – had understood, in a way – but insisted I get over it. *They're your friends*, she'd said. *Let's go be supportive.*

I'd told her that if she really wanted to be *supportive*, she'd stay home with me.

She'd gone anyway. And that was that.

"Damn," Chance said. "She dumped you over a concert?"

I shrugged. What constituted a dumping? It had definitely *felt* like being dumped. Sure, I'd told her that if she went, it meant we weren't going to work out. But that was just a statement of fact. The choice had still been hers, and she'd made it. That she hadn't tried to make amends afterward just confirmed what I'd already feared – that she'd only been interested in band-era me, not the washed-up echo. When it came to a choice between Darkhearts and David, she hadn't hesitated.

Neither had our mutual friends, who sided with her in the breakup. It had been a lonely few months until I met Ridley.

"Shit, dude, I'm sorry." Chance looked genuinely sympathetic.

I didn't want Chance's pity. "It's fine," I snapped.

Chance sensed my mood and shifted gears. "Well, however it went down, I'm glad you two aren't still dating." He grinned. "She's a nice girl. I'd hate to have to steal you from her."

I blushed, then twitched at a sudden thought. "Wait. So the other night ... did you know that was going to happen?"

He raised an eyebrow. "You mean did I carefully plan my own nervous breakdown in order to get you to drive me a hundred miles out into the boonies for the purposes of seducing you?" He actually winked. "Seems like a lot of effort. I like to think I'm more of a 'nice shoes, wanna screw?' guy."

My blush deepened, but I suddenly needed to know. "No, but like ... how long have you liked me?"

"Who said I like you?" He flicked another drop of water at me. "Maybe this is a purely physical relationship."

My mind sparked and went blank. Chance laughed.

"Take a joke, Holc." Wake from a passing speedboat rolled in, bobbing us up and down. "I've always liked you as a friend. I mean, when you're not being a self-absorbed jerkhole."

"Same to you," I managed.

"But like, *like* you like you ..." He dragged fingertips across the water's surface. "Ever since I've been back, I think? Death Putt was pretty much a perfect date, so yeah, I was definitely crushing on you by the end of that." The waves ended, and he found his perch once more. "What about you? When did you start liking me?"

"Um." It was a reasonable question. "I'm not sure."

"Whew." Chance mimed fanning himself. "The romance, it's burning me up." He shook his head. "You're killing my ego here, Holcomb."

"And I'm sure we'll all miss it very much," I shot back. "But I dunno . . . I guess when we were working out? It kinda took a while to process. It didn't all make sense until the drive, and . . ." I gestured vaguely.

Chance smirked. "Until we kissed? You can say it, Holc."

"Until we kissed."

The two of us grinned stupidly at each other. Chance finally reached up and addressed the loose lock of dripping hair, slicking it back out of his eyes. My hands ached to do it for him.

"Well, however you got there," he said, "I'm glad you did. But it leaves us with a new question."

My stomach lurched. "What?"

His grin powered up to maximum mischief.

"What are you doing standing all the way over there?"

My stomach's free fall continued, this time in a good way. Kicking off the bottom in a decidedly unsuave fashion, I frog-hopped over, stopping with my chest almost touching his. "Hi."

"Hi."

We stared into each other's eyes, close enough now that I had to pick one or the other to focus on. Was that weird, to look at only one of someone's eyes at a time? What if I looked at one, but he looked at my other one – would our gazes even be meeting, or would we both be looking through each other?

More importantly, what did I do next? It was the perfect opportunity to kiss him. He'd basically just invited me to. But I couldn't just, like, lean in and do it, could I? Just float over, like some sort of pasty manatee, and push my mouth against his mouth? I felt like I needed to say something. Something romantic, maybe clever.

"So, uh – " I began.

He leaned forward and kissed me.

Thank you, God. I kissed him back hard, putting my arms around him. He responded by wrapping his legs around my waist, clinging to me like the world's sexiest koala.

On second thought, maybe it was best I didn't say anything.

His weight pushed us down, planting me firmly in the muck, our faces just barely above water. Below the surface, my hands roamed the plain of his back, the knobbled mountain range of his spine. His legs scissored tight around me, squeezing, and the restraining mesh inside my swimsuit began earning its keep in a big way. I realized with a shock that I could feel him as well, a hard ridge pressed against my stomach.

His lips left mine and traveled sideways across my jaw, up my neck. My hands slid down, the waistband of his swimsuit thin and slick beneath my fingers. I hooked my thumbs inside the blades of his hips, gripping hard, and the sound he made was like nothing I'd ever imagined. He grabbed my head in both hands and twisted it up to meet his lips.

"God," I gasped. "I—"

A wave rolled over our heads, submerging us both.

We came apart, laughing and sputtering. When we'd shaken the water from our eyes, Chance reached back over and put his hands on my shoulders.

"Holc?"

The word was tentative, vulnerable, his face completely open. My heart beat faster. "Yeah?"

He dunked me.

Sunset found us climbing back up the secret staircase, walking single file to avoid overhanging branches. Chance's shirt clung to the inverted triangle of his back, outlining every detail in wet cotton, and I was enjoying the view. Apparently I had a thing for back muscles? I was learning all sorts of new facts about myself this week.

But at the moment, my List of Personal Realizations had been cleared to make room for several all-consuming points:

1. *Me and Chance were officially A Thing.*
2. *That felt good.*
3. *Really good.*
4. *????*

My insides were roiling, but not in a sick way – more an effervescence. My entire body was a soda someone had shaken. I am become Pop Rocks.

It sounded stupid to say it, even inside my own head: *I like Chance Ng.* It shouldn't have been a revelation. In general, one figures out that sort of tidbit *before* kissing someone, let alone going on a second date. But so much about the last few days had been a whirlwind that I think a part of me had truly been unsure. The attraction had sprung up out of nowhere, without giving me time to process it. What if we'd been a fluke? Temporary insanity caused by the inherent romance of a late-night adventure? Would we bounce off each other in the light of day?

But seeing him again hadn't dissipated the excitement, only

concentrated it. Even now, after hours of swimming and lounging on the bench together watching dragonflies hunt gnats, I wanted nothing more than to run my hands up his bare arms, feeling the cool of his skin. It was like when you spent hours enveloped in a game, or working on a project, only to realize you'd forgotten to eat and were suddenly starving.

Chance looked back over his shoulder at me and grinned like maybe he was starving, too.

We reached the gate and snaked up through his family's yard to the front door. He started to reach for the handle, then shifted course, grabbing my hand instead.

He gave a half smile. "I don't actually want to go in yet."

I matched him smirk for smirk. "Me either."

He stepped in and kissed me. This time there was none of the frenzy of the lake. It was slow and soft – the confident kiss of someone who no longer has to wonder how it'll be received. It was sleeping late on Sunday. It was a summer afternoon with nowhere to be.

I closed my eyes and sank into it.

From behind us came an exasperated sigh.

"Great. This is *exactly* what I needed today."

We whirled to find Chance's manager frowning at us from halfway up the front walk. He closed his eyes and reached up, rubbing dramatically at his temples with thumb and fingertips.

For a moment, nobody spoke. Then he lowered his hand, eyes opening and index finger moving back and forth between us.

"This," he announced, "is going to be a problem."

15

At the first sound of Benjamin's voice, Chance and I had sprung apart like two kids caught playing doctor. Now Chance stepped forward, putting himself between me and the interloper. When he spoke, his voice was surprisingly cold – flat and dangerous. "Why would it be a problem, Benjamin?"

Benjamin rolled his eyes. "Oh, don't go all social justice on me. I couldn't give two shits who you're kissing. But I'm not your audience. We've got to balance this, remember?" He seesawed a hand. "A little ambiguity, a little mystery – that's good for business. Let the fans who want to see it see it, and give everyone else plausible deniability. The more people who think they can date you, the better. But *proof* is different. All it takes is one photo and we can kiss the Bible Belt goodbye."

"I don't care about the Bible Belt," Chance snapped.

"Yeah? Well, your label does." Benjamin shook his head. "But you know what? Screw Arkansas. What about China? Half your audience is overseas. They get one whiff of quote-unquote 'immoral behavior' – no offense –" He acknowledged me with a nod that was one hundred percent offensive. "– their censors will come down on you like a guillotine. You won't just lose fans – you'll be banned."

Chance crossed his arms, but he looked shaken. "That's stupid."

"That's life, rock star." I hated the patronizing way Benjamin said it. His tone softened, oozing reasonability. "Look. Chance.

I'm not gonna tell you two not to hook up. I've managed enough teen acts to know you're gonna do what you're gonna do. But I need to know you two will be *discreet,* all right? No pictures, no social media, no holding hands where anyone might see you. Nothing to start rumors. We've all worked too hard on this."

Chance seemed to collapse inward. For as much as his constant confidence drove me nuts, seeing him without it was worse. He looked like a kicked dog as he said, "Okay."

"Because otherwise," Benjamin continued, his voice syrup over steel, "I'm gonna need to bring the rest of the team into this conversation. Including your parents."

Chance's eyes narrowed, his spine stiffening again. "I *said* okay."

Benjamin studied him, chin in hand like he was evaluating a new couch for his apartment. At last he nodded. "All right. I'll see you inside whenever you're ready to talk licensing." He moved between us and entered the house, shutting the door behind himself.

"Asshole." My fists were tight as I stared at the door.

"No, he's right." Chance leaned back against the side of the house. He brought his hands up, scrubbing at his face, then looked at me solemnly. "We need to be careful. If word gets out that I've got a boyfriend, I'm toast."

The higher functions of my brain overloaded at the word "boyfriend." Fortunately, my anger was there to take over, and it seethed at seeing Chance so defeated. Never mind that a few weeks ago I would have loved nothing more. "It's still bullshit. If people like your music, nothing else should matter. You shouldn't have to pretend."

Chance smiled sadly. "I'm always pretending, Holc." He reached out and took my hand. "Except maybe with you."

That sent my heart bouncing around inside my ribs like a superball, and choked off any chance at a reply.

He squeezed. "I should go see what they want. You have to get home soon anyway, right?"

"Right." My head was still spinning. What time was it? Who was I? What alternate dimension had I fallen into, where Chance's fingers were twining with mine?

"I'll see you soon, yeah?"

That, at least, I knew the answer to. "Absolutely."

Chance smiled – not his cocky stage smile, but a real, happy grin. He squeezed my hand again. "Cool."

"Yeah."

Neither of us let go.

He laughed. "Okay, for real, though. I'm going now."

"So go."

He grinned wider. "Like I said before: You never make anything easy, do you?"

"You like it."

"Maybe I do." He extracted his hand, then opened the door. As he stepped inside, he turned back and shot me one last smile. "Later, Holc."

The door shut.

It was a good thing the privacy hedge was so tall, because otherwise anyone passing on the street would have seen me standing there for a stupidly long time, staring at the closed door like it was an equation I was trying to solve. Only the reminder about my self-imposed curfew finally turned me away. I realized I was still wearing one of the Ngs' towels, and rather than risk a conversation with his parents in my current state, I hung it over the doorknob and slogged back up the cobbled driveway.

Boyfriend. Everything was moving so quickly. What would it even mean to date Chance? So we'd kissed – so what? Any day now, he could disappear again, walking right back out of my life the way he came in. Even if he didn't, we'd still have to sneak around. But then, was that really any different from what we were doing now? Why should I care if anybody else knew about it? My mood soured briefly as I thought of Ridley, and the realization that I still wouldn't be able to tell her anything. Ridley had many lovely qualities, but discretion wasn't one of them. While she'd never intentionally betray me, if she knew I was dating Chance, I might as well call up *Teen Vogue* myself.

But all of that was secondary to the glow rising up from my core, spreading out through my entire body. The giddiness was almost like being drunk, and for a second I had to fight an uncharacteristic urge to giggle. Because in spite of all logic – in spite of years of feuding and the risk of his entire career – Chance wanted *me*. People always said things like "Out of everyone in the world, they chose me," but in Chance's case it was literal. He *could* have anyone.

And he'd chosen me.

I slipped out the gate and unlocked my truck. As I slid into the seat, my elation crystallized into resolve. I set my jaw and turned the key in the ignition.

Benjamin might be right that I was bad for Chance's career. Hell, I might be bad for Chance's *life* – it wasn't like I had a stellar track record with my own. And it had only been a few days since he and I first kissed. For all I knew, in another week, he'd come to his senses and call the whole thing off. Or I'd do something stupid and bring everything crashing down around me.

But it didn't matter, because I knew one thing for sure now:

I wanted Chance, too.

And I'd be damned if I was going to let him slip away without a fight.

16

Benjamin didn't want me and Chance out in public together, but that was fine by me. I had no interest in sharing Chance Kain with an adoring public. It did, however, cut down significantly on the list of places we could hang out.

Which had meant it was time to have a conversation.

"Dad?"

"Hmm?" He'd looked up from where he sat at the kitchen table, reading his phone and eating the same scrambled eggs he had every morning.

I took a breath. "I want to invite Chance over."

Dad's expression didn't change, but it hardened like quick-drying cement.

I tried to make a joke out of it. "Hey, at least this way you'll know where we are."

Wrong move. Dad's face flushed, his chin jutting out with the force of all the words he struggled to contain.

I knew it would have been easier to just hang out at Chance's. But I honestly liked my dad, and hated knowing he disapproved. As much as this was about hanging out with Chance, there was also a part of me hoping that exposure would help Dad get over his grudge, the same way it had for me. (Okay, maybe not *exactly* the same way.) If Chance was going to be my boyfriend – and the word still shot lightning through me – I wanted Dad to like him.

Which was maybe a tall order, given that I still wasn't

entirely sure why *I* liked Chance. Sure, he was handsome, but there were tons of handsome guys who didn't affect me at all. And our shared history was as much a negative as a positive. Was it simply vanity on my part? My Cinderella pride in being chosen by someone above my station? That felt too shallow, and still didn't explain how his gaze could make me blush. There was just something in the way he talked with me – the way he refused to shy away from anything, to skip along the surface. It wasn't just confidence – he'd always been cocky. This was the opposite. Deliberate vulnerability. I'd done nothing to encourage him, had given him shit at every opportunity, yet he kept showing up.

Maybe there was some truth to the old saying about the thin line between love and hate. It felt as if all the same emotional energy from before was still there, just shifted – like we were moving at the same speed, but had slammed from forward into reverse.

Which in a truck would rip out your transmission, so maybe not the best metaphor. But whatever it was Chance had, I knew I needed more of it.

"*Please,*" I pleaded.

Dad shook his head and sighed, looking back down at his phone. "Do what you want."

It was a small victory, but still a victory. I'd taken the win and retreated.

Now it was Friday night. Between family stuff and business, Chance had been booked solid for the last several days, but it hadn't stopped us from texting constantly. It was weird, how quickly we'd fallen back into the old patterns, sending each other funny GIFs and stuff off Reddit and TikTok.

Except that in the old days, my stomach hadn't fluttered every time my phone buzzed.

Chance's last text – headed over – was still up on my phone, sitting beside the remains of an early dinner of Irish nachos.

"At least I don't have to feed him," Dad grumbled.

"Dad, c'mon."

"Yeah, yeah." He cleared away the plates.

There was a knock at the door.

"I'll get it!" I said, even though Dad had made no move to do so.

Chance stood on the doorstep, wind tugging at his hair. He was wearing a wine-colored letterman's jacket with black leather sleeves, the letters *DH* embroidered on the left breast. Underneath it he wore a black collared shirt with a raised spiderweb pattern, plus a skinny tie the same shade as the jacket. The usual black skinny jeans hugged his hips, above Converse with soles so white they couldn't have been out of the box for more than twenty minutes.

It took me a moment to process the jacket's monogramming. "Isn't it gauche to wear your own merch?"

Chance rolled black-rimmed eyes. "Tell me about it. I came straight from a shoot – sorry I couldn't get here earlier."

"It's cool." I moved aside.

Chance wiped shoes already clean enough for surgery and stepped past me. "Hi, Mr. Holcomb."

"Hello, Chance." Dad had a towel and was wiping down the counter.

"Thanks for having me over." Chance shoved his hands into his jacket pockets.

"Thank David." Dad was getting a lot of mileage out of that

phrase recently. He continued scrubbing a nonexistent stain. "I don't control his social calendar." His tone was light, yet I couldn't miss the unspoken *"clearly."* I cringed.

Chance bulled ahead. "How've you been?"

Dad gave the barest hint of an exasperated sigh and straightened, wadding the towel up in his hands. "I'm good, Chance," he said frostily. "How're you." It wasn't a question.

"I'm okay," Chance said. "I mean, under the circumstances."

Dad's demeanor thawed a touch. "I'm sorry about Elijah."

"Thanks." Chance bounced his hands in his pockets. "You were his favorite adult, you know."

"What?" Dad looked taken aback.

"You were always driving us around, watching the shows. We owe you a ton."

"Yeah, well . . ." Dad sputtered a little, unprepared to hear his favorite complaints enumerated so completely. He waved the towel vaguely. "His parents hosted all the practices."

"Yeah, but they were just being supportive. You were the only parent who really *got* the music. That meant something to him." Chance smiled sadly. "Anyway, I just wanted to say thanks."

"You're welcome." Dad blinked, clearly at a loss. He seemed to realize he was still clutching the towel and dropped it onto the counter. "Well. I'm, uh. Gonna watch a movie. You boys have fun." He wandered into the living room, looking like a man in shock.

What the hell was that? In sixty seconds, Chance had totally defused my dad. Had he planned it that way? But I couldn't ask where Dad could hear.

"So, um, welcome." Once upon a time, Chance in my kitchen would have been completely unremarkable, and the formality of it now felt awkward. "You want something to drink?"

"Sure, thanks."

I moved gratefully to the fridge. "What do you want? We've got Sprite, grapefruit La Croix, and water."

"Oh man . . ."

"What?" I peered around the fridge door at him.

His eyes had lit up mischievously. "Should we make Sludge?"

"Ooh." I pursed my lips, considering. "We *do* have everything . . ."

"Let's do it!"

I pulled out the two-liter of Sprite, pointing behind me. "Hot chocolate's in the corner cabinet."

Chance grabbed the container while I dumped ice into glasses. He added scoops of powdered cocoa mix to each, then stood back to let me pour. The result frothed and fizzed, erupting in crunchy beige bubbles.

Chance stooped to watch, stirring to keep the bubbles from overflowing. "I haven't had this since we were thirteen."

"That's because only a thirteen-year-old would drink this." I picked up the glasses and held one out to him. "Shall we?"

"My body is ready." He took his glass and clinked it against mine. "Cheers."

We drank.

Imagine taking Cocoa Pebbles and Fruity Pebbles and mixing them together. Now liquefy the whole thing, add a thousand cups of sugar, and you've vaguely approximated the flavor of Sludge. It's like getting smacked in the face with a full bag of Halloween candy.

"*Gmmph!*" Chance covered his mouth, eyes wide and cheeks

bulging. I saw his throat move as he swallowed, and he bent over. "Oh my god. My body was not ready."

My own stomach twisted a little at the saccharine sucker punch, but I took another swig, just to establish dominance.

"How did we survive childhood?" Chance dumped the rest of his glass down the sink, sticking his mouth under the faucet for good measure. He straightened again, panting a little, and wiped his lips with the back of his hand. "Whew!"

I figured I'd proved myself enough and dumped the rest down the sink. "I guess you really can't go home again."

Chance shook his head in horrified admiration of preteen us. "Okay, well, that's enough nostalgia for one night. So. What should we do?"

For as well as things had gone with my dad, I wasn't about to suggest we hang out with him, which left relatively few options in our small house. "We can chill in my room, maybe watch a movie . . . Or I could show you my woodshop."

"Your woodshop?" Chance's eyebrows rose.

"I mean, *our* woodshop. But yeah. You wanna see?" I played it cool, but a part of me was desperate to show him – had been since before I invited him over.

Chance didn't disappoint. "Definitely."

I led him back outside and down the concrete steps to the basement.

The last time Chance had seen it, the basement had been a damp, spider-filled hole. Now it was brightly lit, the walls covered with rubberized waterproofing and pegboards full of tools. Beneath a dusting of sawdust, the concrete floor gleamed clean and smooth.

"Whoa." Chance ran a hand along the heavy, built-in workbench. "You really gave this place a makeover."

"Yeah. Dad and I did it ourselves." I moved around the room at random, wanting to find words that would convey just how much the space meant to me. "I spend a lot of time down here."

"Yeah?" Chance bent to inspect the blade of a table saw. "What sort of stuff do you make?"

I shrugged. "Whatever." I gestured to a wooden lawn chair in the corner that was still waiting to be stained. "That one's almost done."

"You made *that*?" Chance's eyes went wide. "*Dude.* Where'd you learn to do that?"

"Mostly YouTube. And my dad's carpenter, Jesús. He's gonna take me on as an apprentice after graduation."

"Wow." Chance sat down in the chair, running fingers across the smooth-sanded cedar. I flushed with pride.

"I didn't even know you were into woodworking," Chance said.

"I wasn't. I only really started last year."

"You learned to do this in a *year*?" Chance looked even more impressed. "What got you into it?"

How to explain to Chance? In the wake of the band, I'd found myself without any sort of creative outlet. When Dad had press-ganged me into working for him for that first summer, I'd had no real objection. Dad paid more than Bamf Burger, and didn't make me work weekends. But as I spent time helping him and Jesús, I found myself gravitating to the wood – the clean lines, the smell of sawdust. The satisfaction of having *made* something, even if it was two pieces out of one. When

I'd asked to use his tools outside of work, Dad had been only too happy to oblige.

I shrugged again. "I dunno. It just seemed cool."

"For sure." Chance looked around. "What else have you made?"

"Um . . . Some other chairs like that, a TV stand and shelves for the living room, some boxes. I want to try bowls, but I don't have a lathe." I pointed to a stack of boards and cut pieces on the workbench. "Mostly it's just picture frames for my Etsy store."

"Etsy?" Chance looked amused. "Really?"

My shoulders tightened defensively. "People pay a lot for real wood frames, especially in custom sizes. Plus I can do it during the school year, on my own schedule."

Chance raised his hands. "Hey, no shade – that's awesome." He looked back down at the chair with real envy. "I wish I could make stuff."

The ridiculousness of that statement, coming from somebody with a whole shelf of award statues, might have been insulting, but Chance spoke completely without irony.

An idea struck me. "You wanna make something right now? I can teach you."

Chance sat up straight. "Really?"

"Why not?" I grabbed a long pine one-by-two from where it leaned against the wall. "You wanna make a frame?"

"Sure." Chance stood up eagerly. "What do we do?"

After so much time studying under Jesús and my dad, suddenly being in the teacher role was disorienting – but in a good way. I liked the way Chance deferred to me.

"Well, first we use the table saw to cut the chamfer. That means cutting off one corner at a slant." I bent over and plugged the saw in. "I've already got the blade set at the proper angle, so we can just run it through." I paused, suddenly seeing the sawdust from an outside perspective. "You're gonna mess up your fancy outfit."

"Oh, don't worry, I never wear the same clothes twice."

I stared.

"That was a joke, dummy."

Okay, maybe it wasn't *total* deference. I grimaced back. "At least tuck in your tie so it doesn't get caught and pull you in."

"*International heartthrob Chance Kain found strangled and beheaded in basement,*" Chance narrated, but he slid the tie safely inside his shirt.

I put on a pair of safety glasses and earmuffs, then handed duplicates to Chance. They looked ridiculous with the rest of his outfit. "You ever use a table saw before?"

He shook his head.

"Okay, watch me." I positioned the board, showing him how to use the push stick, then hit the switch. The saw screamed to life, and I fed the board through, neatly carving off one corner. I handed him an identical board and yelled over the saw's whine. "Your turn!"

Behind his glasses, Chance's eyes were huge. "Maybe we should just watch a movie!"

"Come on, you don't need fingers to sing!" I took his hand, keenly aware of our skin making contact, and guided the board to the table. "Just hold it tight and use the stick at the end! You'll never get close to the blade!"

Chance looked a little sick, but firmed his jaw and nodded. Staying as far from the whirring blade as possible, he slowly fed the board through. I moved around to the far side, helping hold the cut section steady. When it was through, I killed the blade and took off my ears. "Nice work."

"Yeah?" Chance looked gratified.

In truth, he'd bobbled it a little at the end, when he had to rely on the push stick, but there was no need to tell him. We'd cut that part off in the next phase.

"Not gonna lie," Chance said. "That saw kind of freaks me out. My feet are sweating."

"Good. That means you're paying attention."

"You won't be saying that when I take my shoes off."

I took the board I'd done and clamped it down to the side of the workbench. "We'll use a router for the rabbet."

Chance leaned against the edge of the bench. "The rabbit?"

"A rabbet's a groove along the edge of something." I was proud of knowing the technical terms. "It's what'll hold in the glass and the picture." I picked up the router, which already had the straight bit I needed. "I've got it set so you can't go too far. Just hold this down flat and move it smoothly along the edge of the board, and it'll do the rest." I plugged it in and set it in place. "Here, hold it with both hands."

Chance took the tool gingerly, switching spots with me.

"Ready?" I asked.

Chance nodded.

I reached over and switched the router on. Chance jumped a little as it buzzed to life.

"Now guide it along!"

The router screamed in irregular bursts as it took random bites out of the wood. Chance twitched each time, jerking the router back.

"Keep it steady!" I urged over the noise. "And flat! Flat!"

The cut Chance left behind was as squiggly as a snake. He turned the router off and stepped back quickly, as if worried said snake might bite him. "Maybe you should do it."

"No way." Seeing him unsure of himself triggered some protective instinct I didn't realize I had. "You've got this. Come on." I pulled the router back to the top of the board. "Grab the handles. I'll help."

Chance reluctantly did so. I moved behind him, reaching around to put my hands over the top of his. I was only a couple of inches taller than him, but he fit perfectly inside the curve of my arms, like those Russian nesting dolls. His back was against my chest, and just like that night under the stars, I could feel his breathing, transmitted from his ribs to mine.

Now it was my turn to sweat. How could he make just *breathing* sexy?

"Ready?" I asked. "Nice and smooth."

"Smooth," he agreed. He still sounded anxious. But was that because of the router? Or me?

I hit the switch, and the router shrieked. Moving slowly, I guided him and it down along the length of the board, then brought them back to the start.

"It's good to do it several times," I said into his muffed ear. "Just to be sure. There's a lot to work through."

We made the second pass, then I turned off the router. We stood there, neither of us moving, the leather sleeves of his jacket cool against my arms where they protruded from my T-shirt.

It was weird how natural he felt there, pressed back against me. I wondered if he was thinking the same thing. A part of me longed to lean forward and kiss him. I could see it happening, craning my neck around his earmuffs, him turning to find my lips as our plastic safety glasses clicked together. But could I actually *do* that now? We'd already kissed multiple times, but did that mean I could just kiss him whenever I felt like it? What were the rules?

But the moment ended. He let go of the router, and I reflexively let my arms drop, stepping back as he ran his finger over the cut.

"See?" I said. "You can totally do this."

"Yeah," he said thoughtfully. "I guess I can."

I showed him how to use the miter saw to cut the angles for the corners. His eyes glazed a little as I explained the math for making sure the inside dimensions were right. But my mind wasn't on it either. All I could think about was the ghost of his back against my chest. The way his eyes narrowed and jaw clenched with determination each time he touched the saw, emphasizing the hollows of his cheeks. I wanted to reach out again, put my hands on his, but worried it would seem too premeditated now – that it would weird him out retroactively.

Distraction and power tools maybe weren't the best combination. After I accidentally triggered the sander, startling us both, I said, "Maybe that's enough for tonight. You still wanna watch a movie?"

"Sure." Chance tried to stifle a yawn and smiled.

Outside, the wind had picked up into a proper summer storm, bending the neighborhood trees and threatening to blow the basement door out of my hand.

"Man, I love storms." Chance stood in the yard with his arms outstretched, letting the wind whip at him. He closed his eyes and leaned his head back, offering himself up.

"Same." But what I was really enjoying was watching him.

He was so *expressive* – not just in his face, but in his body. It made me realize how little attention most people drew to themselves.

"I kinda wanna go run around in it." He looked back at me over his shoulder. "Should we?"

I suddenly wanted nothing more than to roam the empty streets like the teenage kings we were, stretching our shirts into sails to catch the storm. But I wasn't out of the doghouse yet with Dad, and vanishing into the night with Chance again would defeat half the point of having him over. "We should probably stay here."

Chance got it immediately. "Right – damage control. Movies it is!"

Inside, Dad was still in the living room, so we headed up to my room to watch on my laptop. I lowered the door closed behind us, only realizing as I did so the significance of what was happening.

We were in my room.

Alone.

In theory, my agreement with Dad was that the door had to stay open if I had a girl over. But the operative word was "girl." There'd never been any discussion of other possibilities.

Chance clearly felt the sudden tension as well. He put one hand in his pocket awkwardly. "I always liked that you had a trapdoor. It makes it feel like a tree house."

"Yeah." I quickly grabbed my laptop from the desk. "What do you want to watch?"

"Um . . ." He gave it some thought. "*Pan's Labyrinth?*"

"Works for me." I started toward the bed, then froze.

I only had the one desk chair and an aging beanbag. Ridley

and I usually watched movies together on my bed, the same way we did at her house. It didn't mean anything.

Except that this was Chance. And my bed. Chance Ng on my bed. My brain flatlined.

Fortunately, Chance solved the conundrum by dragging over the beanbag and plopping down on it, leaning back against the bed. He gestured toward the slanted roof. "The ceiling is lower than I remember."

"Heh, yeah. Watch your head." I pulled the desk chair over to make a platform for the laptop.

Chance shrugged out of his jacket, revealing sleeves already rolled up to show off his forearms, secured with straps and little silver skull buttons. My eyes went immediately to the bare skin, the fine hairs and movement of tendons as he folded the jacket and set it on the bed.

Why was that so hot? They were *forearms*. Was I suddenly a Victorian lady, that wrists and ankles gave me the vapors?

Chance caught me watching. I blushed, but said only, "Your tie's still tucked into your collar."

"Right." He drew it back out, loosening the neck. Beneath it, the top button on his shirt was already undone. Dress shirts made me feel like a balloon animal, always coming untucked and billowing out in a muffin top, but his fit him perfectly, the fabric tight enough to display the contours of his chest, the tiny raised dot of a nipple.

I yanked my eyes away and pulled up the movie. I knew Chance had seen it before, as we'd watched it together, both of us suckers for del Toro's creature designs.

I flopped down sideways on the bed, propped up on an elbow with my stomach not *quite* touching Chance's head. I wanted to reach over and run my fingers through that black hair, to turn its studied dishevelment into an actual mess and make it my own. But of course I didn't.

After a few silent minutes, he looked back at me and said, "You look uncomfortable. There's room on the beanbag if you want."

There absolutely wasn't. "Okay."

He scooched over, making space. I slid down next to him, managing to squeeze exactly one butt cheek onto the bag.

"Better?" Chance asked.

No. "Yeah, thanks."

A few minutes of valiantly holding that pose made it clear that something needed to change. It was a race to see which would happen first: whether the sting of my right ass cheek falling asleep would become too much to bear, or I'd overbalance and tumble off the bag entirely.

Steeling myself, I reached my right arm up behind Chance and along the edge of the bed, giving myself another few inches of room and a better anchor with which to balance. My ass buzzed with immediate relief.

Chance leaned closer, fitting himself into the crook of my armpit. I'd showered after work, changing into my best jeans and a tight orange-and-white raglan tee that made my chest look good, and I prayed my deodorant was holding. I let my arm relax, coming around to cup his shoulder.

It was a good thing I'd seen the movie before, because all I could think about was the feeling of his shoulder beneath my fingers, the curved muscle and hard knob of bone. No eyeless men or freaky fauns could be as simultaneously fascinating and terrifying. He leaned his head against my collarbone, and I could smell the citrus tang of his styling clay. I rested my cheek against his hair at last, marveling at the thickness of it.

An endless time later, the credits finished their long scroll into oblivion. Dialogue blared as the streaming service's home screen returned, trying to entice us with previews.

"Mmmph." Chance stretched dramatically. "What time is it?"

I checked my phone. "Almost midnight."

"God, I could fall asleep right here." He closed his eyes and curled up like a dog.

"You could if you want," I said. "Sleepover."

"Yeah?" One eye opened, watching me.

"Sure." I tried to play it casual. "I mean, I'm tired too. It'd probably be safer for me to drive you home tomorrow."

"I could get an Uber."

I nodded to the window, where outside the wind still raged. "Would your parents really want you riding with some rando in the middle of a storm? There might be trees down."

He thought it over. "Your dad would be cool with it?"

"Absolutely." Especially since I wasn't planning on asking.

Another pause, then, "Okay. I'll text my parents."

When I went downstairs, Dad was already in bed. I brought Chance a pillow and blanket from the couch, then went back down and brushed my teeth. By the time I got back, Chance was curled up on the beanbag, black socks and pale ankles peeking out from beneath the blanket. I tried not to think about the dark jeans now crumpled atop his jacket on the floor.

I shut the door and clicked the light off. The brief burst of darkness blinded me – and hopefully him – as I squirmed quickly out of my own shirt and jeans, crawling into my bed in just my boxers.

Around us, the house creaked and swayed, shuddering with each gust of wind that whistled around the edges of the windows. I thought Chance might already be asleep, but he said, "We haven't done this since we were kids."

"Yeah." There had been sleepovers in the band years, but they'd always been at Eli's, the three of us passing out in the practice space surrounded by cables and headphones and empty chip bags. The band itself had formed on one such night, in the 2:00 A.M. clarity of utter exhaustion and too much caffeine, as we lay on his floor watching music videos.

There was a long pause, then Chance's voice, soft and tentative. "Was I really that big of a jerk?"

"What?"

"To make you quit the band."

I wanted to dodge the question – to leave the past in the past, and pretend I'd only ever felt what I did right now. But there's something about darkness that demands truth.

"Kinda," I admitted. "You were always hogging the spotlight."

Chance blew out a long, rueful breath. "Yeah, I know. It's just hard, you know?" In the dark, I saw his hands stretch out from beneath the blanket, grasping the air. "I felt like I always had to prove myself."

If I hadn't already been lying down, the shock would have floored me. Since when had Chance Kain – he of the easy smile, the natural swagger – had anything to prove? "To who?"

"Everyone!" He waved a hand. "I mean, you had your guitar, Eli had his laptop. I was just out there naked. The kids in the audience ... they *know* they don't know how to play guitar, you know? They know they can't program like Eli. But everyone secretly thinks they could be the lead singer. I had to be larger than life. How are you supposed to do that at fourteen?"

"I don't know," I said, which was true – I'd never figured it out. But Chance had.

"I didn't understand why you left," he continued. "Not at the time. It seemed stupid. But I get it now. I was always trying to make sure everyone was looking at me – every show, every interview."

He leaned up on one arm, meeting my eyes over the edge of the bed.

"I'm sorry, man."

Two years. I'd never really expected to hear the words, and any part of me that might have had given up long ago. To hear them now – so sincere, so heartfelt – knocked me on my ass.

I managed to get myself together enough to mumble, "Thanks." And then, "It wasn't just you."

"Yeah?"

"Yeah. I was mad at Eli, too." I'd been mad at everybody, mad at the world, for reasons that seemed fuzzy and indistinct now that I was finally looking closely at them. "I was tired of just playing what he told me to play. You say you felt like you needed to prove yourself. I guess I did too." Except I'd done it by walking away.

He nodded slowly. "That makes sense. I never had to fight him for control of my part. Maybe I should have said something."

"Maybe I should have, too. Before I let it get so bad." But it had been easier to say nothing. To just let that pressure build, until the explosion was too big to contain. Escape velocity.

"Maybe that's the lesson." Chance lay back down, not facing me.

"What lesson?" I could just barely see him over the edge of the bed.

He stared at the ceiling. "With everything with Eli … I know bad shit happens, and that it's shitty and self-centered to think it's about me. But I can't help feeling like there's got to be some sort of lesson, you know? Something I'm supposed to take away from this. Does that make me an asshole?"

"No."

"I don't know. All I know is that it makes me think that everything bad – Eli, you hating me for years, whatever – it all comes from people being scared to talk. To say what they need. If Eli …" His voice broke. He sniffed once, hard. "I just don't want to leave anything unsaid, you know? Like, one day Eli's there, and the next he's gone. And not just him – it could be anybody. It could be me." He looked over at me, eyes glinting. "So what the *fuck* are we waiting for, you know? Just say what you need to say."

His gaze pressed down on me, holding me to the bed.

What are we waiting for?

I pulled my comforter aside.

"That beanbag's pretty small. You'd be more comfortable up here."

His eyes went wide. For one endless moment, we hung there, weightless.

Then he threw off his blanket and climbed up into the bed.

He was wearing nothing but boxer briefs, their color too dark to distinguish. They were a black cutout against the moon-white expanse of his chest, the flat plane of his stomach. A line of hair ran down from his belly button, curving slightly to the right. He lowered himself carefully down beside me, as if any sudden movement might send me running.

But I was done running away. I reached out, trailing my hand along the bare skin of his arm, feeling the tiny pebbles of goose bumps.

"What are we waiting for?" I asked, and kissed him.

I'd punctured the dam, and suddenly there was no stopping us. We kissed in a torrent, an avalanche, a river tearing down the mountain and sweeping away anything in its path. We tumbled over and over each other, rolling and turning for no reason except the intensity of feeling, the need to do something, *anything*, with this wild energy. We clung to each other, hands moving, biting at lips. I clawed at the bare expanse of his back, fingers digging into the meat of him. He gripped my biceps, as if shaking me, and it shook me.

It wasn't enough to just kiss. My mouth roamed his face – the ridge of his cheekbone, moving up to the corner of his eye. His mouth was on my neck, breath hot in my ear. He bit the lobe, and I couldn't keep from moaning.

He was on top now, his thigh between mine. I'd fooled around with Maddy, the two of us grinding against each other in this same bed, and this was at once exactly the same and entirely different. Where she'd been soft, he was hard, the strength in his wiry frame shocking as he clung to me. His skin was everywhere, pressing me down, and never mind that I was bigger than him – I wanted it, wanted him to crush me down through the mattress, press himself into me until the bubbles of our bodies burst.

I didn't understand how I could so badly need something I'd never even thought about before, but my body knew. In just our underwear, there was no question of that, both of us wedged painfully against each other, screaming for release. My hand slid down the piano keys of his ribs, onto the sharp ledge of his hip. The diver looking down over the cliff.

My thumb crept inside his waistband, and he made a soft whine. I stopped kissing and pulled back to take in his face.

He was black-and-white, like an old picture. An elegant arrangement of shadows and need. His lips parted in an unspoken question.

"Yeah?" I breathed.

He nodded.

I was so hard it hurt, but I realized with a start that I didn't know exactly what we were negotiating. My junk screamed that I wanted everything, anything, just *something immediately.* But what did that mean?

"What – " I started, then stopped and tried again. "What do you want to do?"

Even in the dark, Chance looked a little wild-eyed, panting. "What do *you* want to do?"

"I don't – I've never done this before. With a guy." In point of fact, we were rapidly passing beyond the edge of what I'd done with *anybody.*

"What, um ..." Chance darted in and kissed me, awkward for the first time, then pulled back. "What sounds good?"

Laughter erupted out of me. "You sound like a waiter." I kissed him quickly so he'd know I wasn't laughing *at* him.

He gave a crooked smile. "The question stands. We can do whatever you want."

Whatever you want. The thought of that blank check and his body nearly ended things right there in my boxers. But what *did* I want? I hadn't watched much gay porn, but I knew the basic idea. It just all seemed so foreign, even as a voice in my

175

head whispered that foreign could be good. And what about protection? I didn't have any condoms. What even *required* condoms? And what if we tried something and I didn't like it? What if it hurt? What would Chance think if I started something and then couldn't go through with it? What if I thought it was gross? What if *he* thought *I* was gross?

I was hyperventilating. Chance put a hand on my cheek.

"Hey." He leaned down until our noses almost touched. "We don't have to do anything if you don't want."

"Um." Anxiety was one thing, but there was no way I was letting this opportunity go. My dick would mutiny. I wrapped my legs around his thigh and squeezed, pinning us together. "I want."

He laughed. "Okay." His hand slipped down between us, fingers spreading out across my stomach. "Hands?"

God, yes. "Hands."

Even though we were supposedly the same, everything about touching Chance's ... god, it felt awkward to even *think* the word "penis" in this context. But everything about his was surprising. His skin was soft, and dry, and delicate, making me think bizarrely of the inside of a dog's ear. Yet underneath was a core of rippled wood, warm and solid.

One thing they never tell you about being with another boy is just how easy some parts of it are. I might have been anxious about my lack of experience, but a thousand hours of solo practice had made us both masters of our craft.

In moments it was over, hands trapped between sticky stomachs as he sprawled flat across me, covering my body with his. I buried my face in his hair, breathing him deep, feeling his weight like a security blanket. The smell of pine blended with our sweat.

"You've got sawdust in your hair," I whispered.

He mumbled his answer directly into the side of my neck. "Marking your territory, Holc?"

I grinned into the darkness and held him tighter.

Outside, the storm lashed and flailed, straining to reach us.

17

The following week was torture, of the best possible kind.

We'd woken early the morning after our sleepover, full of giddy recognition of the lines we'd crossed. The sound of my dad in the shower had let us avoid awkward parental questions, and with a quick kiss at the door Chance had slipped away down the street to call a Lyft. I'd retreated back to bed, to lie fuzzy-headed and content in sheets that smelled liked him.

Now that I'd broken a key seal with Chance, all I could think about was arranging a repeat performance. But the world had other plans. Chance had to catch a plane down to L.A. that night for a cameo in a movie, and wouldn't be home until the following Friday.

Thus began one of the longest weeks of my life. I was comforted by the fact that, if I was ridiculous in my infatuation, at least Chance had it just as bad. Texts hummed through the ether between us, a thousand different subjects that all meant *I'm thinking about you*. Interspersed were pictures of the film shoot (which mostly looked like people standing around with big lights), plus random sights in L.A. and – of course – an impressively stocked craft services table.

One picture was a selfie of him in costume, all ripped denim and fingerless gloves. His hair was a giant rockabilly pompadour that would have made Denny proud.

I texted him a winky emoji. Look at you, Mr. Movie Star.

Hardly, he texted back. Apparently this is how they think high schoolers dress? But hey, at least they cast the Asian kid as the bad boy instead of the nerd, so hooray for progress.

Once upon a time – like, say, two weeks ago – the thought of Chance gallivanting around Hollywood would have had me boiling with jealousy. And I'd have been lying if I'd said a part of me wasn't still there. But for the first time, its space was being crowded by a new emotion: pride. *My* boyfriend was in a movie. I did everything I could to stomp down on the jealous Old David and bulk up the easygoing, enthusiastic New David.

The constant parade of texts did not pass unnoticed by Ridley. While I knew I still couldn't tell her the truth, I paid the Friend Tax by sharing selections from his behind-the-scenes photos, carefully stripped of all context.

"Wow!" She peered eagerly up at my phone from where she lay flopped like a seal on my beanbag, laptop and SAT prep booklet spread out before her. "I can't believe we know someone who's in an actual, real-deal movie-film-for-theaters." She shut the lid on her laptop. "That's really cool that you two are becoming friends again."

"Yeah." If only she knew.

"Seriously, David." She sat up, perching cross-legged on the sack and fixing me with her most mature look, which for Ridley was pretty damn mature. "I know how long there's been bad blood between you two. That's not easy to get over." She reached out and grabbed my foot, shaking it lightly. "I'm proud of you, dude."

"Yeah, well, the Nobel Committee can ship the Peace Prize to my house." But in truth, *I* was proud of me, too. After all this time being angry, I'd suddenly seen a new vision of myself: someone bigger, capable of rising above old wrongs – not out of capitulation, but out of confidence. That person felt a hell of a lot more attractive. And if there was anything I was enjoying at the moment, it was feeling attractive.

Toward that end, I decided to funnel all my frustrated romantic energy – and every brain cell not currently studying or keeping me from falling off ladders at work – into designing the perfect date, taking into account everything I'd learned about Chance from our recent excursions. Thanks to some judicious care and feeding of the parental unit, I was officially off Dad's shit list, and back to having no particular curfew, with the new provision that I promise to tell him if I decided to, say, cross state lines. Fortunately, my plan this time was decidedly more local. By the time I got off work on Friday and went to pick Chance up, I was ready.

He met me at the gate, as was becoming our norm, wearing a long-sleeve button-up in an eye-melting pink-and-purple clockwork print.

"Good god." I raised a hand as if to shield myself from the brightness. "Going for understated today, I see."

"Says the lumberjack. Do they make you sign an oath to wear only plaid when you buy your first table saw?" He waved at himself. "Besides, it's the perfect disguise. Let the shirt draw all the attention."

"If you say so. Get in before you're swarmed by pollinators."

He got in, and before I could start the truck, he was in my seat with me, pinning me to the window with a kiss.

The geometry was terrible – door handle jabbing into my back, shoulder strap threatening to guillotine me. Chance's knee was in the cupholder. On a strictly physical level, it was possibly the most awkward kiss of my life.

I never wanted it to end.

A breathless eternity later, Chance slid back into his seat, looking as cool and satisfied as a cat.

"Okay," he announced, brushing bangs from his eyes. "*Now* we can go."

"Can we?" I blinked rapidly, trying to restart my brain. "I think I might have just forgotten how to drive." But I turned the key. His hand slid to cover mine on the gearshift as naturally as if we'd done it a thousand times.

"So where are we going?" he asked.

I recovered enough composure to waggle my eyebrows.

"Oooh! Surprises." He squeezed my hand. "I like surprises."

As we drove, I asked, "How was filming? Are you the new Robert Pattinson?"

Chance snorted. "Dude, it's a cameo. I have exactly one line."

"Well, what is it? Hit me."

Chance shrank in his seat a little. "Do I have to? It's dumb."

I grinned. "Okay, yes, *now* you have to. Immediately."

"Fine. Just give me a second to get into character." He sat up straight, taking several deep breaths to center himself. Then he turned to me, eyes wide, and in full Keanu surfer-bro accent, said:

"*Whoa – is that cheese dip?!*"

I laughed so hard I almost swerved into oncoming traffic, earning a one-finger salute from a cyclist. "That's it? You spent a week shooting *that*?!"

"And a bunch of background scenes. But yeah – you'd be surprised how many ways there are to say 'Whoa, cheese dip' wrong."

"I mean, clearly. You don't want to accidentally go Excited Cheese Dip when the director wants Trepidatious Cheese Dip."

"Or Sad Cheese Dip."

"Or Seductive Cheese Dip."

"Or Cheese Dip Killed Your Family."

We continued cracking each other up all the way to our destination, delivering the line with ever more unlikely emotions. I made Chance promise to name a future album *Trepidatious Cheese Dip*.

We were back in Georgetown. As I found parking, Chance said, "Death Putt round two?" He nodded sagely. "Of course. Why mess with the formula? Find a date that works and do the same thing every time, that's what I always say."

"Shut up. It's not my fault everything cool happens down here."

We got out and followed my phone down a new street, between a flooring company and a textile factory. As we came around the final corner, the road opened up into a riot of color and noise. Food trucks and retro trailers had crammed into a parking lot, the spaces between them filled with umbrellas, tents, and wildly patterned carpets.

"Behold!" I threw open my arms. "The Georgetown Pop-Up Market and Food Truck Jamboree!"

"Whoa!" Chance said.

"... cheese dip?" I added, and we both cackled. He grabbed my arm and dragged me forward.

My prior experience with street fairs was that they were seventy percent art for rich hippies and thirty percent funnel cake, but this was different. Everything had a punk-rock flavor, from the midthirties clientele wandering around with open beers to the stalls full of fake skulls, scandalous leather, and creepy marionettes. We scooted past a booth filled exclusively with old comics and science fiction novels, then a tent called Sparklepony selling only the most garish fashion accessories.

I tried on a pair of sunglasses with giant bug-eye lenses and long pink eyelashes. "What do you think?"

"Like a slutty Muppet." He picked up a mass of red leather that turned out to be a sex harness with a plastic yard flamingo glued to the crotch. "Wow. How'd they know my fetish?"

I put the glasses back on their googly-eyed mannequin. "Let's get some food."

The trucks were as eccentric as the merchandise, but one immediately stood out. It was airbrushed to resemble a gallery of weird, food-themed paintings – a dude with a burger floating in front of his face, two people with bags over their heads kissing while holding a bowl of pasta. The name on the side read SURREAL BOWL. We stepped up and perused the menu.

"Salvador Dalí," Chance read aloud. "Penne Magritte. Pita Kahlo." He looked up at the heavily pierced woman in the window. "Do you seriously only sell food with puns about famous painters?"

"Famous *surrealist* painters," the woman observed happily.

"And that's a viable business model?"

She shrugged. "It's Seattle."

We ordered. Chance got the Tuna Melting Watch, and I got the Ceci N'est Pas Une Pita, which was, in fact, a gyro. Drinks were lemonades sold as Penny Zinger's Bitter Lemons, and we rounded things out with a bucket of Frites Magritte, which wasn't a pun but was fun to say.

We sat at a plastic table under a bright red umbrella,

squeezing in beside a poloed Amazombie on his cell phone and a dreadlocked woman trying unsuccessfully to feed her toddler. I didn't mind the cramped quarters, as it gave me an excuse to nestle up against Chance, our hips and elbows touching.

Chance took a bite of food and moaned.

"Good?" I asked.

"*Surreal.*"

"Well, eat quick, 'cause this is just the first stop."

We chowed down, watching a girl in a tube top and giant bell-bottoms do tricks with a flaming Hula-Hoop.

Yet not even that was enough of a distraction to save us. Just as we were finishing, a dude suddenly pointed, his finger a few feet from Chance's face. "Hey! It's Chance Kain!"

"Chance Kain?!" Chance made a show of looking around. "Where?!"

But the pointer and his two friends – a girl and another guy, all probably in their twenties – were already surrounding us. Chance slid smoothly to his feet – and, I realized, out of contact with me. I felt the empty space where he'd been like a slap of freezing air.

Of course, a little voice in my head said. *Mr. Famous can't be seen with a normie boyfriend.*

But of course that wasn't fair. I squashed it down hard.

"Dude, you've gotta give me an autograph. Do you have a pen?"

"Sorry," Chance said, patting his pockets dutifully. "Not on me."

"*Does anybody have a pen?!*" Autograph Dude charged off into the crowd. Instantly the girlfriend was sliding in next to Chance, phone held at arm's length. "*CanIgetaselfieokaygreat!*"

The phone made rapid shutter noises before she was even done talking, her other arm wrapping possessively around Chance's waist. He smiled automatically, but I could see his eyes go flat and dead.

"Got one!" The boyfriend bro – the Brofriend – came charging back through the crowd, holding up a ballpoint pen like it was an Olympic torch. In his other hand was a stack of napkins. "Oh man, I'm gonna need a bunch. Start with Mikayla – that's *M . . . i . . . k . . .*"

I watched helplessly as the feeding frenzy commenced. I realized now just how comparatively cool the fans at Death Putt had been. That had been a whole crowd aware of Chance's presence but trying to be chill and respectful. This was only three people, but they stampeded through the mood like cattle, mooing and shitting everywhere.

And they were drawing attention.

The other dude thrust himself in for a selfie as well. "I don't actually like your music," he confided. "But my little sister loves that shit."

Chance smiled thinly. "Tell her she has excellent taste."

It was the last straw. I stood and shoved my way between them, grabbing Chance by the arm. "Yes, yes, thank you all, but Mr. Kain has to go now. He's already late for dinner with Eddie Vedder and Prince Harry. Terribly sorry."

For maybe the first time in my life, I used my bulk to full effect, acting like an icebreaker ship and dragging Chance along in my wake. What would have normally felt mortifyingly rude felt suddenly justified, now that it was for Chance. People moved or got moved, and in moments we were out of the crowd and headed back to the truck.

"Sorry about that," Chance said, looking contrite.

"*Sorry?!*" I realized I was yelling and got myself under control. "You've got nothing to apologize for. Those people were assholes!"

Chance shrugged. "You get used to it."

Would I have gotten used to that sort of treatment? I wasn't sure. "Well, you don't have to tonight. This concludes the public portion of the evening." I unlocked the truck. "Hop in."

This time we drove for less than a mile, back to the top of Beacon Hill, parking along the edge of Jefferson Park. Chance looked both confused and delighted as I led him off the street and through a wall of shrubbery.

On the other side, a maze of bark-chip paths wound up the slope, crisscrossing to create little brick-lined islands of greenery. Some looked like gardens, planted with careful rows of crops, while others grew in wild tangles. In the center stood a wooden gazebo-like structure. Other than an older Black woman weeding a plot downslope, we were totally alone.

"Here we are!" I proclaimed. "Dessert!"

Chance looked around in confusion. "A community garden? Do you have a plot?"

"Nah, dude. This is the Food Forest – everything here is free. Volunteers maintain it, so you can just forage. It's like a treasure hunt!"

Chance still looked skeptical.

I reached out and began picking raspberries. "Look!" I dumped a few in his hand.

He ate them, eyebrows rising in appreciation. "Oh shit."

"Right?!" I started up the path. "Come on, let's see what we find."

As I'd hoped, the joy of discovery quickly got to Chance. Within moments we were running around like first graders, yelling back and forth to each other. There were bushes full of blueberries, and thimbleberries so ripe they fell apart as you picked them. Tiny native blackberries crawled along beneath apple trees just starting to ripen and cherries at the end of their season. There were even things I'd never tried before, like gooseberries and figs.

After we'd picked all we wanted, we sat on the benches of the little gazebo, splitting a plum I'd grabbed. Wooden slats along the sides hid us from the playfields above, granting a modicum of privacy. On impulse I reached out and grabbed Chance's hand.

He flinched, looking around reflexively, and my heart broke a little. But as he saw there was nobody around, he smiled and squeezed my fingers.

I covered the hurt by singing, "'Breaking the law, breaking the law . . .'"

Chance's smile went small and wry. "Did you know the guy who sang that was gay?"

"Really?" That was a little more on the nose than I'd intended.

"Rob Halford. Came out in the nineties."

We sat with that a moment.

"Did you always know?" I asked. "That you liked dudes?"

He shrugged. "Kinda."

"How come you never told us?"

"How come you never asked?" He made a sour face. "I mean, I was basically goth Freddie Mercury onstage. I was waving that banner pretty hard."

"Yeah, but as soon as you got *off*stage, you were flirting hard with every girl at once." I frowned. "*Including* the ones Eli and I liked."

"Yeah." He hung his head. "Sorry. I guess I thought I kinda had to, you know? To make sure nobody thought I was *actually* queer."

"But you just said you were."

"That doesn't mean I wanted *other* people to know!" He looked down in surprise, having squeezed what was left of his plum into a wet mess. He chucked it into the bushes and wiped his hand on the cuff of his pants. "I think ... maybe the stage persona was a way for me to try on being someone else, you know? Without committing."

"So what about now?" I gestured at the empty gardens. "I mean, I know you have to keep it vague in public. But do *you* think of yourself as gay? Or bi?"

He paused, considering, then said, "No. I mean ... I dunno, what do those words even mean? If gender and sexuality are spectrums, doesn't that mean we're *all* bi? Where do you draw the cutoff?"

I shrugged. "Maybe it's like ... if you were gonna be stuck on a desert island, and could only have sex with one gender forever, do you have a preference?"

"But we're not *on* an island." He waved his juice-stained hand. "So like, okay, say ninety-nine percent of the time I choose Team Dick. I'm gay, right? But then let's say I fall in love with a girl, and we get married, and I'm very happy, even though I still – *in abstract* – like dicks better. Does that mean I was lying before, and was never really gay?" He shook his head angrily. "Life is about *specifics*, not hypotheticals. You know?"

"Yeah, I guess."

He squeezed my hand. "Sorry. Didn't mean to lecture."

"It's okay." I bit into my own half of the plum, sending juice running down my chin.

He reached over and wiped it away with a thumb. The gesture Did Things to my assorted organs. "I just feel like people should leave room for the unexpected, you know?"

I snorted and gave him a look. "Tell me about it."

He grinned. I ached to kiss him, but even with nobody nearby, I didn't want to make him uncomfortable. And besides, I wasn't going to get a better segue than that. I stood, hauling him up with me.

"Speaking of the unexpected, this date isn't over yet. On your feet, Ng."

I led him out of the gazebo – dropping his hand reluctantly – and across the grassy edge of the park, keeping clear of the usual crowd of exercisers and frolickers.

Chance looked back over his shoulder. "We're not going back to the truck?"

"Nope. From here on out, we're walking."

We headed north through residential streets. As we crossed a commercial strip, lined with coffee shops and restaurants, we paused in front of a tattoo parlor to watch through the window as someone got inked.

Chance sighed as we turned away. "I love tattoos."

"Clearly." I gave him the side-eye. "Most people don't start with their face."

He gave a too-cool shrug. "What can I say? I don't do things halfway." Then he dropped the act. "Honestly, the first two artists I talked to wouldn't do it – said nobody should get a face tat as their first. But having it on my face was kinda the important part."

I turned to look at him full-on. "Why?"

He grimaced and kept walking, not meeting my eye. "I mean, don't get me wrong, I like the art. And the psychopomp thing makes for a cool story. But really, I just wanted to do something that made me not the perfect star, you know? Something Benjamin and the label both hated. Proof that I own my own body."

"Huh." I thought about the so-called fans back at the food trucks. They'd sure acted as though they owned Chance. I wondered how many people thought they had claim to a piece of him.

"It's not just about them, though," he continued. "Or about tattoos. It's that the whole *world* has opinions on who I should be. And being Asian only makes it worse – because the industry isn't exactly bursting with Asian celebrities, I end up having to represent all of us. Except that nobody agrees on anything." He flopped a hand back and forth, lips thin. "I should speak out and use my platform – but don't offend anyone! Fight injustice – but be easy to work with! If I wear makeup, people say I'm fueling racist shit about Asian men being feminine. But if I *stop*, they say I'm caving to oppressive gender norms. Whatever I do, someone's pissed." He shook his head. "So that's what the tattoo really is: a reminder to myself that I can just be me. That I've got control over my own life." He paused. "Plus a healthy dose of child-star rebellion." He laughed, but his shoulders drew in with embarrassment. "Is that pathetic? Am I a shave-your-head celebrity meltdown?"

"Hey." I grabbed his arm, pulling him to a stop and making

him look at me. "You're not pathetic. You're staking your claim. That's cool."

"Yeah?" He looked hopeful.

"Yeah."

He smiled. "So you're saying it's cool if I shave off all my hair. Maybe get a big skull tat of a spiderweb."

"Absolutely." We resumed walking. "I mean, you'll need to wear a bag over your head whenever I'm around. But I'll totally respect you from the other side of the bag."

"Maybe I'll just get one of those rubber horse head masks. That'll be my new thing."

"You can corner the brony market."

We continued on for most of a mile, homes and hedges casting long shadows across the sidewalk. Most of the other pedestrians were dog walkers, waiting impatiently on their phones for Fido to do his business. Nobody paid us any attention.

By the time we reached the chain-link fence, it was almost dark. "All right," I said. "We're here."

Chance craned his neck back, taking it in. "A church?" He looked back down at me. "Look, Holc, it's been a great date, but I feel like you're moving a little fast."

"You *so* clever." I walked over to the gate's padlock and entered the code. It opened with a satisfying click.

"Oh snap!" Chance's mouth fell open. "This is *your* church!"

"Yup." I hauled the gate open. "Now hurry before someone sees us."

The same code got us through the front doors. Inside, the last sky glow through the stained glass gave everything a dreamlike quality, our footsteps echoing off the distant ceiling.

191

Chance took it all in reverently. "I assume we're not supposed to be here."

"After the Death Putt Paparazzi Chase, I figured you'd appreciate a little breaking and entering."

Chance grinned. Now safely out of sight of prying eyes, I gave in to the desire to kiss him. He tasted like stolen fruit. He took a step backward, half sitting on the back of a pew, and knotted his hand in my collar, drawing me close. I stepped between his legs.

For one long, rapturous moment, I squeezed his sides, walking my fingers up the ladder of his ribs. The shiny synthetic fabric of his shirt slid easily over ridges of muscle, and I was suddenly aware of just how naked he was beneath it.

But there was a *plan*, dammit. I pulled reluctantly free, taking his hand and trying to lead him across the room. "I want to show you something."

"Oh *really*?" He grabbed my hips and dragged me back into him, my ass against his crotch. "Are we gonna make out on the altar? Because that's actually pretty hot."

My pants grew tighter, and only the week I'd spent planning kept me from giving in.

"It would certainly cement your goth cred," I said. "But no, I want to show you something else."

He slid a hand beneath my shirt, running it along the top of my jeans. I paused.

"Okay," I amended. "Something else *first*."

He nipped lightly at my neck. "Sacri-licious."

Behind and to one side of the pulpit, a narrow door opened onto darkness. I pulled two headlamps out of my pocket. "Put this on."

"Uh." Chance looked down at the flashlight with its orange elastic band. "We're not going down into a crypt, are we?"

"What? Don't tell me America's favorite vampire is afraid of coffins."

Chance looked stricken. I let him stew in it for a breath, then laughed.

"I'm fucking with you, dude. It's not a tomb."

Chance sagged with relief. "To be clear, I am absolutely *not* scared of visiting the crypt in a creepy old church where no one would ever find our bodies." He slipped the headlamp on. "I just didn't want to mess up my hair."

"Gotta look good for the Lord." I reached up and clicked on his lamp, the band of which did indeed squeeze his hair into a stupid shape.

The beams of our lamps revealed a narrow wooden staircase, spiraling upward along the walls toward a square of brighter dark six stories above. I started up.

Chance did't follow. He was still staring up at the staircase.

"Don't worry," I said. "These stairs are perfectly good. Jesús gave them his blessing." I stopped, realizing what I'd just said. "I mean my dad's carpenter. But, you know, probably the other one too."

"I'm, uh." Chance looked more uncomfortable than I'd ever seen him. "I'm not a fan of heights."

"Really?" This was news to me. The great Chance Kain, scared of a staircase. How had that never come up before now? I slapped the banister. "You'll be fine. There's a handrail and everything."

Chance still didn't move.

Conflicting emotions warred inside of me. On the one hand, "terror" is generally not the atmosphere one hopes to cultivate on a date, unless maybe it's to facilitate scary-movie cuddling. On the other, this was the grand finale of my magical romantic-evening plan, and I was reluctant to give it up.

And, if I was being honest, there was a tiny, ungenerous part of me that enjoyed seeing Chance off his game. As in the woodshop, there was something deeply relaxing about knowing I could do something he couldn't. It made it feel like we were truly equals. And that, in turn, made it easier to feel romantic toward him.

Liking your boyfriend best when he's scared sounds bad, I know. A psychologist would probably have had plenty to say about it.

Good thing I didn't have one. I held out a hand to Chance. "Just hold on to me with one hand, and the railing with the other. Keep your eyes on my back until we get up there. All right?"

He actually bit his lip – who even does that? – and it was every bit as cute as in the movies. But at last he inhaled, set his shoulders, and took my hand.

"You realize if I die, I'm gonna haunt you forever."

As if he hadn't been doing that for years. I began climbing.

In Chance's defense, the stairs *were* pretty epic. That empty shaft in the center seemed designed for vertigo, with the flights of stairs swirling around and around like a squared-off whirlpool. A braid of dark cables hung down the middle of the tower.

Halfway up, Chance jerked to a halt, grinding the tendons of my hand into the bone. "Oh fuck."

I looked back and saw him staring down over the edge, looking ready to throw up.

"What'd I tell you about looking down?"

He closed his eyes. "We should have gone with the crypt."

I stroked his arm. "Just a little farther."

At the top, the tower flared out again, the stairs giving way to a wider platform. Chance lurched onto it gratefully. "Oh praise Jesus."

"That's the idea."

He looked up at the central joist above us, headlamp shining on the lumpy tumor of PA speakers hanging from thick chains. "There's no bell?"

"Nah. They went electronic in the eighties." I beckoned him over to the chest-high brick parapet that ran around the edge of the open-air belfry. "Here, kill your light before someone sees."

When we were both safely in position, I turned off my lamp.

Beacon Hill fell away beneath us. Out across the valley, the towers of downtown rose up in pointillist spires, stippled out of the darkness by the lights of a thousand windows. I-5 wound through in a glowing ribbon, while out on the Sound ferries glided silently between mainland and islands, tiny lanterns against the black water. I thought of what Chance had said about fireflies.

"This is what I wanted to show you," I said.

"Wow." Looking out rather than down seemed to help Chance's fear of heights. He leaned his elbows on the wall top and gazed out at the skyline.

"Worth the climb?" I ventured.

"I *should* say no," Chance said. "But ... yeah, this is amazing."

We leaned against each other, shoulder to shoulder as we

195

gazed out at our city, and somehow that small contact was as intimate as all our midnight fumblings. I felt a sudden, overwhelming surge of love for the world – for Chance, for this moment, for each and every person out in those buildings. Shining our lights, hoping someone would see us.

Chance sighed. "I'm always surprised how much I miss Seattle. I'll think I'm totally fine, and then I'll be riding home from the airport, and see the skyline, and it's like this weight is lifted. You know?"

"Yeah." I rarely traveled anywhere, but I still knew what he meant. "But I love the opposite, too."

"What do you mean?"

I struggled to find the words. "Okay, so, you know how when you spend enough time somewhere, it starts to feel like home?"

"Yeah?"

"Well, I love when you're coming home from somewhere, and everything's so familiar – your street, your house, whatever. But then, just for a second, you get a little flashback to what it felt like the first time you saw it. The first time you walked up that street. The first day you went to that school. How foreign everything seemed. How exciting. And you realize that the only thing that's changed is you." I waved out at the city. "Underneath the comfort, all that mystery is still there."

Chance pulled away, and I looked over to find him staring at me. He shook his head.

"David Holcomb. And you say you don't like poetry."

"What?"

He looped his arm through mine and pulled me close. "My dude, that metaphor was *hella* romantic."

"It was?" I hadn't really been talking about people, but I didn't refuse his kiss. It was soft, and deep, but just as I was starting to contemplate the logistics of going further in a bell tower, he stiffened – and not in the good way.

I let him break away. "What's wrong?"

"Sorry. It's not you." He didn't let go of my arm, but he looked out at the city again, not meeting my eyes. "They're sending me back out on tour."

My stomach dropped six stories to the church floor. "When?"

"September. Maybe October at the latest. We made the call this morning."

I'd known it was coming, of course. Had known it since before any of this started. But still. September was less than a month away.

"What'll you do without Eli?"

He shrugged. "They'll hire someone. Touring musicians. Producers."

It was almost funny, in that Alanis Morissette, more-unfortunate-than-ironic kind of way. Here I'd spent years thinking Chance had stolen the band from me, and now the band was stealing Chance.

"Listen." Chance squeezed my hand. "I really like you. But I understand if you don't want to . . . this." He gestured at the air between us. "I mean, if it's gonna make it harder when I leave. I know long-distance sucks."

My stomach had made it through the floorboards and was currently burrowing deep into the church's foundation. "Do *you* want to stop?"

"No. But—"

I pulled his body into mine and kissed him hard. There was

a split second of hesitation, and then he was kissing me back just as ferociously. When we finally came up for air, I said, "Good answer."

He grinned goofily. "So you don't want to stop?"

"If I wanted to stop, I wouldn't have started, dumbass. It's not like we didn't know this would happen." I kissed the tip of his nose. "And this is the lesson, right? Stop worrying about the future and just say what you need to say."

"What we need to say." Chance looked into my eyes and ran a knuckle slowly down the side of my cheek. "You make me want to say all sorts of unwise things."

My whole body felt like it was vibrating. "So say them."

"Maybe I will." Another off-kilter smile. "You'll just have to wait around and see."

We kissed again. But even as I fell down the gravity well of his touch, a separate part of my brain was clicking into overdrive, frantically putting pieces together.

I no longer resented Chance – at least, not much. Falling for him had forced me to acknowledge my own role in the band's breakup. Yet while I no longer blamed him for my lack of stardom, I still regretted that missed opportunity. Now here I was, about to be left behind a second time, and it wasn't even my fault. It wasn't Chance's fault, either. Nobody wanted it.

But if nobody wanted it ...

The idea came together. It was almost too absurd to look directly at. Certainly too absurd to broach.

But say what you need to say ...

I broke our kiss, pulling back far enough to see his face.

"What if we didn't have to do long-distance?"

"What?"

I breathed deep and took the plunge.

"What if I rejoined Darkhearts?"

He twitched as if electrocuted, taking a step back. "What?" he repeated.

I rushed forward. "Look, you need a new songwriting partner, right? Maybe that could be me. I know Eli was always the secret sauce, but I still wrote some parts. Nobody they can hire was there in the beginning – they don't know you the way I do. And if I were back in the band, I could go on tour with you." I grabbed his hands. "We could spend every day together."

"Holc." Chance looked shell-shocked. "I. Uh." He blew out his cheeks. "Wow."

"I know, it's a lot, sorry. I honestly hadn't even thought about it until just now. I don't mean to blindside you with a proposal." I squeezed. "But it makes sense, right?"

"Yeah, but ..." In the dark, the expressions that flickered across his face were difficult to parse. "The last time we were in a band, you hated it so much you didn't talk to me for two years."

"You didn't talk to me either."

"That's not the point." He reclaimed his hands, running them down his face, then pressing the palms together like a prayer. "I've been trying to tell you. This life – it's not what you think. It grinds people up."

A flicker of the old anger. "I can handle it."

Chance just looked sad. "That's what Eli thought."

"I'm not Eli," I snapped.

"No, I know." He looked away. "What I mean is, what we have right now – it's *good*. I wouldn't want the band to get in the way of that."

I gritted my teeth. "The band's *already* getting in the way of that. This is a chance for us to fix it. And we're different people now. *I'm* different." I reached for his hands again, drawing him closer. "Listen, I know I screwed up. And I know nobody can replace Eli. We can never be what we should have been. But maybe we can be something new." I stopped just short of saying *something better.* But it *would* be better – at least for me. A band *and* a boyfriend. I didn't really believe in fate, but some part of me whispered that maybe this was always how it had to be. That if not for the pain we'd been through, we'd never have gotten to this place.

I realized Chance hadn't said anything for several seconds, which reminded me that my stomach was currently tunneling through the Earth's mantle.

". . . I mean, if you want to," I finished weakly.

The moment hung. Then Chance let out a long, slow breath.

"I want to," he said.

My heart lurched. "Really?"

"Yeah." He gripped me back. "It'd be super fun to have you on tour."

Tension still radiated off of him.

"But?" I prompted.

I felt his shrug. "But it's also not up to me. Darkhearts is its own thing now – we've got an artist development contract. If you want to rejoin the band, we're gonna have to convince the label."

"Okay, so how do we do that?"

Chance thought about it, then said, "A showcase. We'll write something new together – one song, fast, before the tour starts – and perform it for them. Show them what we can do."

"Perfect!" I felt like my body might spontaneously turn inside out. It was a good thing there wasn't an actual bell in this tower, or I might have started yanking on it like the Hunchback of Notre Dame. This wasn't just exciting – this was a do-over of my entire life.

Chance leaned closer, trying to see my eyes. "You're sure you want this?"

"Positive." I smiled wide.

"Cool."

In the darkness, his own smile could have meant anything.

18

The rest of the weekend was officially Ng Family Time. *My mom's threatening to tie me to a chair*, Chance had said as I dropped him off. But that was fine, because I suddenly had a lot of work to do.

My guitar had spent most of the last two years in its case under my bed, but now I slid it out and popped the latches. Opening the lid felt like opening the Ark of the Covenant – or, more optimistically, Arthur pulling the sword from the stone.

Chrome and rosewood stared back at me, forest green paint swirling around a black pickguard. The case's fuzzy gray fabric molded itself to the guitar's asymmetrical body, holding it up like an offering.

I reached down and accepted, slipping the strap over my neck.

The Fender Jazzmaster: chosen guitar of the Cure, Arcade Fire, and My Bloody Valentine.

And now, maybe, of Darkhearts again.

I cleared dirty clothes and Dad's old Calvin and Hobbes books off my amp, then plugged in and flipped the switch.

The tubes hummed slowly to life. I kept the volume off as I tuned, then took a breath and cranked it.

Distortion roared through the room. I dropped down to E minor and palm muted, chugging to feel the bass in my chest. I tried a couple of experimental bends, then a major scale, feeling my way through the notes.

God, I was rusty. But maybe that could be an asset? Sometimes when you spent time away from an instrument, you came back with fresh ideas. And I'd had plenty of time away.

I ran through a couple of old Darkhearts songs, then began messing around, picking random notes from scales, stringing together chords in search of something that felt appropriately Darkhearts-y. I even put on a couple of newer Darkhearts songs and attempted to play along, trying to get a feel for what Eli would do. His songs were less guitar-focused, but that just meant there was room to make them bigger.

After an hour, Dad popped his head up through the doorway. He'd clearly just come from working on the van, and was eating a bag of white cheddar popcorn with salad tongs to avoid touching it with greasy hands.

"Sounding good," he said, which was being generous. "Nice to hear you rocking out again."

"Yeah." I hit a chord, then rolled the volume off. "It feels good." I was surprised to find how much I meant it.

Dad looked pleased. "What changed?"

There was no way I could tell Dad our plan. It'd either piss him off or get his hopes up, either of which would make it worse if things went wrong. But I also didn't want to lie to him.

I settled for half the truth. "I guess hanging out with Chance just makes me want to play music."

His smile slipped, but he caught it before it could disappear completely. "Well, that's something!" He waved the tongs as he retreated back downstairs. "Anyway, I'm making tacos for dinner tonight. Lemme know if you want anything special."

The rest of the day was a barrage of internet tabs and half-baked riffs, stopping only for food and bathroom breaks. I might have kept going till tacos if not for an email that push-notified itself onto my phone screen.

Subject: Interview?

Hi David,

My name is Jaxon Aldern, and I'm a journalist with Pop Lock. *Rumors are swirling that you and Chance Kain have been spending a lot of time together recently ... would you like to comment on the nature of your relationship? ;)*

Also, if you're willing to do an exclusive interview about it, we could pay a generous honorarium, as well as licensing fees for original photographs or video of you and Chance together.

Thanks, and let me know!

I went back to the top and read it through again. Then I looked up "honorarium." Then read it one more time.

A quick googling revealed that *Pop Lock* was half online music magazine, half celebrity gossip blog – the kind of place where you can tell that the writers want to be *Rolling Stone* or *Pitchfork,* but can't quite keep themselves from posting every celebrity breakup and leaked nude. In other words: total trash.

How had these people even figured out who I was, let alone found my email address? But I guessed it wouldn't be too hard to recognize me. It wasn't like I'd been totally erased from Darkhearts history – I was even mentioned on their Wikipedia page, my sad little unlinked name all alone under "Former

204

Members." And Chance had said these people were tenacious. But we'd barely even been out in public together, and never in an obviously romantic way.

Suddenly I was pissed. We'd been so careful, skulking around, keeping everything on the down-low, and it didn't even matter. People would believe whatever they wanted.

So let them. The impulsive part of me wanted to tell Chance's manager – tell *Benjamin* – where to shove his expert guidance. Just announce that Chance and I were dating, and to hell with the haters. It wasn't like other celebrities hadn't come out.

But of course it wasn't my call. Chance was the one with something to lose, and he'd made his choice clear.

Which, if I was being honest with myself, stung in its own way. I knew it wasn't about me – Chance couldn't afford to gamble with his career. But somewhere, deep down, I couldn't quite dislodge the whisper saying *he's ashamed of you.* Not even ashamed of dating a boy – of dating *me.* Chance Kain should be dating someone glittery and fancy, not a doughy high school nobody with wood glue under his nails.

But that was just one more point in favor of me joining the band, wasn't it? To be a rock star in my own right. Then we could spin our relationship into an asset. Two teen heartthrobs in the same band, and they're dating each other? We'd be icons.

But none of that applied to the situation at hand. I wanted to write back and tell the reporter to go screw himself, or maybe find better things to do with his life than stalk teenagers, but I figured that might not fit with Benjamin's PR plan. At the same time, the idea of saying *nothing* felt profoundly unsatisfying. This sort of invasion of privacy demanded a response.

I hit the reply button. What was it politicians always said, when someone was getting up in their grill?

No comment.

I typed it out and stared at it. It looked good. No salutation, no "Sincerely, David" – just those two words, icy and smooth. A response that said nothing, but with the unmistakable air of *I will not dignify your question with a response. I am above you.*

I hit send and went to eat tacos.

Around noon the next day, I was just starting to get into a groove with a new riff when Chance texted.

CHANCE:

> We've got a problem. Can
> you do a video call?

I grabbed my phone.

ME:

Sure . . . ? What's up?

Chance didn't answer the question, just said, Will email a link. Wear pants.

Fortunately, I was already dressed, but I went ahead and finger-combed my hair as best I could, then sat back against my bed and opened my laptop.

The email appeared. The little *"connecting . . ."* worm chased its own tail.

And then there he was – but not alone. Benjamin hunched in a second window, a hotel room in the background. He gave me the thinnest-lipped smile imaginable.

"And here's our Romeo," Benjamin said. "Thanks for

206

meeting with us. I know you must have a busy schedule stirring the shit."

"Benjamin . . ." Chance looked defeated in a plain black hoodie, his hair a legitimate mess instead of its usual intentional one.

"What are you talking about?" But a part of me already knew.

"Google your name and 'Pop Lock.'"

I opened a new tab, and sure enough – there we were, right on the front page. A photo of the two of us running down the alley outside Death Putt, his hand on my wrist, with the headline A CHANCE AT ROMANCE? I scrolled quickly. Farther down were more pictures of us, all taken at the Pop-Up Market.

"Those assholes at the market *sold* their pictures?" I couldn't believe the audacity.

"Of course they sold them!" Benjamin snapped. "Why wouldn't they? A reporter shows up offering cash for some picture on your Facebook timeline? It's a no-brainer. And speaking of no-brainers . . ." His "disappointed" face was so coolly professional he must have practiced in the mirror. "Let's talk about your response to that same reporter."

I couldn't tell if the heat rising in my cheeks was anger or shame. "I didn't say anything."

"Wrong." Benjamin's tone wasn't even vicious, which made it all the more cutting. "According to the article, you said 'no comment.' Which might as well be 'Yes, absolutely, everything you can possibly imagine is true.' You just told them you've got something to hide."

It sounded so obvious, when he put it like that. Yet rage is a lot more comfortable than guilt. "So what *should* I have said?" I spat back.

"*Nothing.*" Benjamin's hands drew a flat line in the air. "No response at all. Your goal is to be a black hole – their signal goes in, but nothing comes out." He sighed, dropping a little of his professional calm and pinching the bridge of his nose. "Look, rags like *Pop Lock* sensationalize everything. If they get a picture of you with ketchup on your shirt, they'll imply you just murdered a kindergarten. They're squids."

That threw me. "Squids?"

"Squirting ink everywhere." He flicked his fingers, miming a squid spraying. "A bunch of hacks who want to be the next Perez Hilton. They're garbage, but it doesn't matter. Twitter is already exploding with rumors. Some people think you're dating. Others think you're rejoining the band."

"Really?" I perked up at that, but Chance flared his nostrils in a look that said *now is not the time.*

"So what do we do?" It was the first full sentence Chance had spoken, and it hurt to hear him so tired and resigned.

"Chaff." Benjamin made little fireworks motions with his hands. "Smokescreen. We get competing, contradictory rumors going and hope they cancel each other out." He glared at me through the camera. "And we *don't* make any more public statements, *capisce?*"

Thanks to Ridley making me watch *The Godfather,* I knew that last word meant *understand.* "Fine."

"Glad to hear it. So. On to damage control." He steepled his hands. "The biggest threat here is the rumor that you're dating, so that's the one we'll target. And the best way to do *that* is to give people a different potential paramour. A girl this time – someone we can send Chance on a date with, then leak the location, or at least pictures."

"Boy, I sure love being pimped out by my own management," Chance muttered.

"That's what management *does,* rock star. And you're paying me handsomely for it. But relax – I'm not asking you to sleep with her. Just go get dinner, smile for the cameras, and call it a night."

"Who?" My stomach twisted. I might be new to this whole boyfriend thing, but jealousy was old hat.

Chance drew his lips sideways, thinking. "What about Clara Shadid? I could fly back down to L.A."

My intestinal knot pulled even tighter, but Benjamin waved the idea away. "No celebrities. We take this as an opportunity to make you seem approachable. Just an ordinary, hometown girl – someone who makes fans think 'It could be me!'" He dropped his hands. "So who've you got on tap?"

Fake or not, I didn't want anyone taking Chance out on dates but me. But I knew what I had to do. I raised a finger.

"I know someone."

19

"Ohmygod ohmygod ohmy*god*! I can't believe I'm going on a date with Chance Kain!"

In the passenger seat, Ridley bounced in place like a dog doing tippy-taps. She was wearing her favorite outfit, the one I thought of as "fun with scissors": a tight pink Seattle International Film Festival T-shirt with horizontal slits laddering up the side and high-waisted blue jeans that looked like they'd been distressed with a hedge trimmer. She'd pulled her hair up into two big pigtail poofs, like Mickey Mouse ears.

I downshifted, checking the map. "Slow your roll, Lady Marmalade. This is a *pretend* date, remember?"

"I know, I know. You don't have to keep reminding me."

Chance and I weren't *total* dicks. I'd warned Ridley up front that this was purely a PR stunt, wanting to make it seem like Chance might have a local girlfriend. I just hadn't explained exactly *why* we wanted it. Ridley being Ridley, she'd immediately gone into mercenary mode, bullying Chance into promoting her blog in exchange and making Benjamin write it into the nondisclosure agreement. It was all very professional.

So Ridley knew the score. But there was knowing and there was *knowing*, and seeing her so excited made me feel guilty anyway.

"Still . . ." she said. "Even if it's fake, it's still a date. And he's still not seeing anybody else, right?"

I kept my eyes on the road. "Not that I know of."

"Then you never know, right?"

"Ridley—"

"Shush, let Mama have her fantasy. You don't – Oh! There it is!"

I circled the block, looking for somewhere to park, then settled for pulling into a red-and-yellow bus zone.

Zuzu was the latest restaurant from Doug Thomas, Seattle's resident celebrity chef. It was a Chinese-Northwest fusion place, and trendy in the way that meant each stalk of broccoli would cost as much as an entire meal somewhere else. It was the sort of place high schoolers didn't go unless it was prom.

Or a date with Chance Kain, apparently.

Ridley popped the door. "Thanks for the ride!"

"Don't mention it," I said. And meant it, since I suspected Benjamin wouldn't love me being involved even this much. But the light rail didn't run to West Seattle, Ridley didn't drive, and I was desperate to feel some element of control over the situation. Part of me wanted to go full Teen Detective and grab a seat at a nearby table so I could watch it all, but I knew that would only pour gasoline on the fire if someone spotted me.

It was also totally unreasonable. Ridley was my best friend, and Chance was my boyfriend. This whole thing was a scam the three of us were pulling on the rest of the world, not something I needed to worry about. My rational mind knew that. But it didn't stop something deep in my gut from growling that *I* should be the one eating overpriced salmon lo mein, getting the full Chance Kain celebrity-date experience.

A foghorn blast startled me out of my reverie. A city bus had pulled in behind me, the driver gesturing angrily. I ducked an apology and threw the truck into gear.

Back home, I tried to get into the movie Dad was watching, but couldn't stop myself from checking my phone every thirty seconds.

Ridley's Instagram was already filling up with pictures, exactly as planned. Food shots, outfit selfies – and, of course, Chance. My eyes went immediately to a shot of the two of them, Ridley tucked under Chance's arm in a way that could be either friendly or romantic, depending on what you wanted to see. The caption had the same effect:

> @RidleyMeThis: Out to dinner with @ChanceKain. I feel like Cinderella, but with better shoe game. #glassslippersarebullshit #soarepumpkins

I'd initially thought they wouldn't want Ridley posting pictures herself – wouldn't it seem suspicious if she posted selfies with Chance, while he and I avoided being photographed? But Chance had only said, *Dude, half my life is posing for people's selfies.*

The more I stared at the picture, the harder it was to concentrate on anything else. Finally I gave in and texted Chance.

ME:

How's it going?

His reply came in a few minutes later.

CHANCE:

Good! Ridley's actually really cool.
You have good taste in friends.

212

Trust Chance to pick a compliment that stoked both my ego and my anxiety. I tried to keep things light:

ME:

My taste can't be TOO good.
Look who I'm dating.

He replied with a middle-finger emoji.

Oh man, I texted back, this is awkward, but I totally got you the same thing. And added my own middle-finger emoji.

CHANCE:

Great minds. Hey, knock knock.

ME:

Who's there?

Middle-finger emoji.

ME:

They say communication is the
key to a healthy relationship.

From across the couch, Dad said, "You're blowing up tonight."

"Oh, sorry." I put my phone on silent.

"Anything important?"

"No, Ridley's just out on a date."

"Good for her." Dad gave me a curious look, maybe sensing my nervous energy. "Do you like the guy?"

"Definitely." I was becoming the king of technically true statements.

His attention only sharpened. "Are you wishing it was you instead?"

"What?" Oh god, was I that transparent?

"Ridley's a cool girl. Cute, too."

I laughed with genuine relief. "Dad, I set her *up* on this date."

"That isn't what I asked."

I shook my head. "Don't worry, I definitely don't have a thing for Ridley. I'm just invested in how her date goes."

"All right." Dad shrugged and went back to watching the movie.

That was all closer to the truth than I was interested in – and honestly closer than I would have expected from Dad – so as soon as it wouldn't seem like an obvious retreat, I excused myself and fled up to my room.

Ridley's Insta was still going strong, and I was startled to see the number of likes and comments. Apparently even being adjacent to Chance on social media had an effect. Her most recent picture was of her hand reaching for a plate of little dumpling pastry things, while in the background Chance shrugged elaborately with a comical expression that said *welp!*

@RidleyMeThis: Live footage of me grabbing @ChanceKain's sweet, sweet buns. #sorryfolks #notactuallysorry

It was an obvious, juvenile joke, and I was absolutely *sick* that I wasn't the one making it. I texted looking at your buns to Chance, and then, when he didn't respond immediately, texted Ridley as well. How's the fake date going? I fought the urge to put "fake" in all caps.

Ridley replied first.

OMG AWESOME! I knew
he was hot, but he's actually
smart, too??? We spent half
an hour comparing Interview
with a Vampire and Twilight,
and how they're both meta-
phors for religious guilt and
abusive relationships.

Huh. I hadn't thought about it before, but Chance's encyclopedic knowledge of vampire media was actually sort of perfect for Ridley.

I texted back. Yeah, that sounds like Chance.

My phone vibrated.

RIDLEY:

Also, my newsletter has
already gotten like a hundred
new subscribers in the last
hour, and his promo post
hasn't even gone live yet!
This is basically the best night
ever. Anyway, we're gonna go
walk down Alki and look at the
city. For a "fake" date, he's
pulling out all the stops! 😍

My fingers itched to respond that I already knew. Walking down Alki Beach was just another part of the plan – dinner would have given enough time for Ridley's posts to reach the local celebrity stalkers, with Benjamin standing by to send anonymous tips as necessary. As Ridley and Chance walked, they'd no doubt be subject to numerous candid photographs both professional and amateur, making the whole thing seem more authentic and firmly cementing the rumor.

But I didn't reply. I'd done everything I could to stop Ridley from thinking this was a real date, and short of telling her the truth – which was still a grade-A no-no – there just wasn't any more I could do. We weren't leading her on, and she was getting as much out of the arrangement as we were. At this point, if her feelings got hurt, it was because she'd played herself. She wanted the story of Chance more than the reality.

Yet even as I justified it, I couldn't help but feel a little guilty. Not just because I didn't want my friend to get hurt, but because part of me *did*. Never mind that sending her on the date had been my idea – a shitty part of me still wanted to punish her for being with my boyfriend. For doing what I couldn't. It didn't matter that it wasn't rational – my back was up and my claws were out.

My phone buzzed.

> CHANCE:
>
> Sorry you had to see my buns on the internet. If it makes you feel better, they were full of beans.

Followed by the peach and wind emojis. I smiled and texted back,

216

Glad you guys got to talk movies. Just don't
be TOO charming, okay? I'm not good at
sharing.

Another buzz.

Ooooh . . . Getting jealous, Holc?

I sat there for a full five minutes, trying to think up a witty comeback. Before I could, my phone buzzed again.

Oops, she's back. GTG!

And then I was alone again. I lay back on my bed, phone heavy on my chest.

I wasn't really jealous of Ridley. Or at least, not her specifically. She was no different from the photographers, or Chance's parents, or the random fans passing on the street. Just another person publicly laying claim to Chance, in ways I wasn't allowed to.

He belonged to the whole world more than he belonged to me. And he always would.

Unless I did something about it.

20

The next night after work, I waited until Dad installed himself in the bathroom for his standard post-work dump – a phone-heavy activity guaranteed to grant me at least fifteen minutes of privacy – then ran upstairs and hauled down my guitar and amp.

... only to find Dad digging through the storage closet. He looked up in surprise.

"Whoa! Where are you taking those?"

"Gonna go play some music."

He rolled his eyes. "Clearly. I mean with who?"

Here, then, was the conversation I'd been trying to avoid. But screw it – into the abyss.

"Actually ... it's with Chance."

He froze, a roll of toilet paper in each hand. "You're shitting me."

"No, *you're* shitting." The joke was weak, but there was no helping it. "I'm thinking about rejoining Darkhearts."

Once, when Mom was still around, her brother had taken us out bottom fishing in the San Juans. The creatures we pulled up were spiny aliens – lingcod and sculpins and rockfish – but they'd all gaped with the same open-mouthed horror, their eyes bulging grotesquely. Later, I learned that was due to the pressure change: the fish were used to the pressure down deep, and in hauling them hundreds of feet to the surface, we'd made their organs explode.

That was how Dad was looking at me now.

"You want to rejoin the band. After what they did to you."

I clenched the handle of my guitar case and forced myself to remain calm. "*They* didn't do anything to me. *I* quit the band. And anyway, it doesn't matter. This is my chance to fix things. I could be playing *stadiums*, Dad. And not someday. Next month."

"Next *month*?" Dad looked dazed. "What about school?"

"Who cares? Chance is getting homeschooled on the road. I can do it with him, or get my GED, or whatever. Besides, if I'd never quit the band in the first place, I would've *already* left school."

"I don't know how I feel about that."

"Since when?" It was getting increasingly difficult to keep my tone under control. "Would you really have made me stay home while they went off and got famous? You've always said I was robbed of my chance at stardom. Well, now I'm getting it back. I thought you'd be *happy.*"

Which was only half true, but it got through. His frown faltered.

"I mean . . ." He struggled to find the words. "If this is what you want . . . Of course I'm happy. And you're right, it's a big opportunity. Just . . . don't let anyone pressure you into anything, okay? Don't worry about what I want, or the Ngs, or anyone else. Do what's best for *you.*"

"I will," I promised. That much was easy.

We stood there staring at each other, me holding my guitar, him holding his toilet paper.

He let out a breath, then grinned and shook his head. "You sure know how to keep things interesting, kid."

"I know."

He turned back to the bathroom and threw up the devil horns over his shoulder. "Rock out, my child."

At Chance's house, his mom answered the door, and I got to go through the whole thing again in reverse.

"Oh!" She took in the guitar and amp, and her face closed into an elegant, friendly mask. "Hi, David. Chance didn't tell me you'd be playing music."

"I hope that's all right." There'd been no way I was going to host at my house. "We won't go too late."

"Of course." Her eyes missed nothing. I wondered if she saw things I didn't even know about.

"Hey, dude." Chance stood at the top of the curving staircase, wearing a sleeveless black hoodie scarred in long, artful slashes. "Come on up."

I obligingly lugged the fifty-pound albatross of my Marshall up the stairs. "Everything go according to plan last night?"

"Yup. It was actually fun." He grimaced. "Though Ridley invited me to her end-of-summer party."

"Oh yeah?" I followed him down the hallway. "You thinking of going?" I wasn't sure what answer I wanted to hear.

"And spend the whole night being displayed like a sideshow freak? No thanks." He turned and opened one of the doors.

Inside was a bedroom. I would say it was *Chance's* bedroom, but honestly, it wasn't. He had stuff there – a walk-in closet bursting with clothes, a laptop on the desk, a couple of awards on the windowsill – but nothing about it said *Chance*. Ridley's room might be ridiculously tidy, but it was at least expressing a part of her. Chance's old room had been all show posters and replica swords and stacks of horror novels – a shrine to Chance-ness. This place was totally generic.

Chance had bought this amazing house, yet he lived like he could be packed and out the door in thirty seconds. Maybe that was what tour life made you: a guest in your own home. It seemed unbearably sad.

I set my amp and guitar down in the middle of the room. Chance closed the door behind us.

"Sorry if my mom was weird. I wasn't sure how—"

My kiss was half body-slam, shoving him up against the wall with a thud. I pressed against him, squashing him into the drywall, grabbing his hands and feeling his body through the tenuous barrier of our clothes.

Eventually I pulled my face back, panting. "Hi."

"Hi." He was breathing hard as well, his smile goofy. "Holc smash."

"Don't mind if I do." I dove back in.

There was something about having his back to the wall, the way it forced us into contact in ways normal kissing didn't. I wasn't someone who felt powerful very often. But with him trapped up against me, moaning softly into my mouth, I felt at once in command and completely out of control.

His hands slid up under my shirt, but I managed to hold on to why I was there – if just barely – and step backward out of his grasp. "Nuh-uh. That's all you get for now. Business before pleasure."

"Oh my god, you bastard." But he grinned.

"Just reminding you of the stakes." And myself, for that matter. All I wanted to do was tear his clothes off, but we were on a deadline. If we made this work, there would be plenty of make-out opportunities in the future.

And if we didn't, there might not be any.

I unpacked my guitar and plugged in, then sat down atop the amp. Chance settled cross-legged on his bed. We stared at each other.

"So," he said.

"Yeah." I cradled my guitar.

"It feels weird to do this without Eli."

"Yeah." And not just because he wasn't there. He'd always been the conductor, the one running the show on the musical side. I'd written parts, but he'd stitched it all together. "You wanna warm up on something?"

He shrugged. "Sure."

I wasn't quite ready to do old Darkhearts stuff yet, so we ran through some covers – stuff from the earliest days of the band. "Just Like Heaven," Bowie's "Heroes." Even sitting all hunched over, Chance had a more powerful voice than I remembered, richer and smoother. He swayed back and forth with the beat, and each time our eyes met, I had to fight to keep from fumbling the chords.

But eventually we couldn't put things off any longer. I pulled out my phone and opened a recording app, so we wouldn't forget anything we came up with, then set it on the floor.

"So how do you want to do this?" he asked.

I shrugged. "I guess I'll just ... play stuff? And you let me know if something sparks you?"

"Okay." He looked uncomfortable. "And it's okay if it doesn't work, right? I mean, it's been a long time."

It absolutely was *not* okay, but saying so wouldn't help. "Of course."

He let out a breath and popped his neck. "All right, then. Hit me."

I had a few different riffs and progressions I'd been playing with, but I figured it was best to go straight for the prize. I played through the one I was most confident in, feeling the chords burring up from the speaker beneath me.

When I finished, Chance cocked his head.

"That's 'Midnight's Children.'"

My stomach lurched. "What? No it's not!"

"Yeah it is. You're just playing in a different key." He gestured. "Do it again."

I played it again.

This time Chance sang along:

> *"I wanna fly*
> *like a vampire bat.*
> *Don't wanna die,*
> *we're too pretty for that . . ."*

Shit. No wonder it had sounded so perfect in my head.

"It's still different, though," I ventured. "Bands reuse progressions all the time . . ."

"Dude." Chance gave me a look. "It was our third single. You don't think somebody's gonna notice?"

"Okay, okay." I forced a smile. "At least we know we're writing hits, right?" Inside, I felt suddenly wobbly. "Here – try this."

I played another – a punkier blend of riff and chords, with a pick pattern a little more complicated than my rusty right hand was ready for. I winced every time I missed a string. I finished and looked up at Chance.

His expression was totally flat – his Judgment Face. I suddenly remembered a dozen different versions of this same moment, sitting on Eli's couch, watching as they prepared to shoot down my ideas.

"It's a little repetitive," Chance said. "And probably a little too punk for what we're doing."

In the basement of my heart, the old rage monster cracked open the door and peeked out.

I kicked it closed again. *Stay focused.* "Yeah, no, I was thinking the same thing."

I played another. Big open chords, sweet and sad. I looked at the wall as I played, not wanting to watch Chance in robot mode. He was so smooth with fans, or in interviews – why couldn't he use a little of that polish on me? But it had always been like this: as soon as it came to the music itself, he was all business, and to hell with anyone's feelings.

I got to the end and looked over expectantly.

"It's pretty," he admitted slowly. "But a little generic. And kinda cliché."

My simmering anger boiled over. "So? Generic just means universal. Cliché means it works."

"Cliché means *forgettable.*" His face was stone. "These label people have heard everything. It's not enough to just sound good – you have to bring something original." He looked away. "Besides, it doesn't sound like Darkhearts."

He was right – it was probably too soft-rock – but my pride wouldn't let me walk away. "I thought *we* decide what Darkhearts sounds like."

"Yeah, well, not anymore." He closed his eyes, rubbing at one of them. "Maybe this was a bad idea."

You ever have a moment where you can actually *see* an opportunity slipping away? In my mind, Chance receded as if on the stern of a ship, leaving me standing on the pier. My anger turned to fear.

No. I'm not blowing this again. I reached out and touched his knee. "Hey, I'm sorry." I tried to look contrite. "Bad habit. Let's just keep trying a bit longer, okay?"

He searched my face, then nodded. "Okay."

I let out the breath I hadn't known I'd been holding. "Cool."

A stay of execution. Relief made noodles of my arms, yet I was still running perilously low on riffs. I could feel my palms sweating against the guitar's neck, the strings sharp and unfamiliar beneath my fingers.

One idea left. It was the least formed – just a couple of chords, really. Some sort of D thing, but with a root that moved around. I didn't know much about music theory, I just knew it sounded moody. I gave it a percussive strum pattern, almost slapping the strings, letting it rise and fall like the rhythm of the light rail.

I saw it hit. Chance's whole body twitched, ever so slightly. He closed his eyes, feeling it. "Keep going."

Yes! I continued rolling on the progression, watching him bob unconsciously to the rhythm. But after a moment he frowned.

"The third chord is wrong."

My frustration returned. "It can't be *wrong*. I just wrote it."

Chance's eyes opened into slits. "Fine. It's not *wrong*, it's just not *working*. Try something else."

"Like what?"

He threw up his hands. "I don't know! You're the guitarist. Just something different."

I wanted to argue, but hadn't forgotten what was at stake. I swallowed my pride and began inserting different chords into that last spot, choosing more or less at random.

Nothing sounded good. I could see Chance losing the groove.

In desperation, I cut the third chord altogether. Just two chords, alternating back and forth. So simple it was stupid.

And just like that, the groove was back. Chance's eyes shot open, and he nodded vigorously, spinning a finger. *Keep rolling.* Then he closed his eyes again and began to sing.

It was nonsense syllables – complete gibberish. But that was the way Chance worked. First came feel. He'd sing things that weren't even words, but he'd do it in a way you felt in your bones, the notes rising up from the depths of him to float oil-smooth over the waves of the rhythm.

The blending of my guitar and his voice set up a buzz in my legs, my hands, my guts.

How had I ever forgotten this? But I had. I'd told myself I didn't need it, and walked away. But now that I was here again, it was all so clear. His voice running like a violin bow across my nerves. The two of us becoming part of the same vast creature, breathing in rhythm, glorious and terrible in our melancholy.

Suddenly it seemed impossible to play a wrong note. I cranked up the volume and slammed headlong into a triumphant major chord.

"*Yes!*" Chance leaped off the bed as I slid down through the chords of an impromptu chorus. I was flying without a net, discovering each note as my fingers played it, but in our perfection we were untouchable. I rolled out of the new chorus and back into what I now knew was the verse as Chance dove into his laptop bag and came up with a little leather notebook and a pen. He began scribbling furiously.

I just kept going, alternating back and forth between the two parts as Chance muttered lines beneath his breath. At some point I added an ascending line between them as a prechorus build, and Chance jabbed his pen at me so hard he'd have put my eye out if I were a foot closer.

"*Good,*" he commanded. "Do that one!"

I must have played the same thing for half an hour, until my fingers started to cramp and I had to pause. Chance looked at me like a sleepwalker shaken awake. He grinned dazedly.

"I think we've got something."

"Yeah …?" I knew it too, but wanted to hear him say it again.

"Yeah." He laughed and slapped the bed. "God *damn*! This is good!"

"Don't act so surprised." But I was laughing too. It felt too good not to. "I can almost hear the drum line in the verse, too. Sort of a *doot-doot-KSH, duh-doot-doot-KSH.*"

"Doot-doot kitsch, huh?" Chance gave me a playfully skeptical look.

"Oh shut up, you know what I mean." I jerked my chin at his notebook. "You got lyrics?"

He turned shy, hands curling protectively around the little book. "A start, yeah."

"Well, let's hear 'em."

He hesitated, then blew out his lips and stood. "All right." He motioned for me to play. "Gimme a few repetitions to get into it, then four from when I start singing before you go into the prechorus."

"Got it." I started playing.

He nodded along, not looking at me anymore, alternating between checking his book and staring out at an invisible audience. Then he began to sing.

> *"I recognize*
> *it'll never be the same.*
> *And our hands are tied*
> *by choices that we made.*
> *But you*
> *don't want this to burn.*
> *And I don't know,*
> *But I'm afraid that we'll learn . . ."*

A premonition began to build as we moved into the prechorus.

> *". . . that the lights, and the sounds,*
> *and the memories of the friends,*
> *are a life, once lived,*
> *that can't be lived again."*

He's singing about us. My stomach sank even as the music built. Here I was, trying to give us a second chance, and he was saying that our choices were permanent, and there were no do-overs. I didn't know whether to cry or scream.

And then, as we tumbled over into the chorus, he turned and looked me dead in the eye.

> *"But now you're back.*
> *And I'm not backing away.*
> *And I still know what we said,*
> *so let's say nothing instead,*
> *because you're back from away."*

What? He gave me a tentative smile, and I felt a big, sloppy, stupid one spreading across my own face. We looped the chorus a second time, grinning at each other as he changed the last lines:

> *"And I still know what we said,*
> *but we're not done till we're dead,*
> *so let's get back from away."*

I went into the second verse, but he let his arms drop, the book hanging loose from his fingers. "That's what I've got."

"It's amazing," I said honestly. "This is *all* amazing. *You're* amazing."

He blushed, and it was all I could do not to throw my guitar aside and tackle him.

He'd written me a love song. Maybe not the *happiest* love song, but that just made it better. It was a realist love song. We had a history, and it was sad and angry and messy. But now I was back, and he wasn't backing away. He was in this with me.

"It's good," he said, and I didn't know whether he meant the song or something bigger. "But is it enough?"

"It'll have to be." I set my guitar down on the carpet. "How soon do you think you can get us a showcase with your label?"

Chance looked startled. "Already?"

"We don't exactly have a lot of time, here. They're probably hiring your backing band as we speak."

Chance frowned. "I'll try."

"Don't just try." I stood and moved over to him, taking his hands. "It's Yoda Time, dude. This could change everything."

He looked away. "I know."

"Hey." I ducked down into his eyeline. "You've got this." I squeezed his hand. "*We've* got this. Together."

He searched my eyes, and slowly smiled. "Together."

I leaned forward and kissed him, my hands moving up along his arms. There was the briefest hesitation, and then he was kissing me back. I felt the tension flow out of him.

After a minute he pulled away, moving purposefully over to his laptop.

"All right," he said with new resolve. "Let's find a drum loop that works, at least for demoing."

"You think we need one?" Beats had always been Eli's domain, and I was honestly a little terrified of recording software.

"Yes, if the other option is you beatboxing." He gave me a look. "I don't think 'doot-doot-ksh' is gonna cut it."

I clutched my chest. "Whatchu talkin' 'bout? People love my doot-doot!"

He snorted, but couldn't keep a straight face. He sat down in the computer chair. I plopped down onto his lap.

"Augh! You're crushing me!"

"You love it." I wiggled.

"My mom could come in!"

"Your mom loves it too." I was punch-drunk and silly, high on the thrill of creation. "Everyone loves my majestic man-ass."

"Dude, get *up.*" He shoved me off, then gave me the chair and settled himself in my lap. "Let's at least stack by size."

"Fine by me." My hands went around his waist as naturally as if we always sat this way. The weight of him was intoxicating. I leaned forward and inhaled his scent as he pulled up GarageBand.

"Okay," he said, "stop me when there's one you like."

"Stop," I said, and bit his shoulder. "I like."

"Dork." He reached back and shoved my forehead, laughing. "Focus."

"Okay, yes. Focus." I got myself under control. "Let's do it. First, though, I need to know one thing."

"What?"

I slid a hand inside the waistband of his jeans and leaned close, my lips against his ear as I whispered:

"Baby, why you talkin' shit about my doot-doot?"

21

Despite our initial success, any possibility of continuing work on the song was interrupted the next day by Mrs. Ng, who announced that the whole family would be taking a surprise trip to Orcas Island for some Family Togetherness.

The idea of not seeing Chance for five days was physically painful, especially considering our tight timeline. But there was nothing to do but play it cool.

Chance was less sanguine.

She's got us all staying in a one-room cabin, he texted. I'm pretty sure this violates the Geneva Conventions.

Stay strong, I texted back. Don't let them break your spirit.

CHANCE:

Thank god for phones. I'm going to need you to text me constantly, k? Remind me what life's like on the outside.

Despite my disappointment, my heart warmed a little.

ME:

Don't worry, soldier. We will not forget your sacrifice.

And that seemed like that, until halfway through work the next day. I was prying nails out of old studs when my phone suddenly buzzed to life in a string of siren emojis.

> RED ALERT! THIS IS NOT A DRILL!
> WE HAVE A SITUATION.

I stripped off one of my heavy leather work gloves and replied.

ME:

What's up?

CHANCE:

> Mom has just declared that the island
> will be a Phone-Free Zone.

ME:

W H AT

CHANCE:

> I'm texting you from the ferry
> terminal. This will be my last
> transmission before The
> Great Silence.

ME:

Dude. Can you just sneak
away to use it?

CHANCE:

> No good. As soon as we board, the
> Reverend Mother will be locking all
> phones in the glove compartment.
> Including her own.

Mrs. Ng was nothing if not fair. And determined.

CHANCE:

I honestly don't know if I can poop without my phone.

ME:

Seriously!

CHANCE:

It just seems too stressful.

Sitting there in silence, with nothing to think about but the fact that you're dropping a deuce.

"Yup. Poop's coming out now. Gonna be a long one."

plop

ME:

I'm going to need you to stop painting this particular picture.

Speaking of which, what about photos? Doesn't she want pictures of Operation Family Funtimes?

How are you going to post pictures of yourself getting carried off by crabs, or whatever? What if you see Bigfoot?

CHANCE:

She just passed out disposable
cameras.

Our recreational options are
board games, reading paper books,
and staring at each other.

Or screaming into the uncaring void
of the sea. Pretty sure that's still
allowed.

ME:

Oooooof.

CHANCE:

But yeah. Disposable cameras.

Apparently it wasn't enough for
us to just go to an island. We
also have to go back to 1995.

I DO NOT DESIRE TO
EXPERIENCE THE DARK
AGES

ME:

The Land Before Memes.

CHANCE:

No texting. No Reddit. No Insta. NO
PORN.

MAN WAS NOT MADE TO
LIVE THIS WAY

ME:

Okay, true, but you're going
to be in a one-room cabin, right?
Could you actually whack off
knowing your whole family is right
outside the bathroom door?

CHANCE:

I don't know. BUT BY GOD,
MAN, I COULD TRY.

ME:

Such resilience. A triumph
of the spirit.

CHANCE:

I was counting on you to keep
me sane while I watch algae
grow.

ME:

I'll scramble an evac team.

CHANCE:

I wish.

Honestly, I think even Dad is
a little freaked by the phone
thing, but Mother Superior will
not be disobeyed.

The ferry's here. GTG.

ME:

Good luck, soldier.

> CHANCE:
>
> If I don't make it, tell everyone that
> I died as I lived: EXTREMELY
> ATTRACTIVELY.

ME:

And humble.

> CHANCE:
>
> Natch.
>
> Okay, GTG for real. I'm
> getting The Look.

And that was where it ended. For the next five days, I didn't get so much as an emoji.

It was weird: for two years I hadn't even spoken to him, and now a few days without him felt like losing my phone – always reaching unconsciously for something that wasn't there.

When I wasn't practicing guitar, I spent as much time as possible with Ridley, watching weird old movies or helping with covert party prep, which was in full swing. I'd driven us to her brother's apartment to make the booze handoff, then helped sneak it into the crawlspace beneath her porch, where there was now a Roman bacchanal's worth of cheap alcohol hidden behind bags of potting soil. Yet whatever I was doing, my silent phone nagged like the empty socket of a lost tooth.

I was down in the woodshop, working on my party costume,

when my phone finally chimed. I lunged for the workbench where I'd left it.

CHANCE:

Hello, internet.

ME:

YOU'RE BACK!

CHANCE:

Am I? How can I be sure?
WHAT YEAR IS IT?!

ME:

Did everyone make it out
of the Ng Family Octagon?

CHANCE:

Barely. Fortunately, the cabin
had a DVD player. Even Mom
was ODing on togetherness
by the end.

We just got off the ferry.
Driving home now.

The car is silent except for
notifications.

ME:

Well I hope you're rested,
because I'm taking you out
tonight.

CHANCE:

Tonight? We're not going to
get home until like 10.

ME:

Your point is . . . ?

CHANCE:

Oooooooh.

I don't know how my parents
will feel about us going out
that late. :\

ME:

It's called "sneaking out,"
homes. I hear it's a thing
among The Teens.

CHANCE:

Oh dip!

David Holcomb: Rebel.

I like it.

ME:

You'll like it even more once
you see what I've got planned. 🐱

CHANCE:

:-O

Is this a sext?

Are you sexting me right now?

Just text me when you get home.

Two hours later, I pulled up in front of Chance's house. He came darting out from behind the bushes, dressed all in black – what else was new? – with his hood up over his head. With the windows down, I could hear him whistling the *Mission: Impossible* theme.

"So stealthy," I said.

"I am the night." He threw himself inside and shut the door. "The package is secure! Go go go!"

"'The package is secure'? Now who's sexting?"

He leaned over and kissed me deeply, running a hand up into my hair. "Did you miss me?"

"Psht."

He closed his fist, tugging my scalp in a pleasure bordering on pain. "Admit it." He slid his cheek along mine, breathing directly into my ear. "I'm an earworm, Holc. No matter how annoying, you can't get me out of your head."

He wasn't wrong. I turned to show him.

Headlights jabbed through the rear window, lighting us up as a neighbor pulled in to park a few lengths behind. Chance sat back with a rueful grin and nodded toward the street.

I put the truck into gear. "How was Orcas?"

"False advertising. Not a single demon lord."

"What?" I looked over to where he'd leaned back against the window.

"If you name an island 'Orcus,' I expect to see the Demon Prince of the Undead."

The reference clicked. "Did you just make a Dungeons & Dragons pun?"

His Cheshire Cat grin widened. "Sorry. Couldn't help my elf."

"Oh my god. How are you this big of a dork?"

"It's a terrible hobbit, I know."

"I will pull this truck over."

"Whatever, you love my puns. You're goblin them up."

"Prepare to exit the vehicle."

He went quiet at last, and I risked another glance. "You're trying to think up more, aren't you?"

"Honestly, I think that's all I've got. It's been so long."

We both went quiet for a second, thinking of Eli. My dad had bought me a D&D starter box after seeing it on *Stranger Things*, and we'd spent two straight summers playing before the band took over our friendship. Eli had been the Dungeon Master, naturally.

But tonight wasn't about Eli. I shoved those thoughts aside. They *did* bring up the one question I had to ask, though. "Did you get a chance to talk to your label? About the audition?"

Chance's good mood faded. "Not yet. No phone, remember?"

"I know, I just thought maybe before you left. Or if you talked to them on the way home or something."

His shoulders hunched. "I said I'll do it, all right?"

"I know." I reached over and grabbed his thigh. "Sorry – no more band stuff. Tonight is just about us." I squeezed. "So back to the original question: Island life, yay or nay?"

Chance unclenched a little. "Eh, it was all right. Poked a lot of anemones. Played Codenames approximately a million times. Ate. *Mostly* ate, honestly – since Dad can't cook on the road, he went all out. We had salt duck, tangbao, squirrel fish . . ."

"*Squirrel* fish?"

"It's just fried fish, but squirrel-shaped. Kinda like a fish version of a blooming onion."

"Whoa." I tried to imagine it and failed.

"Yeah, so that part didn't suck. And it was good to get time to just chill with Mom and Livi." His tone turned ominous. "But in keeping with her Olde Timey Vacation theme, Mom decided we should rent bikes."

"Cool . . . ?" He was clearly getting at something, but I wasn't sure what.

"Perhaps you've noticed my penchant for well-fitting skinny jeans. Are you aware what said jeans do to one's anatomy on a bicycle?"

"Oooh." I winced. "RIP your balls. Thoughts and prayers."

"It was bad, dude. I didn't pack any shorts, because I was gonna take a vacation from working out, and because I refuse to be less sexy than absolutely necessary. You'd think that would have been the end of that, but Mom Führer had a solution."

"Oh no."

"Oh yes. I spent the entire vacation wearing shorts from the Beach, Please souvenir shop."

"Oh *no*."

"*Khaki* shorts. With whales on them."

I was laughing hard enough that I could barely keep the truck on the road.

"You might be thinking that sounds like a fashion disaster, but don't worry – they also had 'island time, mon' printed on the butt. Because apparently all islands are Jamaica. Or maybe all whales are Jamaican? The shorts were unclear."

"Oh my god! Stop before I kill us both!" I wheezed and clutched the steering wheel. "Also, you're required to wear them on our next date."

"You wish."

"I do. If we crash right now, I'm calling the Make-A-Wish Foundation and telling them that's what I want."

"Sorry, but said shorts are already at the bottom of a ferry terminal trash can. What happens on the island stays on the island."

We merged onto the I-90 bridge, once more traversing the dark plane of Lake Washington. Chance arched an eyebrow. "We going over the pass again?"

"Nope."

He watched me from across the cab. "You gonna tell me where?"

"Nope."

"Such mysterious. Wow." He looked out the window at the lights flashing past. "Feels like it's always night when we're together."

That hit somewhere deep in my chest. He was right – we might hang out in the sunlight, but being *together* was something else. Our romance was decidedly nocturnal. All at once I found myself longing again for the simplicity of the fake date he'd had with Ridley. To let ourselves be whatever it was we were, without a thought for who might be watching.

But what I said was "That's what I get for dating a vampire, huh?"

He gave a polite laugh. "I guess." He leaned his head against the glass. "Is that dumb? The whole vampire shtick?"

I could hear a question beneath the question, but not well enough to tell what he was actually asking. "It's served you well thus far," I ventured.

"Maybe." He tapped a knuckle slowly against the window. "It's just weird to still be trying to be the thing I imagined when I was twelve. I think sometimes we become our characters without realizing it."

"What do you mean?"

He shook his head, looking for words. "Like, sometimes I *feel* like a vampire. I spend all day locked away, only to come out at night and feed on the crowd. Their energy."

"Which is awesome . . . ?"

"I guess." But he didn't sound convinced.

I wasn't dumb. I could tell he was lonely. But that was half the point of me joining the band, right? So we could be vampires together.

Either way, tonight was not for introspection. I slapped his leg. "Cheer up, Dracula. Tonight is a no-brooding zone. Louie Armstrong, all right? Like back in the old days."

"Louie Armstrong," he repeated.

"I don't believe you. Louder!"

He smirked at my half-assed stage patter, but obligingly said it louder. "Louie Armstrong!"

I rolled down our windows, the air roaring in and whipping our hair around. I cupped my hand around my ear. "I'm sorry, what?!"

He put his whole upper body out the window, stretching out his arms to catch the wind, and we screamed together.

"Louie Armstrong!"

*

A short while later, I pulled through the unlocked gates of Lake Sammamish State Park. Out here in the suburbs, there were none of a city park's nighttime dog walkers or people sleeping in their cars – just a thousand empty parking spots lit by tall street-lights, plus the glittering reflection of the distant lake. I found a spot far from the handful of other vehicles and killed the engine. The sudden silence was deafening.

"Another park?" Chance asked.

"Hey, it worked last time." I undid my seat belt and turned toward him. "But we're not here for the park. I just needed somewhere big with nobody around."

"Oh, really?" He tried to play it cool, but his sudden stillness might as well have been a billboard betraying his excitement. In the sodium light, his face was orange and black. "And why is that?"

I leaned over the console, bracing my hands against his thigh, my face a foot from his. Pitching my voice low, I said, "Because I'm going to give you something none of your fancy Hollywood friends ever have."

His eyes went cartoonishly wide. His lips parted, right on the edge of speech, yet nothing came out.

This boy. Beloved of millions, a fantasy made flesh, yet he was speechless at the thought of what I might do to him in an empty parking lot. The incongruity only made it hotter. I let him soak in that anticipation, drinking it in.

Then I exploded with laughter, flopping back against my own door.

"Get your mind out of the gutter, heartthrob."

He blinked. "What?"

The only thing hotter than kissing Chance Kain was making him wait for it. Watching him want me.

I pulled out the keys and bounced them off his chest. "Driving lessons. I'm gonna teach you to work the other kind of stick."

He still looked like I'd hit him over the head with a bat, but his expression brightened. "Wait – really?"

I popped my door. "Come find out."

He bailed out of his side of the truck, and we swapped positions. In the driver's seat, he breathed heavily, caressing the wheel.

"Go ahead and start it," I said. "You'll need to push in the clutch – that's the pedal on the left. Keep your right foot on the brake."

He turned the key tentatively, and the truck rumbled to life.

"Okay, so, first off, you don't need to hold it like that." I reached over and pulled his right hand off the wheel. "That ten-and-two thing is bullshit. You're driving a truck, not a rally car. And you're gonna need this hand for shifting anyway." I drew it down to the knob of my gearshift. "Keep holding down the clutch. Same with the brake. Don't let up."

"All right."

"You're in neutral right now. Move it around. Feel how it waggles?"

He gave the stick the barest jiggle, as if afraid of waking it.

"That was a weak waggle, Ng. Nobody wants a weak waggle. Shake it like you mean it!"

That got the desired laugh. He relaxed a little, shaking the shifter with more confidence.

"Good. Now if we move left and up, that's first." I wrapped my hand over his, guiding it. "Then straight back down is second." I walked him through the gears a couple of times, then had him take off the parking brake. "We're gonna try shifting into first. Remember: If something doesn't work, push in the clutch so it doesn't die. Okay?"

"Okay." He had the steel-jawed concentration of a fighter pilot. It was a good look on him.

"Now give it some gas – not a lot, just enough to hold it at, like, fifteen hundred RPMs. Get a sense of what that sounds like."

The engine growled.

"Okay, now we shift up into first." I moved his hand. "*Without* changing how much gas you're giving it, *slowly* pull your foot off the clutch. Ready?"

"Ready," he said.

"Do it."

The truck lurched and died.

"Sorry!" He looked panicked. "Sorry!"

"It's cool, dude." I shifted us back to neutral. "Ready to try again?"

"Sure."

I could feel the tendons in the back of his hand standing out beneath my palm on the shifter. I squeezed. "Hey. Look at me." I gave my most reassuring smile. "It's fine. I promise."

He smiled unsteadily back and stretched his fingers out between mine, weaving us together.

He started the engine again. Another jerk forward, another premature death.

"Fucking hell!" He smacked the wheel in frustration. "This is a lot easier in *Gran Turismo*."

"It's just muscle memory. You gotta feel it."

"I *feel* like I'm wrecking your truck."

In fact, the cab *was* starting to smell like burnt clutch. But I said, "This truck has seen worse, trust me. Just try again."

He took a deep breath and started the engine.

I squeezed his hand. "Slowly . . ."

The engine changed pitch as the clutch caught. We began to roll.

"It's working!" Chance shook with excitement.

"Okay, that's the hard part." The engine noise rose. "Now do the same thing again – push in the clutch, but this time pull straight back into second. Also, steer."

He did, and the truck rolled smoothly across the parking lot, Chance swerving into empty spaces to avoid the speed bumps.

"Holy shit." Chance laughed with delight. "I'm driving stick!"

"Facts. Now shift back into neutral, stop, and let's do it again."

We repeated the process, over and over, and if Chance didn't exactly get smooth, he at least managed to quit stalling it. Pretty soon he didn't need my guidance at all, and I let myself sit back and watch him.

He practiced with that same quiet intensity he brought to music – not to the performance, but to the writing. No pageantry, no grandstanding, just an all-consuming focus. To watch him with all the excess stripped away – to see him in what I think, deep down, was his natural state – made him feel somehow more real. Closer. I watched the growing confidence with which he shifted, moving authoritatively through the gears, and despite the fact that I'd been the one showing him how a moment ago – the fact that it was *my friggin' truck* – it still sent a shiver through me. I wanted this part of him. This quiet authority. It made me think of that night in my room, the confidence with which he'd moved my body. How good it felt to stop thinking so hard for once. To just lie back and let him drive.

When we'd circled the parking lot for the thousandth time, he pulled back into our original spot and parked.

"Feeling good?" I asked.

"Yeah." His voice was soft, a little awed. He turned, and the lighthouse of his attention rotated onto me. I could feel it on my skin, the heat of his regard catching every hair and pore. My breath seized.

"Thank you." He reached out and grabbed my hand.

The look in his eyes was everything. Admiration. Adoration. Appreciation. On down through the alphabet, a complete glossary of everything one David Holcomb constantly looked for and rarely found. I squirmed happily beneath it, making a half-hearted grab for humility. "It's no big deal."

"Yes it is." His eyes didn't leave mine. I was the one who'd won *him* over, yet somehow now he was the hunter.

His hand slid upward, rising to cup my cheek. "I love—"

My heart lurched like a dying engine.

". . . that you would do this for me," he finished.

My heart snapped back, whipping around into my other organs.

Of course. Had I really thought he was about to say something else? Did I even *want* him to? Wasn't it too soon to be throwing around the word "love"?

But also . . . had he hesitated after that word? Just a little?

I gripped the back of his hand, holding his palm against my face. His knuckles were smooth against my calluses.

"I wanted to," I said simply.

He smiled. Another blast from the lighthouse, guiding me home.

"You know," he observed, "for somebody who tries so hard to be cool and detached, you're pretty good at this sweet-boyfriend thing."

"Yeah, well." It wasn't much of a comeback. I didn't care.

He watched me a moment longer, then laughed. "God, look at us!" He shook his head. "Who'd have thought we'd end up here? Chance and Holc."

"Not me," I answered honestly.

"It's dumb that we spent all those years hanging out, and never had any idea. Yet now that everything's complicated, I just want to spend all my time with you."

I squeezed his hand fiercely. "So do."

"Okay." He leaned forward and kissed me. The seat belt socket dug into my hip as we pressed together, our legs still twisted behind us by the central barricade of the transmission. He hadn't shaved on vacation, and there was the faintest sandpaper stripe across his upper lip. I rubbed my face against it like a cat, feeling the burn across my lips and cheek.

When we broke apart a minute later, he reached up to hide a yawn.

"Wow," I joked. "That good, huh?"

He laughed. "Not commentary, I swear. We just got up early to hike before the ferry."

"Does that mean I should get you home?"

"No." He darted in for a snakebite kiss. "And probably." But he made no move to vacate the driver's seat. "But not until I know when I get to see you again. Tomorrow?"

His eagerness made me smile. "I promised Ridley we'd do our final SAT study session tomorrow. What about Thursday?"

"Can't. I promised Benjamin I'd do this twenty-four-hour charity streaming thing. But I'm open Friday! Or Saturday?"

My stomach sank. This was getting ridiculous. "Saturday is the SATs. Dad's got a special dinner planned Friday night – no way he'll let me go out afterward, before the test. And Saturday night is Ridley's party."

"Oh, right." He frowned. "I've gotta fly to D.C. on Sunday. I'm doing guest vocals on Aventine's new record."

"Jesus." The thought of losing him to the road again so soon was unbearable.

But maybe there was another option. "You should come to the party with me."

He shifted uncomfortably. "I told you, I don't like parties."

"That's not true. That first night we went to Orbital, you said you go to parties all the time."

"Yeah, but . . ." He trailed off, but we both knew what he meant: that those parties were full of other celebrities. He just didn't like parties with *normal* people. Despite the fact that I hadn't forgotten the way he'd been mobbed in public, something inside me still bristled at the idea that my friends weren't good enough for him. That *I* wasn't good enough.

I stomped the emotion down and reached out, hooking my pinkie though his. "Dude, don't worry. It's not the general public, just some of Ridley's and my friends. You already know half of them. Everybody will be cool."

He squirmed, but didn't pull away. "You say that, but it can still get weird. Even with people I used to know."

"So?" I shook his hand gently. "Life is risk. Take a chance, Chance."

He frowned. "Like I've never heard that one before."

"Then stop being a wuss. If you can perform for twenty thousand people, you can get drunk with twenty of them."

He jerked free of my grip, and I could tell I'd pushed too hard. "Why do you even care?" he snapped.

Well. If *that* was how it was going to be . . .

"Why do you *think* I care?" I shoved his knee, not gently. "Because I *like* you, dumbass!" The words tumbled out without thought. "I want to be around you! But you're always gone." His mouth opened, but I cut him off with a raised hand. "And yes, I know, that's the job. And if I can join the band and come be part of your world, great. But I need you to be part of *my* world, too. I want you to know my friends. I want you to be able to hang out around my dad. I want us to be an *us.*" I felt suddenly, dangerously close to tears and turned away, looking out at the darkened parking lot.

I could feel his eyes on me. What would I see in them if I looked? Judgment? Resentment? Pity? Emotion reached down my throat like smoke, choking off my voice and gripping with burning claws.

When he finally spoke, his voice was soft.

"I want that, too."

The pressure in my lungs eased, but I was still too raw to contain all the acid. "Do you?"

"I think so?" I looked over and saw him giving that half smile – the real one, not the camera-dazzler.

I snorted. "That's not much of an answer."

"But it's honest." Now it was his turn to reach out. "Come on, Holc. I'm trying." He touched my shoulder, thumb resting in the hollow of my collarbone. "And if it means that much to you . . . I'll come to the party."

"Yeah?" The tension inside me was a cartoon rope holding an anvil, fraying down to the final thread.

The edges of his eyes clenched, mouth tightening as he nodded.

"Yeah."

The thread snapped, and suddenly I was falling – falling helplessly for this boy who would do something he clearly didn't want to, for me. A boy who, when push came to shove, refused to leave me behind.

I launched myself at him, knocking him back into the door as my mouth found his, my hands clutching at his biceps, his shoulders. He grunted as his head bonked against the window, but it didn't stop him from kissing me back. His hands wormed beneath my shirt, drawing cool lines up my sides. I returned the favor, grabbing eagerly, wanting more – to hold him, claim him. Because he *was* mine. Just mine.

He laughed as my kisses moved down his neck. "Jesus." In that laugh was the wobbly relief of having narrowly avoided a car crash. "You don't make things easy, do you?"

I tugged at the zipper of his hoodie, yanking his T-shirt collar wide to bare more skin. "Would you even like me if I did?"

"I guess we'll never know. I – *ah.*" He gasped as my fingers slid down over the ax-blade ridge of his hip and into the waistband of his jeans. Only an inch, but I could feel his whole body tighten, abs going taut with desire.

No, not desire – *need*. I pulled back to watch his face. Naked. Vulnerable. Watching me as if I were the only thing in the world that mattered. As if he were Saint Walpurga, and I was his divine revelation.

Chance *needed* me.

I reached down and popped the button on his jeans.

"Remember how I told you to get your mind out of the gutter?"

His eyes were bright against the dark. "Yeah?"

"You can put it back now."

I shoved him back against the seat and bent down.

22

In books and movies, there's always a sharp line around someone losing their virginity. One day you're a kid, then somebody puts something somewhere, and presto – adulthood!

This wasn't like that. There were no angels trumpeting, no funky theme music following me around. The David who'd woken up alone in my bed the next day was the same awkward, horny, vaguely sweaty dude he'd been the day before.

Then again, maybe nothing had changed because I hadn't really lost my virginity. What did it even mean to be a virgin in my case? With straight couples, the rules were clear: Blow jobs don't count. By that logic, Chance and I were still virgins. Did that mean we had to go full anal to lose our virginity? I wasn't sure how I felt about that. And even then, everyone had heard about religious kids having anal sex in order to save their virginity for marriage – the so-called poophole loophole. If that sort of technicality was good by Jesus, then was it even *possible* for me and Chance to lose our virginity? I was definitely *less* of a virgin now that Chance and I had gone down on each other, but that had been true when we hooked up in my bed, too. Where was the line?

It was the sort of topic pretty much made for Ridley – sex facts and having opinions being two of her favorite things – but I didn't dare broach it, even as a hypothetical. She'd take one look at my face and it would be all over. I didn't have any other friends close enough to talk about it with, and while Denny was no doubt qualified, I wasn't about to start talking sex with my dad's friends.

What I *really* wanted was to talk about it with Chance. We hadn't really dug into the philosophical ramifications on the ride home, just laughed and held hands and let the moment linger. Dissecting it this way seemed profoundly unromantic, and the last thing I wanted was to give him the impression I was having regrets. In our texts since then, neither of us had mentioned it directly. The closest I'd come had been the next morning:

ME:

I had a good time last night.

CHANCE:

You'd better have!

. . . and then we'd gone right back to our normal banter.

Maybe it was cowardice on my part. I remembered one of the maxims from middle school health class: *If you're not ready to talk about sex, you're not ready to have it.* But at the same time, maybe it was better to just be chill. Certainly I was *happy* we'd done it – was, in fact, thinking approximately thirty-seven times per minute about when we'd get to do it again. So like Denny had said, maybe the labels didn't matter.

These were the thoughts going through my head as I pulled up to Ridley's house at the ass-crack of dawn Saturday morning. She came running out, garage door closing behind her. She flung her messenger bag into the tiny back seat and climbed in, handing me a travel mug of hot bean juice.

"*Woooooo!* Test day! Get hype!"

I winced at her early-morning enthusiasm. "How much coffee have you had?"

"All of it!" She grabbed my shoulders and shook me back and forth. "*Alllllll offffff ittttttt!*"

"Uh .."

"Relax. I'm kidding." She sat back. "You're talking to the queen of standardized testing. I had one cup – the rest is in the fridge, so I can make White Russians tonight. This one's for you."

"Thanks."

She cocked her head. "You okay?"

I forced away thoughts of Chance. "Yeah. Just anxious."

"Don't be. We are gonna rock the *shit* out of this. The graders are gonna be screaming our names." She synched her phone to the truck's stereo and began blasting Queen's "Don't Stop Me Now."

"Montage music! We ride to victory!" She pointed ahead. "Onward to glory, noble steed!"

"Neigh." I sipped my coffee and pulled out into traffic.

The SAT itself was surprisingly anticlimactic. It turns out that when you don't actually have anything riding on a test, it's no big deal. While everyone else was sweating through their pajama pants, terrified each question was going to be the one that kept them out of Harvard, I was just sitting in a school gym filling in bubbles. The biggest test of my life was as low-key as an internet personality quiz.

Ridley, of course, was in her element. Talking was technically allowed during breaks, but the proctors had been so strident

257

in their warnings not to discuss anything test-related that it seemed safer to just stay quiet. That was fine – I could tell Ridley was in the zone, her whole body loose, eyes unfocused in a way that said she was living entirely inside her head. An academic Olympian preparing for her event.

That lasted until precisely ten seconds after the test finished. As we exited out the front doors, she screamed and leaped onto my back, nearly sending us both tumbling down the concrete stairs.

"Did you see that?" She shouted directly into my ear, punctuating each word with a punch to my shoulder. "Did! You! See! *That?!*"

I staggered off the walkway and onto the safety of the grass. "So better this time?"

"I am like unto a standardized-testing *god*!" She took the hint and dismounted, dancing around like a boxer before a match. "The math sections this time were *nothing*. I *Good Will Hunting*'d that shit."

I racked my brain for the appropriate reference. "You're the man now, dog?"

Ridley stopped prancing and gaped in horror. "Those are *not* the same movie."

"Are you sure?"

She crossed her arms and scowled. "Okay, yes, *Good Will Hunting* and *Finding Forrester* both have the same basic premise. And the same director, actually. But Sean Connery was a misogynist douche-basket, and Robin Williams was a Muppet angel sent directly from Heaven."

"I stand corrected."

"You're absolved." She hugged me again, jumping up and

down and forcing me to bounce with her. "And now we are going to get *messed up*. It's time to remove *all* these extra brain cells."

We drove back to her house, blasting "We Are the Champions." We still had hours left before the party, and prep at this point mainly consisted of raiding the Safeway for snacks and mixers, plus helping Ridley choose which teen party films she'd be screening in the background.

"Okay, so, we've got *Booksmart* for the modern day and *House Party* for the classic." Ridley poked at her spreadsheet, because of course she had a spreadsheet. "*Ten Things I Hate About You* fits perfectly in the middle, but I'm wondering if that means I should leave out *Can't Hardly Wait*. I don't want to overrepresent the late nineties. But also, between those and the bro-tacular disaster that is *American Pie*, 1999 was basically the height of the teen party movie." She looked to me, conflicted. "So maybe it would be disingenuous *not* to weight toward that era?"

I lay on the couch bouncing one of Artoo's chew toys off the ceiling. "Ridley. It's a party, not a film festival. Are people even gonna watch them?"

Despite having asked a question, she didn't appear to be listening. She chewed her lip. "You know, I wonder if there's a reason why the late nineties had so many big hedonistic teen movies. Like, maybe something about still being close to the misogynistic sex comedies of the eighties, but with the whole Y2K atmosphere giving people the sense that *something* was about to change. Hence all these movies having that frantic, last-night-on-earth kind of feel . . ."

I could see the blog post coming, so I excused myself and headed out. When Ridley got rolling on a film theory, it was best to get out of the way and let her write it down, otherwise she'd just keep dictating versions to you.

Dad met me at the door as I got home. "How'd it go?"

I shrugged. "Good. No big deal."

"Well, that's great!" He seemed determined to express the enthusiasm I wasn't. "You want to do anything to celebrate? Go get a burger or something?"

Things had been strained between us ever since I'd told him about possibly rejoining Darkhearts. His initial resistance had become cautious enthusiasm, and I'd caught him a couple of times looking thoughtfully around at the house, no doubt thinking about all the things he'd remodel if we could afford it. At the same time, he was clearly trying not to let it show, lest he put too much pressure on me. The result was an awkward artificial cheerfulness, like a waiter forced to sing birthday songs to strangers.

It was exhausting, and I attempted to spare us both as often as possible.

"I actually need to finish up my costume," I said. "I've got Ridley's party tonight."

"Right, the movie party! Of course." He patted my shoulder. "Well, you've certainly earned it."

"Thanks." I took the out and ditched my bag, escaping down to the shop.

The party started at seven, but while I didn't have a ton of party experience, I knew that being the first one there wasn't cool. As soon as we stepped through Ridley's door, I wanted Chance to encounter a Hollywood-worthy party, already in full swing. So at seven forty-five, I parked at his house and buzzed the gate.

Chance's mom met me at the door. "Hey, David!"

"Hey, Mrs. Ng." Her outfit today was brown cords and a slim plaid button-up that was at once eerily similar to my own style and a million times more flattering. For the first time, I noticed just how much Mrs. Ng's hotness was a feminine reflection of Chance's own: the same swimmer's shoulders and narrow hips, same bright eyes and perfect teeth.

I realized I'd missed a question. "Sorry?"

"I said I heard you just took the SAT. Feeling good about it?"

"Oh, yeah." I shrugged again, already tired of the subject. "It was fine."

"Good! Maybe you can convince Chance to actually study for his." Her eyes flicked to the stairs, which were still empty. "So. You two are going to a party?"

"Yeah. My friend Ridley's."

"Where her parents will be present and chaperoning, I'm sure."

"Uh." The worst possible answer, but what else can a mouse say when the owl's shadow falls over him?

Fortunately, she smiled – that same little sideways smirk Chance put to such good use. "Relax, David. I don't want to know any more. Parenting is all about feigning ignorance." Her eyes narrowed the tiniest fraction. "But I want *you* to know that, should you even *smell* alcohol at this party, I expect you to let Chance call you both an Uber afterward. If I suspect that you drove after ingesting any illegal substances, I will personally skin you like a deer, then use your flayed hide to strangle my son. Are we clear?"

"Absolutely."

She grinned. "I knew I could count on you." A door shut upstairs. "And here's Mr. Show Business now."

"Hey, sorry! I'm ready."

I looked up as Chance came thundering down the stairs, and my breath caught in my lungs.

He was dressed as The Bride from *Kill Bill:* neon-yellow motorcycle gear, with black racing stripes up the sides. It fit him like a glove, hugging every line and making him look as sleek and dangerous as Uma Thurman herself.

"Wow," I breathed.

"Right?" He gestured self-consciously at the outfit. "Thank god for same-day shipping." He nodded toward me. "Nice Captain America. You can totally rock the Chris Evans thing."

I most certainly could not, but I appreciated him saying it. All I was wearing was blue jeans, a shirt I already owned with the star-and-bars pattern from *Winter Soldier,* and a couple of brown dress belts looped around my waist and shoulders. "Thanks. The rest is in the truck."

"Pictures!" Mrs. Ng had her phone out, motioning for us to stand next to each other.

Chance raised a hand automatically, turning away from the camera. "Mom, come on."

"Chill out, rock star. If I wanted to sell you out to the tabloids, I've got far more embarrassing pictures. This is strictly the parent tax. Mom-and-pop-arazzi."

"Good one, Mrs. Ng."

She gestured at me. "See? David knows how to humor your mother. Now get closer."

Chance moved over to me, and I put an arm around his shoulders in what hopefully looked more like bromance than romance. Under my fingers, the jacket that looked like leather was clearly some artificial fabric.

Mrs. Ng pinched and zoomed, framing the shot. "Say 'I make good decisions and accept the responsibility inherent in my own mortality'!"

"Jesus, Mom!"

The phone made shutter noises. "Perfect." She put it back in her pocket. "Have fun, you two."

As we walked up the driveway, I couldn't help but think about that penetrating gaze. "Does she know?" I murmured to Chance. "About us?"

"No." He considered. "At least, not for sure. But even if she does, don't worry. She'd be into it."

"You think?" My chest ached. I imagined what it would be like to be totally open at Chance's house. Having dinner with his family. Lying on their couch with my head on his shoulder.

"Dude. She loves you."

I knew that had been true at one point. The idea of it maybe being true again was dangerously appealing. I felt like I was dangling over the edge of a cliff.

We reached the truck, and Chance opened his door. "Whoa!"

I got in on my side. "Sorry, you can throw that in the back."

But Chance didn't. Instead, he held the wooden shield in his lap, tracing its lines with his fingertips. "Dude. You made this?"

"Yeah." I'd built the shield out of plywood, stacking and gluing concentric rings, then sanded the bejeezus out of them to blend it all together. Even having used the cheapest materials, it had still looked nice enough that I couldn't bring myself to paint it, instead staining sections warm or cool, so they implied the Captain America colors without obscuring the grain. "I think it turned out all right."

263

"It's incredible." He placed it carefully in the back seat. "Do you have any idea how talented you are?" Suddenly he was halfway in my seat, kissing me so hard I could feel the curves of his teeth through his lips. "And how *fucking* hot that is?"

"Down, boy." But I was breathing fast, too. "We've got a party to get to."

"Right. Yeah." He sat back with a grimace. "Party. Woo."

I put a hand on his thigh. "It'll be fun, I promise."

"If you say so," he grumbled. But he took my hand.

23

We drove to Ridley's, where the street out front was already parked up. We found a spot two blocks away, and I squeezed Chance's hand. "Ready?"

He took a deep breath and let it out slowly. "Okay. Let's do it."

I grabbed my shield, slipping my hand through the strap I'd made from an old T-shirt and gripping the wooden handle. As we walked, I fought the urge to take Chance's hand again. Everything about this night – cool and crisp, the two of us walking side by side to a party – seemed so perfect that to have to cram that urge back down felt gross. Like plunging a clogged toilet. An ungenerous part of me hoped that Chance was suffering from it just as much. Hadn't he just been all over me in the truck?

But rules were rules, and holding hands in public was a nonstarter. Instead, I led him up the front steps and hit the doorbell. Through the wall, I could hear bass thumping.

The door swung open, revealing Ridley in sunglasses and a long pink bathrobe over shorts and a T-shirt.

"*DUDE!*" Her oversize glasses nearly tumbled off as she gaped at Chance. "Chance! David didn't tell me you were coming! Your costume is *amazing*!"

"Thanks!" Chance's smile was wide and easy, without a hint of the tension from the truck. "So's yours."

"You recognize it?" Ridley beamed with satisfaction.

"Of course!"

She waited expectantly.

". . . Okay, no actually," Chance admitted.

"I'm The Dude!" Ridley raised a glass containing the murky cloud of a White Russian. "The Big Lebowski!"

"Ohhhh, of course," Chance said – generously, in my opinion.

"It's not your fault," I told him. "Ridley only likes movies made before we were born. Especially overrated ones."

"Great art knows no age," Ridley intoned primly. "And also, that's just, like, your opinion, man." She turned and looked me up and down approvingly. "O Captain, my captain! Nice shield, Davey-boy." She stepped aside. "Come in!"

We kicked off our shoes, adding them to an already sprawling mountain in the entryway.

Inside were maybe twenty people, forming two distinct knots. Knot One, gathered in the kitchen, was Ridley's friends from Garfield, her old school. Knot Two contained folks from our school, lounging in the living room watching a teen movie with subtitles.

Despite the obvious division, Ridley's insistence on costumes had clearly paid off. There was a Hermione in wizard robes, a dude in an owl kigurumi and another in a frog one, and a big football-player type from Garfield who made an amazing Terminator, complete with glowing LED eyepiece. Ariel Brady was dressed as her mermaid namesake, snagging everyone's attention with her overflowing seashells. Even folks who looked normal might have been dressed as characters from movies I didn't know. For instance, I was at least seventy percent sure Samira Gupta was rocking a sexy Dora the Explorer look, which was all *sorts* of inappropriate.

But the point was, it was working. The costumes gave people

from different cliques something to talk about, and already there were scouts moving between the two groups, boldly exploring the fertile dating possibilities of a different school.

"Hey, everybody!" Ridley announced. "Look who's here!"

Maybe surprising Ridley with Chance hadn't been the best idea after all. If I'd told her in advance, I could have asked her to play it cool.

Instead, every face turned toward us.

To their credit, most folks were decent about it. They didn't rush us in a mob, tearing Chance apart like medieval peasants ripping relics from a saint's corpse. But recognition lit up half the partiers, who immediately began murmuring to the rest. A couple of phones popped up, snapping photos.

"You guys want a drink?" Ridley asked.

"Please." From the outside, Chance looked totally loose, a slight relief in his tone the only acknowledgment of the room full of eyes.

We followed Ridley into the kitchen, where bottles and cans were lined up along the counter. Football Terminator – whose name turned out to be Jerome – gave me a nod as he moved over to make room, which felt unexpectedly nice.

"What can I get you?" Ridley gestured grandly. "We've got White Claw, White Russians, trashbag mimosas—"

"What's a trashbag mimosa?" Chance asked.

"Like a regular mimosa, but instead of champagne, it's the cheapest white wine the U District Safeway has to offer." She patted the wine's cardboard box affectionately.

"Works for me," I said.

Chance took a White Russian, maybe just to humor Ridley. As with that first lunch at Bamf Burger, I saw him tuck some cash into the donation jar when nobody was looking. This time, however, the gesture triggered a rush of pride. My boyfriend was generous. Which, in a way, was almost like *me* being generous.

The Martinez twins waved from a couch. When Chance made no move, seemingly waiting to see what I'd do, I steered us over, taking a seat on the coffee table.

"Hey, Chance! Long time, no see." Gabe was dressed as Thor, while Angela had the red fangs of Princess Mononoke's tattoos running down their cheeks. Gabe pursed his lips approvingly. "Damn, David. Nice shield."

"Thanks." I nodded back at his cardboard hammer. "Nice hammer." It really was, too. Gabe was an artist, and he'd glued layers of cardboard together in a way that was less cutout and more corrugated sculpture.

"I work with what I got. And what I got is stacks of Amazon boxes." He handed it over and let me heft it. I traded him my shield. "Damn," he said again. "This thing is heavy."

I swapped him back. "Maybe *I* should have used cardboard. Your hammer weighs nothing."

"Guess it finds you worthy," Chance said. "Just like the real Captain America."

"Bruh!" Angela gave him a mock glare. "*Spoilers!*"

Ridley appeared at Chance's side, squeezing onto the table next to him. "And here I was coming to introduce you all. Looks like I'm not needed."

Angela laughed. "We were friends with Chance before you even moved here, Riddles. We used to go to all the shows."

"Yeah, us *real* fans loved you *before* you were good." Gabe bopped Chance's knee with the hammer. "How ya been, man? We haven't seen you since the funeral."

Chance rubbed the back of his neck. "Yeah, I've been traveling a lot."

That surprised me. It had somehow never occurred to me to wonder if Chance was talking with anyone else from our old group – it had felt like we were our own little world. Yet of course I wouldn't be the entirety of his social life. Except now it sounded like maybe I was ...?

"Yeah, us too," Gabe said. "In any case, you should come around sometime. We'll take you boarding!"

"You too, Holcomb." Angela gave me a look. "You can't *always* be working."

"I can, actually, if you only go on weekdays."

Angela shrugged, completely comfortable with their jobless indolence. "Fewer people on the water during the workday. Gotta get that glass."

"You still painting?" Chance asked Gabe.

"Yeah, dude! Mr. Hennessy the art teacher has been helping me apply for city grants. I got to do a big mural down on Rainier."

"Wow, nice! I'll have to check it out."

"I've actually got some pictures on my Insta. Hold on, lemme find 'em ..."

I could see Chance starting to relax, which was nice. But I was still trying to process the earlier exchange. Had he really been avoiding all his old friends except me? It was flattering, but also confusing. I remembered what he'd said about things not always going well, even with folks he knew. But if he was that scared of weirdness, why would he have been so eager to spend time with *me*, the one person guaranteed to be weird around him?

Ridley interjected herself. "Before you get too deep into show-and-tell, I want Chance to meet everybody." She grabbed Chance's arm – a little too possessively, in my opinion. "I'll bring him back, I promise."

"Sure, Riddles." Angela smiled suggestively, and I realized suddenly that everyone must have seen Ridley's photos of their staged date.

Which made Ridley's hand on Chance's arm *definitely* too possessive. I stood up and tagged along.

At each new introduction, Chance did his meet-and-greet bit: relaxed and charming, with just enough unattainable distance to leave you wanting more. Now that I knew what to look for, it was fascinating to watch him play chameleon, predicting what each person would want. He'd gossip with one person, bro down with the next, and give the third the classic brooding vampire. It was like watching someone do impressions, the way he could change the tiniest thing about his voice or posture and become someone else. In three minutes he'd win someone over, pose for their selfie, then move on to the next.

My gut was a roiling cloud of emotions: pride and jealousy at his easy charm, resentment of Ridley for monopolizing his time and making me a third wheel. To be fair, she *did* introduce me as well, to the folks I didn't know. But it was clear who everyone was interested in.

I found myself thankful for my mimosa, which was both filling me with warm fuzz and giving me something to do. The orange juice mostly masked the wine, leaving me with something that tasted slightly fermented, like a juice box left out in the sun. Sipping instead of talking meant it vanished quickly, and I took the opportunity to grab a refill.

Once Chance had been paraded around, Ridley pressured us into helping her start a party-wide game of strip Twister. After all, who could say no when Chance Kain was playing? I could tell Chance was uncomfortable, but too polite to refuse.

While the game didn't result in any full frontal, it did succeed in catalyzing the party spirit. Never mind that the people stripped down to their underwear weren't wearing any less than they would at the beach – in the shifted context, it felt wild and risqué. By the time Ridley finally allowed Chance to retire victorious, having lost only his jacket, I was shirtless and Ridley was down to Wonder Woman underpants and a matching tank.

I was apparently more buzzed than I realized, because I barely even felt myself following Chance to the couch. I floated along like a kite – one he was reeling in without realizing it.

He was just so handsome. So elegant as he flopped down beside Gabe and Angela. His expression was carefully agreeable, but I could see that familiar tightness around his eyes and mouth, and wanted nothing more than to kiss it away.

I squeezed in next to him – or at least attempted to. It was decidedly *not* a four-butt couch, especially not when one of them was mine. I ended up halfway in Chance's lap, arm extended across his shoulders for balance. Which was perfectly fine by me.

"Bruh!" Chance squirmed out from under me. He forced a laugh as he moved up to perch on the couch's back, leaving Angela as a buffer between us. He smirked conspiratorially at the twins. "Looks like Holc gets cuddly when he's drunk. That's new."

Gabe cocked his head sideways and grinned at me. "You turnt already, Holcomb?"

Over his shoulder, Chance was still smiling, but the message in his eyes was unmistakable. *Stop blowing our cover.*

Right, of course. What had I been thinking? *Had* I been thinking? It hadn't really been a decision, just a reflex. But of course it was too risky.

Gabe was still looking at me, curious.

"Ha, yeah, guess I'm pretty lit." I made myself grin. "But that's the point, right?"

"Facts." Gabe handed me a White Claw, and we clinked cans.

I changed the subject, asking Angela about their new boat, and tried not to be hurt at the way Chance kept all his focus on the twins. It wasn't a reflection on me, I reminded myself. It was just necessity. But that didn't make it sting any less.

Across the living room, Ridley leaped up onto the arm of the other couch.

"Let the wild rumpus commence!" She brandished her phone, cranking the stereo volume. "Dance party: activate!"

Lady Gaga thundered through the living room. Ridley charged over to us – or rather, to one of us.

"You wanna dance?" She held a hand out toward Chance.

Before I could even register my disappointment, the two of them were out on the floor, in the center of a rapidly accreting mob. I watched them go.

"Dude," Angela said. "Are you gonna stare like a sad puppy, or are you gonna get out there with them?"

I jerked, panicking that I was so obvious, then saw Angela was talking to Gabe, who looked equally sheepish.

"Wait," I asked, making the connection. "*Ridley?*"

Angela rolled their eyes. "Boy's got it *bad.*" They grabbed us both by the arms, yanking us up off the couch. "Get out there and dance with her, you coward. You too, Holc."

I barely had time to set my drink down before we were crammed into the middle of the dance party.

The modest size of Ridley's living room meant that even though there weren't really that many people, it *felt* like a club. It had that same mosh-pit energy of people moving close together, the starburst nerve flares of accidental contact. Angela put their arms up and wriggled like an eel at a rave.

"Dance, Holcomb!" They bumped a hip against mine, then kicked their foot up behind us, planting the heel firmly in my ass. "Shake that moneymaker!"

I'd always told myself I was built to make music, not dance to it. Where Angela's spine appeared made out of Jell-O, my body felt like dried-up old clay – a solid, unworkable lump. Yet the observation that most of the people around me weren't any better – and that Angela would absolutely continue kicking me – got me moving.

I bobbed to the beat, bouncing my shoulders up and down. Anything I did with my hands felt stupid, but leaving them at my sides was clearly the worse option, so I settled for raising and lowering them in a vague *whatup?* gesture. The combination probably looked like I was repeatedly shrugging, as though saying, *I, too, have no idea what this is supposed to be.*

It was dancing only in the sense that Russian circus bears can be said to be dancing. Yet as I lurched and huffed my way through Ridley's impeccable playlist, the energy in the room and the liquid courage in my veins began to enact a transformation. Sure, I looked stupid – but so did a bunch of us. While some of the guys in the group could move, many were presenting their own takes on my brand of flailing. Jerome the Football Robot was jumping straight up and down, hard enough to vibrate the hardwood floor. Vinh Tran was either attempting to juggle an invisible energy ball or preparing to hadouken somebody. A skinny dude named Andy might actually have been having a seizure. For all my anxiety, I was solidly in the middle of the pack.

With that realization came a sudden rush of solidarity. I was here with my people, the Shitty Dance Gang, and together we were untouchable. I began jumping up and down next to Jerome, and in that moment he wasn't some stranger from another school, but a brother in arms. He whooped and chest-bumped me.

BTS's "Dynamite" came on, and folks spread out to let Vinh attempt the worm, which came out more like a dying fish but earned cheers anyway. Across the circle from me, Chance danced in place with small, rhythmic movements, like the ready stance in a fighting game. He made it look so natural: the tilt of a hand, the gliding of a foot – tiny motions that added up to a mesmerizing sense of *flow*.

He caught my eye and smiled, his first real one since we arrived.

Ridley bounced over to us as the circle dissolved into chaos once more. "You guys having fun?"

"Totally!" Even over the blasting music, Gabe's response was a little too loud.

"You throw a good party, Riddles." Angela shimmied aggressively in Ridley's direction, provoking Ridley to respond in kind, and the rest of the world faded temporarily as my peripheral vision strained to focus on jiggling cleavage without looking directly at it.

When the two of them switched to less debilitating moves, I glanced around for Chance ...

... and found him across the room, pinned against the sliding glass doors by an aggressively grinding Natalie Chambers, a whippet-thin cross-country runner half dressed as Harley Quinn. His expression was the sort of polite tolerance you might use as a friend's dog made love to your ankle.

Ridley crossed her arms, glaring at the scene. "Remind me why I had to invite her again?"

Angela shrugged. "Because I want to eat her ass like an apple?"

"She's straight, Ange."

"Everyone's straight till they ain't."

Angela had no idea how appropriate that was in this case, but Ridley remained unmoved. "Somebody should rescue him before she gives that jumpsuit chlamydia."

"On it!" Gabe ran a hand over his long black hair, then puffed his chest out and bulled through the crowd. As he reached the other side, he planted his feet wide and pointed.

"Ng!" he bellowed. "You! Me! Dance battle!"

Natalie looked displeased, but there was no backing down from a formal challenge. She reluctantly slunk aside along with everybody else, giving the two of them room.

Gabe was one of those mutants whose natural rhythm and confidence make even the clowniest dancing look good. He waited for the beat, then launched into a classic sprinkler, followed by the shopping cart. He finished with an over-the-top b-boy stance, earning a laugh from the crowd.

Chance grinned and countered with a body roll that started at his feet and slid slooooooooowly up his body in a wave that sent rainbows shooting through my internal organs. As it hit his head, he reversed, turning it into a textbook pop-and-lock. Behind me, Angela yelled, "Oh *snap*!"

Gabe just grinned and busted out the "Gangnam Style" invisible horse, melding it into some flossing.

. . . which Chance promptly eviscerated with a moonwalk.

The crowd erupted, and Gabe gave up on playing fair, instead letting his thrusting hips carry him across the circle in a series of little hops until he was solidly up in Chance's business. "Surrender, Ng!"

"Dude!" Chance laughed and tried to dodge, but Gabe just turned around and began twerking furiously on him, pursuing him backward across the dance floor.

"You cannot defeat my booty! My ass is champion!"

Chance was laughing hysterically now, trying ineffectively to shield himself from Gabe's butt-barrage. "Okay, okay, you win!"

Gabe straightened, and Chance grabbed his wrist, raising his arm like a boxer.

"The winner!"

Everyone cheered and flooded the dance floor once more.

If there had been any hesitancy left in the room, Gabe had shattered it. Everybody was flinging themselves around now, letting it all hang out as Dua Lipa shouted through the speakers for us to get physical.

My little knot of friends surrounded Chance, creating a party within the party. And as song bled into song and sweat trickled down my bare torso, I realized that Gabe had given me a gift.

I grabbed Chance and yanked him into a tango, arms

outstretched as we marched across the dance floor. I dipped him, then spun him out and let go, miming casting with a fishing pole. Chance grinned and leaped back to me, wriggling.

People laughed, but even better – they lost interest. After all, Gabe had already played this joke. And in doing so, he'd set a precedent. Nobody needed to know that I was secretly relishing every touch of Chance's body – his hands along my bare back, his hips behind mine as I dropped it low. The more outlandishly provocative our moves, the more we vanished beneath everyone's notice. Just two bros clowning for laughs. Gay for giggles. No homo.

Chance realized it too, giving me a sly smile as we orbited each other. Others joined in our game, taking turns being raunchy or ridiculous. Ridley spun around Chance like she was a stripper and he was the pole, then convinced him to jowl with us for a photo. Natalie graced me briefly with her favors on her way to smash herself against Jerome's truck-grille chest. Yet no matter whether Chance and I were squashing Gabe in a manwich or bouncing together to Walk the Moon, there was no interrupting the connection between us. Even when we weren't dancing together, we were still dancing *together*. I could feel it like gravity, drawing my body toward him at all times. Each time we touched, it completed a circuit, and I could see the same electricity that was frying my nerves coursing through his face. Every time he brushed against my naked chest, it was like jumping off a bridge.

And then Darkhearts came on.

"Hey, I know this song!" Natalie lurched drunkenly toward Chance as Gaga-esque synths joined the thudding bass of "Sick Transit." She prodded his chest. "Tha's *you*!"

"Yep. That's me." Chance gave a tolerant smile and moved smoothly sideways, out of poking range.

"You should sing!"

I saw the light die in Chance's eyes.

Angela put an arm around Natalie's shoulders. "Natty. Girlfriend. The boy is off the clock."

But people were already gathering around. I looked to Ridley to shut it down, but she was staring at Chance with guilty, hopeful eyes.

"You totally don't have to," she said. "But it *would* be epic . . ."

Somebody in the crowd started chanting.

"Chance! Chance! Chance!"

The chant spread, as chants tend to. Chance shot me a trapped look.

"Guys," I said.

But no one was listening. Chance looked around at the expectant faces and saw that the damage was done. He put his shoulders back and flashed everyone his magazine smile.

"Sure. It's cool."

People cheered. Ridley ran for her phone. "Lemme restart it!"

Everyone moved backward as the track began again.

"The dance, too!" Natalie yelled. "From the video!"

Chance's face went blank with concentration, looking suddenly ten years older. His open hands snapped up and crossed in front of his face, bat-like, as he began to sing.

"I think I've got your disease.
I see the sickness in you.
You put me down on my knees.

I let the fever come through.
'Cause your affection ... is an infection ...
'Cause your affliction ... is an addiction ..."

He moved through the choreography – sharp, surgical movements to complement the pointed words. His voice matched the recording note for note, comparing life and relationships to terminal diseases – doomed from the start, so you might as well enjoy yourself. It was a morbid, dancing-at-the-end-of-the-world sort of love song, and it was every bit as contagious as its metaphor.

Another White Claw had somehow appeared in my hand, and I drank steadily as I watched Chance ascend once more to Olympus, right here in Ridley's living room.

It was always like this. Even when we'd shared a stage, he'd always been the one people watched. I'd taken a certain pride in it then, and there was a similar pride now – once again, he was a little bit mine, which made his victory mine as well. Sure, the old jealousy was still there – watching the way eyes followed his every move – but I was bigger than that now. I could contain it, make sure the good feelings stayed on top.

If there *were* any resentment, though ... it would be from the fact that Chance didn't seem appreciative enough of what he had. Didn't he understand that *this* – this moment, an audience hanging on your every move – was everything? It didn't matter if it was a living room or a stadium. This was paradise. They didn't just love him, they literally *begged* him for the opportunity to worship at his feet. To have cultivated that so hard, only to act resentful when it worked, seemed disingenuous. Boo-hoo, rock star – if you didn't want everyone's attention, why'd you chase it for so long? You can't scream *look at me* for years and then get upset when everybody does.

But that was okay, I reminded myself sharply. I could forgive him. I *had* forgiven him. That thought gave me a different sort of pride.

Chance finished the song, ending the dance down in a three-point superhero landing. People clustered around, pulling him to his feet and slapping him on the back.

I graciously decided to give him his moment. I wobbled down the hall toward the bathroom, one hand trailing along the wall for balance, and proceeded to take the most majestic piss of my life. A sudden floaty dizziness required me to place both hands against the wall above the toilet, trusting gravity and providence to handle the aiming. Jesus, take the wheel.

With each gallon that left my bladder, I could feel myself getting drunker. Was that something to do with hydration? Or just bodyweight? If I was losing weight by peeing, then my drink-per-pound ratio was rising, right? They should have put *that* story problem on the SATs.

At last the river ran dry. I washed my hands, startling at the sight of my bare torso in the mirror – *right, no shirt* – and headed back down the hall to the party. Everyone was packed in and dancing again, with one exception.

Chance was gone.

24

My first thought was that Ridley had taken Chance somewhere, a prospect that twisted my stomach all on its own. But no – there she was on the dance floor. I made a beeline for her. Assuming the bee in question was pretty wasted.

"Have you seen Chance?" I yelled over the music.

She pointed toward the glass doors out to the deck. "He went to make a call."

"Okay, thanks."

"Keep the doors closed so the neighbors don't call the po-po." She quirked her head to listen as the next song started. "Oh *hells* yes! This is my *jam*!"

"It's your playlist. They're *all* your jams." But I was already headed toward the doors.

Outside on the elevated deck, the air was delightfully clean after the fug of sweat and hormones. A late-summer breeze iced the perspiration on my skin, tracing cold trails down my torso as the muffled thump of bass emphasized the quiet of the nighttime city.

Chance wasn't on the deck, or down in the fenced yard. I felt a momentary pang of panic – then caught a whiff of strawberry. I walked down the stairs to the lawn.

From the shadows beneath the deck, a green LED flared, then blurred in a puff of vapor.

"There you are," I said.

"Here I am." Chance took another hit off his vape.

I moved in to stand next to him, the concrete patio rough beneath my socks, and leaned against the concrete foundation. "You know, this is the first time I've actually seen you smoke that."

"Yeah, well." He croaked the words without breathing, then exhaled a long, pungent stream. "It's not an addiction. Just an excuse."

I wished he'd chosen a different scent. This close, the artificial sweetness was nauseating – an unholy triad of urinal cake, air freshener, and strawberry Pop-Tart. I leaned back out of the cloud. "An excuse for what?"

The vape glowed as he took another puff.

"Leaving."

I finally registered that the flatness of his voice wasn't just from holding his breath. "You're not having fun?"

He laughed like a dragon, smoky and harsh. "Are you shitting me? Have we been at the same party?"

I bristled. "What's the problem?"

"Christ, Holc, where do I start?" Chance waved the vape. "Getting molested by drunk girls who think they own me because they saw a video once? Having to do a personal meet-and-greet for every kid in the room? Or maybe having the whole party stop to make me dance like a fucking *monkey* for their entertainment?"

I crossed my arms. "People wanted to see you perform. You should be flattered."

"*Flattered*?" Chance seemed honestly flabbergasted. "Is it flattering when panhandlers hit you up for money?"

"Wow. Are you *trying* to sound like a dickwad right now?"

"I didn't mean it like that! The point is, I hate always having to be *on*. And I wasn't warmed up – my voice could have cracked. I could have biffed a move and fallen on my ass. Somebody gets that on video, puts it on YouTube, suddenly I'm a joke. This is my *career*, Holc!"

"Dude, you need to chill. Even if something *had* gone wrong, your career isn't that fragile. Maybe it'd be embarrassing, but it would also make you seem relatable and human." The poison in me couldn't help but add, "Remember being human?"

Chance eyes narrowed. "What's *that* supposed to mean?"

"Just that you seem awfully upset that everyone loves you."

"Everyone *wants* something from me! I didn't ask to be paraded around like the prize pig at a state fair!"

"At least you won the prize." Somewhere in the back of my mind, a warning light was blinking, but irritation was driving the bus now. "This isn't easy for me either, you know. Hanging back while you get all the attention. Having to watch Ridley show you off to everybody like you're her boyfriend."

"Ah, *there* it is." Chance's smirk held no humor. "That classic David Holcomb jealousy. We've got our motive, Detective." He shook his head. "In case you've forgotten, I only came tonight because *you* made me."

"Right, because it's such a sacrifice to hang out with us peasants."

"Don't try to twist this! You were all excited about me coming when you thought it would be *you* showing me off. But now that I'm actually *here*, you're mad nobody knows you're hooking up with Chance Kain."

"Oh, of course! I should be *honored* to be blowing the famous *Chance Kain*." Yet at least half the acid in my tone splashed back, burning like shame. He was right – I *had* wanted everyone to know. Wanted them to be jealous of me. I just hadn't admitted it to myself.

"I knew it." Chance broke eye contact, looking out at the yard. Reflected light caught a shine on his cheeks, and I realized with a start that he was crying.

My anger snuffed out. I reached for his hand. "Dude . . ."

"I told you this would happen!" Chance shook me off and turned away, voice choked. Quieter, he said, "This always happens."

"Hey." I took a risk and stepped up behind him, wrapping him in a hug.

He stayed rigid in my arms, but at least he didn't shove me away.

"You're right," I said, striving for a conciliatory tone. "I *do* wish people knew we were together. Because I think you're great. I've thought you were great since we were ten years old."

Chance huffed. "You think I'm a dickwad."

"That too." I kissed the side of his neck. "You contain multitudes."

He snorted again, but only hunched further inward on himself. "All anyone cares about is that I'm famous."

I laughed. "Dude, you being famous is what I like *least*." I squeezed my arms tighter. "This would all be so much easier if you were just you." I buried my face in his hair. "And I'd still want to show you off."

His shoulders relaxed. He leaned back against me with a sigh.

Finally. Maybe it was the alcohol dropping a rosy filter over everything, but I felt like I'd handled that pretty well. Sure, there'd been some bumps, but ultimately Chance had needed comfort, and I'd given it to him. Plus-ten boyfriend points.

But I was still full of adrenaline from the argument, and that energy needed to go *somewhere*. Now that Chance was leaning against me, it was becoming clear just how thin his jumpsuit really was.

My hand slid up to the zipper at his throat. "This is tempting."

"Dude." Chance grabbed my hand and straightened. An inch of air rushed between us like a moat. "You're gonna blow our cover."

I stepped forward to close the gap. "Out here we don't need cover." I leaned in to breathe in his ear, then twitched as inspiration hit me. "No, wait! I should have said, 'That's not all I'm gonna blow.'"

He broke out of my arms, turning to face me and rolling his eyes. "You're drunk."

"And you're sexy."

He scowled. "I'm still mad."

I pinned him softly against the deck's support post. "I can fix that."

I kissed him, tasting the coffee and cream of the White Russian on his lips. He hesitated, and for a moment I worried I'd gone too far, but then he was kissing me as well, his hands roaming my naked back. I pressed my body up against his, legs tangling, hips grinding together. I wedged a hand between us and found his zipper again, pulling it down ... and down ... and down ...

He bit my lip, then pulled his face away, grimacing. "You can't just fix everything with sex."

I kissed my way down his neck. "Are you sure?"

He shuddered and closed his eyes as I slid a hand down inside his jumpsuit.

From behind me came a single word.

"Wow."

Chance jerked, shoving me off him and sending me stumbling backward. I spun to find Ridley standing by the bottom of the stairs, looking stricken in her ratty bathrobe.

"So," she said unsteadily. "This clarifies some things."

"Ridley." My brain raced. "Chance and I were just, uh—"

"*Don't.*" She seemed to find her footing, tone solidifying. "Please. How long has this been going on?"

"Um." Lying at this point just felt wrong. Wrong-er. "Six weeks?"

"Jesus." Her head jerked as if slapped. "And you've been lying to me this whole time."

"I wasn't *lying*," I protested. "I just didn't tell you."

"And that's supposed to make a difference? It's called 'lying by omission,' David. Look it up. And *you.*" She rounded on Chance. "I knew our date wasn't real – your manager made that *very* clear – but I thought we were at least becoming friends. But you didn't care at all, did you? You just wanted a beard. A girl for the gossip sites, because you're too chickenshit to come out for real."

"Hey!" I raised a hand, even as Chance said, "That's not fair!"

"Isn't it? Then explain why you can fake a date with me, but won't even tell me you're already dating my best friend." Her lip twisted humorlessly. "You're rich and famous, living in one of the gayest cities in America. No one can touch you. You know how many thousands of kids come out every day *without* your advantages? You could be an inspiration for them. But instead you pull this is-he-isn't-he ambiguous act so you can cash in on the queer kids without committing."

"You don't understand," I insisted.

"Oh, I don't?" She pointed to her face, dark skin gleaming in lost light from the party above. "You wanna tell me about living as a minority, David?"

"I don't need this shit." Chance yanked his zipper up and pushed past me, headed for the side yard and the street.

"Chance, wait!" I started after him. "I'll come with you."

"*No.*" His voice snapped like a whip. Seeing my shocked expression, he softened slightly. "I'm just gonna go home. I've got an early flight."

"But—"

Then he was around the side of the house and gone.

I turned back to Ridley. "Thanks a lot, Rids."

"*You're* upset?" She shook her head. "You're unbelievable, David. You *knew* I liked him. How many times did you sit there silently while I made a fool of myself?"

"Um." She had a point.

"That night you disappeared with him – before you left, I asked you flat out if there was anything I should know."

"Well there wasn't *yet.*" Which was almost technically true.

"You're so full of shit, David. You should have told me you were into him. I tell you *everything* – that's the whole *point* of best friends." Her crossed arms turned into a self-hug. "You know I would have supported you, right? You liking boys doesn't change anything."

"I know." I was starting to feel a little sick.

"So why didn't you tell me?"

There were no safe answers.

"Don't you trust me?"

It turned out that staying silent was its own answer. Her eyes went wide.

"Oh my god. You don't." Her voice was distant, almost awed.

"I trust you with a lot of things," I protested.

"But not when it matters." She tugged the bathrobe tighter around her. "I'm just a pawn in your schemes."

"*What?!* You've been trying to get me to set you up with Chance for weeks! How is that any less scheme-y?"

"That's different!"

"Really? And what about the whole Godfather, owe-me-a-favor bit you pulled to make him post about your blog?"

Ridley looked uncomfortable.

"*You've* been using *us.* For your blog, for your party—"

My rebuttal died as Chance reemerged from the side yard. He shot us a look that was equal parts anger and embarrassment.

"Need my shoes."

He padded back up the steps to the deck, damp socks slapping against the wood. Party sounds flared as the sliding door opened and shut.

We watched him go. Ridley shook her head again.

"I just can't believe you'd lie to me."

Chance's arrival and re-abandonment sanded away my last reserves of self-control. "Oh, give me a break, Ridley! You know what you'd have been like."

"What?" She looked shocked.

"You'd have been on me every minute, pumping for details, analyzing, pushing to make something happen. You'd have gone into plotting mode and turned it all into some big dramatic *thing*, with me just getting dragged along. Everything's a movie to you. Everything's a *plan*." I cut myself off and took a shaky breath. "I just wanted to do this on my own, all right?"

She stared. The wind blew between us, smelling of lawns and pavement. Standing shirtless in the cold air no longer felt refreshing. Just exposed.

"Well," she said quietly. "You got that much." She looked back up at the deck, at the party she'd organized for us. "I think you should leave."

"Yeah," I said. "I think so, too."

And I left.

25

I expected to wake to a dozen texts from Ridley. She wasn't the type to let broken things stay broken – if she had a problem with you, she let you know, and kept on letting you know until one of you apologized or you both died of exhaustion.

But this time there was no text. As her silence rolled into Monday and Tuesday, the weight of it began to grind me down, making me wonder if maybe I should break custom and make the first move.

But also: to hell with that. What did I have to apologize for? Sure, I hadn't told her about me and Chance, but was I obligated to tell her every aspect of my life? Just because *she* had no filter didn't mean I couldn't have one. And it wasn't like I'd deliberately led her on – I'd tried at every turn to keep her from getting emotionally invested in her fantasy romance. Plus, she was the one who'd upset Chance at the party, showing him off rather than shielding him like a good hostess. I'd brought him along like she'd wanted – as a *favor* to her – and she'd made a mess of it. Yet somehow *I* was the bad guy?

I wasn't an asshole. I'd accept my share of the blame, the way I always did. But she'd embarrassed my boyfriend and kicked me out of the party I'd helped plan. If she was waiting for me to apologize first, she could go right on waiting.

More concerning was the relative silence from Chance. On his L.A. trip, he'd blown up my phone whenever he wasn't actively working. Now, though, he'd wait hours before responding, and when he did, the answers were practically monosyllabic.

Exhibit A:

ME:

Hey! How's DC? Have they convinced you to run for president yet?

CHANCE:

🙂

Or this thrilling exchange:

ME:

How's recording with the Aventine guys? You coming up with good stuff?

CHANCE:

Yeah. They're cool.

Even addressing things head-on didn't get me anywhere:

ME:

Hey, sorry the party sucked. I'll make it up to you when you get home, I promise. 😈

CHANCE:

It's fine.

I got better conversation out of the spam texts trying to convince me my Social Security number had expired.

Yet perseverance paid off. As I continued to bombard him

with good cheer, Chance slowly opened up again. By Wednesday morning he was sending me pictures of the trip from the airport VIP lounge as he waited for his flight home. One in particular stood out: him in the vocal booth, looking deadly cute in some giant studio headphones. I told him so.

CHANCE:

Deadly, huh?

ME:

Absolutely. I am slain.

On my tombstone, it reads:

"Here lies David, totally dead /
all the blood in his penis left
none for his head."

(I know how much you like poetry.)

CHANCE:

. . .

You think that's romantic,
don't you?

ME:

You're the vampire. Sex
and death, baby. La petit
mort.

(It's sexy because it's French.)

CHANCE:

Oui oui.

ME:

Heh. You said weewee.

CHANCE:

Hey, do hear a crashing
sound?

Oh, that was you breaking
the mood.

ME:

Psht. Whatever.

You just look like you're having so
much fun in that pic. I wish I could
be there with you.

But hopefully we'll get to do
this stuff together again
soon! 🤞

There was a pause, long enough that I thought Chance
might have boarded his plane. Then:

CHANCE:

If you still want to do the
audition, my A&R person is
going to be in Seattle Friday
afternoon.

My heart felt like someone had it screwed into a C-clamp. It
was what I'd been waiting for, but coming now, in the wake of
the weirdness at the party, it felt all wrong. Too rushed, too
sudden.

ME:

But you don't even have a second verse!

CHANCE:

I'll have it ready. Just loop the
same chords.

Deep breath. Apparently it was now or never. There was only one appropriate response.

ME:

Alright. We can do this.

I'll come over tonight and tomorrow,
and we can practice our asses off
and get tight.

Another long gap where I thought I might have lost him.

CHANCE:

I'm actually going to be really
busy.

I stared at my phone. What was even happening?

ME:

Are you saying you can't
practice?

CHANCE:

It'll be fine. I'll update the beat
track.

Also, she says your dad
needs to sign a waiver.

> Benjamin will send it to
> you.
>
> Boarding now. GTG.

And then he was gone, leaving me sitting at the kitchen table with my rapidly soggifying cereal, reading back over the exchange again and again.

None of this made any sense. I understood why he was upset about the party, but that was just one more reason to want me back in the band, right? Right now he was all alone in his stardom, set apart from everyone else. Once I was on the same level, that wouldn't be an issue. And if he didn't want to go through with the audition, he could have just not set it up, or lied and said the label refused. So why was he being weird about it?

I was still chewing it over a few hours later when Jesús leaned against the sawhorse beside me, holding a coffee. "Everything all right?"

I blinked, trying to shove down thoughts of Chance. "Yeah, great."

One bushy eyebrow rose. "You sure?"

Caught. "Yes . . . ?" I managed. "Why?"

He nodded to the stack of boards I'd been cutting. "Because I asked for eighteens, and you've cut all those down to sixteens."

"Oh *shit.*" I grabbed for the battered yellow notepad we used. Sure enough, there was the number eighteen. In my own handwriting. "Shit, Jesús, I'm sorry. I'll pay for the lumber."

He waved away the offer. "Church got plenty of money. And we'll find somewhere to use 'em. But pay attention to the saw, hey? You're gonna miss those fingers when they're gone."

"I will. I promise."

"I know." He took a slurp of coffee. He had one of those weathered Danny Trejo faces that made every action look majestic, even drinking room-temperature lattes. "So what's up? Girl problems?"

"No." Bullet dodged, if barely.

He nodded. "You ever get those, you let me know."

From across the room, Denny snorted. "You've been married three times, old man."

"Exactly!" Jesús grinned. "Talk about experience! I'm a one-man panel of experts."

"Right." Denny looked over from the top of her ladder and caught my eye. "I think Dave-o's just bummed that school's gonna start and he won't get to hang with us all day."

She was giving me an out if I wanted it. But as I joined in their joking, steering away from the issue of my romantic life, I realized she was also right. I *was* going to be giving this up, and not just for nine months for school. If I succeeded in joining Darkhearts, this would be one of the last times I'd listen to the two of them banter. There'd be no more learning woodworking from Jesús. Hell, I wouldn't even be in the same *state* as him most of the time.

Or Dad, for that matter. I hadn't really thought about it before, but of course he couldn't come on tour with me. I didn't expect to get as rich as Chance overnight, and someone had to support us. How weird would it be to only see him a few months a year? Maybe that was no different from all the kids going off to college next year, but moving out had never really been part of my plan. The idea of Dad watching TV alone in the house seemed suddenly deeply depressing.

But there was no time to think about that now. First I needed to have a conversation.

When lunchtime rolled around, I suggested that Dad and I hit up the Perro Feo food truck. As we sat alone in the van eating tortas, I nonchalantly said, "So I need Friday off."

"And I need a million dollars." Dad took a huge bite, salsa escaping across the back of his hand.

"Yeah, but seriously."

"I'm serious. What for?" Dad searched around the cab for a napkin that wasn't already soaked with pork juice.

"I've got my audition for Darkhearts."

"Your *what*?" He turned toward me. "He's making you *audition*?"

"*Chance* isn't," I said quickly. "It's the label. They want to see us together. And I need you to sign a permission slip."

"Un-friggin'-believable." He shook his head. "These people. Making you *try out* for a band you friggin' *started*."

"Dad, it's just the label reps. They've never met me."

"That's my point! They got rich off your work, without so much as a thank-you, and now they want to test you to see if you're *worthy* of making them more money?"

This was going rapidly downhill. "Yeah, but now *we* can get some of that money. You just said you want a million dollars." I tried for an encouraging grin. "And I don't care about the label. This is about me and Chance, and finally getting to do what I should have been doing all this time."

"David." He paused, clearly wrestling with himself. "You making up with Chance ... I respect that. But back when they – when *you* left Darkhearts, you had plenty to say about Chance and his ego. And that was before there was money

297

involved. If you go in there now, you're gonna be working for him."

I hadn't considered that angle. But it didn't matter. "Jesús and Denny work for you, and you're still friends."

"That's true, and I try to keep things casual. But at the end of the day, they know I call the shots. You sure you can handle that?"

"If I have to," I said. "But also, it's not like that. We're equal. And Chance needs someone to help write the songs. He *needs* me."

"Right." Dad still looked unconvinced, which stung more than I expected. If there was one thing I could say about Dad, it was that he always believed in me. It was maybe the only thing in the world I could count on.

There was one more reason Chance wouldn't kick me out, of course. The biggest one. Part of me said to shut up and not make an awkward situation any more complicated, but look how well that had worked out with Ridley. As much as I hated keeping things from her, I hated it even more with Dad. He deserved better than that. And I was tired of hiding.

"Also, Chance and I are dating."

"What?" Dad vultured his neck forward, squinting at me in confusion.

"Dating." I pointed to my chest. "Me. Chance."

He stared, no sound but the quiet *plip* of his torta dripping grease onto the center console.

Then he straightened and shoved the sandwich back into its paper sack. "Jesus Christ, David."

From his tone, you'd think it was Dad who was dying on the cross for my sins. My eyes burned.

He saw it and took a breath. "Sorry, I just ..." He looked around the cab for some sort of assistance. "If you want to date boys, that's fine. But could you have picked literally *anyone else?*"

"Chance is a good guy," I insisted.

"Who, as you just said, *needs* something from you. How convenient."

I was pretty sure that if this conversation continued much longer, I was going to totally humiliate myself by crying. "Look," I demanded, "are you going to sign the waiver or not?"

Dad sat there breathing heavily, a grease stain slowly spreading across the white sandwich bag in his hand.

At last he said, "If that's what you want."

Relief flooded through me. "It's gonna be cool," I said. "You'll see."

But Dad just faced forward and reached for the keys. As the van started up, he shook his head again. "I hope you know what you're doing."

"I do," I said. But inside, a traitorous part of me added, *I hope.*

26

Ahoy Studios was in a surprisingly residential neighborhood. I pulled up fifteen minutes early, just to be safe, and had to check the address twice to make sure I was in the right place.

I wasn't sure exactly what I'd expected. Back when I'd been in Darkhearts – *the first time*, I reminded myself – Eli had recorded all our demos himself in his basement. Everything I knew about studios came from watching documentaries and looking at photos. But those were always interior shots, with the band. They rarely showed you the outside.

This place looked like somebody's house: an old gray single-story, with a line of hedge where the lawn met the sidewalk. There was even a fully occupied chicken coop.

I was just about to check my phone for a third time when Chance came around the side of the house, vape in hand. He met me halfway up the driveway, slouched to one side with a thumb in the pocket of his jeans. "Hey."

I hesitated, wondering if I should go in for a kiss. Just a quick peck. That was what boyfriends did, right? There was nobody else here, and he looked amazing in his usual black denim jacket, letting it hang open to showcase a lace-up shirt with an asymmetrical cowl and a bat-shaped belt buckle. But there was also something defensive in the way he was standing.

He didn't give me the chance to decide. "Got everything you need?"

I raised my guitar case. "Yup."

"All right then. Let's do this." He turned away, walking toward the door.

The front room was still basically a living room, if your living room had gold records from Soundgarden and Death Cab. There were couches, and a TV, and a 1950s kitchen visible through an archway. As Chance led me through a heavy second door, however, all illusions of a normal house fell away.

We were in a carpeted control room. An arc of massive mixing desks squatted beneath a giant glass window looking in on the recording area. Ancient reel-to-reel tape equipment vied for space with top-end monitors of both the video and audio varieties. Yet the most uncanny change was the sound: foam panels textured like egg cartons lined the walls, sucking up noise and leaving the air strangely flat.

"There he is!" Benjamin sat up from where he sprawled on a low sofa. He was all smiles again today, the way he'd been the first time at the theater. It felt even more fake now that I'd seen beneath the mask, but he gave no indication that anything had changed as he shook my hand. "So glad you could make it out."

As if he'd been the one to invite me. "No problem," I said.

"This is Misha, the engineer." Chance gestured to a tattooed girl maybe five years older than us sitting in the command chair in front of the consoles. She waved. "She's been helping me record dialogue for a VR thing."

"We managed to land Chance a cameo in the new *City of Sin* game," Benjamin burbled. "Really cutting-edge stuff." He gestured toward the giant observation window. "Why don't you two set up? Elena should be here momentarily, and you really don't want to keep her waiting."

The door to the studio proper opened with a sucking noise,

like the hatch to a submarine. Beyond, everything was bright wood, our footsteps echoing back in warm ripples as we crossed to an island of Persian rugs in the center. Stacks of amplifiers lined the walls, along with a drum kit and random instruments hanging from hooks.

Chance strolled to a little stand in the middle and picked up a set of headphones as if he did this every day. I tried to match his calm.

"Which one do you want?" Misha inclined her head at the line of amplifiers.

"Um." I raced to take in my options. Half the brands were names I'd never heard before, which probably meant expensive. "Whichever's best?"

Misha gave me an amused look, but not an unkind one. "Not a gearhead, huh? Okay, dealer's choice. You want distortion?"

"Some, yeah."

"We'll give you the 800." She plugged a cable into the gleaming gold faceplate of a Marshall half stack and handed me the other end. "Get you that bluesy Slash tone. There's no footswitch, so just roll down your guitar volume for cleans and crank it when you want the dirt."

"Thanks." I busied myself getting out my guitar and strap, trying to look like I knew what the hell I was doing.

The door opened again, and a new woman stepped in, Benjamin following behind like a puppy.

She was slim and forties-ish, with auburn hair and a deep tan. She wore a knee-length salmon-pink coat with a silk zebra-print scarf and a chunky hippie necklace, yet she wore it all like a business suit – or maybe a military uniform. Confidence radiated off her in waves.

"Chance! Good to see you, honey." She held her arms out, and Chance obligingly stepped into them for a quick hug. As she released him and stepped back, she took his chin in one hand and studied him. "You look good. I'm glad you took this time off to re-center."

Chance shrugged awkwardly. "Thanks, Elena."

But she was already turning toward me. "You must be David."

"Yeah. Hi."

"Lovely to meet you." She gave me a big smile, but her eyes were like an airport scanner, peeling me apart layer by layer. In the same pleasant tone, she said, "Don't exactly match the aesthetic, do you?"

I'd dressed up for the occasion, in my tightest jeans and best-fitting plaid shirt with the sleeves rolled up. It wasn't the vampire look Chance cultivated, but it was still Standard Band Guy.

"David can totally do the goth thing," Chance put in quickly. "He actually came up with it in the first place." Which wasn't remotely true, but I appreciated the assist.

Elena pursed her lips, continuing to scrutinize me for several more endless seconds, then shrugged. "Well, it's nothing a stylist and a personal trainer can't fix." She clapped her hands. "Let's hear this new song, shall we?" She spoke over her shoulder to Benjamin without looking at him. "Have the engineer roll tape. I want to be able to take this back to the team."

"Sure thing." Benjamin turned and waved to Misha through the window.

There was a brief bustle as Misha finished getting us miked up and I got used to the amp. I tried a couple of warm-up riffs – the tone really *was* amazing – but the knowledge that any wrong note could be held against me quickly killed the desire to noodle.

Then it was just the two of us, alone in the bright lights and giant headphones, while the other three watched from the darkened control room.

Misha's voice came through the phones. "Whenever you're ready."

Chance looked to me. My knees felt dangerously unstable, and the neck of my guitar was already slick with palm-sweat, but I nodded.

He looked back to the window. "This song is called 'Back and Away.'"

Huh. That was new – I'd thought the line was "back *from* away." But he was the lyricist, and in any case, I didn't have time to consider it. A metronome clicked us in, and then the drum loop we'd built on Chance's computer thumped to life.

And I played.

My guitar filled the room. Each chord growled as I attacked it, warm and rough as coarse-grit sandpaper even as the higher strings chimed out clean. The bass of my palm mutes chugged percussively, locking in with the simple drumbeat.

Then Chance closed his eyes and began to sing, and my hands switched over to autopilot as every sense focused on him. It didn't matter that getting these chords right was maybe the most important thing I'd ever done. There was no resisting him.

When we'd written the song in his bedroom, he'd been feeling his way through, the lyrics still raw and bleeding. This had that same power – the sense that every word was being said for the first time, straight to you. But now there was polish. Confidence. I snuck a glance at the control booth and saw everyone watching intently, Misha nodding along. Chance was the sun, and we were all flowers turning toward him.

He sailed through the verse, and we hit the chorus together like thunder.

> *"But now you're back.*
> *And I'm not backing away . . ."*

His voice filled me like hot maple syrup. And just like that, I realized that this was what love felt like. Watching him sing, hearing those words – the refusal to leave, the declaration that love was worth fighting for – and knowing it was *me* he was singing about.

Everyone in that control booth could go to hell. We were staking a claim: David and Chance against the world. The intensity of feeling blazed inside me, and it was all I could do to keep playing, making no effort to hide the big stupid grin on my face. I wanted Chance to turn toward me and share it – could see him doing it in my mind, giving me that private smile even as he sang.

But his eyes stayed closed, all attention on the song. I brought myself out of my daydreams just in time to catch the ending drum fill and loop back into the verse. I even felt cocky enough to throw in a bend, then lay back as Chance began the new verse.

> *"And I still fall*
> *for all your usual tricks.*
> *But this song*
> *will be the lesson that sticks.*
> *'Cause you*

don't see me
as mine.
But you'll get yours.
It's just a matter of time . . ."

The bottom dropped out of my stomach.

"When you chase your dreams
and you catch them,
the hurt will teach you
to know when to let go."

I almost fumbled a chord change, barely saving myself.

Okay, be cool. Maybe these lyrics weren't about us after all. Maybe we were just the first verse, and this one was about, like, the perils of fame. Chance knew his audience – of course you couldn't have a *totally* happy Darkhearts song. It didn't mean there was anything wrong with *us*. The Cure had written the most depressing relationship songs ever, all while Robert Smith was happily married to his high school sweetheart. Great music told the truth, but it didn't have to be *our* truth.

Chance had opened his eyes. I stared at him, psychically commanding him to look at me, but he kept his gaze fixed on the control booth as we slid into the chorus.

"'Cause now you're back,
but you're still backing away.
And you've got nothin' to say,
'cause I won't ask you to stay,
because you're back and away."

What the *fuck*? Where was this coming from? I hadn't backed away from anything. But that was good, right? It meant this wasn't about us at all.

They're just lyrics, David. Get your shit together.

I let the last chord ring out. Chance slumped, shrinking back into a mortal again. At last our eyes met, and he gave an apologetic little half smile.

Okay, so he'd taken creative liberties to make our song darker, and now he was embarrassed about it. That was fine. Some of the tension inside me released.

Clapping came through the headphones. I turned to find Benjamin applauding. "Great song, boys! Got kind of a 'Wall-flowers meets Snow Patrol' vibe. Chance, you're absolutely crushing those vocals." Misha was smiling as well.

All eyes went to Elena. The exec sat to one side of the engineer, hands steepled on the recording desk as she studied me.

No one spoke. A drop of nervous sweat trickled down the side of my ribs.

She nodded.

"You've got potential, kid."

Relief crashed through me, and it was all I could do not to crumple to the ground. The blood pounded so hard in my ears that I almost didn't hear her when she followed with:

"But it's not enough."

27

I blinked. "I'm sorry, what?"

Elena gave a tight, professionally sympathetic smile. "Don't take this the wrong way. You've got a spark. You're just not where I need you to be."

The room swam around me as I struggled to match her words to the situation. "But it's a good song." I pointed to Benjamin. "He just said it!"

"Sure it's good. You've got Chance Kain singing it. I could put him over one of those sidewalk bucket-drummers and make a hit." Elena shook her head. "Look, I don't know how many ways to say this. It's not that you're bad. You're just not Darkhearts material."

Chance finally found his voice. "But Holc was already *in* Darkhearts."

She shrugged. "That was before. If he'd been in the band when I signed you, we'd have had years to polish him up. But this isn't a fixer-upper anymore, and you need more than four chords and an attitude. Anybody who's going to replace Eli as your songwriter has to be the full package. Otherwise, we need to go the producer route." She leaned back in her chair. "Chance. Honey. I can get Max Martin and Savan Kotecha in here to write you something. Tayla Parx. *Pharrell.*"

I saw each name hit Chance, threatening to double him over, but he rallied. "Okay, fine. What if somebody else writes the songs? Holc can just play guitar."

I didn't appreciate the way he tossed aside my creative input like that, but at least he was fighting back.

"Hmm." Elena ran her tongue beneath her upper lip. She fixed those dead shark eyes on me and jerked her chin upward. "Gimme an A-flat seventh."

"Um." My cheeks burned.

"That's what I thought." She turned back to Chance as if I had ceased to exist. "Listen, if you want live guitar, there are a hundred touring guitarists who can shred like Van Halen and still look young enough to match your aesthetic. I'm sorry, but bringing on an amateur – an *underage* amateur – just doesn't make sense. It's a liability. In every sense of the word."

"But *I* was an underage amateur," Chance protested.

She nodded agreeably. "And now you're not."

Chance glanced guiltily over at me. "But he's my friend."

Elena spread her arms. "So be friends! This is *business.*"

Chance looked to Benjamin for help, but the manager just shook his head.

"I get it, man, but Elena's right. I respect what David's contributed, but Darkhearts is bigger than that now. Elena and I have a responsibility to the team." He paused for effect. "And so do you."

"So that's it?" The words came out in a snarl as my wall of shock finally crumbled. I glared at the exec in her stupid old-lady hipster scarf. "You get to just decide who's in the band?"

"Of course not." Elena gave another shrug, completely unruffled. "Darkhearts is Chance's band. He can bring in whoever he wants." She tilted her head, peering at him. "But this industry runs on personal connections. It took a lot of work to make Darkhearts this big, and that respect runs both ways. If you snub the people trying to help you, don't be surprised if they focus their efforts elsewhere."

"Right. Like you're gonna walk away from a band making you millions." I turned to Chance, fiercely triumphant. "Hear that? She just admitted she can't stop us. It's your call."

But Chance wasn't looking at me. A cold wave rolled through my veins.

"Chance?" My hands tightened painfully on the neck of my guitar. "Dude. Tell them I'm in the band."

He still said nothing, just stared at the floor.

"David, please." Benjamin's voice oozed false concern. "Don't make this harder than it has to be. It's not personal."

"The hell it's not!" I ripped the phones from my head, dropping them to the floor with a clatter. My guitar cable jerked free with a buzz as I stepped around in front of Chance to look him in the eye. "Chance, what the *fuck*?"

Behind me, Benjamin shoved open the studio door, his voice hard. "Okay, that's enough."

I looked from Chance to his manager. Without the fake Hollywood frosting on every word, Benjamin looked abruptly like somebody's dad. I felt suddenly certain that, for all his slim-fit shirts and designer jeans, I wouldn't be the first person he'd physically dragged out of a studio.

I shouldered past him out the door.

Nobody spoke as I stormed through the control room, but as the outer door swung closed behind me, I heard Elena give a long sigh.

"And, that, children," she said, "is why we work with professionals. Their hearts are already broken."

28

Chance caught up with me in the driveway. "Holc, wait!"

It's a tribute to the monumental stupidity of human emotion that my heart actually rose in the half second it took me to turn around. Here was the Hollywood finish, as clean as if Ridley had written it: Chance chasing after me to say he'd told Benjamin and Elena to screw themselves, that it was me and him all the way. To leap into my arms as the music swelled and the credits began to roll.

But Chance didn't leap into my arms. He pulled up short, looking frustrated and miserable.

I waited for him to say something. When he didn't, I said, "Well?"

"I'm sorry."

"Yeah, I'll bet."

He shoved a hand into that perfect hair, gripping his bangs. "Come on, dude. Don't be like that."

"Be like *what*, Chance? Humiliated? Betrayed?" The magma was still roiling inside me. I clutched my guitar to keep my hands from shaking. "A little late for that, don't you think?"

A reflection of my own heat rose in Chance's cheeks. "Dude! I didn't betray you! You wanted to write a song, so we wrote a song. You wanted an audition, so I got you one. It's not my fault it didn't work out. *I did my part!*"

"I didn't want an *audition*, Chance. I wanted to *rejoin the band.*"

"Jesus, Holc, what do you want from me? You heard Elena. It's a nonstarter."

"Yeah, for *her*. What about for *you*? You're Chance Fucking Kain. You could make it happen if you wanted to."

"Right, and spit in the face of everyone who controls my career."

"Oh, so you can blow them off for a *tattoo*, but not for me?"

He shook his head in disbelief. "Fucking hell, Holc. This isn't some party I can invite you to. This is my *life*. I have to work with these people. I need them on my side."

"I thought you needed *me*."

"I *do* need you." He reached for my hand, but I jerked it back. Muscles stood out along the edge of his jaw as he let his arm drop. "I knew this was a bad idea."

"Which part?" I snapped.

"Maybe all of it." He hooked his thumbs in his pockets again, chin lifting and expression slamming shut. "I convinced myself that maybe you'd be different. We had *history*. It's why I texted you in the first place, after the funeral. I knew you still hated me, but that was fine – at least you *knew* me. But ever since you realized you could use me as a shortcut to fame, that's all you've cared about. Same as everyone else."

"Oh, cut the victim crap. This audition was for *us*."

"Really?" His lips thinned. "And how exactly does it help me for you to be rude to my managers?"

"*I'm* rude?!" I jabbed a finger at the studio door. "They called me an amateur!"

"Dude, you *are* an amateur."

The words drove me back a step. I realized it and forced myself closer. "I've been playing as long as you have!"

"Yeah, and we played, what, thirty shows together?" A frustrated wrinkle appeared between his eyebrows. "In the last two years, I've played three *hundred*, Holc. Elena's right – we're *not* on the same level. Not anymore."

The truth of it buried itself in my chest like a spear. I scrabbled desperately, looking for any way to lash back. "Yeah? Well, at least I can drive!"

He laughed once, short and sharp. "Seriously?"

"Just saying." I attempted to mimic his own disdainful air. "I'm not the scrub constantly begging for rides."

He sucked in his lower lip, biting down on it as he shook his head in wonder. "You really don't get it, do you?"

"I dunno, Chance. What don't I get?"

He hesitated, nostrils flaring, then nodded slightly. "All those times I asked you to pick me up? That was for *you.*"

The way he said it – like a secret he wasn't sure he should spill – lent the words unexpected weight. The ground felt like it was moving beneath me. "What?"

"You were so insecure." Chance looked suddenly tired. "So jealous about everything. It was this giant wall between us. But when you found out I can't drive, you relaxed." He sighed sharply through his nose. "You needed something that let you feel superior. Something I didn't have, to boost your ego enough that you'd stop acting like an immature jerk. That's why I kept asking you to pick me up."

"Bullshit." But my voice shook as I said it.

"Really?" Chance laughed again. "I'm a millionaire, Holc. You think I can't call a fucking Uber?"

I felt naked. I could see suddenly how small I must look, with all my pettiness laid out before him like knickknacks at a garage sale. All those times I'd allowed myself to feel secretly smug, wrapping myself in the few ways in which I was Chance's equal. Except it hadn't been secret at all.

Worst of all, rising slowly over the horizon, was the realization that he'd seen it all and given me a chance anyway. He'd swallowed his pride in order to make me comfortable.

Which meant he really *was* better than me.

And we both knew it.

Hot tears rose up behind my eyes, and I bit down hard to keep them from boiling over. As if from the other end of a long tunnel, I heard myself say, "Maybe we shouldn't see each other anymore."

I expected a flinch. Truthfully, I *wanted* it – wanted to see him feel a shard of what I felt, to cut himself on the broken glass inside me.

Instead, he smiled grimly and checked an imaginary wristwatch. "And here we are again, right on time. Things get hard, so David Holcomb bails." He craned his neck forward, eyes wide. "You're *predictable*, Holc."

"Fuck you. I'm not predictable."

"Oh, you're not?" He laughed, suddenly as calm and cool as the movie vampire he pretended to be. "I wrote our fucking *song* about it, dude. 'Now you're back, but you're still backing away'? I knew you'd react like this. This is what you *do*, Holcomb. Nothing's changed. The moment you don't get exactly what you want, you run away, then tell yourself it's everyone else's fault for not chasing you. But what about what *I* want, Holc?"

"You've already *got* everything I want!"

I stopped short, surprised by my own Freudian slip – I'd meant to say "everything *you* want." But it was true either way.

Chance saw it as well and sneered. "So because I succeeded and you didn't, I'm supposed to spend every minute trying to make you feel better about yourself? That's not a relationship, Holc. You want unconditional love, get a dog. I've been carrying your fragile ego around on a little pillow this whole time, and I'm sick of it."

"Well, you don't have to anymore." I yanked my guitar off over my head. "I'm done."

"Of course you are." Chance waved resignedly toward the street. "Go ahead. Run away if you want. Just don't lie to yourself about who's doing what."

He made no move to follow as I stormed out onto the sidewalk, but his words hung in the air behind me.

"This is all you, Holc. It always has been."

29

There's a famously gruesome, historically dubious Viking torture called the blood eagle. In it, the victim's back is cut open and the whole rib cage cracked apart like a pistachio. As the last step, the victim's lungs are pulled out through the back and stretched wide behind him, to create a grotesque pair of "wings."

That's how I felt now: hollowed out and exposed, all my fear and shame hauled out of me in dark, glistening ropes.

As I opened the door to my truck, I realized I'd left my guitar case in the studio. Screw it – I shoved my naked guitar behind the driver's seat and climbed in.

At some level I must have been seeing the road as I drove, but the job of keeping myself alive was relegated entirely to my lizard brain, that little chunk of stem that remembers to keep breathing while you're asleep. The rest of me played through footage of the audition, over and over again.

I wasn't good enough. I'd spent years believing I'd have been just as famous as Chance and Eli, if only I'd been given the same opportunity. All I needed was my shot, like the *Hamilton* song – the chance to show the world what I could do. And now I'd finally had it.

And I'd fucked it up.

Except that wasn't even true. I hadn't bombed – hadn't fumbled the chords or pissed my pants. I'd written a good song, and played it with everything I had.

But it still hadn't been enough. Because the truth was that David Holcomb just wasn't rock star material.

And Chance had seen it. It wasn't just that he'd watched me fail – it was that he'd *known* I would. He'd never believed in me. I could see it now, as my brain played back every hesitation, every time he'd dragged his feet about the audition. He'd expected me to fail, and let me walk into the trap anyway.

Yet even as my fingers dug new grooves in the steering wheel, I knew I was lying to myself – transmuting shame into anger, the way I always did. Because Chance *hadn't* wanted to do the audition. If anything, he'd tried to protect me from it. I'd laid the trap for myself, by believing my own bullshit. Just like when I'd told myself the band had left me behind, instead of the other way around.

This is all you, Holc.

He was right. It was easier to blame Chance than to admit that the dream was dead – *all* my dreams.

And I was the one who'd killed them.

Outside, it started raining, tiny drops wet enough to blind but not enough to keep the wiper blades from squeaking. They blended with my tears, turning the road to bright smears of color.

Somehow I made it home. It was still work hours, and the house was mercifully silent as I unlocked the door. Upstairs, I shoved my guitar into the corner and threw myself down onto my bed.

Except that was no good. Because despite the fact that I'd slept in this bed every night since I was seven years old, now all I could think of was Chance in it with me. I hadn't washed the sheets, and my pillow still smelled like his hair products.

Fucking Chance. In one night, he'd poisoned my own bed against me.

I moved to the couch in the living room. I told myself to watch TV, but the remote was all the way on the other side of the coffee table, and staring at the blank screen seemed just as good.

The real irony, I realized, was that I didn't even really care about being a rock star. I could see that now. I would have been fine if the band had never gone anywhere, or if we'd broken up like every other teen band. Playing music had been fun, but once the shininess wore off, I'd walked away with no second thoughts.

But then the other guys got famous, and suddenly it was clear to everyone that I'd thrown away a winning lottery ticket. *That* was what galled me. It wasn't that I needed to succeed – I needed to *not fail*. And Chance Kain was a singing, dancing reminder of that failure.

I don't know long I sat there, but suddenly keys were jingling in the lock. The door swung open, and I heard Dad's bag hit the kitchen table.

"Hey! How'd it go?"

I couldn't be bothered to turn around.

"David?"

He came around the couch, and I noticed he was still wearing his concrete-stained work boots – a cardinal sin in the Holcomb household. He took one look at my face and frowned.

"What happened?"

"Oh, you know." I spoke calmly, yet to my horror felt a tear escape down my cheek. "The label didn't want me, and Chance and I broke up. So about like usual."

318

Dad stared. We were so alike in that regard. When presented with an unpleasant situation, a Holcomb always knows what to do: freeze in shock and disbelief. It's amazing our ancestors weren't all eaten by tigers.

Slowly, his frown deepened into a scowl. He shook his head. "Goddammit. I *told* you you couldn't trust those bastards!"

Salt, meet wound. "Yeah, Dad, you did." I stood up, face hot. "You were right. Congratulations." I turned and walked out of the room.

"David—"

But I was already out the door.

I wanted to flee – to run, hide, anything – but it was raining in earnest now, and in any case I had nowhere to go. I retreated down the steps to the basement.

Inside it was quiet, the air cool but with a wood smell that seemed warmer, the way mint tastes cold.

If I had a refuge, it was here. Yet the scattered tools brought no comforting sense of competence. Instead, I was keenly aware that I was hiding in a basement. A rat in its hole.

I'd been so busy practicing for the doomed audition that I hadn't actually been down here since the party, and scraps and sawdust still covered everything. I thought of grabbing the push broom and cleaning up, but it seemed suddenly pointless. I'd just get it messy again. And if *that* wasn't a metaphor for my life, what was?

My eye fell on a stack of cut pine pieces – the half-done picture frame I'd started with Chance. I picked one up, feeling the dusty curve of the finished edge. Remembering the press of his back against my chest as we guided the router down the board.

Why couldn't I be more like Chance? He'd complimented me easily and honestly that night, impressed by my skills – skills I'd *earned* through hard work – without being jealous or belittling. He didn't need to tear me down to feel good about himself.

That was what a boyfriend should be. That was what a *friend* should be. I might not constantly compete with Ridley in the same way, but I sure hadn't spent much time worrying about her feelings, either. I was a human dumpster fire, and both of them were better off without me.

There was a knock on the door, but it swung open without waiting for an answer. Dad stepped inside.

"Hey. Let's talk."

I almost said something snarky, but given that he was maybe the last person who still liked me, it seemed like a bad move. "Okay."

"Okay." He breathed a sigh of relief, but having gotten this far, he seemed suddenly lost. He looked around, as if maybe the table saw would give him some parenting tips, then walked over and sat down in the lawn chair that still rested unstained in the corner. He ran his hands thoughtfully over the armrests.

"This is a good chair," he offered.

"Thanks."

The silence stretched.

At last he leaned forward, elbows on knees. "I'm sorry I was shitty."

I shrugged. "It's fine."

"No, it's not." Clenched fists bonked together between his knees. "I was angry. I can't stand seeing anyone hurt you – it makes me crazy. And I'll admit I was disappointed, too."

"Gee, thanks, Dad."

He held up a placating hand. "Not in you. In myself, for getting my hopes up. I admit, I loved it when you were in Darkhearts. Seeing you up on stage." He smiled wryly. "Typical showbiz parent, right? It's why it was easier for me to blame the other boys when you quit. But that's not my place. This is about your feelings, not mine."

"Yeah, well." I returned his smile weakly. "At least you won't have to be nice to Chance anymore."

"Like I said, this isn't about me." He gave me a level look. "You two really broke up?"

"I think so?" I shrugged again. "I got pissed at him for not overriding the label."

"Can he do that?"

I threw up my arms. "Maybe? Not really? Who knows! The label wasn't budging, and he wasn't trying. I left, he followed, we argued. I told him we were done and drove away."

"Dang."

"Yeah." I deflated backward onto the workbench.

Dad watched me carefully. "You really liked him, didn't you?"

"Yeah." I couldn't look at him. I fixed my gaze on the hedge trimmer hanging on the wall. "Stupid, huh?"

"I don't know about that." Dad picked up a screwdriver, spinning it between his fingers. "Before all the band stuff, when it was just the two of you hanging out again – did you have fun together?"

"Jesus, Dad, are you *trying* to make me feel worse?" I pushed myself up straight against the workbench. "I told you! It's over!"

"Why?"

"What do you mean, 'why'?" I flailed my arms like an angry Kermit the Frog, narrowly missing a metal work light. "I botched the audition, Chance thinks I'm an asshole – oh, and Ridley hates me too, for not telling her about me and Chance. I fucked everything up!"

He nodded calmly along with each statement, as if I were making a PowerPoint presentation instead of throwing a tantrum. When I was finished, he said:

"So fix it."

I grimaced, again failing to meet his eyes. "It's not that simple."

In the ensuing silence, the furnace fan clicked on, filling the basement with its whine. I ran my hands over the dented edge of the workbench.

"Your mother used to walk out, whenever we argued. Just leave the room."

Now it was Dad's turn to look away. He tapped the butt of the screwdriver against his palm.

"If it was bad, she'd lock herself in the bedroom, and I'd have to sit outside apologizing until she opened up."

I squirmed, not liking where this was going. "I don't want to talk about Mom."

"You think *I* do?" He shook his head. "After a while, she started leaving the house. I knew that if I called her phone enough times, eventually she'd answer. If I didn't, she'd sleep in her car for days rather than come home on her own. Those were the rules of her game. And she always won."

He ran a hand over his face. "That's how it happened, the last time. She walked out, same as usual, except this time I didn't call. And she didn't come home." He set the screwdriver down and scooped a handful of sawdust off the table saw, squeezing it into an orange snowball. "The thing is, I never knew if she actually wanted to leave, or if she just needed to be chased. But in the end, it was the same thing." At last he met my eyes again. "You see what I'm getting at?"

I did, and I didn't want to. Heat rose in my cheeks. "You're saying I'm like Mom."

"I'm saying it's a lonely kind of safety." He stood, letting the dust filter through his fingers. "Never sticking around to let yourself be hurt. Makes it hard to build anything."

How many times could my shame geyser erupt in one day? My face was going to burn away. "You don't even *like* Chance!"

"I don't have to." He shrugged. "The point is, I can tell *you* do. And Chance wouldn't have come this far if he didn't care about you, too. Which means maybe you're right about him. Some people are worth taking a risk on." He quirked a smile. "You, for instance."

He stood and moved to the door, then paused with his hand on the knob. "All I'm saying is, you walked away when the band got hard, and you've spent the last two years kicking yourself. Now your relationship with Chance is getting hard. If you decide it's not worth it, and you walk away – well, who am I to give advice there?" He pulled the door open, letting in a squall of wind.

"But if you do," he said, "how long will you spend wondering?"

Then he stepped into the storm and let the door click closed behind him.

30

Dad's words followed me as I parked my truck and popped the door.

I'd spent ten years hating Mom – not just for leaving, but for showing so clearly that I wasn't a priority. Never coming to see me. Always waiting for me to call first. And yet here I was doing the same thing. Had, in fact, been doing the same thing my whole life – with Chance and Eli, with Maddy, even with Ridley. Was it genetic? Was I cursed to be the same sort of emotional leech, constantly blackmailing everyone into validating me?

It was time to stop running away from everything, and start running *toward* something. Some*one*.

I walked up to the front door and knocked.

A shout rang out somewhere inside the house, then the sound of feet thumping down stairs. For a moment my courage faltered, and I wished I'd just sent a text. But some things deserved to be done in person.

The door opened.

Ridley looked out at me and wrinkled her nose.

"You're not pizza."

"Nope."

"Well. That's doubly disappointing."

We stared at each other.

Right – taking initiative. That was the whole point of this. "Can I come in?"

Fingers drummed on the door as she considered. Then she sighed and stepped aside. "Fine."

Inside, the house was back to its usual chaos. One of the more recent Star Wars shows played in the background, the metallic pew-pew of blasters blending with shouts as Kaylee and Malcolm wrestled over a tablet. Mr. McNeill watched the children with benevolent detachment as he stirred a pot on the stove. He waved the wooden spoon in greeting.

I followed Ridley up into her room, the battle for the galaxy cutting off as the door closed behind us. We stood there awkwardly.

"So." Ridley crossed her arms.

"Yeah. Um, hi."

More silence.

"Well, this has been fun," she said briskly, clapping her hands, "but I've got a post to write, so—"

"I'm sorry I'm such an asshole. You're my best friend, and I should have trusted you, and it was totally shitty of me to not tell you about Chance and me when I knew you liked him, and I'm *really* sorry!" The words rushed out in a single breath, using up all the air in my lungs.

Ridley scrunched her mouth over to one side as she appraised me.

"See?" she said at last. "That wasn't so hard."

I gave a rueful smile. "You might be surprised."

"God, I know." She flopped down on the bed. "It's taken all my willpower not to call and chew you out. I literally had to have Kaylee hide my phone for a bit. But it's all worth it now."

Hope thumped hard inside my chest. "So you forgive me?"

"Of course, you dick-wimple!" She threw a pillow at me. "I

325

mean, yes, you've been a human period cramp about this. But . . ." She rolled her eyes and sighed. "I get it. You needed to keep it secret for Chance's sake, and I can maybe get a little carried away sometimes, with the planning and the favors. And it's not like you stole him from me. You legit got there first." She waved. "Besides, he's a little skinny for my tastes, anyway."

My eyebrows rose. "Really?"

"No, of course not, you nuthatch! You could grate cheese on that boy's abs. I'm just being nice. So help me feel good and pretend you're not bouncing on the world's hottest pogo stick while I'm home diddling myself to Robert Irwin videos."

"Okay, first: Gross. And second: *What?*"

"I'm just saying. If Crocodile Junior can find a snake in a swamp, he can find the pearl in my clam."

"Please never say that again."

"You wish. Only God can judge me." She looked up at the ceiling dramatically. "Besides, at least Robbo is one dream-boy I won't have to share with you. Leave a spinster her fantasies."

"Trust me, they're all yours." As I tossed the pillow back onto her bed, I said, "You know . . . I don't want to shit on your Animal Planet fetish, but there might be some boys closer to home you should consider."

"Don't get greedy, Davey. You can't have us both."

"Ha ha. I'm not talking about me."

She rolled over and eyed me suspiciously. "Who?"

I shrugged. "I'm not making any claims, but Gabe seemed *pretty* into it when you took off your pants at the party."

"That's because I've got dumps like a truck." But she looked thoughtful.

I sat down on my usual side of the bed, brushing the skeezy dolphin puppet out of the way. "So we're really cool?"

She snorted. "Provisionally. On one condition." She grabbed the dolphin, and the two of them grinned salaciously at me. "Tell me *everything*."

So I did. With each new story, I felt a weight lifting off of me, even as it sank in just how badly I'd bungled things. Ridley listened with her whole body, barely interrupting except to ask clarifying questions.

When I finished, there was silence again, but this time it was comfortable. She absorbed everything I'd said, tapping her chin pensively with the puppet.

"Damn, Davey. You really dicked the dolphin."

"*What.*"

"'Screwed the pooch' is too crude. Dolphins are kinky, remember?" She waved the puppet, then tossed it aside. "The point is, you messed up. Big-time."

I slumped heavily against the wall. "Tell me something I don't know."

"Okay, how about this: you're not the only one who's been screwing Chance. And not in the fun way."

I squinted. "Whaddaya mean?"

"I mean that guy is a giver. He's constantly trying to give everyone what they want. His label. His fans. His parents. *You.* You've seen how he transforms himself every time he meets somebody new." She shook her head. "It sounds to me like he *knew* this audition would wreck everything. Yet he still went through with it, because you wanted it so bad."

"Yeah." That much was clear even to me now. I scrubbed my hands across my face. "God, I'm such an asshole."

She nodded sympathetically. "You are." Then she sat back and steepled her fingers. "The question is: What are you gonna do about it?"

"I dunno, therapy?"

"David."

I held up a hand. "I know what you meant. But what *can* I do? I mean, apologize, obviously. But this isn't a one-time thing. Even if he did take me back ... I don't know if I can stop resenting him, you know? I'm always going to be comparing myself to him."

"Maybe." She leaned forward, chin on hands. "True or false: I'm a better writer than you. And a better student. Basically all-around smarter."

"True."

"And yet you don't resent me."

I waved away her point. "It's not the same."

"Why not?" She sat up, ticking people off on her fingers. "Gabe's a better artist, and dresses better. Angela's better at sports. Natalie could get laid in a monastery. *Everybody*'s better than you at something, David. So either you get over that shit ASAP, or you're gonna be *real* lonely."

"I know, it's just ... Chance is who I was supposed to *be*, you know? If I hadn't fucked up."

"Says who?" She leaned in. "Davey, I've been your best friend for two years, and I've never seen you play guitar. Maybe that was who you were at one point, but it's clearly not who you are *now*. You need to let that shit go." She sat back again and shrugged. "Or don't. But you're right: if I were Chance, I wouldn't want you back if you're gonna be all the-attitude-formerly-known-as-butthurt about it. You need to choose which you're more in love with – your pride, or Chance."

"Gah." I grabbed the pillow and shoved it over my face, retreating into the dark.

She was right. Why was it so hard to let this go? What was I so scared of?

And in the darkness, the answer came:

Me.

I kept defining myself by what I could have been because there was safety in having been wronged. I didn't have to take responsibility for my own happiness, since everyone could agree I'd already missed my chance. I got to wallow in the comfort of knowing all my problems were someone else's fault. If I let that go . . . it would just be me.

I would always be that guy who used to be in Darkhearts.

But maybe it was time to be someone else, too.

I dropped the pillow. Ridley was watching with concern.

"I wanna fix things with Chance," I said. "But how?"

Ridley gave a very un-Ridley shrug. "That's up to you."

"I know." I took a deep breath and repeated it. "*I know.* And I think I know what I need to say, but I don't know *how* to say it. I don't know where to start. And I need to do better than that."

"I'm sure you'll do fine."

"Yeah, but you just said I need to get over my pride. So here we go." I grabbed her arm with both hands. "Please, Rid. Help me rewrite the ending on this one."

Her eyes lit up as she leaned forward.

"I thought you'd never ask."

31

The next few days were hot – the kind of cloudless, late-summer gift that Seattleites live for. Cyclists branded like NASCAR drivers crammed Lake Washington Boulevard as they puffed nose-to-butt up hills. Along the lake, every patch of grass teemed with runners, dog walkers, and teens trying to squeeze in all the bikini time they could before school resumed. Seattle didn't have a lot of unwritten rules – you didn't carry umbrellas, you didn't jaywalk – but everybody knew that when it was this nice, you *had* to go outside. Anything else was sacrilege.

Evening wind rushed in through lowered windows as I drove, flapping the handles of the paper bag on the passenger seat. I put a hand out to keep it from toppling over as I pulled up in front of Chance's house for what I hoped wouldn't be the last time.

Chance's mom buzzed me in and opened the door. "David. Hi." She seemed surprised to see me, but not in a bad way. I told myself that was a good sign.

"Hi, Mrs. Ng. Is Chance here?"

"He just went swimming." She cocked her head. "You didn't text him?"

"I just got off work, and I was in the neighborhood." And I didn't want to risk him saying no. "I'll go check the beach. Thanks." I turned to leave.

"Hold up." She opened the door to the coat closet and dug around inside, then emerged holding my guitar case. "Chance said you left this at the studio."

"Oh. Yeah." I took it from her. "Thanks."

"Sorry to hear things didn't work out at the audition." She was still giving me that searching look. "You wanna talk about it?"

"That's okay." I had no idea what Chance had told her, and regardless, I didn't think I could handle either sympathy or censure from her right now.

"All right." She paused, then gave a slow nod. "I'm glad you came by, David."

"Yeah." A lump rose in my throat. "Me too."

I made my escape and threw the case in the truck, then headed down the secret stairs, carrying the paper bag.

There was nobody at the little beach, only a folded towel hung over the back of the wooden bench. I set the bag down next to it and shaded my eyes to look out at the lake.

The sun was just starting to disappear behind the hill at my back, and the waves shone like glass. Chance cut through them smoothly, head and shoulders out of the water as his arms swung in lazy, powerful strokes. Water gleamed off his exposed skin, dark hair plastered down across his scalp. I stood and watched him, alone among all that reflected light.

I saw the instant he spotted me. He was too far out for me to judge his expression, but the easy rhythm faltered. For a moment he just floated there. Then – slower than before – he swam back toward shore.

He reached the edge of the lily pads and stood, water cascading off his shoulders, trailing like fingers down the centerline of his chest. He ran a hand through his hair, slicking it up and back in a black wave.

"Hi," I offered.

"Hi." He made no move to come closer.

"I was hoping we could talk."

His face was a painting, flat and unmoving. "And I want to talk to you why, exactly?"

"Because I'm an immature asshole who came to apologize?" I winched my cheeks up into a smile and gestured to the bench. "And because I've got your towel?"

He shook his head, but came forward anyway. Mud clung to his feet as he stepped up onto the goose-shat grass, stopping well out of reach. He waited expectantly.

I took a breath. "I wanted to say I'm sorry. For everything. I know you only put that audition together for my sake, and I was a total dipshit about it."

"Yeah." He crossed his arms. "You were."

Three days ago, that would have been enough to make me snap back. Now it just confirmed what I already knew. I picked up the paper Safeway bag and held it out to him. "Here."

He raised an eyebrow, suspicious. When I didn't say anything, his curiosity got the better of him, and he stepped close enough to take it. As he withdrew the object inside, his other eyebrow rose as well. I risked stepping up beside him so we could look at it together.

It was a small wooden picture frame, golden pine with a stripe of red cedar inlay. Across the top, I'd used a dremel to carve out the shape of Chance's bird tattoo, filling it with the same red cedar. Behind the glass sat a printed-out picture of the three of us: me, him, and Eli. We were standing on the edge of a stage, sweaty and grinning. Chance stood in the middle with the mic cable looped around his neck, arms thrown over our shoulders. We looked young and happy and indestructible.

"It's us," he said softly, wonder in his voice.

"Yeah." I ran a finger lightly across the varnished wood. "And it's the frame we worked on together."

He stared at it a moment longer, then moved his stare to me. "Why?"

"Because it's the same as the band." I gave another strained smile. "Something we started together, and finished on our own."

All softness vanished from his face. "Goddammit, Holc. I can't keep doing this."

"No!" I grabbed his shoulder. "That's not a dig! The band is yours." I realized what I was doing and let go, raising my hands in surrender. "The band – you were right, Chance. The band stopped being mine when I left. It's time I stopped acting like I have a right to it."

Chance's frown lessened, but he still shook his head. "I appreciate it, but maybe you were right at the studio, Holc. Maybe this is just never going to work. I can't deal with your constant jealousy."

"And you shouldn't have to." I touched his arm again, lighter this time. "But I'm done being jealous, Chance. Because I don't care about being famous. I never really did."

Chance looked skeptical.

I sighed and sat down on the bench, looking out at the lake.

"When I left the band . . . okay, yeah, the whole dynamic had gotten on my nerves. But it was because I felt unnecessary. Eli was the musical genius. You were the frontman everyone loved. I was just . . . there. So when I left . . . it was sort of a test. Not consciously, but I wanted to know you guys needed me. When you let me walk away, it felt like proof I didn't matter. Like you weren't really my friends."

333

"Jesus, Holc." Chance sat down beside me. "You realize how messed up that is, right?"

"I do *now*." I gripped the edge of the bench. "It just seemed like that's how you know someone loves you, you know? If they'll fight for you – even if the person they're fighting *is* you." I shook my head. "But I see now that I've been so focused on figuring out whether people love *me*, that I never bothered showing I love *them*. I've just been taking, constantly." I reached over and took his hand. "And I'm sorry."

He bit his lip, but didn't pull away.

"I know I've been a terrible boyfriend," I said. "But I wanna change that. I wanna be the kind of boyfriend you deserve. Because this summer with you . . . I don't want it to end."

"But it *will* end." Chance looked like he hated the words and was saying them anyway. "In a couple weeks I'll be back out on tour. You won't see me for months at a time."

The thought wrapped an iron band around my heart, but I said, "So send me pictures. I'll work on my emoji game."

He squeezed my hand hard. "And I'm not gonna stop being famous. Not if I can help it, anyway. That's always gonna be there."

"I know." I smiled. "Like I said, I don't care. Being famous seemed great when it meant the whole world loving me. And I still wish we could stop pretending in public and just tell everyone we're dating. But I don't care about everyone." I lifted his hand and kissed the back of it softly. "I care about *you*."

"You're sure?" Chance looked like he wanted desperately to believe, but couldn't quite let himself. I felt a new rush of shame at how badly I'd messed this up. But on its heels came a reassuring sense of understanding.

It's my turn to chase.

"I'm sure." I turned toward him on the bench, taking the picture frame and laying it gently aside, then taking his other hand as well. "I don't need to be you, Chance." I squeezed. "I just need to be *with* you."

Chance looked deep into my eyes, evaluating. Then his lips twitched upward in that lopsided smile – the real one. "So are you gonna kiss me or what?"

I kissed him, his hair flopping down to drip lake water on my forehead. One wet end speared straight into my eye.

"Ow!" I pulled backward and rubbed at the injured orb. "You got duck pee in my eyeball."

"That's what you get!" Chance laughed and grabbed me, crushing me against him as the water droplets from his chest soaked through my shirt. He shoved his way onto my lap, damp swim trunks wicking directly into my jeans. "That's what you get for holding my towel hostage!"

"Congratulations, your boyfriend now looks like a pants-wetter. Someone call the paparazzi."

As I ducked back in for another kiss, fingers running up the drop-spangled expanse of his back, I felt something inside me release, like a balloon cut free from its string. For the first time in I didn't know how long, I was happy to just be where I was – to be *who* I was.

Things would still be hard. I wasn't a dummy. Having a boyfriend who lived primarily on my phone would be grueling. But in between, in those stolen moments . . . we'd have this. He could go be Chance Kain, and I . . . I'd be here. Finishing high school, learning a trade. Figuring out who exactly I wanted to be.

335

And all of a sudden, that felt all right.

I'd spent the last two years feeling like a failure, cursing myself for my one big screwup. But if it led me here, to Chance wrapped around me and nipping at my ear . . .

Maybe I hadn't screwed up at all.

32

The thing about being backstage at a concert is that it's not much different from a construction site. There's scaffolding, and cables, and big metal road cases you definitely don't want to stub your toe on. There are a lot of burly beardy dudes, and everyone's just trying to do their job. It's manual labor.

Yet there's no escaping the sound – and not just the speakers. When you get enough people in one place, they don't even have to talk. Just the motion of twenty thousand people shifting in their seats roars like a plane gearing up for takeoff.

And right now nobody was sitting still. Even through my earplugs, the sound of the crowd was a physical force, pushing against my skin in gentle waves. I stood in the shadows, just behind the curtains blocking the gear from view, and looked out at the show.

Chance stood center stage, incandescent in the spotlight, skin blazing against the perfect black of his outfit. Red light pooled out around him, drawing the outline of his crow tattoo on the floor: the new Darkhearts logo, for its new incarnation. He stood with mic raised overhead in a fist, chest heaving as the song finished and the crowd's adoration avalanched over him.

I realized that, from their distance, they'd never see that he was breathing hard. Never see the sweat running down from his scalp, over the transparent cords of his in-ear monitors. To

337

them, he was perfect, mythical – an idol to be worshiped. The idea of Chance Kain, so much bigger than the boy himself. They'd never smell the reek of his armpits as he collapsed onto a couch after a show. They'd never see him honking and gagging as he used a neti pot to clear out his sinuses beforehand. They'd never know the real Chance.

And that was just fine. They could have Chance Kain. I'd take Chance Ng over him any day.

He spread his arms, soaking in the crowd's approval, and for a moment I could see him the way they did: a reflection of all their hopes and dreams. I saw the way he turned it back on them, becoming what they needed, and felt a fierce sense of pride. On its heels came gratitude: to be able to be here, watching my boyfriend do what he was born to do. To support him as he shined.

It was enough.

A long-haired sound guy wearing a headset clapped me on the shoulder. "You good?"

I breathed in deep, my whole body buzzing. "Yeah."

"Cool. I'll take you live as soon as you step out there, so just turn up the volume when you're ready."

I nodded, not trusting myself to speak further. He grinned and smacked my shoulder again.

"Rip it up, brother."

Out on the stage, the band went quiet as Chance moved down to the very front, putting a foot up on one of the angled monitors. Below him, security guards made a wall between him and the fans crushing themselves rapturously against the steel-barred barricades.

"Thank you so much, everybody." Chance's words came

smooth and easy – the calm in the center of the storm. "You've been an amazing start to the tour. It's been a hard few months. Everything's changed. But all of you ... you make me feel at home."

He smiled into the cheers.

"So tonight, I want to give you something special. Something no other city is getting. One night only. Would you like that, Portland?"

The crowd lost its mind. In the face of that chaos, Chance turned and looked back.

At me.

The sound guy tapped my back. "That's you."

I stepped out onto the stage.

The stadium was a sea of people, curving up and along the walls in every direction. My brain tried to process that each of those little dots was a person, and promptly shorted out. Somewhere in the back of my skull, the dude from *Princess Bride* shouted "*Incontheivable!*" I had long since fear-sweated through my undershirt, and hoped the panic stains in my pits weren't showing on my plaid button-down.

I might have thrown up or passed out right there, if not for Chance. His smile was an anchor. I hauled myself along it until I was standing next to him. Faces stared up at us.

Chance put an arm around my shoulders.

"This is David Holcomb. He started Darkhearts with me and Eli, back when we were in middle school. Without him, there would never have been a Darkhearts. I think that deserves some applause, don't you?"

The thunder was deafening, people stomping and clapping and whistling. Nothing felt real.

"Holc here drove all the way down from Seattle so we could do a song for you – a new one nobody's ever heard before." He lowered the mic and spoke just to me. "You ready?"

I swallowed and nodded.

He grinned encouragingly. "Just pretend we're playing the Kirkland Teen Center."

I smiled back. He dropped his arm as he raised the mic.

"This song is called 'Back and Away.'"

Amplifiers hissed as I rolled up my guitar's volume knob. He nodded to the band, and the drummer clicked us in.

It was the biggest sound I'd ever made. The chords boomed out through the arena, matched immediately by drums and bass as the band dropped flawlessly into rhythm with me.

And then Chance began to sing.

It was the same song we'd written in his bedroom. The one from the audition. Yet it was different now. The words were the same, but there was no sense of dread. Yes, it was about us. But it was also about a moment in time. And that time was past. The song was the same, but we were different.

It was just a song. And we were so much more.

The music flowed. Chance didn't run around the stage, or hype up the crowd. We just stood there, side by side, and played our music. His voice and my guitar, flowing and blending. Not competing, but complementing each other.

I tore my eyes away from Chance and looked out at the crowd, memorizing that sea of faces, trying to burn the scene into my retinas. *Remember this.*

This would never be my life. I would never be a star like Chance. But I could taste it, just for a minute. And nothing would ever be able to take that away from me.

Yet as we moved into the final chorus, I found my attention drifting away from the crowd and back to Chance. Watching his eyes close on the high notes, the strands of hair falling down across them, begging to be brushed away. And as the last note faded and his eyes opened again to meet mine, I knew: here was what I really wanted.

It didn't matter that nobody could know the truth about us. It didn't matter that I'd be back in school on Monday, the same old David Holcomb. I liked hanging out with Ridley, and working in my shop, and learning from Jesús on weekends. I didn't need to be anybody else.

And I had Chance Ng. My beautiful secret.

The audience cheered, and Chance grabbed my hand and raised it high above us, presenting me to the crowd. "David Holcomb, ladies and gentlemen!" The cheering intensified.

I turned back to him as we lowered our arms. "Thank you, Chance." I squeezed his hand once, invisibly, then let go.

But he didn't. He kept holding my hand, giving me a strange smile. A memory clicked, and I realized where I'd seen it before: on the way up to the church's bell tower.

Chance Kain was nervous.

A bead of sweat ran down his cheek. He licked his lips.

"Thank *you*, David Holcomb."

And he leaned forward and kissed me.

Speakers hissed. There was a rush of air as twenty thousand people gasped.

And then they *roared*.

ACKNOWLEDGMENTS

Publishing is a team sport – and a rough-and-tumble one, at that. This book would never have made it out into the world without a full band of wonderful people on my side.

Infinite thanks to my agent, Josh Adams, and the whole team at Adams Literary, for this absolute fairy tale of a partnership. I feel so fortunate to have you in my corner. Along the same lines, I owe a tremendous debt to fellow Adams Lit compatriots Amie Kaufman and Jay Kristoff for making the introduction and vouching for my character. Thanks, friends.

My editor, Sara Goodman, is everything an author could hope for. Within the first five minutes, I knew we were on the same wavelength, and at every step it's been a joy working together. Thank you for making this book happen. Thanks as well to Editorial Assistant Vanessa Aguirre, and Authenticity Editor Kayla Dunigan for lending her expertise. Copyeditor Terry McGarry did a stellar job of calling me on my grammatical foibles, and Managing Editor Eric Meyer kept everything on schedule. I'm also deeply grateful to my UK editor Chloe Sackur and the rest of the team at Andersen Press, for believing in this book and helping it reach readers across the world.

This gorgeous cover was brought to you by Senior Art Director Kerri Resnick – who, in addition to being amazingly talented, was *extremely* patient in listening to my amateur graphic design thoughts – as well as artist Sivan Karim, who captured Chance and Holc so dynamically. We shot for the moon in trying to create a YA romance cover that *also* felt like a Darkhearts album cover, and I think we hit it. Designer Devan Norman turned raw text (and texts!) into finished pages, and Production Manager Chris Leonowicz and Production Editor Carla Benton made it all into the beautiful object you're holding. (If you're listening instead, that's thanks to Audiobook Producer Ally Demeter and narrator Ramón de Ocampo.)

This book would have been a lot rougher without the efforts of my generous beta readers: Jessica Blat, Susan Chang, Katie Groeneveld, Charlie N. Holmberg, Amie Kaufman, Aprilynne Pike, Kat Tewson, and Shannon Woodhouse. Renaissance man Dave Markel gets points for helping inform the woodworking scenes (which is probably a nice change from me asking him all my gory medical questions).

A thousand thanks to Wednesday Publicity Manager Mary Moates and Publicity Assistant Oliver Wehner, as well as Associate Marketing Manager Lexi Neuville, Marketing VP Brant Janeway, and Marketing Assistant Austin Adams, for spearheading the push to get this book in front of people.

At this point you're probably thinking "Good lord, how many folks does it take to make a book?" Well, buckle up, because the answer is *more*. You wouldn't be reading this without intrepid sales reps like Rebecca Schmidt, Sofrina Hinton, Jennifer Edwards, Jennifer Golding, Jaime Bode, and Jennifer Medina, or their assistants Julia Metzger, D'Kela Duncan, Isaac Loewen, and Alexa Rosenberg. Creative Services – the people who make the ads and keep the marketing from just being photos of me looking desperate – are Britt Saghi, Kim Ludlam, Tom Thompson, and Dylan Helstien. And to all the other folks at Wednesday Books and St. Martin's Press, whose names I've yet to learn: thank you, from the bottom of my heart.

If this were an awards speech, they'd probably be hauling me off the stage with one of those giant vaudeville hooks right about now, but just as important as everyone who got this book up and running are all the folks who keep *me* up and running. Thank you to all the Wabis, who continue to show me every day what a supportive community can be. Thank you to my publishing friends, especially the crew of the Screamin' Hole – you both inspire me and help me stay grounded. Thank you to my housemates, the Mooncastlers, for hikes and puzzles and not murdering me after several years bottled up together in a pandemic.

Thanks to my family, for their unwavering support in all my wild endeavors. My father, Jim, and my brother, Anthony, deserve a special callout for this one – Dad for his contractor knowledge and catchphrases, and Ant for suggesting scraping paint as the most mind-numbing job one encounters when growing up on a worksite.

Last but not least, thank you to my wife, Margo Arnold. When I'm the panicking chicken from *Moana*, she's the coconut helmet that calms me down. She constantly encourages me to pursue the projects I'm most passionate about, even when it means leaving a dream job or base-jumping into a new genre. So thanks, babe. Business Pig couldn't have gotten the gig without you.

Not MY PROBLEM

CIARA SMYTH

Winner of the
WATERSTONES BOOK PRIZE FOR OLDER READERS

When Aideen agrees to help ambitious class swot Maebh
Kowalska deal with her crazy workload, she doesn't expect
to end up reluctantly pushing Maebh down the stairs. With
this, Aideen becomes the school 'fixer': any problem a student
has, Aideen will sort it out, from stealing confiscated mobiles
to breaking into parties. All she asks for is a favour in return.
But Aideen's own life is a mess. Spending more time with the
uptight (but annoyingly cute)
Maebh, Aideen starts to wonder:
can every problem be solved?

9781839130854